THE HEART IS AN
INVOLUNTARY MUSCLE

monique proulx

THE HEART
IS AN
INVOLUNTARY
MUSCLE

translated by
DAVID HOMEL & FRED A. REED

DOUGLAS & MCINTYRE
Vancouver/Toronto

The author would like to thank the Canada Council for the Arts and the Fonds Gabrielle Roy for their support.

Douglas & McIntyre Ltd.
2323 Quebec Street, Suite 201
Vancouver, British Columbia
Canada V5T 4S7
www.douglas-mcintyre.com

National Library of Canada Cataloguing in Publication Data
Proulx, Monique, 1952–
[Coeur est un muscle involontaire, English]
The heart is an involuntary muscle/Monique Proulx;
translated by David Homel and Fred A. Reed
Translation of: Le coeur est un muscle involontaire.

ISBN 1-55054-991-X

I. Homel, David. II. Reed, Fred A., 1939– III. Title
PS8581.R6883C6313 2003   C843'.54   C2003-910273-4
PQ3919.2.P763C6313 2003

Cover and interior design by Peter Cocking
Cover photograph © Skan/9/Getty Images/Photodisc Green
Typesetting by Lynn O'Rourke
Printed and bound in Canada by Transcontinental
Printed on acid-free paper

We gratefully acknowledge the financial support of the Canada
Council for the Arts, the British Columbia Arts Council, and the Government
of Canada through the Book Publishing Industry Development Program
(BPIDP) for our publishing activities.

for France and Gustave, departed

Fame is like a dictionary.
A dictionary is like a door: it opens and shuts.
RÉJEAN DUCHARME, *Le nez qui voque*

Beneath my feet, I know that roots are growing,
and soon they'll join those, I know, that are growing
beneath yours, and soon they'll become as one.
RÉJEAN DUCHARME, *L'Océantume*

No father. We didn't know what that meant. When
we found out, we couldn't figure out what good it was.
RÉJEAN DUCHARME, *Les Enfantômes*

THE DISORDER OF LIFE

I HAD NEVER BEEN alone with him before. Now I am, though it's a little late. His icy hands steal the warmth from mine. His forehead burns like a furnace gone mad. The disorder within him has begun to unravel all that was so tightly wound. The parts of his being lose their coherence; each takes off in its separate panic. What part truly remains, what part can still receive my encouragements or prayers? I petition his feverish head, and from it issues the steady, shallow breathing of sedated sleep. I'm waiting for a miracle, and that's what I tell him. I am waiting for him to flick open his eyes and give me a fraction, a ghost of a look. I am waiting for him to blurt out my name in a voice both clear and filled with pain. *Florence, Florence.* If he would say my name, even in silence, even in the hiss and sputter of fever, if he only just thought my name, I would hear it. Even if it were the last glimmer in a dying molecule of his brain, I would hear it. *Say my name, Pepa.*

He opens his eyes. I swear he does. He opens his eyes to speak to me, since I am all he can see, clinging to his bed like a shoot sprung from his ribs during the night. *It's me, Florence, speak to me, say my name, say something.* He opens his eyes and sighs gently. His lungs hang in his chest, empty of air, and calm. His gaze is mute. It tells me that the house below is emptying, that it had emptied without my knowing it. The last traces of humanity are vanishing from his brown eyes, his hazel eyes, the golden brown of his eyes tarnishing like an oxidizing copper roof. That is all. That will be all, forever. A shame. There is nothing more to say about such a calm, submissive death. I close his eyes. I kiss his warm forehead that still smells of life and red blood. I cry a little, effortlessly. Suddenly I'm so calm that I'd take out the intravenous needle from the wrinkled flesh it needlessly inflames, I would make myself useful, sweep the room, change the sheets, lie down beside him to watch the orange slash of the sun climb towards heaven. Today, again, the sun will rise in the sky and day will break. And no one will remark on this astonishing magic, no one will greet this extraordinary ordinariness with enthusiastic applause.

I STEP OUTSIDE. Beyond the room, another world rushes and vibrates with panic. Creatures dressed in white or green hurry through the corridors shouting orders, wheeled stretchers brush against my legs with creaks of distress, voices in imperative tones flow from the walls and ceiling, demanding the presence of people who are not there. All is noise and confusion. For a moment I stand stunned, wondering which way to run, and how to protect myself from the catastrophe that has fallen upon this place, a fire, the impact of an asteroid, an earthquake. A woman speaks to me, but I cannot hear. I tell her my father is dead. That must be the thing to say. The universe has slowed enough that I can recognize it. Nothing is out of place, no particular catastrophe. Normal life in a hospital, the disorder of life as it struggles to stay alive. The woman, a nurse, has wide blue eyes, and she swathes me in their benevolence. "Ah, yes, room 2029," she says softly. She touches my shoulder, suggests coffee. A man in white—another nurse, or the doctor on duty—touches my other shoulder. Their affectionate touch numbs me pleasantly. As if from afar, I hear the man's voice, trembling with commiseration, I see his liquid eyes shining like friendly planets. "Your father," he says. "Your father spoke at the beginning of the night. *The heart is an involuntary muscle.* That's what he said, quite distinctly, *The heart is an involuntary muscle.*" I say, "Oh, really?" And thank him warmly, though I don't know why. His tenderness and presence, perhaps. I like this place. You feel so much like a child, all fussed over.

Suddenly my mother and my two brothers are there. We step back into the room, pink now with the light of dawn, to find an ancient dead body that hardly resembles Pepa.

My brother Bruno hugs my mother by the waist and I snuggle against her. My other brother Stéphane enfolds us all in his massive arms. That's the fleeting image that most often comes to me from that night of vagueness and void. Our four bodies joined in a single warmth, cast by grief into a massive, throbbing sculpture.

IT WAS NOT an intolerable death, the kind of absence that would suck the air from your lungs. In a few days it was over. For lack of stamina, the sadness disappeared. Bruno and Stéphane took care of everything, the ceremony and the ashes, the sorting of shirts and sweaters, the pipes, the collection of skin magazines, all the intimate, insignificant possessions accumulated over a life of eighty years with little exaltation. Mother, her eyes as bright as a young girl's, took me aside to confide things I had no wish to hear. They made love for the last time, she and my father, just before my birth. After, never again. "Never again," she repeated, three or four times, each time with a different tone, her magnificent, defeated eyes flashing on me, as if she were bequeathing me precious jewels. That finished me off. I forgot everything. It's still the easiest thing for me to do. *Log off.*

Papa. Papapa. Pepa.

What do other people feel when they think "Papa"? How do they make something warm and strong rise within them, or even anything at all?

If someone asks me about that night, when everything between us could have burned in brilliance, but instead he chose to flee as he had so many times before, I will lie. I will say that my father suddenly opened his eyes in the midst of his terminal coma, not to die but to speak to me for the first time in my life.

2

MAHONE INC.

NOTHING IS SIMPLER than to step through the doors of the universe. First, you switch on your computer. Then rapture begins, when you teeter on the edge with the world at your fingertips, gaping open like a gigantic box of candies that your two hands and your one lifetime could never hope to exhaust. Hardly the kind of thing for small minds, or paper-eating mice cowering in their holes. It's rapture for condors, galvanized by space, and not diminished by it. Condors, and the young.

Which is why our business cards, Zeno's and mine, carry the image of a soaring condor.

When I turn on my computer, the threshold of an infinite world, I always find Zeno blocking the gate. Growling, sniffing, tenacious as a guard dog of virtual space, he's a cyber-Cerberus transformed into a lamb by the first caress. This time, five messages, each more peremptory than the last, were not self-expression enough for him. He had been waiting for me on-line for days, and he let fly with a flurry of indignant keystrokes as soon as I showed myself.

WTFAY!!!? (Where the fuck are you?)

I answer: DID. (Dad is dead.)

Stunned, he let ten seconds pass, ten huge unproductive seconds lost and gone forever.

;-(he said at last. (I'm really sorry.)

;-) I answered. (It's okay.)

G? He asked. (When do you want to meet at the Greek's?)

G! I told him. (Right away, if you like.)

WE LIKE TO GET to the point, Zeno and I. We don't have patience for the telephone, that crackling dinosaur that devours time and excretes small talk. The precious water of time leaks in swollen rivulets from the pockets of failures, leaving them poor and shriveled in their arid wasteland. The two of us treat time with all the consideration it warrants. We save so much time that our virtual coffers are heavy with it, our temporal ingots clink together in magnificent abstraction, waiting to materialize in some form we can't yet imagine.

"The Greek" is a Greek restaurant like the millions that proliferated before they dropped out of fashion, as blue and white as a family vacation brochure, generous in its portions of fried potatoes and feta, slow-simmering the same rudimentary dishes that the primitive mouths of philosophy's bearded founders once gulped down. The kind of nourishment that's proven itself, the nourishment of history. At The

Greek's, there are the regulars who've become part of the furniture. Most of all, there's ageless Therios, regal as only a venerable man of the land can be, negligent enough to let us set up our headquarters in a far corner of his restaurant in trade for a Web site designed for him by Zeno. He gave it everything he had, Zeno did, and the site works wonders, bringing Therios customers from Japan and Denmark, who leave in disgust after tasting the same greasy souvlakis they could find at home.

We meet there to keep abreast of things, the boss and the sole employee of Mahone Inc. There and not at Zeno's place, where his girlfriend lives, the one who's a bit hard to get along with, and most certainly not at my place. My place is burned. Zeno lived there for a year while we tried to be lovers. The walls, that have a memory of their own, start oozing with grievances the minute he walks through the door.

One day, before I hit thirty, we'll have a real office on the fashionable part of Sherbrooke Street, providing Zeno doesn't futz everything up the way he usually does. We'll have an office made of mahogany and glass that our computer screens will bombard with spatial luminosity, behind a facade with no less than five windows, against which a condor will spread its massive brass wings. Our secretaries will be enchanting and our clients will sink deep into armchairs as forgiving as a mother's breasts.

In the meantime, we're stuck with Therios and his blue and white tablecloths, plus free ouzo whenever he doesn't have anyone else to talk to.

Sitting in our usual booth, Zeno was drinking his third cup of coffee. Twenty olive pits were laid out in three straight rows on his plate. With great application, he added a twenty-first to the middle row as I took my spot across from him. Behind his little round glasses, his silken, fearful gaze appraised the extent of my grief. His voice had that stilted tone it gets when he doesn't know what to say.

"What did your father die of?"

"He died of being eighty-three years old."

"Eighty-three!"

He rolled the enormous figure in his mouth along with an olive pit. He was as astonished as I am that human beings could hang on that long, after God only knows how many shameful capitulations. A cold weight started to settle in my stomach as Pepa's face flickered on my inner screen, but I kept it at bay, and it eventually faded.

"So," I said.

End of subject. I switched on the mini-recorder that I use to keep our official conversations from sliding off into digression.

"So," repeated Zeno, delighted at having gotten off so lightly. "Here we are."

He laid before me the fruits of his harvest. We had three new customers. Three new egos to tart up, to melt down like gold coins in the immensity of the Web. One was a sculptor, the second a gospel singer, the third an author. Artists had begun flinging themselves into our arms. Because of Zeno's hot pursuit, but mostly because they couldn't stand the anonymity that enveloped their careers. We designed them eye-catching Web sites, we offered them a spotlight on the world's greatest stage, we were made for them like fleas for a dog and maple syrup for hypoglycemics, even if not everyone knew it yet.

"Just this once, you'll be looking after Gina Da Sylva, the writer," Zeno said.

"Oh, shit! How come?"

"Because I'm asking you to."

He put on his soft, warm boss's voice, a full octave lower than the voice of friendship. Which meant I'd be handling the writer, period. Which also meant he'd already handled her, in his fashion, complete with fraudulent promises.

"I have some knowledge of her," Zeno confirmed, his eyelashes fluttering behind his glasses. "She'll be more comfortable with you."

Hands off the customers until they've paid up; anything else might ruin the transaction. That was our agreement. Zeno, you lecherous little runt. We'd agreed that writers weren't my line. Strange: Here was a guy who shone when it came to images but got tangled up in words, but he adored writers, he navigated through their endless books as if he were snorkeling tropical waters teeming with coral and rare fish. I was supposed to be the in-house stylist. I liked to write and I wrote gracefully—so he told me—but I couldn't stand the heavy-handed arrogance of books. In a 300-page book, there are always 250 pages too many. Reading books slows you down, it softens you, it wipes you out. When you open a book, a particularly underhanded book, you're neutralized for hours, the captive of this corpulent mass that isn't even true, a creation that some neurotic fabricated out of the worst of his neuroses, the better to unload it on you and get it out of his life.

"Zeno Mahone, I'm warning you. It's going to cost you double, triple my usual rate if you expect me to whip this shit author of yours into shape."

"Don't raise you voice, Flora, please."

"Don't call me Flora."

I was yelling for real now. Okay, so I agreed to use *Flora* on my business card because it sounded more international than Florence, a subaltern *Flora* beneath a gigantic Mahone Inc. like a piece of condor shit. But I wasn't going to let him throw it in my face whenever he wanted to, like a member of the gentry pinching one of his retainers. *Flora-at-your-service.*

We glared at each other, like in the good old days when hate and love walked hand in hand, destroying one another, giving birth to indigestible pap. I switched off the recorder.

"Here, this should calm you down. It's your advance."

He dropped an envelope onto the oily olive pits and got to his feet, all five feet two inches of him, full of exaggerated self-importance. He headed for the toilets with an intolerably tragic air. You don't realize how small he is until he stands up. But he remakes the space around him, malevolent homunculus that he is, and convinces you that the world is at his feet.

I opened the envelope. It contained a single bill, a portrait of Queen Elizabeth II as a pinkish doll. One thousand dollars. In spite of myself, I burst out laughing.

"Make room for me, my little heart!"

Therios appeared with a bottle of ouzo and three glasses. I stuffed the pink queen back into her sheath. He sat down beside me and tapped the recorder with his fingertip.

"Is it on? I want to sing into the machine."

Usually he was happy just to talk to us in those sunlit gutturals that betrayed his origins, and that sounded like a prelude to a piece of oriental music. But to sing for real, to break

into song for no good reason? Into the Mahone Inc. machine
at that, where the only thing you'd hear were figures, contracts and official shouting matches? I didn't touch the glass
of ouzo he poured me, and shoved the tape recorder towards
him. People are always surprising me with their juvenile
whims, people older and more immature than me.

Therios grabbed the table with his huge, rough-cut hands
and began to sing, without preparation or throat-clearing.
Words in Greek flowed along a monochordal melodic line, a
stuttering wave breaking free. *To kalokairi, to kalokairi,* he repeated, three, five times over. A dark tide of sadness hit me
like a hammer and I stared at him, transfixed.

What was he doing to me? How handsome he was! I had
no idea he could be so handsome. Even in his everyday skin,
stained like an old screen, even with his heavy swarthiness, his
belly that ballooned over his belt and his puffy forearms.
What was so handsome about him? *To kalokairi, to kalokairi,*
he sang, leaning on the table as nonchalantly as if he were
handing me a fish. It seemed to be so simple to be Therios.
That's what was handsome, he was handsome beneath his
skin, where complete self-confidence reigned, majestic. I saw
the essential Therios, his crystalline self that flowed with his
song, that damned song that shattered me to pieces.

It must have been a love song. Only love makes you lose
your bearings like that. Or so they say. I don't know much
about it, no one ever undressed me like that, no one ever let
me undress him to the very marrow of his bones. That
damned song of his, that damned way he sang it. He is a king,
while I am nobody. How I would have loved to be Therios for

a moment, how I would have loved to be the woman he sang for and who made him magnificent.

Fortunately, the song didn't last long. He went back to being the workaday, non-threatening Therios, while I became the woman with the bright future. We traded embarrassed smiles. Zeno was standing silent behind us, also transfixed by the truth of Therios. But he couldn't think of anything subtler than applause, as if Therios were an actor or a production number. Therios stopped him with a wave of his hand.

"It's for my father, Dimitrios," he said. "He died twenty-five years ago today."

He raised his glass to Dimitrios. We all raised our glasses to Dimitrios, but my hand was shaking so badly the ouzo spilled onto the table. Zeno gave me a knowing glance, and for a moment I stopped breathing, terrified by what he would say. But he didn't say, "Florence just lost her father too." He said nothing. He touched my shoulder, hardly at all, the briefest contact, but enough to bring tears to my eyes. Tears of relief and hopeless gratitude.

One day, when Zeno and I are grown up, but still not old, we'll invent something more ethereal than love, more burning than friendship. Some refuge where, day or night, we can repair everything that has been broken.

Meanwhile, we were stuck with this little package of passion and prickliness.

"To work, to work!" Zeno decreed. "Come on, Flora, I'll give you a lift in my tank."

And so he rescued us from soft-heartedness, at the last minute he pulled us from the swamp into which we were about to sink. Therios rushed off happily to welcome a customer by pummeling his shoulders with a virile flurry of fists, and I finished up what remained on the table. The backbone of the day was straight again.

YOU COULD SPOT Zeno's van a mile away. It's the one parked in the no-parking zone, rear-end far from the curb. It's the one with the ugly dog on the front seat and a parking ticket on the windshield.

"Bastards!" Zeno erupted, tearing the ticket from the windshield. "Why do they persecute me like this?"

"Because they personally hate you. What other reason could there be?"

Pokey the dog greeted me with desperate whimpering and a gush of grateful saliva. You can't be more dog than this dog. Stinky, stubborn, libidinous, servile. For the millionth time he shoved his muzzle between my thighs, and for the million-and-oneth time I pushed him to the other end of the seat, but before long he was at it again, and with no compunction, so great is his incomprehension of all that is not dog. A raw-boned mutt, a coat that grates like old steel wool, hindquarters half-paralyzed, head hung submissively, the sum of his parts a total failure. And old. So old that Zeno has to help him up the stairs when they get home, so old he snores even when he's awake.

"How come you don't put him out of his misery?"

That question snuffed out our brief relationship. That question turned into a fight, because I couldn't stand the stink of the dog's rancid coat whenever he stuck his drooling snout into my crotch. The same question Zeno's girlfriend was beginning to ask, poor thing. She didn't understand the totalitarian passion that united Pokey and his master. Not yet.

"Nice doggy nice nice doggy nice doggydog, yes, so nice."

They actually started kissing. Disgusting. I turned away so as not to interrupt their idyll. Zeno's van was crammed full of his passions in concentrated form. In addition to Pokey the dog, there was his laptop, the stacks of CD-ROMs, little bags of tamari-flavored almonds, a styrofoam cooler full of cans of cherry Coke. And books by Pierre Laliberté, his favorite writer, which he carried with him wherever he went and leafed through respectfully, as if they were sacred texts.

Recreated Creatures, Morbid Martha, You Love You. Provocative, inspired titles, Zeno insisted. Bullshit, I told him. I would open one of them at random, any one, and the words would blow up in my face, sumptuous words beyond number, a fistful of wordstones that rattled like hail. A deadly inertia would sweep over me, dragging my eyelids closed. It wasn't the words themselves, it was their incontinent mass, the reinforcements of words that kept pouring in, surrounding me, strangling my spirit, more kept coming, more sumptuous and sticky, weaving their spider web around me. No way out, no air hole, no way for the light to get in. Quick, get me out of here.

"TAKE *Recreated Creatures,* powerful stuff. Every time you read it, it destroys you in a new way. Look on page 25. I made a note in the margin. Read the passage where Annie and Anna go their separate ways while shooting stars rain down on them. That's on page 25, right?"

"Yes, Zeno. Yes."

What limitless devotion. And who for? A phantom, a mirage, a non-image, a rumor. Pierre Laliberté was the mythical writer whose face no one had ever seen, who lived secluded like a leper while awards tarnished and fell to dust, waiting to be collected.

Pierre Laliberté. What a banal name. There were three columns of that name in the phone directory, the name of a cuckold, the name of a clerk in the income tax department, or a furniture manufacturer. *Pierre Laliberté, cubbyhole maker.*

Thousands of people adored him the way Zeno did. Tens of thousands, who, through some curious perversity, admired his self-conscious underground existence as much as they did his books. If all artists were like him, petrified by fear, invisible, repelled by what constitutes the salt of existence, Mahone Inc. would vanish like a patch of mold in the sunlight. The Web would lose its magical wings, and life would become completely boring.

When I tell Zeno that, he stares at me a moment with a look of supreme affliction in his eyes. "It's terrible, Florence," he says. "You don't admire anything or anyone." Which is utterly false, of course, and profoundly unjust and cruel. I'm forced to burst into tears to prove how wrong he is.

This time, we gave the literary minefield a wide berth. We switched on the radio, music without words, and pulled into the traffic.

We drove to my place in silence. My head was propped against the door frame. His was in the clouds. Five times out of ten when he drives me home, he misses the off-ramp that gets you to my neighborhood without going through down-town, and suddenly there we are, caught up by the river and the brilliant North American sunlight, moving rapidly away from everything on a wide highway with the scent of damp uncut hay, alongside herons tearing themselves from gravity and beckoning us to follow.

"Oh, shit," groaned Zeno.

We needed another fifteen minutes to reach the exit that would bring us back to our lives, fifteen wasted, enchanted minutes. Head against the door frame, leg braced to keep Pokey's lecherous snout at bay, I drifted off into the same old sugary adolescent dream, stuffed with caramel like a cheap chocolate bonbon. Zeno isn't Zeno and I'm someone else. We're a new entity, something called a couple, a modest little couple, mouths agape with love and the marital state, and that hairy, drooling hulk between us is a child who will soon be frolicking on the golden sands of a beach. We're driving full speed towards paradise surrounded by flying creatures and sea-scents that wipe away our ambitions and useless projects, and I am nothing in the face of this euphoric, onrushing *we,* I attain the mindless happiness of being nothing, and finally I am rid of myself.

"Hey, Flora! Florence!"

Already? Already! There was my apartment. My old iden-tity stood before me.

In memory of the good old days, we quickly kissed on the lips, and I pried myself out of the van before Pokey could rouse himself from his senile slumber. We had no idea when we'd see each other again. In two weeks, maybe three, when there would be new contracts, and new shouting matches. Zeno went home to his girlfriend Maud, and I headed for the realm of possibilities. The sugary dream vanished with Zeno's van and nothing remained, no nostalgia, no clinging dust.

Once you figure it out, that it's all in your head, all the dreams, the love, once you know that everything is created in the huge, high-voltage workshop of our minds, you're saved. You just stop the thing before it gets started. You switch off the turbines, turn off the fantasy machine before it gets out of control. You can turn it on for a test run just to see what it'll do, the flush of new blood, the trembling, the hammering heart. That can be dangerous, you can forget where the off switch is, you can forget everything and tumble into the dream, into love, as if it were a reality that came from the outside, from others.

3

BENEATH THE EARTH

---

*G*INA DA SYLVA was a writer.

Writers write. They build walls of words to shut out the clamor. Each word sends up shovelfuls of earth until the windows of ordinary life are covered over. And on they write, they burrow deep into words, they tunnel into their words until each one gives up its inviolable secret depth, sometimes pain, other times trance, it depends on their temperament, or their astrological sign. In those lonely, dark depths they lay out their imagination and begin polishing their creation.

That's how those 300-page books of theirs come to be.

That's how writers forget that there are people out there, waiting at the other end of the tunnel. People willing to read their books, but who still hunger and thirst, who are afraid of dying without having known love. To those people, hungry for normal life, writers have nothing to give, not a drop of water, not a brotherly embrace, nothing but words, the beautiful and frigid words of their subterranean domain.

IN HER PHOTOS, the first thing that strikes you about Gina Da Sylva is that barrier of oil-black hair that hides everything but her two phosphorescent eyes, glowing like braziers of fury.

When she answered the door, that's what I got first, the acid shower of her burning eyes. She was tall and slender, with a few discreet wrinkles, dressed entirely in black. Hair, sheath of clothing and ankle boots included. I thought of a stick of licorice, minus the sugar.

"Mahone Inc.," she repeated, suspicious, looking over my shoulder for he who was not there. "He's not with you?"

He, meaning Zeno the First, the Dark Master of Snatch.

An aggressive aggregate of gears and sharp spines was masquerading as a sculpture in the center of the foyer. Things went quickly downhill as it ripped a patch from my coat as I attempted to sneak by. "It's a Vaillancourt," she said, as if that could absolve it. "Superb," I agreed, "superbly effective against thieves." We traded exaggerated smiles as we looked each other over cautiously.

It wasn't going to be easy to like her, even enough to work with her. What about that transsexual starlet's first name? Why did she dress in black like a crow? Why write novels instead of treatises on computers, robotics, cryogenics, the new economy, resolutics, domotics or some other essential discipline?

As she walked ahead of me, black and monkish, I imagined the two of them, Zeno and her, impaling themselves passionately on the Vaillancourt's spikes, more naked than a pair of fakirs.

Jealous? Not me. I've got nothing against Zeno for being a man genetically in thrall to his hard-on. But her! At fifty-five, letting herself be mounted by a gnome who could be her son!

Fifty-five years old. Twenty-eight books to her name. A stack of literary awards no normal person had ever heard of. Twenty-eight times 300 pages: that's no laughing matter. That's not just an edifice, it's an entire subterranean city she constructed in darkness. That city has only one inhabitant, always the same, surrounded by cardboard figures and abstract scenery. Her. Always her. I'd skimmed over enough passages to size up the swollen contours of her ego. She can write only about herself, but she's not good enough to disguise that fact. Her heroines are named Helena, or Mina, or Bella. They write, they paint, they translate or they teach. They're all beautiful, wounded, alone, and growing older with every book. They travel extensively, but almost nothing happens to them: a man or two, some sexual gymnastics, a well-turned quote or two and great effluvia of intellectual angst. Then, like a sudden spasm, an unexpected tragedy smoldering beneath the ashes bursts into flame: they die, they are raped, they discover some terrible family secret, they murder someone. And the book ends. The consolation is that every book ends. That's the best part.

Of course, it's all very sculpted. "A powerful, impeccable style where every word counts," say the critics and the prize awarders.

The words are there, standing at attention. What else can they do? They've been issued their orders to stand guard in the underground city, and repel any intrusion of imperfect life.

SHE ASKED ME TO SIT DOWN. Then sat down herself.

Would she ask if I liked her books? They can never help themselves. They're always looking for approval, admiration. On principle, I never give handouts to beggars. Neither money nor false compliments.

But she asked nothing. She waited. From close range, her tiny, piercing eyes were more intense than angry, as though equipped with x-rays constantly scanning everything they encountered. In response, I pulled the digital camera from my bag and pointed it at her, and around her, in hopes of intimidating her.

"Photos?" she said. "What's this with the photos? We were talking about a Web page."

"On a Web page," I told her, "you need lots of images and sound, but the fewest words possible."

"The fewest words possible," she echoed.

Then, unexpectedly, she burst out laughing.

"Fine," she said. "That's fine with me. That means I won't have to talk."

"Far from it. Talk. You have to talk. I need your words to know which ones to eliminate."

"But my books are full of words."

She didn't ask, *Haven't you read them?* She scanned me with her x-ray eyes and I saw how she saw me, all prickly with hesitations and reservations, and that she wasn't even upset.

"People your age don't like what I write. Too bad for me.

My publisher thinks if I exhibited myself on the Internet, I'd convince young people to like me. I don't write to be nice to the young, or the old either. I don't write to provide nourishment for anyone. I don't write because it gives me pleasure. If I didn't write, if I hadn't written, I'd be dead, that much is certain. It's the only thing that keeps me alive. I write for myself, I write about myself, I don't know how to do anything else."

She's black, the absence of color I hate the most, and she's getting old, her books are encyclopedias of narcissism, and Zeno slept with her. But right then, at that moment, she spoke without filters, and the resentment that had been blocking my view fell away, and I began to see her. Now I could work.

I photographed her, examined her, recorded her in a state of total neutrality. She liked that. It made her want to talk.

"I have two children," she said. "They live in Toronto. Both of them. I never go to Toronto.

"I don't like writers," she said. "Neither do you, you don't like them either. Writers are no more neurotic than you are. It's just that they hold up their neuroses for everyone to see.

"My latest misadventure with writers," she said, "there were ten of us, from ten different countries. We were in France for a reading on the subject of failure. The idea was to read something we'd written, supposedly a failed text. But no one can face a diminished image of himself, we were all frightened to death, all of us were madly scrambling to display our talents without making it look that way. Everyone read a magnificent text, claiming it was a failure. It made for a horrible evening. The painful pride of the writers shone through like a bleeding wound on center stage, and the neurotic spectators applauded wildly.

"I slept with your boyfriend," she said. "Congratulations—as a lover, he's got potential. Neurotic though, terribly neurotic. He reminds me of the Bishop Syndrome in Pierre Laliberté's books. You haven't read Pierre Laliberté, of course. It felt good to sleep with your Mahone. I hadn't slept with anyone for six months.

"Do you want a whisky?" she said. "You do? If you don't want to talk, at least you can drink with me.

"Pierre Laliberté," she said. "We all envy his anonymity. It protects him from ball-breakers of all kinds. These days, no one would dare be invisible like him, it would be like committing hara-kiri as an author. Besides, deep down, who wants to be invisible? If you want to be invisible, don't publish books. Keep them in your drawer, and take them out once a week and caress and despise them. Every Friday, for instance. I have nothing in common with Pierre Laliberté. Except my sister. He's been living with my sister for the past twenty years.

"Let me say a word about my books," she said, "even though I know you don't like them. Each of them contains one character who represents death. Not death as you imagine it, morbid and despairing. Death as deadpan. Death can have a sense of humor. It does, in fact. Each of my books could be subtitled: *Death Laughs Somewhere Near.*

"Is that your natural hair color?" she said. "Poor thing. No matter what they say, blondes never get anywhere in life, especially in love."

WHEN SHE DISMISSED ME several hours later with a warm, firm hand, and steered me around the Vaillancourt, upon which I was just about to disembowel myself, I was stunned and livid. I walked aimlessly for an eternity, wondering which way led towards home.

It was the whisky. I never drink whisky.

Night had fallen, or so it seemed, though in my spongy state I couldn't swear by anything. Maybe night had fallen only on me. I eventually made it home. My house had been whistling at me like a dog, and finally I heard it.

There's no place like home for being sick. I collapsed, sweating, relieved of any semblance of dignity. I couldn't manage vomiting. My stomach was quivering with weakness. Maybe it was hunger, but I couldn't bring myself to eat. My body had become so foreign to me that I didn't know whether to fill it or empty it so it would leave me in peace.

I never knew how huge my place was, and how empty, how terrifyingly cold it was when you're at death's door. I was going to die without knowing what I was dying of, too young and unknown to be wept over by anyone. I was in such suffering, and now I would die and Zeno would never look at me with those beautiful, desperate eyes we reserve for those we're about to lose, and I couldn't even enjoy the hurt I would cause him for the first time in my life, Zeno you dirty dog.

Keep your sense of humor, whispered my condor, my immortal condor soul. Keep your sense of humor. Who else has a sense of humor? Death, that's what *she* said. Death has a sense of humor.

I got up and straightened my contorted body. Keep your sense of humor. I sat down in front of my computer. It's *her*.

Not the whisky, not my body that's too youthful to make me
suffer, it's my head I have to set free. My head's been poisoned
by *her,* her rasping alcohol, her tarantula venom. Gina the
black widow. In my inoffensive state of neutrality, she imprisoned me with her calm voice and watchtower eyes, and forced
me to swallow all her bitter bile.

That was how I hit on the design of her Web site, and for
hours I worked hard to build it, as curtains of murky fog fell
one by one from my mind.

First her head appeared in a big close-up. No ordinary head,
that you can tell immediately. Hair too black, eyes too fiery.
Black surrounded her like a natural halo. Joined to her head
was a body just as black, scurrying swiftly towards the center of
a spider web. You couldn't find a more weblike Web page.

As you tracked Gina the spider across her web, you could
access twenty-eight hyperlinks, twenty-eight intersection
points, each giving the title of one of her twenty-eight books
followed by a three-line excerpt, and a critical note that broke
off as soon as it started making sense. Each time, twenty-eight
times over, you'd hear Gina's lovely voice over a requiem (perhaps Mozart, or Arvo Pärt, I've got to check with Zeno, he
knows all there is to know about that kind of spectral music)
speaking these words: *Death Laughs Somewhere Near.*

A beautiful sentence, *Death Laughs Somewhere Near.* Even if
she did write it.

NOW THAT EVERYTHING was perfectly clear, I was exhausted, my body craved sleep. Gina Da Sylva was losing her
aura, her venom, fading away like those outdated products
that have given up their essence and that can be kept alive

only by technical means. I lay down. My sleep would last a hundred years, like that of an insipid Sleeping Beauty, untroubled by dreams or moist kisses.

Noise at the door. Someone was ringing, then knocking. There were still some fanatics who acted as though there was no such thing as electronics, and who stubbornly insisted on knocking on people's doors to sell them calendars, carpet cleaner or fear insurance. I won't answer, not even to curse them out.

A voice added to the din. Was that my name being called? Some door-to-door salesmen stop at nothing to get you to open your door, they even call your name as if we'd once played show-your-thingy together when we were kids.

Whose voice was that?

Zeno's?

The last time I saw him hanging from my doorbell was in another life, when he lived at my place and had lost his keys again, and I'd given up waiting for him because I'd waited too long, too much sobbing in the bathroom.

My face was pale with surprise and fatigue. His was in shock. Something serious must have happened to his computers.

"Florence, you've got to help me."

"What time is it?"

"Who gives a damn?"

If I were a respectable person, I'd have stood up without arrogance, wrapped in the dignity of my self-love, and said, "I do. I give a damn, Zeno. I'm exhausted, I'm sick. Can't you see I almost died?"

But I hung there, silent and servile, ready to do anything to lift the mask of distress from his face. He didn't speak until I'd touched his hand.

"Pokey's dead."

As soon as the words left his mouth, they turned against him, stabbing instead of releasing him. He didn't weep—it was much worse. He was pale and dry like a tower of plaster slowly crumbling into dust. We wrung our hands, and for the next five minutes we didn't dare speak for fear that our words would join forces with the ones we'd already said and destroy him once and for all.

"What do you want me to do?" I finally asked.

"Help me. I've got to bury him."

IT HAD BEEN NIGHT for so long that something must have gone wrong up there, where they manufacture the light, unless someone else's war—which we couldn't care less about in these parts—had plunged us into nuclear winter. Anything could have happened. The air crackled with cold, the gray earth awaited the snow, and like zombies we slogged our way up the carriage path along the flank of Mount Royal in the dim light from the city below. Pokey was on his way to let his old bones and all that remained of his coat decompose by Beaver Lake, under the ancient maple he so loved to sniff and perfume with his piss. And we were seeing him off.

Zeno was towing the corpse behind him, wrapped in a handsome tartan blanket of cashmere and virgin Shetland wool, in a small wagon. I knew that blanket. It was a gift from me, for the back seat of his van. I was carrying a knapsack that dug into my shoulders; in it a shovel and some other tools clanked funereally at every step. We did not speak. Whenever we hit a hole or the wagon collided with an obstacle, Zeno looked back and said, "Come on, old boy, come on." It broke my heart.

There's only one Beaver Lake at the top of Mount Royal, and that's where we were heading. But there were a good dozen ancient trees looming out of the darkness, and any one of them could have been on the receiving end of Pokey's prodigious pee. Zeno chose one of them by some mysterious process, and hurried towards it with the wagon, as though going to meet an old friend.

"Here," he said.

I gave him the knapsack, took the flashlight he handed me and directed the light as he set about digging into the half-frozen ground. Beneath its surface, there was much less earth than rocks and roots. Zeno wielded the axe as much as the shovel, then scraped away the soil with his bare hands. I stood there uselessly, keeping the light on and shivering. I was a stranger to the love between Zeno and Pokey, superfluous from beginning to end.

"Here's where we part company, old dog."

He lifted the blanket, revealing Pokey in the glare of the flashlight, like a dramatic, theatrical corpse: stiff, patently fake, head stretched out as if still begging for a pat, which Zeno gave him. He ran his slender hands across the coarse fur, and I understood just how alive Pokey had once been, with his foul-smelling breath, his old dog's rasping and snoring, how his declining life had truly been life in all its splendor. Now that he was disconnected from reality, Pokey became real to me, poor Pokey, poor once-living creature I never appreciated, poor sack of fur reduced to silence and decomposition.

Zeno wrapped him in the blanket again and dropped him into the fresh-dug grave. The soil did not return the slightest sound. He squatted close to the hole and started filling it up with fistfuls of dirt. Those gestures seemed to flow so harmoniously—where did he learn them?

All the time I stood there, shivering with my petty concerns, training the flashlight on Zeno. I had no thoughts of grandeur, only a sudden, sorrowful reflection about my lovely blanket, cashmere and virgin Shetland, condemned to the stains of the soil and others, worse yet, of Pokey's putrifying juices. I managed to keep my mouth shut. Lighting technicians are not authorized to speak during the performance.

Zeno's voice gradually blended with the silence.

"Sleep, old dog, sleep in peace, I won't forget you. You were a brave dog, a fine dog, no dog was ever as fine as you. You have the right to sleep, your dog's body has the right to rest without suffering. You got off to a lousy start in life. You could have been fierce, you could have been vicious. People treated you like a dog, but you never hated them. Your first master's children, they dreamed up ways to torment you, they hit you with baseball bats, hung you by the tail, drove nails into your paws, stuck you in the refrigerator. What a wreck you were when I adopted you, old battle-scarred Pokey, I had to bind your wounds and nurse you back to health. And when you met those little monsters again, you yelped with delight, poor old Pokey, there wasn't an ounce of malice or rancor in you. May those children, wherever they are, receive all the pain they gave you. That's my wish today. You see, I'm not as kind as you were, old dog, handsome ugly old dog, mistreated dog who loved me so much."

I knelt on the ground, my legs suddenly cut from beneath me, then dropped the useless flashlight and began to toss fistfuls of earth onto my lovely wool blanket. The poignant music of Zeno's voice pervaded the night.

"You weren't much for looks, Pokey. That's why I loved you right off the bat. The pretty ones get all the petting, but they end up dying of boredom. You were so happy when you got a pat on the head, like you knew what a rare and precious gift a caress was. When I touched you, I think you burst out laughing. It was so easy to make you happy, and making you happy made me so happy. How can I live without that? Pokey, my gimpy old dog! What good are we if we can't make anybody happy? Go to sleep now, don't think about me, go to sleep, don't worry about a thing. I didn't put you into a box, you see, so you can blend in with the earth. I don't believe in anything, but I'd like to believe that your spirit will lift itself away from the earth. Even if I don't believe in anything, I'd like to believe there'll be another life for your dog's spirit. It will be an easier life, a better life, and we'll meet again. Next time we'll meet sooner, that's a promise."

When Zeno's voice finally fell silent, you could hear the wind that springs up at dawn, and the sound of me shedding warm tears. Zeno's voice, true and loving like I'd never known it. The pain, the hurt that shelters everywhere on this earth and in the earth. As Zeno finished filling the hole with generous gestures—so calm, so fitting—that seemed to be an extension of his voice, I wept. I wept, wept, I who had never cared for Pokey, who didn't like him, I wept for all the tormented creatures, for all the love condemned to float aimlessly, then wither away forever, unrequited. Where had all that water been before it poured from me, how could I send it back where it had come from? I wept so pitiously that Zeno interrupted his gravedigger's work to take me in his arms.

"There, there, Flora, forgive me, I shouldn't have, forgive me, Flora, you've just lost your father . . ."

It worked. It brought my sobbing and my miserable tear-shedding to a screeching halt. *Pepa?* What did *Pepa* have to do with it? He never came anywhere near Mount Royal. Anger welled up in me. I pushed away Zeno and his tender, loving arms.

"I'm cold. I'm tired. I'm thirsty."

"Wait. I brought some cherry Cokes."

Together, we got to our feet, and together we felt the presence behind us of something big, something terrifying and very much *alive.* There were two of them. In the gray dawn light, we saw two monsters, two mythical creatures, two enormous Pokeys returned to devour us. Perhaps our grave-digging work had not been done according to the rules; perhaps the offering of tears had been insufficient. I took shelter again in Zeno's arms, too afraid to scream. One of the monsters began to speak:

"All right, what are you doin' here?"

That snapped us back to real life, where there are fewer specters than ass-kickers. The two monsters turned out to be two horses, astride which were two policemen, one of whom, considering the five-thousand-volt beam he shone upon us, irradiating us to the marrow, was no amateur when it came to special effects.

"You can't be in the park at night. What are you doin' here?" repeated Horse Number One.

"Looks like they're buryin' something," commented Horse Number Two.

Horse Number Two had a more gentle voice, a female voice. Thanks to parity and sexual non-discrimination, the pigs now come accompanied by their sows, the stallions by their mares, gentler but unfortunately more inquisitive. Horse Number Two spotted the shovel and the grave, at which she aimed her spotlight long enough to reheat Pokey's coagulated blood. Our goose was cooked. Now we were going to have to do it all in reverse, exhume the poor critter and risk his chances of reincarnation, simply because his master could not distinguish between a park and a cemetery.

"Please, you're blinding me."

Zeno assumed an authoritative stance, arms folded across his chest, a block of granite suddenly grown taller by a foot, that kept on growing. The beam of a light disappeared a moment, then returned, more intense than before.

"What did you bury over there?" asked Horse Number Two.

"Rocks," replied Zeno, calmly. "Every new moon, we bury rocks. It's a Mohawk ritual, to renew the earth. This is Mohawk ancestral land, in case you didn't know. Your horses are trampling the burial ground where my forefathers made their wampum."

"What's he talkin' about?" wondered Horse Number One.

"He's an Indian," sighed Horse Number Two.

They talked things over in low tones, perplexed and frustrated, and probably too sleepy to want to handle what could be an explosive situation. The spotlight snapped back on, setting us aflame from head to toe. The beam came to rest on me.

"I suppose she's an Indian?" asked Horse Number One with the last vestiges of an aggressiveness that did not want to die.

"She's my girlfriend," said Zeno in his serious voice.

Miraculously, that's where it ended. The ample hindquarters of the real horses began to move off, and the barked command of Horse Number One reached us, muffled by distance.

"You got ten minutes to finish your business, then beat it."

"Yes, sir."

Zeno's skill left me breathless. I turned towards him to congratulate him, maybe even kiss him. Then I saw the look on his face, tense, furious, ready to spit or bite, or worse, scream. He did scream. Shit. He screamed at the cops, they weren't that far away, they would hear him, they're going to turn around, come back and give us trouble without end.

"Fuck you fucking bastards ass-fucking dogs FUCK YOU!"

"Shut up, will you!"

I leapt on him and tried to muzzle him, and for a couple precious seconds I succeeded while he was figuring out where this unidentified adversary had come from, and how to pry himself from her grasp. He figured it out in short order and sent me flying, but that's okay, the cops were gone for good and the fall didn't break my bones, not the most obvious ones anyway.

Afterwards, we stood there for an eternity, saying nothing. I watched him burrow into his knapsack and extract three cans of cherry Coke. He opened one and handed it to me. I turned it down. He placed it at my feet. He poured the other over the freshly turned earth that covered Pokey, slowly, with the same movements as before. The third he emptied down his gullet in the wink of an eye, with an irresistible glug-glug that reminded me how thirsty I was. When I started to drink too, he broke the silence.

"Did I hurt you?"

"Yes."

A second eternity elapsed. Might as well take my lumps. He'd offer no further excuses. I sat down beside him, grimacing in put-on pain. He rubbed my back for a long time. I made no effort to stop him. The day was entirely upon us, illuminated by a cardboard sun that gave no warmth.

"Not bad for a made-up story," I finally said.

"What story?"

"The Mohawk thing. You, a Mohawk."

The whole thing seemed so preposterous, so comical that I burst out laughing. I could have laughed for hours. He wrapped me in his indulgent look.

"It wasn't all made up," he said.

"How's that?"

"My mother's Mohawk."

"Your mother?"

His mother. I pictured her, though I had very little to go on: a tiny, copper-skinned woman in a dress several sizes too large for her, bustling this way and that around Zeno, brushing the dust from his clothes and nibbling at his cheek as I moped, waiting for her to say hello to me. There had been nothing Iroquois about that little suburban bungalow and its machine-trimmed cedar hedges, or about Zeno's silk shirts.

Still.

You never really know anyone. You might have touched every centimeter of his skin, memorized the shadings of his voice, his emotional highs and lows. You might study, compare, analyze and end up believing that you've succeeded in isolating a human being in a test tube, labeled and classified him. But you'll never really know anyone.

It's enough to discourage you. Or make you want to start all over again.

Crushed and mute with fatigue, we wound our way down Mount Royal, Pokey's ghost lying like an invisible weight in the empty wagon. I forgot to think, and asked a question I hadn't asked for a long time.

"Want to come over to my place and rest for a while?"

He'll say yes. His entire body says Yes, intensely, his eyes, his hand as it burns my shoulder, the sudden swelling at the base of his belly, everything but that flat, expressionless fragment of a voice he lets escape from his mouth.

"Maud's expecting me."

4

THE TENANT

$\mathcal{I}$N OUR HEADS ghosts lurk, so unobtrusive we forge they're there. We walk around, eat, all the while we're carrying them with us, weightless as angels, enveloped in the silent sheets of our nerve endings. Then a holy place looms up before us, a place of the accursed, a place that belongs to them but into which we've intruded, out of absentmindedness or stupidity, and suddenly they rouse themselves and come tumbling from our heads, hitting the ground with a ferocious roar, the din of awakened ghosts.

We deserved it.

I hadn't been back to the family table for a long time. Necessarily, at the family table, it couldn't be any other way. There he was, propped lopsidedly against the window, a hand stretched out on the tablecloth with all its veins and living, famished blood. Pepa. The old man called Pepa.

He was ignoring me. Nothing new there. He toyed with the multicolored pills lined up in front of him on the tablecloth. It's true, they were cute: red, yellow, blue, round, rectangular, opaque or transparent, with their adorable tiny logos, you couldn't help but want to touch and play with them if you were a little girl. But you're not allowed to. All those years. All those years of watching Pepa toy with his pills as he waited for his nourishment to be placed before him.

He was served first. He would start eating, and not stop, even when the plates were not yet set before the others. His sons, his daughter. His wife. Or the odd time, a friend of his daughter or of his sons. He would look at the other guests' plates. Enviously. He craved the contents of the other plates, the meat that was rarer, the vegetables that were more tender, the sauce more copious. He wanted what his sons, his daughter and his wife were eating. If he could, he would have taken the last bite from each of their mouths and put it into his mouth. His mouth, his.

Be quiet, Florence. He's an old man. He's Pepa.

Pepa had always been an old man. Not so, according to his wife. He was one hell of a lover, she claimed, until not all that long ago. Until their daughter was born.

Hard, hard to imagine.

Words like "one hell of a lover" lose the battle for credibility. But why would his wife lie? Sometimes she'd show pictures, photos of the Hell of a Lover as a younger man. But even the photos weren't believable. Like caricatures of Pepa as an old man. The young Pepa, the Hell of a Lover, false youth preparing for old age.

Be quiet, Florence.

Pepa always acted like a tenant. What's a tenant? A tenant is someone who feels no sense of responsibility for the place where he lives. Someone who can get up at any time and leave the table for no good reason. He can choose not to speak to anyone. He can claim that no one is there. He has the right. He hands out the money, hands over his entire salary, and in exchange he gets a table at which to eat and a bed in which to sleep. The other tenants might become a little invasive at times, but he tries to pay no attention. Whenever he finds them insufferably alive, he retires to the basement, and makes them vanish until the next communal meal. *Log off.*

Who did it? Who inflicted the silent wound from which he could not recover, that kept him cold and silent, even in moments of warmth when food should have filled him with well-being? Who made Pepa old and indifferent for all eternity?

His wife, maybe. Maybe Bruno, or Stéphane.

Maybe you, Florence.

It could only have been me. The coincidence was too overwhelming: birth of the Daughter, death of the Hell of a Lover.

Pepa stood up. He'd finished his dessert, cast an envious eye at the plates of the other guests until he'd been served a second portion and, having eaten his fill, he got up. Slowly he made his way towards the basement without a backwards glance, with that curious walk he'd invented. Arms folded across his chest, shoulders hunched forward, his entire body curled like an armor-plated shell around the precious kernel that his innumerable enemies threatened with attack. The heart, his heart.

If a heart is well enough protected, there is no reason why it should die.

No one else watched as Pepa disappeared into the basement. Not my brother Bruno, or my brother Stéphane, or my mother. Even before he became a ghost, I alone watched his sudden desertion, his flight in the heat of combat.

Had he looked in my direction, had he bothered to acknowledge my existence at least once, he would have read these tender words in the eyes of his little Florence, both girl and woman: Coward. Deserter. Good riddance.

And other similar niceties.

MOTHER LINED UP the birthday presents in front of me. It was my birthday, after all. A few days ago, in any case. It's tough to be alone on your birthday, and protect yourself against everyone's festive rage. Still, most times I manage it. I imagine a greater celebration taking place somewhere else, an immoderate celebration with people who love me immoderately. There's no other recipe for survival. No one, not even the people to whom you are most indifferent, will allow you to spend your birthday in conversation with yourself. All day long, Zeno kept dialing me up on the computer. I didn't answer. I was spending my time in the company of the Web, with billions of Web surfers around the globe. Not alone in the slightest. Totally in phase with myself, instead of being forced to *celebrate* in the company of foreign bodies, *celebrate* by absorbing liters of alcohol that always remind you that you want to forget, not to mention make you sick as a dog.

No drink for me. I never drink unless I'm forced to. I'm not dependent on anything. Not wine, and not psychotropics. Not nicotine or caffeine or sexine or lovine. To be cold turkey in this universe of anesthetized druggies can only be regarded as heroism. That's me: A heroine without a heroin habit.

MY BROTHERS Bruno and Stéphane, and I, their little sister. What changed in our family deposit box? Apparently nothing. Pepa deserted the table the way he always did. Bruno folded napkins into paper airplanes. Stéphane pinched my leg under the table. Mother was serving dessert. We laughed loudly, like children who know nothing of the world's solitude and hunger.

But something about the youthful lead characters rang hollow. Someone replaced Stéphane's curly hair with a preposterous pink shower cap. Then they stuffed spindly Bruno with paunches and protuberances that defeated his well-cut clothes.

My two older brothers came down with old age, the illness from which there is no recovery.

We'll have to rewrite the family meal scene totally. Find new actors to play the kids.

Why are we just the way we were ten years ago, twenty-five years ago? Where are our wives, our lovers, our children? Why are we sterile? Why haven't we sent out living feelers, rootlets or rhizomes?

Bruno was the only one of us to go through a divorce as official as it was trying. He and his ex-wife had no children, but now she was working on a second with her second husband. My brother Stéphane was gay without gaiety; he repelled the frivolous young men whose love he craved. No offspring from that quarter, unless some momentous change occurs. Then there's me. Nothing to hope for from me either. I'm so blond, so young and so beautiful that it must be terrifying for anyone who casts his eye on my alluring carcass. I haven't considered the sperm bank yet. I've never liked frozen foods.

Whereas my mother.

Mother twirls round and round in her low-cut dress and serves me a glass of champagne I will not drink. Mother is radiant. Mother at fifty-eight has a new lover. New for her, that is, for he is a graying, worm-eaten specimen who has already made the rounds, but who's counting? She has someone to stroke her, someone to lean her creaking bones against. Not a clue how she did it. Bruno and Stéphane, who visit her every week, know no more than I do, but they haven't the faintest idea from what hidden closet she pulled her arthritic Romeo—Alonzo by name—who urges her to splash florid perfumes like a little girl and has her wear skirts well above her knobby knees. All quite mysterious, and vaguely disgusting. Temptresses on the comeback trail are everywhere, their aim is true with their sagging tits that they go on flaunting as if they were juvenile jewels. When are they going to stop blocking the fast lane and let the sportier models zip past? *Delete. Log off.*

Keep quiet, Florence. You're a cynical, envious monster.

Open your presents and keep your mouth shut.

These are the people who love me. Three, to be exact. They gave me birthday gifts. They provided me with a tranquil, uneventful childhood. Even the fourth person, he who is no longer at the table and whom I continue not to cherish, never interfered with my existence. Never threatened me with violence, never demanded anything either difficult or easy, never raised a hand against me. (Never touched, never caressed, never rocked, never kissed, never never.)

If I'd been mature and well-adjusted, I wouldn't have asked for more. But I have a nasty little heart, due to a lack of attention, even from strangers, from anyone worthwhile. Each gift that I strip bare, bestowed by over-intimate strangers, locks me into my own pettiness. A mauve silk negligee that will no doubt set my computer's pulse racing, a portable television to add another screen to my adventurous life, a magnifying mirror in which to contemplate the glorious wrinkles that will soon be crossing my face. Thank you, thank you, it's all too much, may I go home and cry now please?

My mother doesn't see it that way. She went on swathing me in the cloying scent of flowers and concentrate of love. She patted my head for no particular reason, ordered me to drink champagne, insisted I try on the mauve silk negligee. Several times I caught her glancing furtively at the kitchen clock. She was expecting another guest, and the guest was late. No doubt about it, she was expecting that personal someone of hers. You can never be too careful with fifty-something nymphettes. Who knows, maybe she'd planned a gigantic family orgy at which her late-bloomer, her long-toothed lover-boy, would put in an appearance. That was him ringing now, coming through the door to the tune of her bawdy banter, rolling right up to us, tiny and invisible, hidden behind an avalanche of white flowers. I never imagined him so short of leg, so minuscule, almost as minuscule as . . .

Zeno.

Him again. Forever and always.

He deposited the flowers on my lap. Kissed me on the lips. Everyone laughed at my open-mouthed amazement. I was

well and truly had. Zeno brandished a beribboned gift, a book
or maybe a box of chocolates if luck deigned to smile upon
me. He dropped it among the flowers on my lap, mutilating a
few in the process. My mother handed him a glass of champagne, my brothers made room for him. In no time, he had
figured out where the best seat in the house was, with the
laughter and the champagne. There I was, alone with my astonishment that was no longer justified, too entangled in the
bouquet to feign a semblance of good cheer. I needed to find a
vase big enough to handle this overpopulation of flowers.
There was nothing in Mother's tightly packed cupboards, so
I jammed them into a plastic bucket. Good riddance. Now,
open the gift-wrapped box everyone seems to be ignoring. I
tore open the wrapping for the sheer delight of ripping
something with scant ceremony.

It's a book. Oh joy.

While my mother and brothers conspired with Zeno, who
quickly became what he always was, the center of attention,
charming and adorable, I decided I couldn't stay here one
minute more. The depth of their betrayal mortified me. They
have no right to do that, neither my family nor him, especially
him, my ex-amorous illusion, they have no right to throw a
party for the express purpose of excluding me, they have no
right to pretend they like being together, as if a group could
exist that would include the five of us. Zeno's got Maud,
Stéphane has his fairies, I've got nobody, and Mother's got
her new old lover who's pawing impatiently at the ground
somewhere nearby. They have no right, I kept repeating. I
didn't ask for this artificial reunion in the first place. One of

my inviolable rights has been violated. I got up. Where could I go that would be immediate and effective? I got up and stomped off towards the basement. My step lacked assurance on account of who lurked down there, on account of the tenant, the tenant's ghost. How would he react to the intrusion of the Daughter into his protected domain?

Zeno cut short the breathless suspense.

"Where are you going, Flora? You didn't even look at your book. It's a Laliberté. Didn't you notice? A Pierre Laliberté. What a title, eh? *Falterlust.* What a twisted title. It's his latest, his first in six years. I tore through it in three hours, it's terribly powerful, stirring, magical. I got you a numbered copy, it's worth a fortune."

If it's worth a fortune, I could always resell it. Or so I told myself as I returned, falsely contrite, to the book lying on the table amid splashes of sauce and wine stains. Zeno was holding it in his hands, waving it high like a monstrance. Titillated by curiosity, my mother and my brothers attempted to lay their hands on it, but he wouldn't let them. He would surrender it only to me, alas, into my unclean hands. I was the one who would forever be laden with this powerful, stirring and magical object.

Not even a picture on the cover. A white communicant's dust jacket with the ridiculous title printed sideways in red letters, and the name Pierre Laliberté in large type, also in red. From the weight alone you could tell that it was going to run some 320 pages.

"What's a *Falterlust?*" Mother asked in that inflamed, second-youth voice of hers.

"It's something that doesn't exist, at least not in the dictionary," I replied, dripping sarcasm.

But Zeno brushed aside my objections with a joyous toss of his head.

"It's a compound word, a fabulous compound word of the kind that fabulous magician is always inventing. *Falterlust* is a combination of *falter* and *lust,* and that's exactly what the novel is about. But you have to read it, you have to read it, that's all I can say."

Since my mother and brothers were relatively normal people, they knew nothing of the spectral existence of Pierre Laliberté. Zeno undertook to educate them, and launched into a highfalutin exposition on the clandestine life and work of the object of his admiration, sparing not a detail of that which already long ceased to interest me. Happy birthday, *Flora-at-your-service.* I returned to my place at the table, resigned and placid, and poured myself a glass of champagne and drank it to the last drop.

Since the book had attached itself to my hands, weighing them down, I decided to open it. Since it was open, why not read a little? In my own fashion, minimalistic and precise. The first and the last sentence would be quite sufficient. All the rest being, as we know, nothing but indolent development, small talk and redundancy.

The first sentence read like this: *The hospital was meadow green, swamp green, green like birch when their leaves are one day and a few minutes old, and this was why we made the hospital our meadow, our swamp, our forest of young birch quivering with birdsong and the smell of sap.*

With an opening like that, just try to find a sensible story, the kind that can stand on its own two feet. I knew better than to hope—I leapt across the useless chapters and the 320 pages, and abridged the delirium.

The last sentence read like this: *The heart is an involuntary muscle.*

What kind of sentence is that? Where did that sentence come from, and why did it catch me like a right to the gut? Opaque silence closed in around me, though two seconds before there had been sound and people all around. I slipped into the silence that became a nightmarish sea so troubled that I could expect nothing but horrific shipwrecks full of stench and pain. In the silence, someone very old and very dead floated to the surface. It was Pepa, of course, returned from the basement without a sound. He may have been very old and very dead, but he spoke, and said, *The heart is an involuntary muscle.* The words were ridiculous, as out of place in his dead-man's mouth as they would have been had he been living.

Pepa could not have spoken those words. No words in the world could have been further from Pepa. The proof? They were sleeping in the pages of a book, and there is no possible relation between the pain of Pepa's death and books.

SUDDENLY THE WATERS of silence became limpid enough for me to see everything without terror. I saw the hospital, and the night during which those words were born, someone stepping between Pepa and me and pronouncing them, a doctor, a man in a white lab coat with liquid eyes who touched my shoulder with great compassion, as if I were the one who had just died.

I rose to the surface, into Zeno's words. Zeno was still talking, and my mother and brothers were listening to him with
an attention that had begun to falter. It took me forever to
stand up, and all at once my legs were twice as old as my body.
The champagne. I never drink champagne.

"We don't know anything about him," said Zeno. "No
one's ever seen his face, no one knows where he comes from,
what he likes, what he does when he's not writing."

"Pierre Laliberté is a doctor," I blurted out.

Zeno chattered on, then fell silent, then asked me to
repeat what I just said. I repeated. He burst out laughing.
Everyone burst out laughing, me included. Nothing is as
easy as being funny when you don't know the reason why. Far
below, beneath my failing legs, I heard laughter from him
who never laughed.

5

FALTERLUST

I WAS SITTING IN a hospital corridor, eleven o'clock at
night. Around me the walls were green. The last time I
hadn't noticed they were green. I'd always thought white was
the default color in the limbo of sickness. I thought that only
white possessed that perfect neutrality. Maybe green was
found only in the corridors and on the walls of the floor where
I was seated. I'd have to check, ask questions, get up from my
straight-backed chair, an enterprise as exhausting as it was
daunting. Maybe white was appropriate only for those floors
where life resists and lifts its head, reinvigorated by surgery
and combative medication. Not here. This was the floor where
life hung by a thread and where threads were constantly
breaking. The floor of death. The walls were death green.

At the other end of the corridor orderlies were bustling
about, busily retying the severed threads for an hour or two, a

minute or two. What gentleness, what extraterrestrial devotion. I recognized the maternal nurse—she didn't recognize me, of course—who had brought me coffee and led me to this quiet extremity of the corridor, like a noise-sensitive decorative fixture. She put logbooks and computers at my disposal, tracked down the names of the two men on duty in this fateful wing the night Pepa died. The first was Dr. Woggan; he would soon be arriving. The second was a male nurse who would begin his shift in two hours, by the name of Bertrand Poach. One of the two wrote books using the pseudonym Pierre Laliberté, but she didn't know that. Before assigning me my seat and my coffee, she called me *dearie,* in a universal maternal voice that made me want to weep.

I waited for Dr. Woggan or male nurse Poach, whoever smiled first with the liquid eyes I'd recognize right off. I waited and I listened. What else could I do? From the rooms closest to me came the rattle of death, the circumspect music of shallow breathing, the gentle purr of a waiting room. As I waited, I imagined I was in an ordinary waiting room, like in an ultramodern airport. Travelers wait lying down, each one in an individual cubicle. The ultimate in luxury. Better than first class, where at best you can stretch your legs. This is supreme class: each passenger has an entire aircraft to himself to reach his personal destination. Passengers are not requested to proceed anywhere; the departure gate will come to them.

I was dying of fear.

Not because of Pepa. Or room 2029, where a new torture victim lay at whom I barely glanced as I walked down the corridor. The thought of Pepa's death didn't frighten me. To tell the truth, I wasn't thinking of Pepa at all. Pepa wasn't here.

He was rocking himself in the dream-like basement of our family home, strolling through some infernal shopping mall placed at the disposal of errant spirits, hiding in my head or somewhere else, but he wasn't here.

Here was where terror lay, in this green, groaning presence, where I stood alone with fear.

There was nothing healthy here. Only expiring cells and malignant humors devouring the remains of the living. How could I protect myself? I'd always been one of those people who attract itinerant bacteria and viruses, the first to catch those exotic flus that pop up unannounced in North America. What if it was catching? What if death was catching? I mean the idea of death, the germ of the possibility of the beginning of death. What if it was catching, what if after catching it lurked, crouching, whistling softly, waiting for a propitious channel, a complacent vector, an opportunistic little ailment that would let it make its way into me, to take up residence in the marrow of my bones?

At last, a man. A man showed up at the nurses' station. His baritone voice surged through the corridor, sweeping away the threatening miasma. I hurried towards the owner of this hygienic voice, but the closer I got the clearer I could see that he wasn't the one. He was eighty pounds too heavy, too tall, too bulky, too blond. Still, I walked up to him. You never know about memory.

It was Dr. Woggan. He listened to me with total attention, his pale eyelids beating time slowly as I stammered out my stupid questions. No, he was definitely not the man. No, he gleaned no poetic words from the recently departed. No, he

had clearly not written a novel or kept the company of novel-
ists. No, he had never seen me or spoken to me. He swore he
would have remembered as a vulgar gleam glistened between
those blond eyelids, then immediately switched off, for he had
no time for trifles. It must be Bertrand, concluded the maternal nurse, who hadn't missed a word of our conversation. It
was Bertrand for sure, opined Dr. Woggan before abandoning
me for a pile of files less alive than me, but more essential.
This time, no one offered me coffee, and I returned downcast
to my chair at the far end of the corridor to wait for Bertrand.

So, a male nurse. The fantabulous author, the clandestine
idol of Zeno and several thousand other people was a modest
male nurse who collected piss-bottles and swabbed down the
yellowed skin of poor decomposing bodies. If the place
weren't so oppressive, I would have giggled. But why? Wasn't
it an edifying thing, something authentically professional, to
plunge one's hands into the phlegm of humanity to find out
what people are made of before dissecting their intellectual
obscurities, their illusions and lies? I declare, in this section of
death-green corridor, on this lugubrious night when my heart
beats, in spite of itself, in rhythm with the death rattle of unknown ending lives, that Pierre Laliberté goes about his work
in admirable fashion, and that any writer who intends on
dealing with the human soul should follow intensive training
as a nurse, a garbage collector or an embalmer before being
permitted to write a line.

The noise of the dying grew louder. The wheeze of swollen
lungs, the growl of animals as they slipped into the inorganic
state, the music of suffering and spasm that cannot go on

much longer without ending, even whole words poured from the nearest door, two meters away, *my God, Christ, nurse, ah no more no more.* I shrunk down on my chair, I would have run away if I thought I'd have the courage to return. What do you expect me to do, what do you expect all of us to do? There can be no consolation, your number is up, be a good sport about it, circumspect and proper, if you please. If you please.

Worst of all was the smell. I hadn't noticed it before, but they had one, all right. Collective, subliminal, a fine mist of pain that filtered up through their personal emanations, wafted down the corridor of their whispered supplications, a toxic gas that contaminated the space and would contaminate me before my time, the almost two hours I had to wait for Bertrand Pierre/Poach Laliberté. If I had my computer, I could escape. But nothing so useful occurred to me. I brought no portable exit. Except for the book, his book. *Falterlust*

I picked it up, opened it, dove into it. I would read all of it, at top speed, without skipping, not a word. The sooner the book swallowed me up, the sooner nothing else could.

The hospital was meadow green, swamp green, green like birch when their leaves are one day and a few minutes old, and this was why we made the hospital our meadow, our swamp, our forest of young birch quivering with birdsong and the smell of sap. Everything had to be unbuilt, of course. So we unbuilt everything. We razed the hospital, tore down the corridors, the partitions, the nurses and most of all the bad odors that always accompany enclosed things. Afterwards, against a backdrop of green, we were free to invent nature.

This nature of ours cared nothing for zoning or temperature regulations. In our birch forest were oaks and palm trees because we liked oaks and palm trees. Although bright sun was hard for us to tolerate, our vines thrived in the shade and produced grapes that ripened in a few hours. Our moose had fluorescent antlers so we could watch them from a distance with eyes on the edge of expiration. We never encountered birds that were completely orange, so we made all our birds orange, even the ravens and the bald eagles. All performed a spectacular ballet of fire at sunset over mountains of eternal snow. And our hens had teeth at last, in answer to the question of when that would occur. There was nothing exceptional about that, actually. It only meant being bitten when we tried to gather their eggs.

Us. Vito. Nero. Ginger. Nina. Babelle. Grande Jeanne and Lou. Seven of us, like the seven deadly sins, the colors of the rainbow, the seven branches of the candelabrum, the seven times that we should measure before cutting once. Seven of us, united against death and disenchantment, which is worse, far worse than death.

I read on. Reading was easy enough. You just need to cling to the bottom and hold your breath. What kind of crazies were these people? *We.* Who is speaking, which toothless mouth? Because it was obvious that their mouths were toothless. They were old, very old, the species closest to nonbeing. No one wanted that kind of hero, that kind of story could only torture you, and fill you with pain whose existence you never even knew about. I closed the book. Around me I heard the deceitful silence that preceded the moaning, and then the moaning returned, wrapped in the stench of decomposition. It was better to dive back into those subterranean depths. I read on. *We* bound my hands and feet, perforated my head, nibbled at my brain. *We,* three men and four women. Seven entities united in baroque hallucination. In the paradisal countryside they recreated anew each day. Heaping together ferns, lianas and prehistoric creatures, the component parts of *We* played at reliving their past failures and transforming them into victories. Vito found reconciliation with the son who killed himself, Babelle found her pre-war fiancé, Lou learned how to stop drinking, Grande Jeanne finally screwed as she'd never screwed before, a collection of pathetic little psychodramas I couldn't care less about, that I'd love to care less about, but I had no more judgment with which to judge. As I read, slowly I became empty, I was stolen from myself, my rational asperities smoothed away. I turned into a flatland swept by powerful, biting winds and there was nowhere I could crouch and keep warm. After an eternity, when the paradise of *We* became a nightmare, it was worse. By then, I no longer existed to know cold or gasp for air, I had become *them,* those made-up creatures with their paper names and their crushing destinies, I felt each burst of laughter or despair, the slightest of their twitches, *Vito, Nero, Ginger, Nina, Lou, Grande Jeanne, Babelle,* as if they had stuck to me, as if they had become me.

They did stick to me.

This book is about *them*—the very people I was trying to escape, the dying at my side, and others still, breathing their last in the same beds, the same rooms. All of them dessicated on their pallets like so many tiny heaps of bone, injected with tubes and liquids on which the tatters of their lives depended. But their spirits were vibrant, they were buzzing in silence thanks to drugs, or pain, or the mystery that separates life from death, and again their spirits rallied, gathering into a powerful force, raging and triumphant, transmuting misery into a luxuriant paradise, the final flutters of existence into apotheosis.

Now we are alone. We, Nina, burying Ginger beneath the spruce trees on the hill, her face turned skyward, her words frozen forever beneath her tongue. Now there are not mouths enough, words enough to keep our enemy from advancing, from laying waste our beautiful savannah. With us, Nina, the trees and brooks will slowly disintegrate, the grapes will shrivel on their vines and the soft earth will dry and crack until it becomes an icy tiled floor again, a hospital floor. We do not want to go this way; we beg our enemy to relent. But our enemy is within us. He always betrays us in the end, he always refuses the delirium of love, and we can do nothing against him. The heart is an involuntary muscle.

Then it was over. I closed the book. It weighed empty on my knees, inert, harmless. I put it in my handbag. But the harm had been done. The book had impregnated me and now I carried it like some monstrous fetus. I knew it. Open a truly dangerous book and you cannot easily close it again.

I rose among the constant moaning of pain. I did not want to go into the first room, five meters away, from which the sound was coming, but that was exactly what I did. I pushed the door ajar. I had to see them.

At first glance, there was nothing to see, nothing melodramatic or terrifying. Just a room bathed in the artificial glow of a night light, a minuscule green dormitory where troubled sleepers lay. The metal tubing of the beds gleamed in the penumbra like a promise of cleanliness kept. White curtains masked the heads of the beds, where the respiratory devices and survival serums gurgled, and where the upper bodies writhed, that part of the human body that is the most dangerous to watch. A narrow escape. There was really nothing to see after all; only the bulges drawn by legs beneath the thin covers. Four beds, eight legs: Everything accounted for. I could go now.

The first curtain, the one closest to me, began to move, as if of its own volition, but things don't move by their own volition. Slowly, a hand opened the curtain. There was still time to flee, but the spectacle of this hand, no longer a hand, petrified me. The hand was fleshless, reduced to an outline, a child's drawing with five crooked lines. Then the head appeared. "Bertrand?" the head said, very distinctly. "Bertrand, is that you?"

A few tufts of hair, lips, a magma of bones and drooping flesh. But the eyes, my God! Living eyes exploding with distress. The hand reached out towards me as if expecting me to take it, suspended in midair, quivering, soon exhausted by waiting. "I'm not Bertrand," I said, but the hand and the head remained turned in my direction. I repeated, louder, "I'm not Bertrand," to cut short this intolerable exchange. Then I surrendered. Bertrand or not, I had no choice but to take the hand, this memory of a hand, and grasp it.

It was hard, knotty, warm and cold all at once. The effect was devastating.

"It's time for my drops, Bertrand," said the lipless mouth, "it's time."

On the bedside table lay paper tissues and cotton balls, but no juice, no liquid except for what was gurgling above her head, imprisoned in sacs and the tracery of tubes that vanished into her body, moistening nothing as it flowed. "I'll get you some water," I said. But instead, I went on stroking her calcified fingers, endlessly, and then, in the middle of that dessicated face something incredible appeared, a hole took shape, a smile. *She* smiled. For in that withered envelope, once a woman had lived.

It was too much. I wasn't ready for this. Not for a meeting with the unendurable.

Damn that book, damn Pierre Laliberté! I didn't want her to be a woman, I didn't want them to be humans, they can't belong to the same realm as I do, I refuse. You're not part of my family, I can do nothing for you, don't you understand? You're not real, you're a nightmare. If I close my eyes, the nightmare will dissipate and my condor soul will lift me upward, back to my own kind, the smooth-skinned, the beautiful, the eternal. But I went on stroking the bones of this remains of a woman who went on smiling at me, and nothing could resist her, neither virile anger nor healthy repulsion, just softness, a liquid quality, an immense liquid pity for her and for me.

"Oh! Look who's here!"

I turned. He was standing there. Short, thin, dark complexion, white smock. It was him.

"So, we have late-night visitors, do we?"

He spoke to her in a loud, cheerful voice, as if to a person in the best of health, and she reacted. She dropped my hand and extended her arm towards him in a feeble suggestion of movement.

"Bertrand! My dewdrops . . ."

"Yes, dearie. Your dewdrops are here. Who wants a dewdrop?"

You don't stroll into a room full of semi-cadavers with that rumbling voice. He'd wake them up, the lot of them. There, he's done it, from the other three beds rose moans of pain.

" . . . *It hurts . . . my God . . . Bertrand . . . a dewdrop . . .*"

"I'm coming, I'm coming, hold on . . ."

With quick little gestures, he unscrewed a flask and poured several drops into her IV solution, right in front of me. Our eyes collided.

"You don't come to see her all that often," he said.

"I don't know her. I don't know anyone here."

I watched him closely, with changing emotions. It looked like him, it had to be him, that hair, those cinnamon-brown eyes, the frail shoulders. The image of him from that distant night took its time surfacing. Suddenly my certainty faltered. Something was missing.

"Are you Pierre Laliberté?" I asked, choosing from among all possible questions the one least likely to draw an answer.

"I'm Bertrand Poach."

The velvet was missing from his voice and eyes. The respect, too. But tonight, he had no reason to treat me with respect. He turned his back on me and slipped behind the curtain of the neighboring bed, abandoning us, the envelope of the woman and me, to our mutual ignorance of each other. I stared at the old hand that had closed upon the sheet next to its twin, her ancient face hiding its mysteries.

"No one's come to see her for a year," he told me from the other side of the room.

In a weak voice I repeated, "I don't know her," and I heard her emit a soft rattle, a kind of cooing. Then she opened her eyes and looked me up and down. To my surprise, she laughed.

"Very good doctor," she said, shaken by laughter, feeble but genuine.

She gave a great peal of laughter, so long I was tempted to laugh too, though with less pleasure. Laugh we might, the discomfort persisted, even intensified. Out of the corner of my eye I watched Bertrand Poach move rapidly between each bed, then return to me.

"So what are you hanging around here for? Trying to set up a death relationship, too, are you?"

"I beg your pardon?"

"It's true, you're too young. It's a baby-boomer trip mostly, when they start getting guilt feelings about being alive."

Bertrand Poach began to chortle. This time I looked into his eyes and clearly saw that it wasn't him. I read something else, too, something hard to pin down that looked like gaiety, but it was too forced.

"They all read the same books. Accompany the dying on their final journey—nonsense. Screw 'em! It'll be an uplifting experience, they think, it'll turn them into saints. Let me tell you, they last a couple of days, then they're outta here. You think it's uplifting to hang around old wrecks who nobody cares about anymore and listen to them gasp for their final breath, then all of a sudden you can't hear them gasp anymore because they've gone and croaked? She's the only one who isn't going to croak."

He took the hand of the old woman beside me. Then he shook it like a rattle. She squeaked, she hiccoughed, and laughed her choking laugh.

"She should have died a year ago. But you're not going to croak on us, are you, dearie?"

"That's right, Doctor, that's right," she babbled.

"Love is forever, love undying, love . . ."

He began to hum and she joined in, and little by little, from the other beds, rose a heart-rending chorus of quivering squawks worse than the worst cries of pain. This place was a true chamber of horrors. A nightmare. Then it hit me. It was the dewdrops.

"What are you putting in their IVs?"

He sized me up mistrustfully with his half-acid, half-wild eyes. I realized he was as high as they were, stoned to the bone.

"Something to help them."

He was drugging them. That's all there is to it, and suddenly I felt comforted. That confirmed it: Beneath every mystery slumbers an explanation, and all you have to do is dig deep enough. Let's get it over with, Florence, dig up what there is to dig, and let's get the hell out of here before the light of dawn transforms you into an old crone.

I pulled the book out of my handbag and held it up before Bertrand Poach's glassy, cinnamon-brown eyes.

"See this?" I told him. "I'm looking for this writer. He had what you call a death relationship in this very place."

He took the book from me carefully, impressed by the white dust jacket, or maybe by the sudden, cold efficiency of my voice. His eyes traveled between me and the book as silence settled in around us, broken occasionally by piping cries and beatific sighs.

"Yeah," he said.

He opened the book, then closed it. A few endless seconds passed.

"I think I know who it is. Yeah."

"You do?"

I waited, full of impatience and hatred for the slowness that stole over him.

"A short, dark-haired guy, close-mouthed. Yeah, yeah. A hell of a business."

He laughed. Opened the book again. Just so he doesn't go and read the whole thing at the same languorous pace he used to drag out his sentences.

"I should have guessed. He was the only guy who stuck it out a whole month. Took notes, he did. He actually helped me, too, for real, all kinds of help. He washed 'em. Gave 'em morphine. Yeah, yeah, Pierre. That's him, that's his name. Pierre. A hell of a business. I thought he was taking notes, but he was writing a book."

"Where is he? How can I get in touch with him?"

He nodded over and over again, struck by the revelation that slowly worked its way into him.

"Haven't the slightest idea. We never follow up that kind of thing. They come, they go. I stay. Poor Pierre. Too sensitive. Every night he'd pick one out and stay by his side. He didn't say much to me, but he spoke to them all right, yeah, he really spoke to them. In a low voice, so I couldn't hear. Then he wrote in his notebook. He saw at least a dozen of them die. Cried every time. Crying around here, it's not a good idea, it doesn't help anybody. I cry inside; after all, we can't be demoralizing the troops. Can we, Nina?"

He began speaking to the old woman, so softly that his words did not even crease her ancient face, sealed now by the shadow of a smile.

"We don't cry, not us, but it hurts just the same. Isn't that so, pretty little Nina?"

"What did you call her? What's her name again?"

My overexcited voice rang through the room, where for an instant even suffering had fallen silent. Bertrand Poach hushed me and handed me the book, as if to put an end to the story.

"Nina. Nina, Nina, love is waiting . . ."

He hummed and stroked her hair, smooth and white like a stone on the shore.

Nina.

We, Nina.

Nina, who had real hair so long ago it could have been in another galaxy. Nina didn't answer because she had drifted into sleep. An appearance of sleep. Her spirit was moving into a place we could not reach, that much was true, her spirit had joined her traveling companions and was gamboling through the luxuriant vegetation while orange-colored ravens wheeled overhead on phosphorescent wings.

I handed the book back to Bertrand Poach.

"Keep it. He wrote it for you."

6

IMAGINA

$\mathcal{T}$HE TABLE WAS LADEN with my favorite things. Olives, grilled squid, garlic shrimps, crushed eggplant salad, feta with olive oil and savory bread. And a carafe of tap water.

"Don't you want a little retsina? An ouzo? A glass of champagne? Shit, Flora, just once, a glass of champagne, okay?"

"Easy, Mahone. Eat, while there's still food on the table."

Zeno was treating, and I was packing it in. Zeno had lost possession of himself, and could no longer master the petty little movements necessary to the consumption of food. He was floating high above common nourishment. He got up, sat down, filled my glass with water, spat out an olive and swallowed the pit, burst into laughter, then stopped laughing. He would have burst out sobbing had tears been in his repertoire.

He knew about Pierre Laliberté. He knew what I knew, which was not much, but this microscopic knowledge was enough to make all his private circuits short out.

"What's his chin like? With dimples, or not? What about his hair? You didn't say how long it was. Would you say he's good-looking? Shit, Florence. Talk!"

"My mouth is full."

I had nothing to add to what I already said. The man who treated me with so much solicitude late that night was as un-extraordinary as Pepa's death. Brown eyes, brown hair, average complexion, average build, gentle expression. That was Pierre Laliberté, in all the splendor of his brilliant banality.

"Find me a detail, there must be a detail. You say you'd recognize him on the street—he must have something special. Try harder, Flora dearest—sorry, Florence—tell me that one thing about him that makes him unique."

That one thing. I went on chewing and swallowing, but my stomach was starting to contract. That one thing. That thing, Zeno, you maniac, is that he isn't a car or an electric iron, that's the thing, he's unique, we're all unique, because the combination of ordinary components always produces extraordinary results for people who aren't assembled by GM or IBM. That's the miracle of genetics, the complexity of life on earth, and it's utterly uncommunicable.

"What a shame," Zeno sighed. "What a shame you can't draw a picture to save your soul."

Finally he sat down to catch his breath. He was calming down. He was happy just to gaze at me, and something ineffable and inexpressibly tender flowed from his nearsighted eyes to mine. Suddenly it hit me: I remembered when he used to look at me like that, for no reason at all, and I remembered how much I remembered the time when he looked at me like that.

"What a shame," he said again, edging closer to me and touseling my hair, "What a shame the program doesn't exist."

"What program?"

"The one that would let you download the images from your mindscreen onto my computer's hard disk."

"A little lobotomy on the side, while we're at it? Mind-screen yourself."

"Don't you understand, Flora? You *saw* Pierre Laliberté. You're one of the few people on the face of the earth who have ever seen Pierre Laliberté."

Every time he pronounces the name, his voice changes perceptibly. He says "Pierre Laliberté" the way others say "The Dalai Lama" or "Our Lord Jesus Christ." And that irritated me to the point of hyperbole.

"What about it? I'll never see him again."

"On the contrary. You *will* see him again. And you *will* recognize him. You're the only person who can recognize him."

"I'm going to forget him. I'm going to do everything I can to forget him."

Zeno dropped into the chair across from me. He caught my hands in his, his eyes blocked all escape routes, and his voice started punishing me.

"Stop behaving like an idiot. That's enough! It's unwor-thy of you. Something momentous has happened to you, whether you like it or not. You have no right to squander it. There are people out there who would pay a fortune to know what Pierre Laliberté looks like, a fortune, you hear? You're sitting on a gold mine, you're sitting on the beginning of the start of the end of the world. You've got a nuclear detonator in your hands."

He fell into silence. Dropped my hands, and my eyes. But I didn't feel any freer. Quite the opposite. I collapsed under the ten tons of what he said. In a moment, my life was brutally torn asunder, the old part flapping in the wind like something marvelously light about to leave me, the new part demanding, massive, tenebrous, its black maw gaping like a precipice at my feet. I recoiled with all my strength. The first thing is to smile at Zeno to dispel the pathos, and restore the lost innocence of the atmosphere. Okay, okay, I'll do nothing to forget Pierre Laliberté's face, I'll cherish it and polish it within me like a holy icon. Okay, okay, I'll cross his path again one day, for chance is an all-powerful master. I'll follow him and trail him and let Zeno know, even if it's the middle of the night, even if he's busy screwing that saccharine Maud of his. Now that we've exhausted the subject, can we display a little more efficiency, pick up some customers and some sites and get down to work, since that's what we're here for, right?

"Your job from now on," said Zeno in his don't-talk-back boss's voice, "is to find Pierre Laliberté. That's what I'm paying you for. That, and nothing else."

"You're firing me from Mahone Inc.?"

"I'm not firing you. I'm promoting you."

He's crazy. He's gone stark raving mad from reading all those nutcase books. It's time he was attended to by a psycho-

analyst who would touch off the right biofeedback, the one
that would set him free from his Lalibertarian phobias.

"And how do you find someone you only saw once in a
place you know he'll never return to again?"

"You'll go back to the hospital and talk with that Poach
guy again."

"No way. Never never never."

"I'll come along."

"Zeno, no."

"Flora."

Flora. When he says "Flora" that way, there's none of the
mellow ecstasy that suffuses his voice when he says "Pierre
Laliberté." Not a bit. It's like he's turned on a faucet in my
side, and everything that's precious to me goes gushing out.
Quick, turn off that faucet of condescension and scorn. I
plead time-saving, our old hobbyhorse. I plead the useless-
ness of knocking on Bertrand Poach's door again. He's been
squeezed dry; there's nothing left but a dry shell. I plead for
the power of the imagination, the pressing need to invent
other solutions. I don't tell him that returning to the hospital, to that green floor where earthlings metamorphose by
suffering into extraterrestrials, would kill me. He'd find a
way to force me to go back, for sure.

"Very well. Then you'll hang around outside the hospital,
walk the streets, take the subway, the bus, position yourself at
intersections, and watch, watch, watch."

"Excuse me? What if Pierre Laliberté lives on the other
side of town? What if he's in Victoriaville, or Saint Cinnamon,
or New York City?"

"We'll start with Montreal. Then we'll see what happens." That's the way he treats me. I'll resign before I do any such thing, and slam the door on the way out. I'm not about to waste the best years of my youth pretending to be a derelict, I'm not going to walk the streets eyeballing guys who'll reward me with promiscuous familiarity. I stood up, sorely tempted to upset the table and send its load of leftovers right smack into Zeno's lap. But Therios chose that very moment to show up and disarm me, to remove from the table everything I could already imagine staining that little creep's stylish ocher shirt.

"How come you don't eat everything? It's not good, maybe? Sit down, my little heart. Time for some Metaxa."

"Sit down, my little heart," Zeno repeated, smiling suavely.

I was about to boil over and he knew it. The diversion suited him. You'd have sworn he secretly arranged the whole thing. Dogs, the lot of them, those members of the other sex, lolling around, complacently sniffing each other's hind end.

"Three Metaxas," Therios instructed the waiter.

Then he cleared the table, and wiped off a space in front of me with his rag. In his other hand, he held an envelope. He opened it and emptied the contents on the table. Photos. How did he know we were dying to see, at this very moment, kitschy Mediterranean landscape photos?

"Look at this, pretty, no? And this? A lot prettier than slush and skinny trees in Saint Louis Square?"

I like Therios, don't get me wrong. His fried squid are deliciously indigestible. But I don't much like the way he plunks himself down in the middle of a private matter, without warning, without paying any attention to the crucial file we were studying, from which he immediately deletes all information with that booming, earthy, food voice of his. *Log off.*

And we have no choice. It's either this, or ten thousand dollars a month office rental.

"Look at this, my little heart. Pear trees, fig trees, trees with real fruit on them. Real, sweet fruit, not like the apples you grow around here that turn your tongue inside out they're so sour. You, I bet you never picked real fruit straight from real trees. Yes or no?"

"Real fruit like lemons?" I asked perfidiously.

"Even the lemons are sweet in Cephalonia."

So, they were photos of Cephalonia, an island like Montreal, minus the concrete, and even more Greek. His birthplace, where Therios has a plot of land with a shed that his brother looks after for him, like the mirage of an oasis in the eyes of a man dying of thirst. In the photos, there are his brother's grandchildren in faded work clothes, so blinded by the sun that their faces are reduced to tiny, shriveled masks. Therios's white shed is all surrounded by trees with twisted trunks. He swears they're fruit trees. We have to take him at his word because the fruit is invisible. Then there's that expanse of blue in the background that catches the eye, fragments of the sea that even the miserable quality of the photographs can't devalue. The sea. Who can criticize the sea? Not Zeno and I. We looked a little longer at the photos of the sea, but ended up discarding them just like the rest.

"I can't die here. A man can't be buried in snow when he was born beneath the olive trees."

Olives? I thought we were born in cabbage patches.

Therios and winter still haven't worked things out. Every winter, he starts out moaning and groaning and fearing the worst, even though he can see that you don't die any sooner here, where you freeze your ass off, than where it's hot. On the contrary, actually. But Therios fears the cold with such intensity that his apprehension turns to pleasure when the bad weather really sets in. When the cold arrives, when absolute evil is upon him, he can relax, and watch the rise and fall of the thermometer as if he were watching a football game. He turns into a weather fanatic and shivers with delight when they predict a blizzard, or an ice storm or, even better, when they talk about the Windchill Factor. Ah, the Windchill Factor, "Fifty degrees below zero with the wind-chill factor!" he jubilates, and in his mouth the Windchill Factor becomes a character of monstrous truth, a kind of thermometric Dracula who grips the throat of life, sucks its blood and makes it unlivable, yet curiously exciting. At the end of every interminable winter, he's just as discouraged as at the start, not to mention the exhaustion, like a soldier returning from the trenches.

That's where we stand now. The month of March, the same old late-season lamentations, time to recall the lost paradise of Greece, and despair of the glacial New World.

Zeno, more sociable than I am, clinked his glass of Metaxa against Therios's and downed it without a grimace.

"Look," sighed Therios, "Vassilis took these photos in February, and the trees are already in flower. We're sitting here talking, and the weather is as gray as the inside of a garbage can, but over there the poppies are flowering in the fields. What do you say about that?"

"I don't like flowers," Zeno answered.

"You!... You, all you like is pine trees, right? Pine trees, that's all you have here, you're all born with sap in your veins!"

"The pine tree is an excellent remedy for scurvy," said Zeno, straight-faced.

"I'm not talking to you, I'm talking to her. You, my little heart, you know how pretty you'd look over there? Can you see yourself with the sea breeze in your lovely hair, like a little blond flower in among the red flowers . . ."

"Florence," Zeno said suddenly, taking my hand, "Florence, if you want to go, I'll take you there. I'll take you anywhere as long as you introduce me to Pierre Laliberté."

He was serious. Good God, so serious there were tears in his eyes.

"You'll take Maud and me both?"

Okay, it was a low blow, but if you don't use your enemy's weaponry, you'll never win.

"Who's this Liberty you're talking about?" Therios grumbled, unhappy because we'd set aside his poppy fields.

"If you give me Pierre Laliberté," continued Zeno, still clutching my hand, "my debt to you will be eternal, Florence, my love for you . . ."

"Shut up, Mahone, before you say something really stupid."

The worst part was that he really meant it. At that very moment, he was completely sincere. In his heart, Pierre Laliberté and I occupied the same vast, passionate and authentic territory, but the moment will pass, shoved aside by others, which will propel each of us back into our natural habitat. Of course,

Flora-at-your-service will end up as far from Mahone's heart as it's possible to get, wondering what the hell ever became of the total sincerity of that stupid, long-gone moment.

It's happened before.

"So, are you going or not?" Therios insisted. "If you go, the keys to my house are yours. You'll get them off Vassilis's wife's brother who's living there with his kids. My house is your house whenever you like, there's water and electricity, almost, and the sea is five minutes away by foot, fifteen at the most, and while you're at it you could find me a mason. I've been thinking of making the front of the house bigger, my brother says he's a mason but his hands are soft like sponges, you could find me a mason in the next village called Lourdas, L-O-U-R-D-A-S, here, let me write it down for you..."

In the midst of the hodgepodge of images Therios poured down upon us—squid poppies house mason wall sea kids—I caught a glimpse of a dark-haired head, not Greek at all, but it could have been, with its sharp eyes and belligerent, oracular profile.

Gina Da Sylva.

This time, I grabbed Zeno's hand and twisted it.

"A lead, Mahone, I've got a lead. Pierre Laliberté lives with Gina Da Sylva's sister."

Zeno's eyes turned as wide as flying saucers, as wide as a two-year-old's seeing Santa Claus for the first time.

He flung himself at my feet like a fool and covered my legs with kisses.

"I adore you, Florence, I adore you!" he shouted.

I laughed a little, Therios laughed a lot, suddenly there was a lot of noise for such a small place, and the other customers, always on the lookout for a cheap show, snapped their heads in our direction. When they realized it wasn't violent, or even a real love scene, they quickly turned back to their kabobs and their business talk. Therios was the only one who appreciated our little act.

"When are you two getting married, eh? What do you got against marriage?"

"Nothing!" Zeno the zero vociferated. "Will you marry me, Florence, will you will you will you?"

He kissed my arms and hands like a man possessed. I had to pummel him to calm him down.

"You two," Therios sighed. "Never serious about serious things. I'm asking, seriously. How come you're not in love?"

"It's the pine trees," Zeno explained. "Too much pitch in our veins."

We laughed. Nothing like laughter to dilute the syrupy misunderstandings that Therios, among others, insists on calling *love.*

Love love love. Find me one single person who's been happy long enough to be worth talking about, happy in love, I mean, that fake nest lined with steel wool they call love. Not very likely. If there is such a person, they must be blind, blinded by their terror of being alone, so blind they can't see the blood pouring from their gaping wounds.

Anyway. Anyway, Zeno and I get along a lot better now that we don't have to.

SIDE BY SIDE in his van, silent as the seats we're sitting on, we watched the brightly lit windows of Gina Da Sylva's apartment. We said not a word as we shared a can of cherry Coke that did double duty as a mental lubricant, and concentrated our thoughts on how not to botch the next phase of the operation. Gina Da Sylva was expecting us. One of us or both of us. Actually, she was expecting Mahone Inc., in whatever form it might materialize. Gina Da Sylva, our worrisome shrew, she of endless surprises. Gina Da Sylva represented the greatest literary success story in our short history. Her site, dictated to me in the middle of a semi-nauseous stupor, had attracted sixty thousand visitors to date. Was that because of her genius, or mine? The question was meaningless. When train dispatchers do their job, the trains stay on the tracks and the passengers are happy. Real flesh-and-blood train dispatchers no longer exist. They have been replaced by us, the masters of infinitesimal movement, tamers of chips the size of microscopic fleas. Trains themselves still exist because we activate, propel and uplift their inert mass.

I snuck a glance at Zeno. He was thinking about Gina Da Sylva, too, with a kind of tension that hardly suggested the ecstasy that once drew them together, or drove them apart. He did the talking, at a careful distance this time. By telephone. He suggested we devise a new site to deal with the success of her first site. She agreed right away, having quickly sized up the mercantile nature of the man. Strike while the iron is hot nothing succeeds like success nothing ventured nothing gained. (Providing you get in touch with Mahone Inc., those redoubtable young people who will put you on the map of a brand-new world.)

"Do you like her books?"

My question caught him off guard. He took off his glasses and pretended to wipe them.

"There's something about her, that's for sure. Something solid, you can't deny it."

"Yes, but do you like her books?"

"That's not the point," he snapped at me. "Like or dislike, that means nothing. She writes powerful books, that's what's important. There's power in her."

"You can't stand her any more than I can. Admit it."

"Flora. Don't let me hear you utter the slightest reservation, the remotest hint of a remark that might be interpreted as disparaging when we're with her. You know what? I feel like leaving you out here in the van."

"Why not? What could be better? I'll wait here, take your time, you two get it on, enjoy yourselves. I'll take care of Pokey, I mean, I'll take care of—oh, forget it!"

It was all because of the dog hair that Zeno had hung from the rearview mirror. A long, wiry tuft pulled from Pokey's tail, a shed relic that went dancing to the blasts of air from the defroster or the heater.

Because Pokey loved so much hearing his name, and because I had spoken it out loud, his flea-bitten carcass leapt up onto the front seat between our thighs, his breathless panting swept our faces again, his small, round, affection-starved body trampled all over us and licked us. The vision lasted for all of a second, then vanished, swallowed up by emptiness that brought us back to life. I felt Zeno shiver next to me, a bolt of his pain ran through me. How long does it take to fill a void, the void in your stomach left behind when something is cut out, something so much part of us we thought it *was* us?

"This summer, Zeno, I'm going to buy you a dog."

He pinched my arm gently to show he wasn't mad at me. "You can't just buy a dog," he said. "Either they come into your life, or they don't. Come on, Flora, let's go. It's time."

GINA DA SYLVA opened her door wide.

Dressed in black as always, eyes like coal and penetrating, but considerably less hostile than last time, she cracked a thin smile in my direction.

"I thought you'd come alone," she told me.

Paff! Right in the kisser. But our blasé lover-boy extended a courtly hand as though he'd heard nothing.

"Hello, Gina. How nice of you to give us a little of your time."

Distractedly, she took his hand, then immediately released it.

"It will only be a short time, I'm afraid," she said, her eyes on me alone.

Once inside the vestibule, I was on familiar ground. The guard-dog sculpture lay in wait with its multiple puncturing extremities, but to my surprise, just behind it, another large black installation had been set up, as invasive as the first. Then I recognized it as a man, a man standing so motionless he could have just as well been stuffed with straw.

"Anthony," she spoke.

The installation barely stirred.

"How do you do?" Anthony answered.

He was young, even younger than us, with hair clipped close to his skull, dressed in black to conform with house regulations, gigantic and running with muscles as if he'd escaped from a bodybuilders' convention. Zeno stuck out his chest as he stepped past him, and let fly with one of his machine-gun looks that are supposed to intimidate, but the low level from which he was aiming meant that he only managed to hit Anthony in the solar plexus. Zeno moved past like a parade that was being rained on, without a single brass band. Out of compassion or indifference, Anthony gave no sign of following us into the room where Gina awaited us.

"So you've hired a monster bodyguard?" Zeno said ingratiatingly.

"He offered *me* his services," Gina corrected him with a smile.

She said no more, but forgot to wipe off that smile that summed up everything I knew about her. The image of a hard candy came to mind, one of those English candies that are slow to deliver their goods, but sooner or later you reach their soft center by sheer patience and saliva.

"Life certainly is funny," she told me. "All my books have been reprinted. In English, for the most part. I have a lot of new readers. *Young* readers. Did you know that?"

Following no particular cue, we brought out our cameras and mini-recorders as discreetly as possible, our inner antennae quivering as we homed in on our prey, all the while assuming a casual air, the way true professionals do before they gun you down. Above all, we mustn't startle her.

"Yes," I said. "It is surprising."

I felt the arrows of Zeno's disapproval sink into my back, but Gina, who was far less impressionable, hardly noticed.

"Surprising, as you say," she said cheerfully. "They're twenty, twenty-five years old for the most part. Never opened a book in their lives. At least, that's what I think. All of a sudden, I've become a necessary part of their initiation process. It's all so terribly comic, or pathetic, depending on how you look at it. And I've chosen to look at it and laugh to my heart's content. For the time being. Would you like a whisky?"

I thought I'd sensed a vague threat waiting to take shape. Zeno accepted the poison even before I'd had a chance to turn it down. Before I knew it, Anthony was before us, in his black uniform and Zen haircut, bending the skyscraper of his torso, the better to fill our glasses to overflowing.

"What about him?" Zeno asked aggressively, "is he one of your readers?"

"Oh, Anthony?" Gina repeated. "Thank you, Anthony."

She laughed, then patted him on the arm to dismiss him. I caught a glimpse of the childishly animal look in his eyes, overflowing with admiration. Gigolo, yes; reader, no—anyone could see that.

"Anthony is the president, the director, in a word, the head of my fan club," she said with a smile. "I have a fan club, you know. Laugh if you like, I'll understand, for me there's something old-fashioned and burlesque about the expression, as if I told you I tap-danced, but what other name can you give to a group that meets on the Internet to . . . how do you call it? To chat about you? The group calls itself Imagina. Imagine that, Ima-Gina!"

She burst into hearty laughter, an enthusiastic but slightly raucous laugh that produced the same sound as a rarely used pulley. We followed suit.

"ImaGina is really more like a game . . . But you must know all about it, since it all began with your site . . . Right?"

"Wrong," Zeno said, sober as a judge.

Follow-up is for bureaucrats. Zeno and I never follow up on anything. We never waste a minute on files from the past; we're too busy leaping from peak to summit in search of something new. But try to tell that to someone who's spent her whole life rewriting the same book.

"I don't like games," she declared. "I can't understand them. It sounds to me like Dungeons and Dragons, where the players make their way through my books, as if they were crawling under barbed wire and facing other such ordeals."

I couldn't have described her books any better myself.

"The goal is to find Death. The character that represents death. On account of that slogan you chose, remember? *Death Laughs Somewhere Near.* So they search for the place where death laughs, in every book. But that's not all. There's the final ordeal, where all those deaths meet in combat, challenging one another in tournaments that have nothing to do with my books. According to Anthony, there are real encounters, every month, between virtual players. Comical, isn't it? I mean, you write, you're a serious writer, you write for some reason, I don't know what in hell for, but what can you do? It's a matter of survival, and then, all of sudden, you're being read for all the wrong reasons, but you're being read, and there's nothing you can do about it, I suppose. My publisher has nothing to say, except 'Write another book,' even though he used to tell me I wrote too much."

Zeno listened to her, as fascinated as I was, because when you get right down to it, she was talking about us. Mahone Inc., the ones responsible for the landslides and flat tires that determine tiny destinies like hers, that would have remained tiny otherwise. We didn't exchange any looks, but we did silently congratulate each other. For a moment she gazed upon us as if she could read our minds, that sorceress.

"I should thank you," she admitted, her smile turning thin and sardonic. "Yes, thanks to you, I have several thousand additional dollars. And readers, too. Strange readers, I admit, but readers just the same. But the most comical thing about it, the most stupidly comical thing, is that for the first time in my life, people are impatiently waiting for a new book, and for the first time in my life, I cannot bring myself to write it."

"A classic case," Zeno pointed out. "The Success Syndrome. You'll get over it. The syndrome, I mean. And your next book will be all the better for it."

What could he possibly know about such things, that sycophantic whippersnapper? She could have destroyed him with a word, with one solid sarcastic word, but no, she drank in his insipid words like they were honey wine.

"You think so? Perhaps you're right, Zeno. Perhaps. You could call it success. I guess I'll have to learn to live with it."

"And you have Anthony," Zeno hissed, his insolence out of control.

Suddenly he slipped in between her and me. They began to feel out each other with meaningful gazes, recalling that they'd shared something a good deal more torrid than superficial conversation. They were rapidly turning into a royal pain in the ass. Irritated, I gulped down the contents of my glass. Good for me. Good for them, because in a few seconds I'd be rolling around at their feet, a bothersome, vomiting and probably unconscious mass. But nothing happened. Their eyes disengaged, and a delicious inner warmth flooded over me, there where the whisky had come to rest.

"Anthony," said Gina. "My publisher set up an E-mail address for me; I check my messages once a week. That's how I found Anthony. He wrote me every day for two months. That kind of tenacity is touching, don't you think? He comes from a little village somewhere in Arizona. He doesn't call himself American, he calls himself Gothic. Charming, isn't it? He think I'm a priestess, a powerful demon. And a woman, too, which boils down to the same thing, and that really isn't hard to take."

Anthony strolled into the room, as if he were walking on ball bearings, with the expressionless face of someone who doesn't understand the language being spoken. He bent over behind Gina, low enough to reveal the top of his near-naked skull, on which a tiny tattoo was visible. I heard the hushed click of Zeno's miniature camera, as if reminding me not to lose sight of our work.

"It's nine o'clock, Gina," said Anthony in a grave voice.

He must have spent years training his voice to produce that solemn timbre, and his hormone-swollen muscles puffed up as he did. He was mimicking, playacting, clumsily copying a role he'd pilfered somewhere. I didn't understand the first thing about his character.

"Anthony," I asked him. "What . . . what . . . just what are you doing here?"

All of a sudden, the whisky caught up with me, turning me muddier than the bottom of a pond. Anthony wrapped me in an endless stare of perplexity, as if I were the strange one here. Gina smiled at me with a touch of pity.

"Anthony has informed me that I should be leaving soon," she announced. "I've been invited to one of their little tournaments, tonight. It's the first time one is being held in Montreal."

Panic brought me back to earth. How can she leave us? We haven't had time to lure her onto the pragmatic terrain of Name, Profession, Family, Childhood, Sister, Sister, what about her Sister?

Zeno jumped to his feet, revitalized by the deadline, all smiling efficiency.

"We'll go with you. It's important to incorporate this experience—the game inspired by your site—into your next pages."

She stood up, more deliberately. She questioned Anthony with her eyes and immediately found a very clear answer.

"No. I'm so sorry. It won't be possible."

Out of service, I turned to Zeno. It was time for him to stop the earth in its tracks and get us utopia on a silver platter.

"Very well," he said. "We won't be keeping you any longer, Gina."

He's gone crazy. I wanted to put in a word, but all I could manage were some surrealist stammerings, to which no one paid the slightest attention.

"If you don't mind," Zeno put in, "before you go, could you give me a few useful addresses? As I told you, to complete your portrait, we don't need you so much as we need what people say about you. Don't worry, we'll show you the pages before they're posted on the Web."

"What is it you need?" she asked cordially.

"Just a few things," Zeno said, "but they're essential things. I need the addresses of your sons, you have two sons,

right? The addresses of a few close friends, if you have any.
Oh, and the address of your sister, of course. That would be
enough to start with. I'll be back in touch later."

She swung into motion. She grabbed her black handbag
and shawl, and was moving quickly towards her small writing
desk when she stopped in midstride, as if hobbled. She turned
towards us and looked at each of us. Then a wide smile broke
across her face.

"You want Melody's address?" she asked.

"Melody? Yes . . . Among others," Zeno said.

She laughed, the creaking of a runaway pulley. Her laughter was unreliable, suspicious. Zeno and I waited for the sky
to fall on us.

"So that's it," she concluded when the laughter was over.
"You almost got me. The whole time you were after Melody,
it was Pierre Laliberté you wanted."

"You're wrong," Zeno began.

"Shut up, you little twerp," she told him. "Who do you
think I am? Do you think you're the first one who ever but-
tered me up in hopes of nabbing the Great Invisible Hero?"

Tipped off by her voice, Anthony returned and blocked
the doorway, a guard-dog look in his eyes, ready to leap and
devour us at her command.

"Flesh-eaters," she thundered. "You're two little flesh-
eaters, two unscrupulous little carrion-eaters. Ready to eat
anything, as long as it's raw and dripping with blood, right?"

Zeno was frozen in surprise. I shook his arm to restore his
mobility.

"Come on. We're not going to stay here and let her
insult us."

Insensitive to humiliation, he made no move. Or maybe he was too greedy to drop the piece. When he finally did stir, it was to take a few steps in her direction instead of slouching towards the door.

"You're being unfair," he said, and his voice was so soft I had to stretch my whole being, my entire circuit board of flesh and nerve endings, in order to hear his words. "Unfair and paranoid, which is undoubtedly essential in your line of work. Your publisher hired me, remember? It never occurred to me, when I began to design your site, and even less, when I became intimate with you, Gina, that you had anything to do with Pierre Laliberté. Otherwise, I would have kept my distance. Mythical beings mean nothing to me. I prefer building my own myths myself."

It took that kind of nerve, and music of such touching sincerity, to stand a situation on its head—starting with Gina's hostility, which immediately melted away.

"I don't believe you," she said, but her voice was small, submissive, a crumb of a voice, and she gazed at Zeno as if she were about to kiss him.

Then she turned away abruptly and rummaged through her writing desk, looking for something, a pistol perhaps, or a dagger, which would be more in keeping with her antiquated style. When she came back to Zeno, she was brandishing a postcard.

"You want this? I just got it. From Melody, from New York. If you want it, I'll give it to you. Why wouldn't I give it to you anyway?"

She waved the card instead of handing it to him.

"I can wait for her," Zeno said, imperturbable. "Tell me where I can reach her when she gets back."

"No one knows if she's going to return. With artists, you never know."

She slipped the card into Zeno's shirt pocket.

"My sister is an artist of a kind," she said. "A backstage artist of matrimonial servility. But there have to be people like that, and there are advantages. After all, she is in New York."

She invested her words with a tenderness that made them even more poisonous, and I wondered what Gina's sister could possibly be like, what kind of gall genes *she* could have inherited. But I said nothing, and watched Gina stroke Zeno's chest as she buttoned his pocket. My discretion was beyond reproach. If I could, I would have held my breath so as not to disturb their concentration; I knew how important the insignificant, mute spectator is to actors as they play out their roles. Two of us were acting as foils: Anthony stood on alert at the threshold, waiting to be summoned, understanding even less than I, poor colossus, and beginning to lose patience.

"Let's go," she tossed in his direction, like alms.

"As far as your sons are concerned . . ." Zeno ventured, playing the probity card to the last.

"That's enough," she declared, and her voice meant it. "That's enough and you know it. Let's just say we're even. Let's just say that I've paid my debt."

This time, she looked at me. She winked at me, whether in complicity or commiseration I couldn't say. It was clear to me, even in my state of total drunkenness, that she wasn't fooled by us in the least, and that she never had been.

7

EAST SIDE, WEST SIDE

––––––––––

New York. The words are powerful hallucinogens.

Say New York and conversations come screeching to a halt. Magical mirages flicker across the eyes of those who have never been there, and those who have never come back.

Zeno said, "We're going to New York."

Suddenly my mind was filled by a rush of frenetic fantasies. But at nine o'clock in the morning, when your freedom has not yet been encroached upon, I was in top shape, so I kicked the whole gaudy procession straight out the door.

What is New York, after all? A tiny fragment of land converted by speculators into a mutual fund, a place so small, so glutted with human greed that they had to build upward to accommodate all the yawning maws. I suppose we'd have to go into ecstasies over the skyscrapers?

So as not to be surprised in a state of ignorance, the day before our departure, I hitched up my best search engine and headed top speed for the most exhaustive (*the most, the best, the greatest, the New Yorkest New York Web site in the world*) Web site on the megalopolis.

A two-hour stroll, I told myself.

I spent the night wandering the sidewalks of New York.

I began by the water, for it was by sea that all those agitated, desperate people full of hope arrived, in search of an island where they could plant their madness. For a time I floated on the East River where it joins Manhattan, and something like an island slid towards me, but it was really a forest of hard, brilliant tree trunks, squeezed tight against one another, a forest of constructions impaling the sky with its triumphant pinnacles, and just as surely plunging its immense roots far beneath the water to grip the seabed. A mineral, earthly, aquatic, aerial forest made up of all realms. A total artifice.

And the lady alone on her islet, photographed, iconified beyond satiation, reduced to the flash of propaganda. The lady, I had to admit, had a powerful attraction.

Artificial, artificial, I kept repeating.

The next thing I knew, I was at the southern tip of the island where the peaks are at their tallest, and I set myself to climbing one hundred and ten stories to the summit. Far below my feet wound canyons of concrete and glass so deep that the eye panicked, and the crewelwork of masonry flowering three hundred meters above street level seemed there for the picking, like strawberries. From the top of the World Trade Center, you could not quibble with the magic of the skyscraper, that magic had slipped free from human hands and shone, sovereign, over the tiny appetites that had unknowingly set it loose upon the world.

Before wonder could overwhelm me, I made my way down.

I clicked on Fifth Avenue. The first images carried me to the Upper East Side, the district of the immensely wealthy, where all the winning conditions for the anti-bourgeois revolution could be found in concentration. Slowly I drifted past the neo-Georgian, post-Gothic or pseudo-Renaissance facades of private mansions, the better to summon up indignation at the dollars shamelessly squandered. But the perfection of the color and design of their structures, the harmony ensconced in the minutest details of their manicured shrubs, their marquees, their doormen in shiny uniforms kept intruding, and it was all I could do to coax my cursor into movement until I spotted, in the distance, the silhouettes of the great bird-like buildings soaring above the leafiness of the immense park. Search though I might, I could not see the money, that dirty, vile, venal money.

Money laundered by beauty.

I clicked on Times Square. Here, at last, I would not be disappointed. Kitschy, bigmouthed and brassy, American as only America can be, Times Square by night splashed me with its dazzling propaganda, the gigantic NASDAQ billboard side by side with Lite Beer looming above seedy midnight cowboy look-alikes, black punks and tourists searching desperately for full-throated Americanicity. There in Times Square, where aesthetics surrendered to real life, I stopped staring at buildings and began to watch the crowd.

People. *People who need people.* So many of them, so many industrious, bright faces, old, young, colored, pale, all pushing towards the banquet table to tear a bite from the magical, inaccessible fruit before none remains, wandering through the termite colony blind to the path to the center, to the delectable heart of the Big Apple, constantly seeking, finding for a brief instant, losing it once more, then setting off in dogged pursuit through the Bowery, Greenwich Village, Battery Park, along Broadway and Canal Street, hopes and fears as countless as human faces. I drifted for hours on end, clicking on *People,* and finding only faces to serve as landmarks, this truly brilliant site (*the most, the best, the greatest, the New Yorkest site in the world*) gave me all the harrowing close-ups I could endure, lifted me from place to place and year to year before I could figure out what happened, and suddenly the clothing changed texture and cut, and the years fled by backwards, 1938, 1902, 1865, 1712, and the buildings deconstructed themselves and shrunk in size, but the faces told the same story of daring and fear, always, the faces showed human history as a single piece of frayed but unbroken cloth. Immigrants at Ellis Island somber as they awaited the verdict, steamer passengers weeping for joy as they drew near the island and the statue of dignity became possible, Irish rioters enflamed by despair, the fury of justice on the faces of blacks, the blood-soaked intoxication of freedom won by the North, by Washington's troops entering Manhattan, desire and dread, dread and desire in infinite succession. Time moved backwards, retreated into its last bulwarks, and now the faces belonged to people who lived in a *Manahatta* given over entirely to real trees and to primordial nature, the faces were those of the Indians once known as the Lenapes, they too caught in the grip of desire and dread on that morning in 1609 between the century-old elms and oaks as the Dutch three-master bore down on them, towards their wild island, with its total revolution and the undetectable germ of future skyscrapers.

Suddenly it was five o'clock in the morning. Zeno would be here to pick me up in an hour, and I hadn't even thought of sleep. But what was the point of being young if you couldn't be indefatigable? At 6:15 on this May 10, 2001, suitcase and laptop at my feet, I was as firm and fresh as the Chrysler Building in the glow of the rising sun.

Now it was 6:29. I was as firm and fresh as ever as I heard Zeno's van pull up outside my door.

His eyes were bloodshot, and even with a perfunctory kiss, I felt the stubble on his cheeks scratch mine. He lifted my bags onto the back seat without a word. It didn't look like he got a lot of sleep either, and he's much the worse for wear. In a foul mood, it's better to leave him alone. We drove to the airport in silence. Normal people would be squandering their energy in idle chatter and excited anticipation. Not us. We sped along in silence, in harmony for all our dissonance, a tandem-in-spite-of-itself that would not give up the ghost. Head resting against the door frame, I surrendered to the gentle rocking of the van and the daydream that rose in its wake. Zeno had stopped being Zeno, and God knows who I was, but at least we were out in the field instead of stagnating in offices and factories, we were picking up speed before taking flight for something better than a sea teeming with viscous beasts, more passionate than the seashores of death, we were taking flight for our date with the City of Cities, with the forest of glass and steel that pierces the clouds to bring down upon it golden rain, delicious mysteries, adventures as hilarious as a Woody Allen picture, and there are two of us, the magic number, two of us making sure we would not miss a thing.

This was going to be our first trip together, Zeno and me.

True to form, he parked in the wrong place, the short-term parking lot. He unloaded my suitcase and my laptop and locked the doors. Only then did something strike me as wrong: he had no luggage. He took me by the shoulder, and before I could react, he pushed me towards the terminal.

"You're going to go by yourself. I'll be there in a couple of days. Something's come up, something I have to look after, it's vital. I'll explain later."

"No. Oh, no. No, no."

That was all I managed to babble as he guided me up to the counter, burying me with instructions, supervising the check-in and getting my boarding pass, sweet-talking the lady behind the desk in the process—all fifty years of her, you never know when she'll come in handy.

"Are those really your eyes? When you get there, take a taxi, go to the hotel, the address is in the envelope, don't lose it. Rosie, what a pretty name, it fits you like a flower. The U.S. cash is in the envelope, don't spend it all if you don't have to. Take photos of him, that's all. Don't try anything too daring, whatever you do, don't mess things up, just follow your hunch. I trust you. You're wearing Godiver, right? I knew it, I can always spot Godiver women. Come on, Flora, smile a little. You're going to New York, not the Arctic, for God's sake. We'll talk tonight. You're not afraid of flying, are you?"

How should I know? I'd never taken an airplane in my life, I'd never been so abandoned as I was now, how should I know whether it's the airplane or the abandonment that's floored me, and left me feeling more helpless than a ten-year-old?

I let him kiss me on the mouth, let him lead me to customs, and when he turned to leave, that's when I regretted not having scratched out his eyes or crushed his balls. Fury carried me past the luggage inspection and the passport check, all the way to the departure lounge, where I paced back and forth in silence, all eyes upon me as if I were a sunset, burning brightly with rage.

Calm down, I told myself as I slouched across the floor. What's so different about this time compared to all the others, when he threw me away like a dirty Kleenex, what's so exceptionally upsetting now? It was only one more time, but it was once too many. Blame it on New York. Blame it on the treacly dreams that New York had planted in my weakened brain, entangling me in the nonsense of waiting. That was my fault. Sitting and waiting like a near-normal passenger, I was struck by a sudden revelation. It was my fault, *mea culpa,* the terrible suffering every time Zeno went predictably astray. I was guilty of suffering for nothing. Why this repulsive attachment to someone with whom nothing will ever be possible? Why this mindless cowardice that keeps deluding me into thinking that the two of us make up something distinct, compact, a real entity? Enough of Zeno and me. *Zeno and me* doesn't exist, it never did exist. That alloy of words will be forever banished from my mind.

Now what? Should I forget the whole thing and not leave? Rush back to my apartment and hole up, ruminating over complex plans for breaking up?

A computer-generated voice announced that Flight 742, destination New York, was now ready for something—to be highjacked or vandalized, the words were lost in the whine of the public address system. The people around me stood up and moved forward, as though they'd just heard some excellent news.

Very well. Leave. Leave and find Pierre Laliberté in immense and chaotic New York, track down Pierre Laliberté and keep him for myself, I and I alone, *Flora-at-your-service.*

I got into line and promptly stepped on the toes of an arrogant little guy who vaguely reminded me of Zeno. Behind me, my condor wings were spread wide.

EVERYBODY'S TAKEN the plane at least once before they're twenty, I know. But not me. What can I do? Where was I supposed to go, what was I supposed to look for? Isn't everything contained in the here-and-now? Even New York, past and present, was contained in a few invisible bytes in my computer.

I had a seat by the window. Next to me, Zeno's spot was taken up by my resentment for him. Which left me room enough to put my laptop and part of my legs there. All around me, people chattered away as if they were at a garden party, a glass of Cinzano in hand. But the clouds were lower than we were. We were floating in thin air, eleven thousand meters up. Life itself, in all its pomp and works, scurried comically beneath us, far below, like the leaping and coupling of fleas. The earth really was round, just the way they'd always claimed it was, and there was no doubt now, around us and within us stood the void, nothing but emptiness. So how could these people chatter on as if they were standing in a garden, glasses of Cinzano in hand? I was mesmerized with awe at the shadow of the airplane as it imprinted itself on the clouds, and the clouds themselves as they traveled alongside us, huge, opaque, gracious, sniffing fraternally at us like porcelain dogs, like dogs of thin air. Then the same virtual voice as before, or another produced in the same factory, informed us that we were not meant to float on eternally in space. In a few minutes, we would be landing. My heaviness and anxiety returned, I tore open the envelope left to me by the Unreliable One and saw with relief that it contained only what had been promised. Four five-hundred-dollar bills, that I solemnly swore to plow through in a week. The address of the hotel in huge block letters, as if intended for a visually deficient moron. And the postcard from Melody, the one indelicately revealed by her sister Gina, that other unreliability. Its message was laconic, Melody's handwriting round and infantile. *Hi, Gina,* she wrote. *Well, here I am again at the heart of the storm. At the Washington Irving Hotel, 339 MacDougal. You can write me. Or even come see me.* xxx. The card depicted my favorite New York structure, the Flatiron Building, looking like a weathered transatlantic liner. I saw in it a favorable omen, as a sign of possible cordiality with a woman who was both sister to a monster and wife to a madman, whom I was preparing to tail and no doubt betray, ever so slightly. I would see anything I wanted to in it—I was that alone and vulnerable in this airplane beginning to descend, better to relieve itself of its cargo.

I felt tremendously tempted to close my eyes. I resisted. No way I was going to miss my own death when it was as spectacular as this. Then I caught sight of them. The first skyscrapers. Rectangular, gray, stretching high into the sky. A bit disconcerting. Seen from above, from the clouds, they looked exactly like gravestones.

There's no way you can be timid here.

The energy comes at you from every direction, pushing you on, no matter what shape you're in, keep on keeping on, impose yourself. Nobody cares about the rest, that accent they can't quite name, whether your clothes are sewn from rat hair or human viscera, whether you mouth inanities or demand the unobtainable, whether you're completely at odds with reality, nobody could care less. They've seen it all before, nobody gives your little self a second thought, not like in Centerville, or even Montreal. Nobody has time to wait for your first mistake so they can destroy you. Begging is the only thing you're not allowed to do here. But I hadn't planned on doing that.

In Washington Square, as I waited for my hotel room to free up, I looked around, and was sorry I didn't have more eyes in my head. Not that there was anything particularly extravagant or remarkable to see. Little groups of young people talking and milling around as in any university neighborhood. Blacks in close-knit bunches making music. Strollers strolling, sitters seated, chess players playing chess. Dogs running and sniffing each other in a park, while their masters admire them. Scenes from parish life. But how can I describe it? Here, space is palpable, all living things are enveloped in an aureole of space that proximity cannot erode, a broad and gaudy backdrop that gives them all ample opportunity to shine, or be dull, just be themselves. Each carries his realm inside him, each is the ruler of his world, no matter how tiny, how flawed, how poor, each one walks, bearing the proud stamp of his own uniqueness.

In this park, Pierre Laliberté was nowhere to be seen.

He could have been here, scribbling feverishly in his notebook as life unfolded around him. After all, the hotel was only a few steps away. He could have been here, but that would have been too easy, too much too fast. Besides, my thoughts were elsewhere. I wanted nothing that might remind me of my previous existence. I wanted my mind to be here, in the intoxication of reality. What did I care about the plot of novels, or their last sentences, or some famous writer who only wanted to hide? If that's what he really wants, let him hide, everybody should be free to exhibit themselves or hide, on earth as it is in heaven. I sat on a bench in Washington Square, nodding off like a real native, with a big, broad, I-don't-give-a-damn grin on my face.

Already I'd received two messages from Zeno. One at the hotel, the other by E-mail. He's not going to get anything in return from me. No *Hi*, no *Hello*, no *How-are-you.*

I told the hotel switchboard operator, a black woman with an aggressive chewing gum habit, that I'm not available for anyone. After making me repeat my message, to make sure she grasped the essence of my pidgin English, she answered "Not over my dead body!" Fake serious from head to toe, she promptly forgot my request and my existence as soon as I turned my back.

On a giant billboard between Fifth and Sixth Avenues: *First on the lifeboats. Another great reason to be a woman.*

Now what?

NOW, MELODY.

Melody isn't Melody Laliberté or Melody Da Sylva. Melody's last name is Ferretti and her hair is artificial blond, as artificial as the black hair of her hypothetical sister, but that's where the similarity ends. Nothing looks less like Gina Da Sylva than Melody Ferretti.

She's blond, that much has been established. You wouldn't call her sultry, or even particularly eye-catching, more pleasantly maternal than anything else, with a small, round, soft body enshrouded in an outsized khaki shirt. A curious appearance, simultaneously on edge and laid back. When she walked into the dining room, she paused to examine the guests who were already seated before choosing, not so much a table, but the quality of the tablemates. She bestowed her smile on an elderly couple nearby, Asians from whose necks dangled a variety of high-tech cinematographic gadgets designed to film everything, no matter what, whether it was raining or pitch dark. I took a seat while she showered her attention on them, bent on wolfing down the bagels and cappuccino I'd been dreaming of since dawn.

Everything was easy, everything went smoothly. At six o'clock the next morning, I left a message at the desk for Melody; unfortunately I'd forgotten her last name. "There is only one Melody Ferretti here," my good friend the operator barked. I then set about watching from a safe distance who would pick it up. A very safe distance, to avoid the suspicious eye of the operator, a needless precaution because she really couldn't have cared less. I settled in for a lengthy siege, maybe Melody would be sleeping alongside her Pierre until noon, then take breakfast in bed, maybe she would never even come near the desk, I might miss her during a microsecond of distraction as I was scratching my knee. Perhaps HE would come downstairs first, in which case her existence would become inessential and superfluous.

She arrived at seven o'clock sharp, alone, skipping along on leather sandals, dropped her keys at the desk, where my pal the operator with the extreme sports gum-chewing style flipped her my message—it was actually an advertising flyer scooped up from the street. She opened it and, smiling, crumpled it into a ball, which she deposited on the counter. So that was where we were at.

On the threshold of nowhere is where we were at. I didn't know what to do with her. Accosting her was out of the question. I watched her instead. She ate her breakfast in absentminded style, pulling apart her bagel above her cup of tea with lemon instead of chewing it, completely absorbed by her Asian Kodak-speaking neighbors. She said nothing to them.

She switched them on and they talked. She pointed at one of the machines adorning them and they launched into endless explanations, and she listened with rapt attention, mouth open, eyes fascinated, and I figured there were only two possibilities: either this crumbling, Nipponifying couple truly was captivating, and therefore a certain optimism regarding touristic humanity could be allowed, or Melody Ferretti was totally off the wall.

The digital couple stood up, bowed to her several times and departed, too bad, but they were visibly exhausted by their own oratorical performance. And the day was still young. An ideal family then sat down at the table. Father and mother as healthy as Scandinavian trees, their blond-headed children a credit to successful cocooning. Curiously, Melody didn't so much as give them a glance. With no warning, she withdrew into her inner reaches, calm and absent, almost somnolent, leaning against the back of her booth. Then a twinkling of life flitted across her face, she distributed warm smiles that sought no specific recipient, from her purse she took a pen and notebook and began scribbling energetically.

What next? That is the question. Should I follow her when she leaves the hotel, or should I wait until Pierre Laliberté decides to appear to excite his superheated brain cells? This is when the figure two comes in handy: one to follow Melody, the other lying in wait for Laliberté. And this was where, once and for all, Zeno Mahone lost whatever claim he might have had for reasons of criminal absenteeism.

I decided to tail her. The rococo little breakfast room with its sweetish scent of bagels had begun to titillate my angst. In any event, something tells me that *he* won't be coming down for breakfast, *he* has already come down at the misty hour when paranoia can hide its face, say, at around five o'clock in the morning, that maybe she is just now hurrying off to meet *him*.

She set a brisk pace, but she stopped to observe a thousand anecdotal scenes: a city worker underneath a manhole cover, a young sandwich woman distributing ads for the Zimbabwe Club Med, a man selling watches, the window of a Thai restaurant. Not only did she stop, she established her presence and persevered, and with smiles and questions, she managed to extract from the passersby a veritable conversation. A conversation as she understands it: They stand and deliver, she listens transfixed, mouth agape and eyes wide open.

A snoop, that's what she is. A professional busybody who, beneath her greengrocer's good humor, conceals a web of curiosity as tightly strung as a fishing net. Suddenly I pictured her sister Gina, so different, as cold as this one is warm, but whose intelligence is likewise directed outward, a massive antenna sucking up signals, both of them manipulating other people to extract their vital juices. I pictured Pierre Laliberté, as described by Poach the male nurse, bending over, notebook in hand, wringing confidences from the dying and writing it all down, weeping compassionately the whole time, which in itself was an unacceptable detail that blurred the whole picture. What is it about them? What is this ferocious fascination with other people? What is so delectable about them, so necessary for their own existence? I was so deeply perplexed that I almost missed Melody as she moved off again at her brisk pace.

We made our way down Thirty-fourth Street without another stop. She sped along smartly and I hurried close behind,
until we reached Avenue of the Americas. She crossed it on a
yellow light, me puffing along in her wake, then she made a
beeline for a tiny triangle of green wedged in between inter-
secting boulevards. She stepped into the microscopic enclave
bordered by a wrought-iron fence and took up position there,
at a small metal table.

Shit!

Just as if she'd sought asylum in a church and I was the
Gestapo, stopped cold on the doorstep. *Eintritt verboten!*

No way could I go into the square, which was about as big
as an elevator. She'd notice me, she'd call me over, she'd scrutinize me and turn me inside out like a pocket.

I skirted the clock that stood in the square, a preoccupied
look on my face, and crossed over to the bus stop on the other
side of Broadway. There, I waited. Around me, nothing but
superlatives. On the right, Macy's had just opened the doors to
its treasurehouse of useless objects, and an armada of women
was bearing down upon it. Shoe-horned in across the street
stood the Empire State Building, once the world's tallest structure, the only one worthy of King Kong's attentions, but just a
has-been now, overshadowed by the World Trade Center. I
waited in the company of workers who were waiting too, but
they abandoned me for any one of the southbound buses.
Other people took their place and kept me company for a time,
then inevitably they left me to pursue their own dynamic business, and so it went, hour after hour, huge divisions of com-
posite humanity battened against my unmoving flanks and

moved on, snatched up by air-conditioned buses and rushed off towards destinations that must have been captivating as I stood there waiting for nothing to happen, on legs that were turning rubbery.

The attractions of espionage are highly overrated.

Meanwhile, the designated victim, she who was being tailed unbeknownst to her, was enjoying herself immensely. The tiny square where she'd set up house was an island of calm in a stormy sea, a handsome ocean liner breasting the waves, imperturbable. On either side, the city spewed forth torrents of automobiles and passersby, while she sat drinking in the spectacle, sitting straight-backed on her metal chair in her quiet garden, where petunias bloomed and sparrows twittered. A wrought-iron fountain gleamed in the sunlight, a well-dressed man seated a bit farther on was reading the *New York Times*. When the large clock on the little square chimed eleven, then noon, two bronze figurines sprung into action and began striking a bell with a hammer, producing a sound far more disorienting than the cacophony of the boulevards, something like a country carillon. Melody hardly moved. She wrote a few words in her notebook, crossed and uncrossed her legs, didn't try to catch the eye of the other resident of her island. She was the sole owner of the space, and obviously expecting no one.

A busybody and a sensualist.

The next step will be the right one. How can the next step not be a restaurant in which her invisible gentleman friend Pierre Laliberté is languishing at this very moment? Pierre Laliberté will, I hoped, be as hungry as I am. We will sit down to eat, and celebrate the happy outcome of my detective work, and their reunion. Time to be together to share the boredom—what else is a couple for?

I brought along a disguise. A short, rust-colored punk toupee so flamboyant I can't possibly wear it more than once, and a baggy coat to cover my clothes that were undoubtedly x-rayed by her penetrating eye. In the middle of a line where five other people were stagnating, I pulled the gear out of my handbag. They stared at me briefly as I struggled to shove my rebellious locks beneath the hairpiece, and a woman standing beside me speculated in friendly fashion, "It's too small, it'll never fit." They returned to their foggy contemplation of the boulevard while I carried on in lonely combat. It was too hot, my head was sweating, my fingers were like limp rags. Finally I got the thing to settle into place, and recovered some of my lost dignity. This dime-store Mata Hari was ready for the next step. As if she'd been waiting for the signal, Melody leapt to her feet, roared out of her refuge and merged onto Sixth Avenue, heading north, forcing me to dash across the street like a kamikaze on a light just turning red. We went striding along, the buildings steaming towards us like so many majestic *Titanic*s, we strode along and encountered bicyclists traveling in packs rushing north, then groups of demonstrators marching south, forcing us to the other side of the street, but not before Melody stopped one of them to ask their purpose. Young people under police escort who, in their debonair manner, were making sure no one exceeded the strict geographical limits allocated them. The troupe, flanked by uniformed guard dogs, tramped on their way, chanting circumspectly, holding raised banners that identified their cause: the seven, silly-looking, little green leaves of the cannabis plant. It was all too much like 1970, some faded documentary on the pot-heads of Woodstock.

At Forty-second Street, Melody veered right, along what I recognized as Bryant Park, and for a moment I wished might-ily that she would slip into one of the inviting outdoor snack-bars from which the scent of grilling meat wafted across the sidewalk. Instead, unfortunately, she turned onto Fifth Av-enue again and continued northward. We flirted with Dia-mond Alley, passed Rockefeller Center, Sak's, Cartier, stores so luxurious that the mere act of looking at them overwhelms you with feelings of poverty, but on we went, northbound. Melody walked with purpose, as if she might be seriously late for our meeting with Pierre Laliberté.

At Fiftieth Street, she stopped at a sidewalk vendor's and bought a pretzel, that curious variety of chewy dough that not only looks like a life preserver but almost certainly tastes like one. My hopes of an intimate little restaurant where I could stretch out my legs and order a huge American steak as I feasted my eyes on the face of Pierre Laliberté had started to evaporate.

At Seventieth, we were well into the Upper East Side, amid superb residences where not even the shadow of a restau-rant could be found. The billionaires who live here have no such need; these are folks who employ their personal three-star chefs to whip them up chateaubriands for breakfast. For a time, Central Park in all its magnificence accompanied us, as if we'd left the city far behind. I was so hungry I hated every bit of it. Melody angled off to the right and made a beeline for what at first glance seemed to be a private residence, with a colonnaded facade and a garden in the local manner, but at second glance turned out to be a museum. A museum. All these erratic steps, all these cramps in the tibias and the devouring hunger . . . for this?

These must be the kind of people who live on art and pretzels, and meet at lunchtime in places where no risk of sustenance lurks. I took a few steps inside. Visitors were few—they were all hard at work, tucking into *entrecôtes béarnaises* in more nourishing parts of town. She waited in a short lineup, then flashed a pass. As if she were at home. She was just about to vanish when, in a sudden onset of heroism, I bought a ticket that let me follow her inside, in all my suffering.

An odd museum it was.

I figured I would have been welcomed with a glass of champagne—either that or stylishly dressed bouncers giving me the bum's rush—so strong was the feeling that I'd stepped impertinently into the inner sanctum of some nabob, some aristocrat, or some mafioso with a veneer of culture. In this eccentric personal palace, everything, or so it would appear, was on display: the woodwork, the lamps, the writing desks with their bulbous legs that ostentatiously identify them as dating from the reign of Louis-the-whatever, the marble-topped tables, the sculptures, the carpets, the dimensions of the rooms themselves, as extravagant as concert halls. Not to mention the rare paintings hanging from the walls, scattered here and there; after all, a classy joint like this wouldn't try to throw everything at you at once. I lost Melody, but something told me I'd find her soon enough. I trotted through the rooms, photographing everything that caught my eye. Then I found myself on the banks of a pond sunk right into the dining room floor, unless it was the living room, all decorated with flowers, rocks and fish. A pond. How come they never thought of the birds, maybe two or three herons standing among the water lilies, or a few roseate spoonbills seen through the marsh grass? I sat down on a bench, out of breath. All this hodgepodge was beginning to have an effect on me.

In the next room I found Melody, in an immense hall as big as a gallery, with numerous paintings hanging from the walls, and austere benches just as numerous for contemplating them. Melody was seated in front of a painting. Only her back was visible, straight and alert; I could barely make out the painting that attracted her attention. A portrait of a man from a bygone era, a venerable object that must have been worth millions, even if it was painted in a studio crushed by poverty. Considering the way she was sitting, with her entire body strained towards the painting, as if inexorably drawn to it, I realized she would be sitting here for hours to come, and that she was entirely given over to an intimate ritual upon which no one else could intrude. She had no appointment. Pierre Laliberté would not be coming to meet her. Mata Hari was dismissed.

I was almost relieved. With a bounce in my step, I made my way to the exit, where I pulled off my wig from my over-heated scalp. I went running off like an idiot, the kind nobody pays attention to, because nobody could care less. I headed towards the southern reaches of the island, that teemed with delectable spots where they served lobster thermidor, dishes that seem to have stepped right out of Old Masters paintings.

WASHINGTON IRVING was a cheeky young man. Under the pseudonym Diedrich Knickerbocker, he wrote a book about New York's Dutch heritage full of fabrications and wild-eyed inventions. It paid off for him. The book became American literature's first bestseller, and at least one hotel bears his name, the one where I was staying. Cheek always pays, I said to myself as I put aside the front-desk prospectus that chronicled Washington Irving's triumphs, and rang for the receptionist, a black man with glasses who had taken over from my gum-popping friend. Could there be a man in Melody Ferretti's room, a man who sleeps, eats, writes and never comes out? The desk clerk gave me the once-over, the kind of look that very much does care; obviously, he disapproved of my curiosity. He then proceeded to hand me three messages with my name on them. "This guy has been phoning you every two hours since I came on," he said. Subliminal message: "You should mind your own business."

Thank you so much, sweetheart.

I tore up the messages without reading them, and sent them hop-skipping into the wastepaper basket at the end of the counter under the censorious and myopic gaze of the desk clerk, to whom I dedicated a gracious smile. At least he wouldn't be able to accuse me of lacking cheek.

THE TRAIL WAS beginning to smell like a dead-end. It was doing everything possible to elude the magnifying glass of *Flora-at-your-service* and disappear back into the jungle of disorder to which it had always belonged. Luckily, the American dollars were still in their envelope, and with them, the euphoria of being here, at the smoldering center of civilization. In the heart of the storm, as Melody put it.

I spotted my first rat. He spotted me first, as I was passing a low mound of garbage. He let out a squeal of panic and fled into a drainpipe, leaving his interminable tail dangling in clear view.

I spotted my first cockroach. If he spotted me first, he gave no indication, staying right where he was in the middle of my bathtub, brown, placid, as fat as a crab.

I took my first trip on the New York subway, a network of tubes like the belly of some factory, but without any of the dangerous sensations the travel brochures warn us about.

I went out walking late at night, side by side with endless variations of human beings kept awake by fear and desire. I brushed up against a thousand universes in a single minute, each one different, forever parallel. The gold of New York isn't its skyscrapers. It's the people.

Now what?

Now, Melody.

Day dawned on the bagels and cappuccino of the Washington Irving Hotel, and found me sitting across from her. By now my defenses and strategies had become meaningless. I expected nothing from Melody. If I were a full-fledged spy, I would have discovered some way of sneaking into her room and sniffing out the traces of a masculine presence. Being an amateur sleuth, I did discover that her room corresponded to the section where there were single beds. I won't say how; we get bogged down in details. The conclusion was obvious: a total lack of male phantoms hiding under her bed. With less effort, even half-competent spies achieve the same results as perfectionists. But what should I do with the knowledge that I am no longer on Pierre Laliberté's trail?

I had all but finished my bagels and was halfway through my perplexing thoughts when Melody appeared on the threshold of the breakfast room, swathed again in an oversized shirt, purple instead of khaki. She stood and swept the room with her gaze, scrutinizing each of the guests in search of the best concealed jewels. Our eyes hardly met, but suddenly she headed in my direction, rushing straight towards ME. My heart stopped beating.

"Do you mind if I sit?"

Her voice was pleasing, her eyes friendly. Then I remembered that she singled me out, and for her it's nothing but a game, she chose me from among all others to share her breakfast and satisfy her avid curiosity for other people. That made me feel better.

"Of course not."

She spoke to me in French. Anxiety returned in waves: the fear of being found out, the annihilating breath of retribution. I couldn't quite summon up a pleasant facade. She picked it up immediately.

"Perhaps you prefer to eat alone. I can understand that."

"No, no. It's just that . . . I lost the habit. I haven't spoken to anyone in two days."

"Is that so?" she said, sitting down. "How did you manage that?"

"I don't mean, 'Hello, do I have any messages, I would like to buy some apples.' I mean really talking."

"Yes," she agreed. "Even though it is possible to really speak your mind by saying, 'I would like to buy some apples.'"

And so began our conversation.

She was much better looking close up than from a distance. Close up, everything banal about her, her round face, her gray eyes, her fine straight nose, her plump silhouette, became sisterly and comforting. She looked me right in the eyes, as if holding back nothing for herself, as if she were completely at my disposal. Like a compact little heater whose sole function was to keep me warm, and to hell with the rest of shivering humanity.

"I know you're from Montreal," she said. "I recognized your accent."

I didn't recall having opened my mouth in her vicinity; I was too busy maintaining a safe distance. Careful, careful, this friendly little space heater is an experienced snoop who's trying to get something out of you. Well, I'd give it to her—why not?—as long as she gave me what I wanted. Human relations become so much simpler when everything is clear and up front.

"I noticed you, too," I said without hesitation.

"Really?"

"Not that many women travel alone."

"Alone," she echoed with a knowing smile. "We're never really alone. Or else we always are."

She laughed, I laughed, I offered to buy her a coffee, she accepted. Pals, come hell or high water. She pointed her chin in the direction of my laptop.

"You work in management, in computers?"

"I design Web sites. I've got a small business. Two of us."

"You're the boss?"

"Yes."

I couldn't resist the delicious lie—but was it really a lie? Aren't I the one running herself into the ground for Mahone Inc., while the other guy, that ne'er-do-well, is screwing everyone with a double-x chromosome in her gene pool? Isn't it about time to shift the scales in my direction? For a delectable eternity, I explained our work methods to the delectable Melody, as if they were mine and mine alone: to take the world's stage by storm, pull artists from their void, find the image and the formula that perfectly sum up the strength of a particular human being, and all the rest. No one ever listened harder than Melody Ferretti, no one ever raised so high the art of respectful and loving attention. I could have talked to her for hours.

"Are any of your customers writers?"

A tiny red light flashed in my head, bringing my egocentric flights to a screeching halt.

"No," I said. "Just actors."

"Ah."

Her smile was as friendly as ever, but the red light continued to flash on my inner screen. She waited for me to go on, but I wasn't going anywhere. I shot the ball back into her court.

"Don't you want anything to eat?"

"I never eat in the morning."

Nor at noon either, I could have added, knowing of what I spoke. The smile was still there, but a veil of melancholy settled over her, unless it was disappointment at her failure to entrap me. She continued sending me warm and furtive glances, as if to encourage further expressions of trust, but I pretended not to notice.

"Do you have much free time?"

"Plenty," I said enthusiastically.

She fell silent. As I did. Despite my stumbling ways, could this be the breakthrough of my career? Is Melody Ferretti, the visible half of the invisible Pierre Laliberté, the above-water segment of the iceberg, about to offer her services as guide to the megalopolis?

"How well do you know New York?" she asked.

"Not very."

"Too bad," she said. "Someone is coming to meet me today, and we'll be leaving for Maine. Otherwise, I'd have been happy to be your guide."

"Don't mention it," I reply in a flat voice. "Here, everything's worth looking at."

"Everything is worth looking at, but there are two places you mustn't miss. First, there's this adorable little square just north of here, where you can feel the pulse of New York, its fever, its immensity, the time passing, the extreme condensation of energy."

Herald Square holds no secrets for me, my lovely.

"I'm going there now," she offered. "That's where I'm meeting my friend. You can come along if you need help finding it."

"No. Well, maybe. Okay."

"You just need to sit there," she said, "and let the city overwhelm you. Then there's the Frick Collection. Promise me you'll go to the Frick and meditate in front of Rembrandt's *Self-Portrait* for at least fifteen minutes."

"What does he have to do with New York?"

"Because the painting is here. Only in New York can you can sit down in front of such a marvelous picture."

Sit down, sit down, meditate: the only words she knows. I'm not in the mood to sit down, not when everything around me is moving. I'm not fifty years old like her, looking for excuses for physical exhaustion. She picked up my disapproval, even though it was as light as the air.

"In New York you have to sit down," she said gently. "People are always running off in all directions, trying not to miss anything, but that's a mistake. You have to sit down to keep from being swept away, to keep your balance, and understand how things move."

Then she shook her head like a puppy and began to laugh. She ran her fingers through her hair, obligatorily blond, trying to flatten her coiffure. Did I say fifty? I actually had no idea how old Melody Ferretti was. There were juvenile parts of her side by side with parts that seemed to have lived several lives. How to average them all out?

"Anyway," she added, "it would be a pity to make you follow anyone else's path on this kind of trip. Follow your impulses. But if you take a moment to sit down in front of the Rembrandt, if you just take the trouble . . . there's such rawness in that canvas, such understanding of humanity, you're bound to be moved."

She laid her hand on mine and squeezed it.

"Off you go," she said. "And good luck."

Still smiling, she went off. My hand stayed warm long after hers had withdrawn. Everywhere else, the cold came creeping back. I felt a sharp, irrational pang of regret as I watched Melody Ferretti walk away, leaving me with a few particles of her warmth. And here I was, a stranger who had wished her ill. I felt such a longing for love in any shape or form, a love that would ask nothing in return, and I was devastated. I finished my cold coffee, kicked myself, called myself names under my breath. Florence, you cantankerous old mule, you damned slug, Florence, you gob of rancid butter. It worked. Sterner stuff staged a comeback. I got a grip on myself again and made it to my feet, cold and clear as an ice cube.

I didn't rush off to Herald Square. Everything was just where it ought to be, within easy reach, and I felt no exaltation. It's always that way when you've desired too strongly, and too long. Measured against desire, against its incandescent heat, all else seems tepid, lusterless, even fulfillment itself.

I could reach the little park before he did. I would see Melody sitting straight-backed on the wrought-iron bench, floating calmly on roiling waters. I would wait until Pierre Laliberté pushed open the gate and stepped forward to meet her. A few moments later, I would pass through that same gate, with the fragile look of someone who has everything to learn about roaring cities. She would be happy to see me, I'm sure. That radiant smile, and since space would be at a premium on our little island, she would invite me to join them at their table. She would introduce me to Pierre Laliberté. "I would like you to meet Pierre." Just "Pierre," that simple. And then—I don't know. That's where the film gets confused, and the heart beats more furiously. No one knows what kind of film it will turn out to be, a terrifying thriller or a tale of passion.

Everything happened just as I'd pictured it, at first, in any case. From a distance I saw Melody sitting alone with the contented air she carries with her wherever she goes. Cars surged along Broadway and the Avenue of the Americas in perfectly orchestrated chaos. Miraculous that everything works as well as it does, that the connecting rods and circuits of such a gargantuan creature could function so superbly. The din of the city reached my ears like a triumphant hymn to the glory of civilization. Then, on the Avenue of the Americas, a man stepped out of the group portrait, and Melody straightened on her seat. She waved her hand vigorously. The man responded with the same emphatic gesture. I checked the zoom lens of my camera, that I had carefully hung on my handbag. The man crossed the boulevard. He was wearing a cap and a scarf that streamed along behind him in the wind. His expensive clothing seemed to be cut from silk. He hurried towards the square, but once through the gate, he slowed his pace. She stood up. They were only a few feet apart, but they were taking their time, savoring the short and steadily diminishing distance between them. Slowly, slowly, their arms and bodies came together. They embraced and stood still, as one, then stepped back to gaze at one another. I could see Melody's face, laughing, transported with emotion. They embraced again. I've never really enjoyed love scenes, especially those in which I play no part, so I decided to add a note of melodrama. I moved quickly towards the square and stepped through the gate, almost at their side. Something strange happened: Melody did not recognize me, she did not glance at me, she did not even notice that a foreign presence had slipped into their bubble. But the man threw me a brief, euphoric glance as if to say, "Excuse us, we're crazy."

He wasn't Pierre Laliberté.

JUSTICE DOES EXIST, and not only for Melody Ferretti. At the hotel, it was my turn for a scene of passionate reunion. No sooner had I walked through the door than a tiny devil leapt up from the lobby's only armchair. Zeno didn't attend the same academy of seduction as the man with the scarf; he can't be bothered with the slow approach. He took two strides and set upon me, shaking me like a fruit tree.

"Good God, Flora! I was dying of worry. What got into you? Why didn't you send me word?"

I hung loose, waiting for him to calm down. It took a while. Zeno stepped away from me and considered me in silence.

"You're looking fine. Wonderful."

"Sure, sure. Why not?"

"Shit, can't you understand? It's the first time we've been out of touch for two days."

If what he said is true, then I've buried something monstrous from which I'll soon feel liberated. Right then, all I felt was fatigue, an immense lethargy that kept me from displaying the new woman that I am.

"I missed you," he declared, managing to lift me off the ground, even though inertia has doubled my weight. "Let's go eat somewhere. You're treating."

HIS GOOD MOOD did not survive my news. He asked me ten times over whether I was sure that the man in the scarf had nothing to do with Pierre Laliberté. Ten times over, he turned as dark as a skyscraper in a power failure. The tenth time he slammed his fist on the table, and our two plates of steak and French fries jumped into the air in a state of panic.

"That slut!" he fulminated. "That no-good bitch!"

That was Melody, my own personal soul-heater. The insults were so out of place that I erupted in turn.

"Frankly, Zeno Mahone! You! Since when do you have the right to be scandalized by other people's infidelities?"

He glared daggers at me.

"That has nothing to do with it! If I was with someone like Pierre Laliberté, I'd never even look at anyone else."

How nice for me, for us, for all the women he betrayed with the indifference of a stud bull. Before I could prepare a suitable reply, he attacked again. Nose thrust into the money envelope, he mentally counted the remaining bills.

"What have you done with five hundred dollars in a day and a half, if you don't mind saying? That money I gave you belongs to Mahone Inc. What the hell have you done with Mahone Inc.'s money?"

My reply was going to be as terrible as it would be definitive, and would include references to double-dealers who deserve worse than death, and my disgust for him that would long outlive our separation, that would take effect immediately. But I needed time to fit the words together, and Zeno abruptly put his hand on my forearm, shattering my concentration.

"Forget it," he said. "Bygones are bygones. We'll start all over. Keep the money, it's part of your salary, you've done good work. We'll turn over a new leaf. Pierre Laliberté is over and out. Pack your bags, we're going back to Montreal. I've got two new clients for you. One of them is totally crazy and filthy rich to boot, you'll love him."

He smiled. Kissed me on the cheek, ensconced himself in his chair and purred like a cat. He disarmed me completely. Even stole my precious irritation.

"I can't leave right away," I told him. "I've got a couple things to do."

"What?"

"None of your business."

"Fine."

He waited a second, maybe two. He tickled my forearm with his fingertips.

"Can I come with you?"

HE HAD IT COMING. Instead of spending our last New York hours in the tumult of Times Square or in Greenwich Village, there we were, sitting studiously together on a hard bench in the West Gallery of the Frick. Facing us, Melody's Rembrandt stared at us austerely, enjoining us to silence. Zeno spoke first in a voice so soft it barely stirred the weighty, cathedral-like atmosphere.

"I didn't tell you why I couldn't leave," he whispered.

"I'm not interested," I answered in a voice lower still.

"It's not what you think it is. I know what you're thinking."

"I'm not interested."

"I'm going to tell you anyway."

The canvas was large, more than a meter square. The colors were muted, with persistent shades of red and gold showing through the darkness that shaded the man's forehead. The man was Rembrandt himself, as far as we know. Fine. He was seated in what seemed to be a throne, and his hand held something that could have been a scepter. His clothing was curious, half oriental, half rustic, while a strange yellowish apron held in place at the waist by a red sash covered the front of his body. He was wearing a hat. Looking directly at us. Old. He had the skin of a man who could have benefited from a leaner diet and some anti-wrinkle cream, but his piercing gaze let us know that such matters did not concern him. How long did Melody say you had to meditate in front of this canvas before it began to yield its secrets? I felt as if I'd been here for centuries. I had learned nothing, not a single thing.

"It's my mother," Zeno whispered.

If he couldn't stop himself, let him talk. Let him talk, and accept the fact that his words were being swallowed up by a desert where there was no echo, no willing ear to hear.

"My mother tried to kill herself."

"Your mother!"

"She swallowed more than four dozen sleeping pills. Then she built a fire in the middle of the living room with newspapers, wood from the chairs, torn curtains. A pile of kindling in the middle of the living room, just like a campfire. Luckily, a neighbor who wanted to borrow a saucepan turned up just as the campfire was getting started."

That voice of his, still whispering, empty of any form of emotion. How could he say those things in that church-mouse voice? How could he even be here? How could he have eaten and laughed only minutes ago? I gazed upon Zeno, that total stranger. He looked right back, and I saw him as he is: divided. Behind his lively facade, a state of collapse lurks inside him, so deeply rooted it would take a microscope to see that devastated land.

"Don't you worry," he said, taking my hand. "Don't you worry, she's all right now. She says she's going to try it again, but I don't think she will."

"Why did she do it?"

"It's complicated. It's because of her Mohawk blood. She wants to move to the Oka reserve, something she got into her head after her menopause, but they don't want her. She'll get over it."

He turned to the painting before us, as if everything that needed saying had been said.

What's this world coming to when prim and proper mothers start trying to kill themselves? How will people who are only a little bit tormented hang on? I was so shaken that I clutched Zeno's hand as if it were the only patch of solid ground on this earth, and he clutched mine, for the same reasons, I thought. In the midst of our wordless desolation I felt a strange sense of calm settle over me, like a shield being lowered, a respite in this fight to the finish.

In that hushed respite, without warning, the painting opened up before me. Surely it had been open all along, but I had not. It didn't matter. Finally the man seated across from us said what he had to say. Unspoken words I'd already heard in a thousand different ways, hope and fear, hope and fear without end, the absolute turmoil of living and soon ceasing to live without ever overcoming the turmoil. I listened as the pained gaze of this Dutchman who died more than three hundred years ago spoke, I heard him clearly, in the surrealistic modernity of New York, May 2001. And my flesh crawled.

Zeno got the same message I did. I felt his body sag and his breathing grow labored.

"Let's get out of here," he muttered.

But we did not move. He had us now and he wouldn't let go, this man who once had lived, and who was staring at us. The least we could do was accept the parcel of authentic pain he communicated, burning from its passage across so much time and space.

8

PIERRE LALIBERTÉ,
FINE CUBBYHOLES

————————

*T*HERIOS WAS LEAVING.

Just as we were beginning to recover, our minds freed from our impossible quest, just as we were getting our summer legs, he went and did that to us.

Was this any kind of a time to be leaving? When everything was returning, everything that could claim some degree of intelligence, right down to the white-throated tweetie-bird and the rosy-breasted what's-its-name? Why not wait until the next cold season, when beauty faded again? How dare he miss the first strawberries, the first morels, the first salmon trout, the first young ladies with their plunging necklines, the first bellowing blasts of car horns on a Saturday night?

"I know, my little heart, I know," sighed Therios. "But when it's time to go, it's time to go."

Eleftherios Kaklamanis sold everything: his house on the Plateau, his restaurant on Saint Denis Street, the safe harbor that did double duty as our office, his northern immigrant soul. He was leaving to bleach his bones on that sun-scorched island of his where the poppies grow even in winter. But man cannot live by poppies alone, dammit! And nowadays the sun gives you cancer, how could he not know that?

"I know, little heart," Therios sighed again. "Don't make things more difficult than they are."

He sighed for the sake of appearances, to spare us the distress, we faithful customers with faces drawn long by disappointment, but deep down he was bursting with excitement. His visage was radiant in anticipation of the sun's cancerous rays.

"Come and see me when it's thirty below."

I had never thought of him as Eleftherios Kaklamanis. Eleftherios Kaklamanis, son of Dimitrios Kaklamanis, born fifty-nine years ago in Argostoli, on the Ionian island of Cephalonia, was returning to inhabit that part of his life that had always been foreign to us. It's as though Therios, our Therios, were fading away, as though he were suffering a brutal death at the hands of this stranger who returned to this earth. Damn that stranger. What right did he have to come and steal our Therios, his big, powerful hands always bearing fattening victuals, his massive, comforting shape by the kitchen door, his voice as abrasive as oriental music, his land-bound harbor open until late at night to welcome any storm-tossed vessel?

Maybe that stranger actually had the right to reappear and lay claim to the light, because we did not love Therios enough, we did not want to know anything more about him than fit the stereotype of the jovial restaurant owner, we never took his melancholy seriously. We didn't even know whether he had ever married, or why he was single now.

"Come on, what are you talking about?" Zeno interjected. "Married twice, divorced twice. He must have told us ten different times. You never listen when people talk to you."

"Very well, Zeno Mahone. So will you please explain to me, great insulting mind reader, why a man, who everybody loves and who's lived in one place for thirty years, suddenly gets the irresistible urge to pack his bags and clear out?"

"Easy. It happens every day. It has nothing to do with us."

Considering his record as a deserter, Zeno hardly qualified as the ideal partner for sharing this kind of self-flagellating anxiety. No one would ever convince him to swallow the tiniest drop of guilt. He didn't need to, anyway, with so many of us ready to raise the cup. Still, for all his bravado, he was as heartbroken as I by Therios's precipitous departure. There were a good three dozen of us victims scattered around Therios's restaurant, the three dozen or so regulars Therios selected to whom to announce his departure.

"I don't want any hangdog looks," he thundered. "I want to celebrate! Show me you know how to have a good time, you bunch of pale-skinned Quebeckers. We're going to have a party, I said. Push back the tables, we're going to drink and dance!"

Platters of grilled eggplant poured forth, plates of stuffed vine-leaves, taramosalata, tzatziki, shrimp, feta, squid, olives, and enough ouzo and retsina to drown us. His new life, at the rate things were going, was going to begin deep in debt.

"That's what you think!" he burst out. "Your bill will be waiting for you at the door."

Two musicians equipped with electric bouzoukis materialized from the kitchen and plugged in their instruments in what used to be our booth, making themselves comfortable in what once was our office. That was it, there was no escape, we were stuck in the soundtrack of *Zorba the Greek,* while Therios and another Hellenic pal of his actually executed the steps of a *syrtaki* in the middle of the floor. All that was missing were the goats and the bone-dry hills and the postcard I would never buy. We hesitated between consternation and amusement, we sophisticated customers who consumed local color only when it came in pastel tones, on the border of non-existence. Maybe it was the joyful kitschiness, maybe it was its own pride in itself, but this thing, this picturesque Greekness started to take hold of us, and our feet began to shuffle in spite of ourselves, even if no one was drunk enough to dance yet. A blast of sea spray washed away our North American mental constipation, and drunk or not, we were transported to the Cephalonian plateau, clutching one another's shoulders, lifting our legs to the beat, stiffer than arthritic geese.

You're never as happy as when you never intended to be.

Therios extricated himself from our sweating, disheveled company to take the microphone. He was going to speak. And he did.

"My friends," he said. "My friends. *Fili mou.*"

He couldn't find the words, so he began to sing. A Greek song drawn from his tearjerker repertoire, a song about love or parting or faded flowers—you figure it out. Our ignorance of its exact meaning made it even more touching. Our legs felt full of lead. Just as we were about to become so heavy we would all sink together, he started to speak again. His voice was fine and salubrious and carried the conviction that, all things considered, life, in spite of everything, remained a positive experience.

"That was a song of welcome. I am telling you that you are all invited next year, at the same time, to the sunniest island in the world, and you must not offend me by not coming. My house is your house, and I have extraordinary plans for my house. I am telling you that I am opening an inn in my house, the most Quebec-like inn in Greece, with mattresses stuffed with peacock feathers, or with ibis feathers for those who prefer a firmer mattress, and delicious roast baby lamb you can feed from a bottle before you eat it with a fork."

As we wondered whether or not to applaud this invitation to descend into carnivorous barbarity, Therios moved on in a more serious tone, and a more vegetarian one at that. He spoke of roots, how his roots remained there even though his heart was here, and how a heart deprived of roots ends up beating in a vacuum.

"I love all of you," he said, his voice dropping. "I love Montreal and I even ended up loving the snow, devil take it, but for a long time I've been torn and I can't explain it, I feel like setting my feet on hot dry ground that smells of the sea, I want to see myself again like when I was a kid and I used to fish for octopus and beat them against the rocks to soften them up, I want my father's bones to recognize me and say 'hello,' I need to recover something that's always been there even if I don't know what it is. But I swear I love you all, even more than my family back there."

He began to cry, finally, and finally we gathered around him and mingled our tears with his, but because there were a lot of us and only one of him, we ended up jostling the person next to us, who jostled the person next to him, and that created a bouquet of disparate heads shaked by the same emotion, a kind of huge, multiheaded octopus already so tenderized it needed no whacking against the rocks.

The music began again, as Therios enjoined it to, for he would not let the celebration slip away. As the musicians struck up, we disentangled ourselves and considered one another, we the guests at this farewell revel, a little bit surprised to find ourselves liquified in one another's embrace after years of mutual ignorance. There was a little of everything at Therios's place, the young and the decrepit, people with tattoos, others with their yuppie pens, blue denim and fleece, ugly girls and handsome older gentlemen. The only thing we had in common was Therios, and perhaps an irascible, solitary soul, for most of us seemed to be alone, but a little less desirous of solitude after tasting the spicy sauce of solidarity. Take that skinny redhead Zeno zeroed in on the minute she walked through the door; even as we speak he was leading her into a quiet corner of the room, that lubricious dwarf. But I couldn't care less. Hang on to your condor's soul. Then there's that striking older woman in a long red dress engrossed in conversation with a biker with peroxided hair, and there's even a man giving me the once-over and—I'm not saying this to toot my own horn—a guy who's looking long and hard enough at me for me to give him the once-over myself.

Slender, brown-haired with patches of gray at the temples, wrapped in a cocoon-like, shapeless, forest-green sweater, brown eyes focused on me more like a deer than a predator, soft liquid eyes ready to release me at the first sign of refusal.

I moved towards him. I did not say to myself, *Good God, it's him, how can it be, what a stunning coincidence.* Not a single word worked its way through my mind, not a single thought took hold. I moved towards him in a state of utter tranquility. I knew this man. I knew he could be trusted.

We stood before one another and gazed into each other's eyes, frankly and freely.

"How have you been all this time?" asked Pierre Laliberté.

"Fine, and you?"

"Fine as well."

His face and voice were so unremarkable that it was easy to stay close to them, and become immediately familiar.

"Which table did you usually sit at?" I asked him.

"This one. And you?"

"That booth over there."

He redirected his eyes for a moment towards the spot where I had been for all the years we had never seen each other. That was the only opportunity to try to piece together in my memory the few striking details of his features. One eyebrow slightly more arched than the other. The hollow beneath his chin that could be from an old scar. Short, slightly wavy hair. The beginnings of a pot belly distending his sweater, ordinary ears, an average nose, a roundish face, average complexion. Try as I might, his face slipped away and memory eluded me. When he turned his eyes back to me, I realized they were the only memorable thing about him, the peculiar liquidity of his eyes, so brown, so pleasant. A forest marsh, a swatch of damp velvet, a creamy chocolate sauce.

"I remember," he spoke. "You were always off in your corner arguing with someone in a loud voice."

"Yes," I said. "That's the way we work."

"I see. Did you used to work here too?"

"Some of the time."

"It was a perfect place," he said. "For everything. For work, and for just sitting."

Now I recognized his voice. From that night of confusion I recalled the tone of his voice, and his eyes glowing like a comforting light in the darkness. No words were more important than the warm tone of that voice as it told me, without speaking, that my grief meant something to him, that my life as a complete stranger meant something to him.

It seemed like so little, but it was everything. In the end, that's all we ever really need. To face whatever may be, we need nothing more than the occasional illusion that our life means something to someone who knows nothing about us.

"Did I thank you at least, that time?"

"Of course," he said, embarrassed. "It was nothing, really."

"What you told me. The words. Do you remember?"

A sudden current of concern stirred the calm chocolate of his eyes. He was slow to answer.

"Yes, of course."

"Well, you were wrong. My father could never have said those words. You must have heard them somewhere else, in another room."

His concern dissipated, he looked at me with both curiosity and benevolence, mostly benevolence, until a touch of acidity began to gnaw at my stomach, as when a third slice of overly sweet cake is plopped on your plate. Thanks but no thanks, I'm in no need of benevolence, benevolence is too rich for me, and needless too, now that I'm neither poor nor sick nor afflicted by anyone's death.

"It was very kind of you," I added, my voice rougher than it should have been, "really very kind, but there are some things we know for certain, and that is one of them. My father could never have spoken those words. Besides, he was in a coma."

"Even so," he said, smiling, "room 2029 was your father's."

"Twenty twenty-nine. Yes, it was. I was in that room myself. The whole night."

"There was no one there when I went in."

"I was there, I tell you."

"It was the beginning of the night, around eleven o'clock, midnight."

He extended his empty glass towards a bottle of retsina that was making the rounds. At the bottle's other end was a drunk, intense and mirthful Therios who found the perfect excuse to stop, knead my shoulders with his free hand and smother my neck with wet kisses.

"This woman," he said, turning Pierre Laliberté into his witness. "Ah, this woman. If I was twenty years younger, let me tell you, I'd have gone after her myself. Is that a sad sight or isn't it? A pretty little sweet-smelling flower like her, and smart too, not married or in love or anything, always typing away on that damned computer like she was old and ugly as sin. Figure it out if you can. The women in this country, they drive me crazy on account of I can't figure them out. I bet the two of you don't even know each other, eh? People in this country, they're totally northern and wild, so nice and polite that no one talks to anybody on account of they're afraid of getting kidnapped. Isn't that so? So I'll introduce you, if you don't mind. This is Pierre. He was my best, my biggest eater, a guy who wanted to know everything, who never left a bite on his plate. You can be sure he's a remarkable guy, he knows how to enjoy life, and over here, this is my pretty little flower Florence who no guy has ever had the balls to add to his bouquet, and if that isn't a shame . . ."

Enough, Therios. Down, boy.

Luckily, other empty glasses demanded Therios's attention and he abandoned us to one another. Pierre Laliberté sipped his retsina with a cautious half-smile, and pretended not to notice my embarrassment, reeling as I was before this sudden attack of Mediterranean virility that put my sense of humor to the ultimate test. He waited until I'd stopped forcing myself to laugh idiotically. I appreciated his discretion, northern and wild though it may be.

"I was walking down the hall," he said, glancing at me furtively. "A voice I heard stopped me cold. I remember it. It was the voice of someone who's already gone but hasn't reached the other side yet. He was right on the line between two worlds. There's nothing more riveting than being able to touch a space that's so close by, but so distant. So I went into room 2029, your father's room."

He paused. I said nothing. No questions, no reaction. He continued.

"Your father was speaking. In fragments, tiny broken sentences, as if he were arguing with someone. As if he were taking time to observe something, a show or some curiosity, before commenting on it. There was no pain in his voice, no physical or moral pain, I can assure you."

He paused again to let me absorb this vital information, vital for him and most certainly for Pepa. But it left me absolutely cold, and each element he added piled another icy stratum on top of the immense polar magma settling over me. How much farther will it advance, I wondered, this ice field paralyzing my mind? Where will it end, and how? Will it become so intense that it will turn into its opposite, and burn me worse than fire?

"I couldn't understand his words," he said. "It could have been a foreign language. Maybe it was. Maybe he was speaking in another language he learned a long time ago, ancient Greek or Latin. Did he know the rudiments of another language?"

"I haven't the slightest idea," I told him.

"Maybe sounds stop sounding like themselves in the space between life and death. Maybe there's a different language for every level of consciousness. But maybe I'm just making things up."

"Maybe you are."

"In any case, your father was speaking. So I went up to him, right up to him. I leaned over him. I touched his hand."

"I see. You touched his hand?"

"Yes. He opened his eyes. He looked at me."

"He looked at you?"

My voice was smooth and pleasing. I might even have been smiling. But inside, the iceberg had grown so huge I was amazed I still had room to breathe.

"And then, at that moment he said those words, very distinctly. As he looked at me."

"What words?"

"You know very well. The words you know."

"Repeat them."

"The heart. *The heart is an involuntary muscle.*"

"I see."

"Then he closed his eyes. I think he slipped back into his coma."

Slipped back into his coma. Fine. Pierre Laliberté stopped talking, he'd finished his piece. So then, all's well that ends well, especially the *deus ex machina* final twist in the shape of a coma. It adds up to a perfect story, a very visual one too: Pepa, the main character, emerges from his perpetual aphony to deliver his poetic testament—and his last look, let's not forget that last look—to a perfect stranger who happened to wander into his room, and immediately after, when the near and drear draw nigh, in the form of his Daughter, he withdraws anew into the cloisters of silence. No, there's nothing more to say, the story is perfect as it is. Nothing would be gained by grafting on idle questions, but let's try it all the same. Where the hell was the Daughter when the lead character was exhuming those rare and precious words from the cavern where they'd lain fallow his whole life? Was she not on duty that night? Ah, yes, of course she was, somnolent, more dead than alive, but standing guard nonetheless, except for a few moments, those few moments when she stepped out for a cup of coffee, or a muffin, or some other insignificant victuals in the hospital cafeteria. Ah, ah, ah! Another idle question perhaps? A last one, but a tough one.

If the Daughter had not left the room for a few minutes to gulp down a coffee or a bite of muffin or some other insignificant victual in the hospital cafeteria, would the lead character Pepa have spoken those rare and precious words, would he have bestowed his last glance upon her?

No answers, please. An answer would only undermine the perfection of the story.

"You're looking pale," Pierre Laliberté said. "Aren't you well?"

"No."

"Come on. Let's get out of here."

I was right about one thing. I knew that my brain, petrified by cold, would begin to boil over at any minute, and that's exactly what it was doing. Boiling heat follows cold if we are to be consistent with global warming, and frozen liquids inevitably melt. How reassuring it is to know oneself.

From a distance I saw Therios, whom I would certainly never see again. From a distance I saw Zeno, whom I was condemned by fate to see my whole life long. They meant nothing to me, neither of them. I was seized by something boiling and bubbling that managed to choke off any warmth. The cold in me was boiling. Probably that's what they call rage. I was infected with the icy heat of rage. If rage could kill at a distance, no one in this room would get out alive. Not even the man beside me, so soft, so considerate, the man who was holding my arm like I was a paraplegic, and guiding me towards the exit. Zeno spotted me leaving on the man's arm. He turned away from the girl he was pawing in our former booth and gave me a wide-ranging look, both complicity and friendship. I could hear the words rushing through his mind. Finally, he'd be saying to himself, finally she's going to get laid by some guy, finally she's acting reasonable. Make off like I didn't see him. That's the best policy.

IF YOU'RE ALLERGIC to oxygen, the air on Saint Denis Street is as unbreathable as anywhere else. I pushed forward, then all of a sudden I would stop, to see if that made any difference. I wanted to kill someone, that's what I wanted. As I walked, I managed to crush a few of the billion or so microbes and micro-organisms that thrive on the sidewalk, as I breathed I neutralized the bacilli copulating quietly in the atmosphere. But the carnage was too well concealed to give me any relief.

The one I wanted to kill was already dead.

Pepa never gave me anything. Nothing, not a thing. Not even alms at the end, which would have cost him nothing. Which he gave to some guy, not me.

"Would you like to go for a ride? I have a new kind of car. Would you like me to show you something beautiful?"

I looked at him with astonishment. Pierre Laliberté. All the while, he'd been holding me by the arm, as light and supple as a fifth limb that had suddenly sprouted. All the while, he had stopped when I did, sped up when I did. My feeling of nausea intensified and grew more complex. Florence, you pathetic rubbish heap, Pierre Laliberté the Great Invisible Hero is next to you, holding you by the arm, and you let yourself be devoured by petty thoughts. It was all his fault, actually. What was he doing there, perched on top of Pepa's burial mound, in the first place?

"Where is this beautiful something?"

"Not far from my place, but not at my place."

Like the first time, his eyes glowed with infinite solicitude, reassuring me that I was not venturing alone into darkness. I must have really been in a bad way to warrant all that attention and expenditure of energy.

"Am I red?"

"No."

"Strange. That's how I feel: red, scarlet red."

"You're pale, but a little less than before. Don't worry. It looks good on you."

I started walking again, in step with him now, following his lead. He let go of my arm, and I felt doubly orphaned. We crossed Saint Denis against a red light, so slowly that at least five cars had to screech to a halt to keep from hitting us. Brimming over with stress, the drivers peppered us with horn blasts and invective. Off to a fine start. We slogged along until we reached a narrow side street, and the vehicle, half Jeep and half Oldsmobile, rusted to an approximate red.

"Is that your new car?"

"It's not new," he said. "It's a new kind of car."

"How far is not far from your place?"

"Forty-seven minutes from here at ninety kilometers an hour."

"You'll drive me home after?"

"I'll drive you home after."

"Let's go. But I don't feel like talking."

"I'm not much for small talk myself."

And that was that. He started the engine and off we went, and before long my head was propped against the door frame, as trusting as if I were in my own house. We kept our word, and did not speak.

Something familiar and sugary enveloped me, and closed my eyes. A smell. That was it. The car was impregnated with a smell I knew by heart, and as our motorized silence pierced the night, I let the smell carry me off into cozy melancoly. Because of the smell, a tiny nostalgia fraught with sighs, silky to the touch and warm, rose inside me. Zeno. That was it. The smell of Zeno's van.

Head against the door frame, I snuck a glance at the rear seat through half-closed eyes. Two cushions covered with Mexican fabric, a gray wool blanket, a black imitation-crocodile briefcase, bottles of water, a knapsack. Nothing remotely resembling the squalor that surrounds Zeno, nothing that could possibly exhale the same slightly tepid, slightly foxy, slightly living smell. Except. Except for Pierre Laliberté.

Could Pierre Laliberté's books, that fill Zeno's van, smell of Pierre Laliberté himself? Could they have carried in their words, in their very intensity, their sweat and black magic, the fragrance of the primordial essence of Pierre Laliberté himself?

In amazement and terror, I straightened up in my seat. Pierre Laliberté was driving cautiously, as prosaically as possible, as attentive to the road as a fastidious accountant motoring homeward with his progeny. How does he do it? How does he carry off that unimaginable sorcery, infusing his books—the copies soiled by printers, distributors, booksellers and God-only-knows what other smell-saturated middlemen—with his own indelible odor?

Sensing my eyes upon him, Pierre Laliberté turned towards me and smiled a soothing smile.

"We're almost there," he said.

Poor Florence, you poor mosquito brain! I spotted the fur, matted and enmeshed in the fabric of the seat, weaving its way triumphantly into his sweater and now into my skirt, like a crawling, creeping leprosy. Yellow hairs, masses of yellow hairs. Pierre Laliberté's automobile was impregnated with the smell of dog, smelliest among all smells, with the lingering stink of Pokey.

WE FINALLY ENDED UP somewhere. At forty-seven minutes from Montreal, this particular somewhere was desolate indeed, as cut off from civilization as the moons of Jupiter. When I stepped out of the car, stifling darkness and concentrated humidity assaulted me. This must be what they call the great outdoors, if memory serves. There was a road, on which at least one automobile traveled, our automobile. There was a house fifty meters farther with two lighted windows. There was a strange silence that wasn't really silence, more a continuous electric hum, the kind of silence produced by humus and mildew when they seize the solid universe and reduce it to mush. I stood next to the car, a packet of nothingness, without any landmarks at all, and no way of knowing where to go, and if there were even any right ways in a world of such utter loneliness. Then Pierre Laliberté was there beside me, wrapping me in a wool blanket, the gray one from the back seat, that was surely crawling with yellow dog hair.

"I have another one," he said, "if you're still cold."

"Why is it so dark?"

"Because it's night."

"Aren't there any streetlights here?"

"Nothing of the kind."

There was a note of amusement in his voice, the only element of his being accessible in this universe of the blind. Suddenly I could not tolerate his voice.

"I don't want to be here. I want to go home."

I went to open the door. He grasped my arm and pulled me away from the car.

"Come on, come on," he said, his voice amused and hateful. "Stop complaining. I'll lend you some rubber boots. Come over here, they're in the trunk."

"I never wear rubber boots. I'm allergic to rubber."

I wasn't just being frivolous. Some people are allergic to rubber, they suffocate and die horrible, painful deaths if you so much as wave anything made of hevea under their noses. For other people it's peanuts or dog hair, but let's stick to rubber for the time being. If you're going to die of something, why not die of rubber instead of love, right? I had downloaded it all from a ridiculous Web site called latexo.com, designed to convince criminal skeptics like him who refuse to listen to people like me at the possible cost of my life, who thrust dirty boots upon me as though there were no possibility, even the most remote, that I might be telling the truth, that I might collapse, as if struck by lightning, into the black muck.

"The ground is wet. You'll catch your death with those little evening slippers of yours."

"I don't feel like walking."

He headed towards the house, quite prepared to abandon me, numb and asphyxiated. I hurriedly pulled on the boots and followed him. What's good about rubber, despite its drawbacks, is that dog hairs don't stick to it.

"This beautiful something of yours, where is it?"

"We're almost there."

"This is your place?"

"Yes."

"But you said we weren't going to your place."

"We're not."

"No?"

"No."

So be it. We'll just stand around outside, I suppose. What are we going to do in the pitch-blackness and suffocating damp? Where will we rest our eyes exhausted from seeing nothing?

In the oversized boots, my feet slipped and slid, and the footing was treacherous on the rough terrain. I stumbled, making laborious headway, until Pierre Laliberté took me by the arm again, his grip rock-solid in the precosmic slime. We squished along. Finally, in front of us loomed a structure that seemed to be unavoidable. An immense, barn-like construction plunked down in a clearing a hundred meters behind the house, half garage, half shed. Dry at last, maybe even warm, and minimally lit—a dim light gleamed in a small window at the front of the building. No lock on the door. He pushed it open and we stepped inside.

We were greeted by the smell, the smell of Pokey to the tenth degree, not to mention light and warmth. And the sound of whining.

"Come closer, come closer. I'd like you to meet Blondie. The others are Uno, Dos, Tres, Fourth and Fünf. They're temporary names, just like everything that's just born."

Sure enough. There, on a thick mattress laid directly on the floor, covered with rumpled blankets and unmatched sheets, lay the dogs. A big one, a female, lying on her side, clearly having just whelped, and the little ones crawling all over her, squirming and sucking, each one more vigorously than the other, dog larvae with a scanty fuzz on their minuscule larval bodies. I stood there with my mouth open. Pierre Laliberté knelt in front of the mattress, laughing. Blondie the bitch got halfway to her feet as he came near, throwing her thirsty brood every which way onto the bedclothes. She licked his face, laughing as well in her wheezy dog voice. The pups threw themselves again at their mother's flank, and she lay down docilely, her belly offered in sacrifice. A nice-looking dog, you could say, with a lustrous coat that never suffered rejection or parasites, like Pokey's did. A big, yellow-haired and surely very gentle animal, the prototype of the slave who adores his enslavement, a dog of the fluidly affectionate variety, who slathers you with saliva more often than you swallow your own. Pierre Laliberté looked up at me, waiting for my reaction. I attempted a smile. He picked up a larva from the wriggling mass, paying no heed to its peeps of distress, and offered it to me. I might be smiling, but that doesn't mean I'm prepared to commit myself to just anything. I patted the head of Uno, or Segundo, they all look the same in that chaotic existence of theirs, and I left it at that.

"You don't like dogs?" he asked with his smile.

Telling a dog lover you don't like dogs is as good as a declaration of war. I broadened my smile.

Then I wriggled my way out of it, using a sentence Zeno used until I'd gotten sick to death of it, during that very short time when we'd tried to live together in harmony. For once, it did the trick.

"You can't not like dogs."

Pierre sat me down in a shaky chair and left me alone to stew in silence, cultivating all the ill feelings I wanted to, as he squatted down to take in the show at close range. I watched him watching the dogs. He did a lot less than Zeno. He didn't pretend to talk to them in those preposterous peeps and squeaks we affect for lower beings; actually, he didn't say anything. Blondie rose to her haunches from time to time to make sure he was still there. He nodded at her, which set her tail wagging, and that seemed to be enough for her. Then she flopped down among the greedy guzzles of her little piglets, pardon, puppies, to let them drain her dry.

"You're feeling better, right?" he asked abruptly, without looking at me.

I had to admit it. Yes, I was. Not because of them, that's for sure, all sticky and dependent as I never imagined anyone could be at birth. So how come? It must have been the entertainment. Yes, I was completely entertained. I had nowhere to hang my personal gripes.

"Come with me, there's another part."

He stroked the dog's head and whispered a few words I didn't even try to understand. We left behind the odoriferous canine world, which was just fine with me. On the way out, he picked up a half-unrolled sleeping bag. A tiny concern, an amused concern all the same, popped up in the back of my mind. What if he wanted to rape me, here in this bog? The hypothesis didn't withstand scrutiny for more than a second or two, it was even more ridiculous than the idea of dying from rubber poisoning. I followed him outside, about to move into the next phase of the entertainment.

Which took place outdoors. More and more outdoors, farther and farther from the house and its outbuildings with their shining lights and rustlings of life, canine though they may have been. Suddenly I thought of Melody. Could she have been inside the house falling away behind us, curled up in the hollow of those lights, growing ever fainter? It was hard to picture that little space heater languishing away in this water-logged wasteland, after she'd strode so deliberately across the pulsating New York cityscape. Just in case, I put the question to Pierre Laliberté.

"Do you live by yourself?"

No reply. He quickened his pace as if to put more distance between us. Then, when I'd stopped expecting an answer, his voice came floating back:

"No."

There was enough light for me to make my way without leaning on him, or on any other crutch. We followed a wide pathway pockmarked with puddles that my valorous rubber boots easily vanquished. Trees of medium size, branches bare well into May, lay in wait in the darkness, unaware that the leaves had already come out in Montreal and other civilized places, that green, bushy dresses were what well-dressed trees were wearing these days. And then we must have arrived, since he came to a stop. In front of us was a bench, and in front of the bench, a stretch of water small enough that all the raw-boned nakedness of the trees on the opposite shore was in plain view. Water, more water, as if the moisture in the air had not already saturated us to the core. He spread the sleeping bag on the bench, meaning that this stop was obligatory on our circuit. He sat down. I sat beside him. Now what? Where are the dogs, the monsters, the ghosts hired for my entertainment? Maybe he was expecting them at any moment. Maybe they would emerge at a preset time from the murky waters, according to a schedule known only to him.

Normally, silence should have surrounded us, for silence is one of the obligatory attributes of the great outdoors, but it wasn't like that at all. That same electric hum filled our ears, intruding on the silence, then pitilessly demolishing it.

"What's that?" I asked. "What's making that noise? Is there a power station around here?"

He took his time answering again. I saw his shoulders shaking. I'll be damned, he's laughing. He turned in my direction with a joyful face, a smile from ear to ear.

"It's the frogs. The bullfrogs. It's their mating season. Haven't you ever heard the sexual concert of bullfrogs?"

Bullfrogs!? What's he talking about? Since when do frogs talk to one another? If frogs could talk, we'd have heard about it, there would be dozens of Web sites where frogs could speak for themselves.

"They're not talking," he said. "They're singing. Of course frogs sing. You can hear them, right?"

This time, I really listened. This was no undifferentiated background noise, but an enormous clamor made of innumerable tiny cries, dozens and dozens of tiny strident voices, one atop another, answering and adding to one another until they had composed a dizzying, immense, discordant chorus. My toes curled inside their rubber protection. Frogs, an entire population of frogs wriggling in obscurity in the cesspool at my feet. Ugh.

"How many are there?" I asked in a low voice.

"Dozens," he said. "Hundreds, for sure, if you count all the swamps in the area."

He spoke in low tones too, to avoid attracting their attention, for singing frogs are, by definition, in a position to hear.

"Don't be so tense," he told me. "Lean back. Lift your head a little. No, keep your eyes open."

I awaited his next series of instructions. They did not come. Now what? What other beast would emerge, winged and repulsive, from the blackness? I waited and waited, and since there was nothing, I finally saw the stars. A fireworks display frozen in full flight. Like a virtual Web page on a colossal screen. Like the dream of a manic depressive in the manic phase. Where did that nebula of tiny, indiscriminately focused lights come from?

"The thing," Pierre Laliberté pointed out, "is to see that they're not outside of us, as if we were spectators, but everywhere around us. In front of us, behind us, beneath us. The thing is to see that we're part of it."

"What?"

"People say "the stars" as if they were of no concern to us. But the truth is that we come from them, every chemical particle in us comes from them, and we float exactly like them, with nothing to hold us down. Everything is floating in space. The stars, the frogs, you and I. It's crazy, but it's the truth."

If there's any kind of talk I'm really allergic to, this has to be it. All the mumbo-jumbo about space and the stars, and pretty soon, about the great Oneness and an infinitely infinite God, if I don't put a stop to it. I gave him a mocking smile, but he motioned me to keep looking skyward in my uncomfortable position.

"Do you have a cigarette?" he asked point-blank.

"No."

"At night I always get the urge to start smoking again."

"Fine. But what's the connection? The frogs, the stars, the dogs, what's the connection? What are we doing here?"

He cogitated for several minutes, then sighed impatiently.

"I don't know what to tell you. The answer is right here, in front of us. Don't you see anything?"

"What do you mean? What am I supposed to see?"

"It's not easy. I don't know if you'll get there. If you don't, I'm afraid you'll be upset with yourself, and that might put you back in the state I managed to pull you out of."

"Don't worry. I might be angry with you, but not with myself."

"Ah! That's not so bad."

We laughed briefly. Two deeply retarded individuals, warm and cozy in their dog coats, making hifalutin small talk while the frogs do the nasty in the water, and where everything floats away with the stars in the middle of everything else. A night out of hell.

"Okay," he said. "Okay. Let's begin at the beginning. You sit down the way I told you. Jesus, you're as stiff as a board. Face to the sky. Eyes open. Relax. What I mean is, don't try to think about anything. Just listen. That's all you do, you listen. You don't hear one voice, you hear thirty, a hundred. Listen and you'll start to hear each one, in detail, like the separate voices of a choir."

"That's crazy, it's impossible . . ."

"Be quiet. Concentrate. Listen. You'll hear everything. Now it's louder, now it's clearer, to your left the voice is deep, it's a bullfrog for sure, you hear everything, nothing escapes you. And then, when you're there . . . are you there yet?"

"No."

"When you're there, look at the sky. I mean, really look at it. You hear everything, and at the same time you become very aware of the sky, the space of the sky, its immensity, its depth, its stars, its planets, all that. And then . . . you dive in."

"I dive in?"

"Yes."

"Where?"

"Right here. Here's where you dive in, and here's where you surface, totally here, in the only place where we could possibly be, on a huge ball of earth full of bullfrogs, dogs, water, people and cities, floating and floating in space."

Silence now. Maybe he decided to keep quiet for good. I heard his soft breathing. Where has he traveled to, in what parallel universe is he floating, leaving me far behind? Though our respective warmths were almost touching, it was clear to me I was alone, stranded on this wooden reef. His instructions were incomplete; I had no idea what to do with the sky and the frogs, so absurdly twinned together. The silence was unbearable. I pictured myself very well, tiny and stiff and alone, lost in the immense blackness of this flooded wasteland, a poor tiny stiff little thing forsaken forever on the bench of existence while everything floats around me, blissful and ethereal. I pictured myself so pathetic that tears started to flow. Luckily, my condor, never too far, sized up the situation and threatened me with his talons. Florence, you fat noodle, you whimpering marshmallow, what's all this treacle? Come on, give it your best shot, connect with the frogs, of course it's ridiculous, but when you come right down to it, what infinitely more stimulating alternative does the present moment have to offer?

None. So, frogs it is.

I know nothing about frogs; I never ran across one on Saint Catherine Street. What's a frog's life like? Cold, comfortable, short, nebulous, viscous or none of the above? Is real pleasure, pleasure that's aware of itself, accessible to frogs? What about pain, and sensual ecstasy? When the male attracts the female after croaking himself hoarse, and takes her from behind or from the front and deposits his seed in her, which of the two enjoys the greatest transport, the bomber or the bombee? What is a frog orgasm like? Is it hot, painful, stimulating, dark green, juicy, hyperbolic or none of the above?

Shit, Florence, LISTEN. So I listened. It's hard to listen without thinking about what you're listening to. I listened. What I heard was indescribable. Was it music or cacophony? What I heard came from everywhere and extended in all directions, and in the end it gave birth to an uproar almost harmonious, metallic, as hypnotic as a mantra.

I began to hear soloists emerging from the great chaos. Each, in this unlikely choir, was a soloist, assembled by an unlikely conductor, a hard-of-hearing primitive. Whew! There were way too many of them for me to pick out one in particular, but I stuck to it doggedly.

What do I do about the sky? What do I look at it with, now that my attention's entirely taken up by frogs. I had no energy left over for the sky. Too bad. It'll just have to be happy with me looking at it the way I can.

Looking? No. Not exactly.

Better this: Seeing it from within. Say "within" and acutely you feel how each star corresponds to the voice of a frog, how the audio belongs to the visual, how everything is of a piece, inextricable. Ah, so the choir is much larger than I imagined. Everything is part of the score: what I see, what I hear, even what I feel. I'm part of the score. It's a perspective thing, nothing really, just the entire universe I suddenly perceive in a big bang of lucidity, the perfectly synchronized universe that has no trouble accommodating the fictional borders created by the puny human imagination, including my own. I-me-Florence has no real boundaries, I-me-Florence is no more than a single beat in the immensity, the vast vastness, the void.

I retreated. It was too much, way too much.

I retreated, but I was moved.

"You see?" said Pierre Laliberté. "I knew you could. I knew it right away. That's why I brought you here."

Soundful silence. I waited for the rest. There has to be a rest. When something is as gigantic as what I've just glimpsed, there has to be an explanation of what's hidden behind the swinging doors he pushed open for me. How can he expect me to lead my life as if nothing happened, as if I wasn't a microscopic particle of sky.

"Now what?" I asked, almost respectfully.

"I don't know about you," Pierre Laliberté said, "but I could go for a hot chicken sandwich and a big side of fries."

AND SO IT WAS that we returned the way we'd come, leaving the mystery behind us. Not a word about the sexual habits of the stars or the supernatural powers of frogs, though I was completely ready to accept the worst, the most inconceivable. Not a move in the direction of the house of dogs, which by that time I considered hospitable, nor towards the real house, now in darkness. No doubt Melody was sound asleep. Ah, to slip into the kitchen still warm from wood consumed by the authentic woodstove, to sit down at the spot where Pierre Laliberté ruminates over his masterworks, to be served a steaming cup of coffee or even a gut-wrenching shot of liquor by a disheveled and warmhearted Melody, to linger in the magical lining of the night in the company of those accessible magicians.

Instead of which, Pierre Laliberté strode over to the dog-hair-matted automobile and helped me in without a glance.

We headed towards Montreal, greater strangers than before. I peppered him with questioning looks, but he drove on, end of story, an inexplicable scowl on his face. Very well, we'll discuss it all in due time, over soggy hot chicken sandwiches and limp fries. But no, he brutally brought me back to earth.

"I'll drive you home. Where do you live?"

He's dumping me. I've been dumped. After the initial disappointment wore off, I propped my head against the door frame in a ferociously philosophical mood. Don't forget, he doesn't owe you a thing, he's already given you more than you could have reasonably expected, don't forget he's Pierre Laliberté, the mysterious writer, a well-established nutcase in his own right. Head against the door frame, body shifted as much as possible towards the segment of sky that's visible to me, with all my strength I evoked everything he had given to me, the feeling I felt so recently, so terrifying, so inordinate. Nothing. The sky hung there, dotted with innumerable stars, but it had closed in upon itself once more, as claustrophobic as a subway sky. No more connection between me and the sky, each of us has retreated into our narrow limits. The frogs must have been a crucial part of the exercise, but what kind of godforsaken exercise depends on the presence of stinking, bacteria-laden batrachians? I gazed upon Pierre Laliberté, barricaded behind his earthworks. He wasn't going to get away so easily.

"You do understand that I should have been the one to hear those words."

It had returned, more virulent than ever.

"What?"

His brown-eyed gaze was startled but not bitter. It was indifferent, which was worse.

"My father's last words. I should have been the one to hear them, don't you think?"

A small, annoyed silence.

"Yes," he said cautiously.

"What did you do with them? Did you repeat them to anyone else?"

Now we'd see what kind of convoluted lie he'd come up with at this crucial moment. Now we'd find out all there was to know about him in spite of his obfuscations and his concealments, and we'd act accordingly.

"I could have," he said evasively.

He wasn't entirely dishonest. But what did that matter, once the duplicity has been committed? Just because he's not entirely dishonest doesn't mean we'll let him off the hook, now that we've gotten hold of a vulnerable piece of flesh that may soon taste of blood. Florence, you she-dog!

"It was my inheritance," I told him in a soft voice.

"What do you mean?"

His voice sounded apprehensive. I kept silent, my eyes caught up in the dark landscape outside, my head in my hand like a heroine afflicted by melancholy.

"Those words were my only inheritance," I said once more. "You entered my father's room the only time I was absent, and he delivered my inheritance to you."

I could feel him squirming on his seat.

"What can I do about it?" he muttered. "I'm terribly sorry."

"You owe me something."

"What do you want? Do you want money?"

He regained his composure, and gave me a sidelong glance with a hint of amused provocation, like a boy playing with hand grenades. All at once, the gravity of the moment lightened by a notch, and I caught myself laughing.

"No," I answered. "Not money. Anybody can see you don't have any."

"What?" he said, feigning offense. "I'm rich. I have a house. I have a stereo. I have a car. I have six dogs."

He doesn't say *I have a wife.* And he was right. Melody also belongs to the man with the expensive scarf who held her tight in Herald Square, which means that Melody belongs to no one.

"Give me some tips. Show me things you know."

It came over me as abruptly as my outburst had a few minutes before, and just as inexplicably, taking root as though it were crucial to my existence.

"Tips?"

"Teach me something. At your age, you must know some things I don't."

"Come now," he countered. "I don't do things like that. I don't teach anything."

"You do. Like tonight. Tonight you showed me something I'd never seen before. Show me something else. Please."

"Come now," he said, irritated. "If you want to learn, there's no lack of books. All you have to do is read."

"I never read. I can't stand reading."

"Oh, really?" he blurted out.

"Really."

He was driving faster now, hands clutching the wheel.

"Just one or two little things," I repeated humbly. "One or two things you know that make life less difficult. What's it to you? For me, it would mean everything. It would be worth an inheritance. Please, I'm begging you."

"You're serious?"

He looked away from the road completely and gazed at me, perplexed. I was prepared for any inspection he might care to perform. My sincerity was total, or rather, my hunger, for he had awakened in me a terrible hunger for a kind of nourishment I had never imagined, for unknown varieties of bread and water to satisfy the hunger of the Third World inside me. He had revealed the emptiness within me. All this time I'd been starving to death and I didn't even know it.

9

THE BISHOP SYNDROME

IX TIMES THREE HUNDRED makes eighteen hundred. One thousand and eight hundred pages.

To read.

If I could just swallow the whole thing down like a snake, and let it decompose slowly inside me, and lie inert until digestion had worked its way through its fibrous mass. No such luck. I had to chew everything, one word at a time. Twelve words per line, thirty lines per page, 320 pages per book. Maybe I'm hung up on figures, but I have my reasons. It's like an endless journey on donkey-back, and along the way, I will be spared no pestilential odor nor emotion.

On my desk, the works of Pierre Laliberté awaited me in their monstrous totality.

You Love You. Morbid Martha. Go Run Fly. Recreated Creatures. Raspberries.

And *Falterlust.*

Fortunately, I'd already read *Falterlust.* And fortunately, Pierre Laliberté didn't suffer from logorrhea, not like Gina Da Sylva and her incontinent colleagues, who every year put entire forests to the axe, and force-feed libraries to match their frantic pace.

I've done it before, so I can do it again. I can. I do. I opened *You Love You.* It was eleven o'clock at night, and I had no interest in sleep. Eleven o'clock. Maybe that was the right time to get to know Pierre Laliberté.

I dove into the jungle. The most difficult part was penetrating the curtain of dense foliage and thornbushes, and finding a roadway, the hardest part was to persist, scratched and disoriented, even though no practicable pathway appeared and none may ever materialize. One hundred times I found myself wanting to give up, one hundred times I goaded myself on. And then came the moment when I no longer needed goading. That which I feared most had come to pass. I lost everything. My self-control, my freedom. The book destroyed my willpower and moved forward on its own, carrying me with it like a soulless rag, with no resistance.

ON I READ, delirium be damned, tracking the characters servilely as they drifted their aimless way. The Bishop. Here's someone called the Bishop, because at the beginning of the story he was a bishop by trade. We never learn his first or last name, even when he isn't a bishop anymore, which happens early in the book. A bishop who will lose his bishopric without losing his faith, and for his troubles will win a magnificent woman named Loiselle, whom he will also lose. From total loss to holy infamy, there is but a single step before he graduates from holy infamy to spiritual crime. He will become head of the North American Mafia, in which capacity he will order his own assassination. There, in a few pithy words, is the story of the Bishop, take it or leave it. We take it, of course, because we have surrendered the faculty of refusal, we take it because the nerve endings that govern critical judgment have been severed by the pen or the computer, a perfect creative crime that leaves not a trace.

Presenting the story in schematic form explains nothing, because the plot is no more than a brass plate upon which to serve the main course, and the main course is wild emotion carried along by the words themselves. How can words on paper be transformed into heat and violence? Who knows? It is a deep mystery one step removed from sorcery.

Afterwards, I couldn't sleep. I don't just mean the night that followed the book, which was a total loss. I mean several nights after, when all I could do was catch a few disparate scraps of sleep, that were constantly torn to let in the cries and moans of the Bishop.

This man does not exist. This man is a hallucination propagated by the perverse mind of a writer, yet this fictional man weighs more heavily than real beings whose memory he obscures. This man hammers fragments of something into me, but I can't quite piece them together, like a wrenching puzzle I have to try to solve anew every night.

Over and over I watch him fall. He reaches dizzying heights where all will be his, only to fling himself down without provocation or external cause, and down, down he falls. What makes his fall more terrifying is that it would never have happened if he hadn't willed it.

THE FIRST FALL takes place in Rome, at his moment of glory. He is soon to be named a cardinal. Seated on the throne, in the midst of a disquisition on love, he begins to disintegrate. An unknown spirit has taken hold of his tongue. "Cease to love!" he bellows at the assembled apostles of fanatical love. "Cease pretending that you are able to love, for love is never for one's neighbor, and only for one's *self self self.*" The rustling of sacerdotal silks, hubbub, scandal. He is hurried out.

The second fall takes place 150 pages later. He has returned to the laity long ago. His heretical pronouncements on the love of one's neighbor which is never the love of one's neighbor have been forgotten. For the last hundred pages, he has been passionately pursuing a different kind of neighbor, and that magnificent neighbor has now fallen into his arms, murmuring *my love my love,* as he had always dreamed she would, and he with burning eyes feels the monster rise up in his heart and speak through his mouth, saying, "You stinking rotten whore bitch I don't give a fuck about you," instead of the burning words of love on the tip of his tongue. Shivers beneath the silken dress of the lover, dismay, horror. She exits.

He falls for the third time 150 pages further on. By now he has become a don among Mafiosi after an astonishing career. The whole world quakes at his feet. He could order the assassination of the president of the United States, or Saddam Hussein, or the Dalai Lama, name the guy and he's dead meat. Once more the monster within him rises to the surface and, this time, he welcomes him with relief, like a long-lost relative. In his voice of dark efficiency, the monster orders that the man who will be standing in front of the church at eight o'clock sharp tomorrow morning be killed. (In this part of the city there is one church that has not yet been converted into yuppy condominiums, even though it opens for religious services only twice a week, hosting bingos, charity bazaars and concerts in which Bach is massacred by amateurs the rest of the time.) We encounter him at the church on the dot of eight, having expelled from his impromptu refuge the young junkie who had threatened to steal his death, and now he stands waiting for the black car from which the sawed-off weapon will take aim. The car draws up. It's a blue Honda, since times have changed and the dark aesthetics of Al Capone are no longer in fashion, but the weapons have remained the same despite minor changes in their crude technique, and death is always the flower that blooms at the end of their steel barrels. He receives the discharge in the shadow of the church and falls to the ground, and as he does, he catches one last glimpse of the inner assassin hastily freeing himself from his side. His suicidal alter ego that had always betrayed him at his moment of triumph. Now he is running to safety, his work of sabotage complete. In amazement, as the fleeing killer turns to look at him one final time, he recognizes the impish face of himself as a child.

Why? Why is this contorted, impossible tale so painful, why is it so frightening, why does it produce such toxic substances? And why invent stories in the first place? Isn't real life full enough of outlandish events that poison us and distract us from the essential tasks at hand, without inventing any more?

On my fifth sleepless night, Pierre Laliberté's very ordinary face appeared on my mindscreen, with those tender deer-eyes of his that wouldn't hurt a fly. I called upon him to answer my questions. Pierre Laliberté, who is the Bishop? To whom does he belong? Why is it that I—neither man nor priest nor Mafioso, and nothing of what he is—feel his presence like an arrow lodged in my flesh? Worse, like a part of my flesh that has been pierced by an arrow?

Pierre Laliberté's ruminant gaze, instead of answering, beams my question back to me like a mirror.

My intimate acquaintanceship is not with the Bishop. It is with his private monster, his inner assassin. I know the voice that hisses, *Jump* when I come near a precipice. *Steal that scarf,* when I go shopping in a high-class boutique. *Say No,* when it's so vital to say Yes. *Hurt him,* when the caresses have begun. I know it all too well. I have him in me, we all do, all us self-styled non-crazies, we all have a part of the Bishop nestled at the heart of our hidden dementia, we all carry, incognito, a suicidal little Bishop of our own who lies in wait for a moment of inattention, when he will destroy us.

"What's the matter with you?" Zeno finally got worried enough to ask when, on the tenth day after my ninth sleepless night, we met for work. We had relocated Mahone Inc.'s business to new, temporary quarters, an Italian café not far from my place, with a nasty owner who popped up every fifteen minutes to inquire what we wanted to drink, a rather translucent way of suggesting we leave if we don't drink more of his dishwater tea or poor-man's espresso. "What's the matter with you?" asked Zeno, eyeing me critically. "Are you coming down with mono, or maybe it's a touch of leukemia?" My appearance was hardly reassuring. I had dark circles under my eyes. I was pale right down to my fingernails. I was hooked on Pierre Laliberté, but now was not the time to tell him so. Zeno was worried about our contracts. The candidates for fame jostling impatiently in the lineup, anxious for us to give their brown, unfired clay a vivid new hue, and transform them into precious objects. That was his worry. Zeno bit off more than he could chew. Zeno was gripped by greed. In addition to glassblowers, retired crooners and other pathetic has-beens who have squeezed the last tablespoons of moisture from their dehydrated talents, he's taken to designing personalized Web sites for the most arid of ultra-dry professionals: notaries specializing in last wills and testaments, dentists dedicated to complex cavities, inventors of underwear with holes in all the right places, translators in search of texts in Nepalese and Swahili. Instead of being driven by true genius, Mahone Inc. has turned into a dating agency of the third kind. We were becoming rich and tired, a direct consequence of our turpitude.

"This is no time to get sick," Zeno fretted. "We've got work and plenty of it, but it's only temporary. I'm hiring three interns. What do you say? You'll be the idea woman, you'll think up the concepts and leave the nuts and bolts to them. Plus, I've turned up these incredible digs on Sherbrooke at the corner of McGill. A brokerage firm just deserted the first floor of a neo-Baroque building, all six hundred square meters of it, okay, maybe it's too big, but what the hell?"

"I see."

"It's just what you always wanted, right?"

"Isn't the rent exorbitant?"

"Sure it's exorbitant, what did you expect?" he said, irritated. "We're getting exorbitant ourselves, that's how far we've come. We can't turn back now that the contracts are raining down on us. What's your problem with being exorbitant anyway? Isn't your salary exorbitant enough?"

I hadn't noticed. The zeros on paychecks and bank statements are nothing but zeros, the very opposite of plenitude. So far, I haven't had time to cross-dress them as useless hard goods, as inescapable realities.

"Flora, you're not trying to pull *that* on me, are you?"

"Pull what on you?"

"Crying poor on me, putting on your hair shirt," Zeno complained. "A lot of people, once they get a taste of success after working like crazy, a bunch of spiritual paupers and genetic failures, they begin to freak out. Not you, right? I won't put up with it from you."

"So success, according to you, is designing far-out Web sites for ear-nose-and-throat specialists and orthodontists? Is that the magnificent destiny of Mahone Inc.?"

Score one for me. For a brief moment Zeno's pallor attempted to match mine, but quickly gave up for lack of depth.

"Why not? We agree, all egos are alike, all egos are hot air. Don't we agree?"

I mumbled under my breath to avoid the answer.

"You miss the artists, is that it, Florence? Which of our artist-customers do you miss most? The soon-to-be-washed-up, the has-beens or the never-will-bes?"

His turn to score a point. But I felt like a very bad loser, and too exhausted to play fair.

"What's the matter?" he repeated more gently this time, scraping the bottom of the barrel for all the sweetness that was moldering there for lack of use.

I should tell him. I should say, Zeno, right now I couldn't give a shit about all your notaries and orthodontists trying to improve their visibility. I've caught a bad case of Pierre Laliberté and I don't know what to do with him except read his books and get my fragile brain tied up in knots, and remember what you told me once, remember? That I'm sitting on a gold mine, on the beginning of the start of the end of the world with a nuclear detonator in my hand.

I only managed to deliver the first part of my mental collage, of course. That was good enough for him. He edged towards me, better to run his fingers through my hair.

"You're right, of course you're right. Listen. We don't give a shit. We don't give a shit, Florence. Nobody's kidding us. Everybody's the same, what do you expect? A notary or a creator, their hunger is the same, the same miserable appetite for the heights, the same certification of their own insignificance. That's our bread and butter, Florence, our usefulness. We work with that hunger and that appetite, we give these poor angst-ridden narcissists a color that's better than the real one, it looks like what they might have been, we soothe that anguish of theirs. Think about it: as a trade, it's great, it's generous. And it's starting to pay dividends. But nobody's kidding us, that's for sure. We're not expecting any extraordinary individuals to come knocking at our door. When you're someone extraordinary, you don't need anyone else to proclaim it for you, on the Web or anywhere else. Take Pierre Laliberté, for instance."

Ouch! Dropped that way, with all the offhandedness of ignorance, the name of Pierre Laliberté made me go even paler, or redder. Succinctly put, it brought a suspicious glow to my face. Zeno stepped back and examined me carefully. Luckily, the café owner came up at that very moment, bless his mercantile heart, and carried away our dishes, fingering the bill that was lying there unnoticed, and wiped his rag incisively across our table as if to sweep us beneath the table along with the crumbs. Zeno turned his bloodhound eyes upon him. I glimpsed a rapid darkening of his eyes, a sign of the approaching storm.

"Mi'spiace, Signor, ma questa maniera di trattare i clienti . . ."

He wasn't speaking Italian, he was bellowing it. The owner, as stunned as I was, dropped his rag to the floor before leaping into the verbal arena. Suddenly they were exploring all the explosive nuances of this operatic language. I managed to catch the odd outburst, *offesa, perché* and *ragazza,* spat three times in my direction by Zeno as if I were somehow involved in the dispute, while their ferocious hands speared the air in search of victims. Neither of them realized that they were caricatures, actors in some time-worn melodrama, and as a result, serious as popes—most of whom, as we know, are Italians, except for the last one who for some strange reason insists on being Polish. Finally the owner turned on his heels and Zeno got to his feet, gathering up our stuff. "Come on," he hissed between clenched teeth. Then the owner returned, carrying two glasses filled to overflowing, and plunked them down on the table and—why not?—they unleashed another torrent of words as vehement as the preceding one, except this time they were grinning. Zeno sat down. Whew. *Che commedia.* I didn't order anything, and now there I was, forced to swallow a potion that contained all the deleterious characteristics of alcohol.

Zeno dropped back into his chair across from me, ready to resume the cross-examination where he had left off. I wasn't going to let him get away with it.

"You speak Italian. How come?"

He shrugged.

"I'm Italian. On my father's side."

"Your father!"

"*Zeno* is an Italian name. You never read Italo Svevo?"

"Italian, Mohawk, what's next? You'll do anything to surprise me."

"I've only begun to surprise you," he threatened with a thin smile.

"What about Maud? Is she Italian too?"

The question was as inept as all impromptu exit strategies are. Still, it produced the desired effect. Zeno's face darkened.

"Maud is no longer part of my life," he said curtly.

"Since when? What happened?"

"Nothing."

He wouldn't say more, but I knew how wide a territory that "nothing" of his covered. For three nights in a row he didn't come home, he never offered any explanations or excuses, he forgot all the important dates, including birthdays and the anniversary of the night they met. He brought that redhead with the bug-eyes back to the house to sleep, a friend from work, but he obviously had more in common with her than work. He neglected, concealed, misled, profited. Plausible hypotheses abounded, but never a complete explanation, never an excuse, he never understood how murderous his little peccadillos were, he couldn't even remember having committed them for that matter. And when Maud, or was it Florence, cleared out one fine morning, or was it evening, depending on their preferred time of day for the sweeping gesture, he watched them go with astonishment bordering on indignation, as if to say, What the hell's gotten into you?

I didn't know what to call that part of Zeno that, sooner or later, makes the hurt he inflicts on others turn against him. Now I knew.

It was called the Bishop Syndrome.

"Florence," he said, cautiously guiding our silence in another direction, "Florence, you wouldn't do *that* to me, would you?"

"Now what?"

"Find Pierre Laliberté and not tell me."

Pearls of emotion scintillated in his handsome dark eyes. In his handsome dark eyes I saw Maud's vanished reflection, prostrate somewhere as her waters broke. I grinned at Zeno.

"Of course not," I replied. "I would never do that to you."

HE WAS MINE.

I had never had anything important all to myself, something extraordinary and rare. I didn't know yet what you were supposed to do with something no one else had. But I'd learn. I'd learn to cultivate that state of plenitude: he belongs to me,

I need seek no further, I need not cast upon him the nets of my greed. He is mine because only I know he exists in that fleshly form, he is mine abstractly, far more than any tangible form of wealth I could lock up in a chest, than any warm body I could lie down with in my bed.

Abstract goods are not for sharing.

Pierre Laliberté was mine and mine alone.

PIERRE LALIBERTÉ climbed out of his hybrid automobile just as I reached my front door. He didn't call my name, he made no sign. He stood there beside the open car door to show that he had been waiting for me, and if I didn't notice him, that was my problem. I did notice him. I walked towards him, towards my buried treasure. I was so moved that I left all forms of civility entirely up to him. Good morning, good evening, how are you, I've been thinking a lot about you.

"Listen," he said abruptly, "I came to tell you I can't do it. I'm not what you think, a teacher or a master of anything, I'm just an ordinary guy. I've got nothing to teach you."

He was wearing the same green sweater as the last time, though the weather was warm and dry. His eyes blinked in the bright sun. What was different about him? The light. Night suited him better. Day made him more ordinary, it disfigured him and revealed his tiniest fissures, his slightest blemishes. What had he done? What did he let happen? Why did he let his skin collapse, so that it separated from his bones, independent in its decrepitude? Anger swelled up inside me, and I insulted him under my breath. Use face cream, for God's sake, or tanning lotion! Get a facelift! Sell your soul to the devil! Stop this!

How old is he? Forty . . . fifty . . . fifty-five? Or older? He finally managed to see me through the dazzling sunlight, and detect my enormous disappointment.

"Come on," he said. "At least we can talk a little."

I invited him inside. At my place there was nothing to drink, except for Japanese tea and tap water, but my miniature Canon had been gathering dust, waiting for something worth photographing. Like pictures of him. But he refused right off, as if I had made him some vile offer.

"Let's go for a walk," he decided. "We can get a drink somewhere."

"Wait for me. I have to drop off my laptop."

When I returned, without laptop but with Canon, I saw him from the back. I was struck by how youthful he looked, his faded jeans and white running shoes, shifting from foot to foot, and whistling. From behind, he seemed to be thirty, or maybe fifteen. He could have fooled anybody. But he turned in my direction, offering me the ruined frontal view, except for his eyes, which gave off an ageless, distant light.

Remember that, Florence, when your time comes, if it ever does. The eyes don't age. They might die, but they don't grow old.

WE WALKED. I had to keep slowing down to stay abreast of him. Walking slowly is sheer torture for me. We moved so slowly that we seemed to have no destination at all, or if we did it wouldn't appear for another hundred years, when the city's people and landscapes would have changed so much that I wouldn't be able to recognize where I was, nor in

whose company, I'd have stagnated in this immense interme-
diate space while time sped by around me, to the profit of
everyone else. I'll have lost all my clients and with them the
marvelously neo-Baroque office on Sherbrooke Street at the
corner of McGill College, some cunning, quick-witted inter-
nauts rushing towards success will have taken it, while we,
we, we—FASTER!

"Are you in a hurry?" Pierre Laliberté asked.

"No, no, not in the slightest."

Maybe he devised this tortuous pace, so ill-adapted to my
own rhythm, as a form of exercise. Maybe slowness was back
in fashion, who knows? I forced myself to stroll along nonchalantly, trying to figure out why anyone would want to
waste his life force in immobility. But doing nothing seemed
to be the practice here. All around I saw half-naked creatures,
young, unkempt, slouched over park benches, leaning
against walls, seated directly on the sidewalk, singly or in
groups, or both at the same time. Summer had swept the
dead bodies from inner spaces and offered them up to the
highest bidder.

The greatest waste was the silence between us. The man
walking beside me was overflowing with vital information,
yet I was not allowed to extract it from him.

Why was he hiding? What was he running from? Why
did he write? And why publish? Who is the Bishop? Why the
Bishop? Why death, and not life, triumphant, shining, life as
the true subject for fiction? Was he unhappy? Or in love with
Melody? What could love be like with her? Without her?
How many times per week? What does he prefer, the living or

the dead? (Human beings or books, I mean.) What was he thinking about this very minute? What did he think of me?

I attuned my silence to his, and waited for him to open a door. I did not have long to wait. At the first corner, he turned to me.

"Let's say," he said, "let's say you have a choice between eternal beauty and learning how not to give a damn about it. What would you choose?"

I hazarded a smile. You never know. What was he after? An ill-conceived pass? A saintliness test? As my nerves galloped off in search of an answer, I gave him an indulgent little smile to let him know I was entering quite consciously into his fluorescent trap.

"To start with, I'd have to be convinced I was beautiful."

"You're evading the question," he said. "Answer it. No evasions, no lies."

"Very well. Eternal beauty, of course. No woman would answer any differently, even though the second choice is clearly the best."

"Oh, really? And why is that?"

"Because not giving a damn whether you're good-looking, old, ugly or hairy means being powerfully free. If we had one ounce of dignity, we'd prefer freedom. But because we're dim-witted, masochistic and feminine, we choose beauty."

I could have told him that women choose beauty because they're choosing love, that you can't have one without the other, whereas freedom, that's different. There's plenty to say about freedom, which I kept to myself. Freedom without love tastes of sour verbena and the bottom of the barrel.

Maybe he was pleased with my answer, or overcome by a surge of gallantry, but he took my arm as we crossed the street, in full view of everyone. We strolled along so slowly that the picture we presented to those we encountered was that of a real couple frozen in love's promiscuity. Suddenly I felt the warm flow of the sun on my back, I passed through the scent of lilac barely disturbed by carbon monoxide, I understood the necessity of naked bodies offered euphorically to the god of heat. Summer, the season of condors and youth, came over me like a majestic revelation, and I became summer itself, I, Florence, young and beautiful, on the mythical arm of Pierre Laliberté, he whom no one else knew.

On the other side of the street he dropped my arm and stopped. We had reached a square where an unruly multitude of drummers, sun worshippers and flabby gawkers were fighting for the few centimeters of new grass that was unlikely to survive its popularity. I observed Pierre Laliberté observing the crowd. What brought that hint of a contented smile to his face?

"Shall we go this way?"

He pointed towards the center of the square, the core of the multitude, where electrons and protons hummed crazily, apparently blocking the way. How could a person whose profession was rugged individualism suddenly become so sociable?

"All right," I said, though without much enthusiasm.

He took my hand, with good reason this time, since our fragile association was threatened with being torn apart. Joining hands, we dove in, soft as eels or unyielding as granite, depending on the resistance we encountered. We strode into the maelstrom of gesticulating lives that again and again tried to tear us apart, but finally it propelled us through, our appearance a mess but the rest of us miraculously intact, into the eye of the storm. There, curiously, all was calm. Is that what happens in the true core of all cells? An area of complete calm surrounded by turbulence. Everywhere, tiny Herald Squares.

A fountain was gushing, casting droplets of water on the benches where people were engaged in civilized conversation, playing chess, stoking their nostalgia with a harmonica or a joint. There was even space on one of the benches.

"Is this okay?" Pierre Laliberté asked.

"Yes."

He hadn't let go of my hand. There were no subtle messages, and not a shadow of desire. He had simply forgotten. When he realized the incongruity of my hand in his, he deposited it delicately on the bench, with no further comment.

"Well," he said. "If you really insist, I could show you some little things, trifles I've discovered along the way. But for me to call that teaching is too presumptuous. I couldn't bear it if you took anything I said as instruction."

"I don't venerate anything, and you know it. Why would I venerate you?"

"Indeed. There's no reason to."

"It's normal for you to know more than I do. Just give me some hints on how to get through life more skillfully. I'll take them for what they are: hints. And I won't try to camp out at your feet, I promise."

"You're laying it on a bit thick," he smiled. "I'd like a little respect all the same."

Curiously, we were replaying that night not so long ago. A wooden bench worn by rain and sun, water again, but this time far more rollerbladers than frogs and not a single star to be seen; but dogs, yes, lots of dogs. What would emerge from this hodgepodge of colors and lives? What magic would his voice work in the raw light of day?

"First and foremost," he began, "is curiosity."

"Curiosity?"

"Curiosity is a matter of life and death. It drives all discoveries and all experimentation."

"Yes."

"You have none."

"Me?"

"You."

"I'm not curious?"

"I'm so sorry."

"How can you say that? How do you know?"

"For example, at the hospital, the first time. When I repeated your father's words to you, such extraordinary words, you didn't ask a single question, you didn't seem surprised or even interested. And that was only the first time. It's quite clear. You don't have any enthusiasm for other people, for their hidden zones, which we call curiosity."

Whoa. I didn't like what he was telling me, especially that cowardly and totally unexpected broadside about Pepa, and that sententious "It's quite clear" like a nun's nunnering. I didn't like it one bit. If his precepts were going to end up as blame, he could shut up and clear out.

"What do you know about my father and me? What do you know about my feelings back then, and my feelings now?

What gives you the right to interpret silence as a lack of curiosity? Ever heard of shock? And since when is curiosity more important than discretion or respect?"

I was shouting. The nostalgia circle turned to stare. I clammed up, mortified at having made this peaceful place a disaster area.

"I'm sorry," said Pierre Laliberté. "I didn't mean to hurt you. Let's just stop."

"Yes. Let's stop."

He stood up and looked away, as if we were strangers. I got up too. Fine, I've had enough. Heard enough, read enough, caught enough hot air from this clandestine crackpot who knew nothing about the sophistications of modern existence. Had he ever switched on a computer or written an E-mail? No, he insisted on concocting his poisonous works by hand, as if we were still living in the eighteenth century. And he's old, besides. What could he know about life, about my life? Grab a couple photos of him, quick, quick, with my almost invisible camera, then make myself scarce, that's what I'm going to do. Afterwards I'll give Zeno the photos in exchange for a fabulous sum, that's the deal, then I'll leave the two of them to slosh around in their mythomaniacal follies.

But my fingers had morphed into nonfunctional sausages. I palpated my handbag, then tore it open. I'd whip out my camera and KO the Great Invisible Hero without even putting on the gloves, since he didn't bother to do it either. I spilled the contents of my bag onto the ground. Pierre Laliberté, who had been looking for a path through the crowd, eventually got interested in my panicked search.

"Have you lost something?"

"Something's been stolen."

The electrons and protons that we'd pushed our way through were far from the neutral particles they seemed to be. Now, one of them was strolling through the magnetic field with one extra charge in his positive or negative bag, a tiny digital Canon PowerShot S110 that retailed for a cool thousand. I always hated physics.

Pierre Laliberté came towards me, a sad shadow in his eyes. I met his eyes, defying him, and my anger melted away. Anger is too hot and completely useless in this sunlight. There was no desire to cause pain in those worried deer-eyes of his. There was only truth.

No more Canon.

But worst of all, no curiosity.

"What did they steal?"

"Something useless."

"What do you want to do?"

"Talk about useful things. Like curiosity."

"Don't take it that way. It's not an incurable condition."

"You mean it can be developed? Like a muscle?"

"Yes, yes. Exactly right. Like big biceps."

He bursted out laughing, enchanted by the image. He must be imagining me laboring under the dumbbells in some virtual Nautilus where they offer emotional weight training. I laughed at the sound of his laughter. It surprised me: it sounded like anybody's laughter. Coming from someone so off the wall, his laughter was perfectly normal.

I always surrender to people who laugh. People who laugh

grant me brief membership in their tribe. What is laughter, after all? An outburst of shared childhood. Humanity patches up its differences and smooths its wrinkles in laughter.

If only Pepa had laughed more often, he wouldn't have grown so old.

But I digress.

Instead, let us return to the bench in the park. Pierre Laliberté has just stopped laughing, and now he is preparing, judging by the way he looks at me, to deliver a few elements of his non-teaching.

"Here's what you could do," he says. "But of course the final decision is up to you."

10

CURIOSITY

EVERYONE ELSE, and then me.

They're there, and I'm here. The distance between us can't be measured. We don't share the same territory, we never touch the same ground at the same time. One of us is necessarily the projection of the other. How could the two of us ever hope to merge?

To merge with others would mean that I have agreed to disappear.

Which is exactly what Pierre Laliberté is proposing. He wants me to select two individuals, and in choosing them forget my own existence, give them life to the detriment of my own. For as long as the exercise lasts, a half-hour at the most.

His words seem benign enough. Stay close to them, do not speak, use nothing but your eyes, insinuate yourself into their space. And then, he added, "Don't think about yourself."

That's no small matter. The return trip is not guaranteed. If I lose sight of myself for even a half-hour, what's to guarantee I'll find myself again?

IN THE PARK, a little farther on, I tried to pick someone from the crowd who seemed worth the effort, and who inspired some basic interest in me. There were good-looking girls and handsome guys; fat, pale-skinned men and oldsters displaying their remains; smooth, tanned skins and timid normal types dressed for the office; teenagers with spectacular tattoos. For all their apparent disparities, they seemed as identical as cut-out figures, as if they had been placed there like walk-ons. Why choose one over another? Which of them is worth forgetting myself for, even for a moment?

Florence, you're a monster.

Pierre Laliberté was right.

I felt no attraction to other people, to their zones of concealment. The strangeness of strangers bored me. Let them nurture that concealed zone of theirs in secret, let them pickle in their unknowable brine. Don't worry—I won't steal the recipe.

As far as I'm concerned, they can all croak.

It's not my fault. It's not me. Deep down, I'm soft and kind, and saddened to tears at having no extra sympathy for my unknown fellow-man. My condor is speaking through my mouth, my solid brass soul, the most trustworthy part of me, bulwark against complacency and despair.

At last. My first Other would be a girl. She was pacing back and forth in front of the fountain, so self-absorbed that, with total impunity, I could examine her as if she were a piece of meat. Girl it is. Sixteen, maybe seventeen years old. Auburn hair, dyed, short and spiky. A sleeveless super-tight pink tank top, and underneath, two aggressive little breasts. Exposed navel, around which one of her hands was fidgeting. Matching little skirt, very short. She paced: five steps right, turns around, five steps left. One hand on her belly button, the other holding the side of her head. Was she sick, a terrible migraine, was she expecting someone, did she have a stomachache? I moved closer, to the far extremity of the methodical orbit she described. She was talking on the telephone.

"No, like I, me, you know. Yeah, like I. Cool! No, like me, I go. Oh, gross! Yeah, like I . . ."

Monosyllables shot from her mouth in a low, impassioned voice. Hard talk was coming from the other end of the line. A girlfriend, probably, loitering a few meters away. Not a boy, I could have sworn, a boy would have kept her body from going slack, forgetting itself, those absentminded steps in their mechanical regularity, right hand playing with her navel. A boy would have made her self-conscious, caught in the pitched battle of seduction.

Red sandals on her feet, eight-inch heels. The tiny cellphone glued to her ear was red too. Toenails painted maroon. Maroon fingernails too, gnawed to the quick. A ring in her eyebrow, like everybody else. And another in her belly button, just the thing to keep her right hand busy.

What else? Lunar pale skin. Dark eyes, shadowed by mascara. No lipstick on her small mouth, half-open at all times. Imitation lizard-skin handbag, swinging from her shoulder to the stuttering rhythm of her steps.

I tried to find a word or a concept that would sum her up. Or, at least, something that would describe her well enough so her picture would last, however briefly, in the mind of someone who would never see her. Sexy? Streetwise? Ingenue? Laughable? Vulgar? Moving? Interchangeable?

A city girl, June 2001.

I couldn't find anything more specific. She wasn't defined enough, she was built upon too many mixed and contradictory models, each pulling her, her mind not made up yet. The way she was, chaotic, under construction, her image couldn't be pinned down. She wouldn't leave a picture for posterity. Tough. Posterity isn't for everyone. Think of the crowd if it were.

She had no idea what to do later in life, or even if there was anything worth doing. She was going to school anyway. Fashion design, communications, nursing, early childhood education, computer science. No, not computer science. She was doing everything possible to hide the fact that she was a student, which was why she looked like one.

She lived with her parents. In a modest downtown duplex, or maybe in the suburbs, a place like LaSalle or Longueuil.

She hungered for everything, but without judgment. She squandered that hunger at raves, in clumsy telephone conversations, in daydreams, in fantasies of sex and love. She'd made love a couple times, indiscriminately, but her appetite remained unfulfilled. Maybe she'd never gone all the way, maybe she was still at the marketing stage, displaying her merchandise in full, too unsure of herself to put all her eggs in one basket.

No steady boyfriend. Her brothers and sisters younger than her. Worked in a supermarket on weekends, or in a secondhand clothing store on Mount Royal Avenue. Saving all her money for plastic surgery for big breasts and bee-stung lips.

Dreamed of being a pop singer, an actress, a model, a rock star's mistress, a hockey player's wife. Determined to be somebody even before she knew who she was.

She didn't like herself much.

I stood there, wavering, on the edge of a yawning chasm. Why didn't she love herself? Who was to blame? There had to be a guilty party. I stopped myself. You had to stop somewhere, otherwise you'd disappear into the void of other people, all of them were bottomless pits, all of them. I saw that now: even the most anecdotal among them, the most homogenous.

I released her back into anonymity. My mission complete. For someone so bereft of curiosity, I didn't do all that badly.

She looked like a Maribelle, or a Lisa.

What was her father like?

Enough about her. Her father must have looked like the man undressing her with his eyes, sitting Buddha-style on the grass, leaning against a tree with a book as cover. That man would be my second Other, a natural extension, a satellite orbiting in Lisa's gravitational field.

Forty-five, fifty years old. Maybe less, but excess weight seriously undercut what remained of youth. Fine blue eyes barely breaching the surface of his smooth face the way a periscope breaks the surface of the water. A nascent bald spot; fortunately for him, his hair agreed to leave its normal itinerary and be drawn across it. Casual but expensive clothing.

Stretch jeans, a pale blue silk shirt, darker blue under the arms where sweat had imprinted two half-moons. Soft leather sandals of the thick-soled variety that let you walk kilometers on concrete without dislocating your spinal cord (but the soles were new; he was more the type to spend hours lounging on the grass). Hairy feet, clipped toenails, impeccable. Hairy chest too, judging from the thicket of hair that clamored for air through the open collar of his shirt. His legs crossed lotus fashion, a spectacular position for a well-padded body like his. On his knees a book that had lain open to the same page for the past ten minutes.

A professional, or a recently promoted executive. Maybe a teacher or an administrator at Lisa's school. You never know, chance can do strange things. Married with two young teenagers. A condo in Outremont, a summer house up north, distinguished friends, higher interests, philosophical conversations, an independent wife who combined post-feminist success with a return to family values, meaning she juggled two jobs for the wages of one. They screw once a month, on vacation.

He watched Lisa. *Watched* was hardly the word. Too weak, too wishy-washy. He undressed her, pawed her at a distance, nibbled the best parts, in particular her butt and her pointy little breasts. From time to time an attack of serenity or modesty tore him away from his virtual feast, and for a few heroic seconds he lifted his book, long enough for me to catch a glimpse of the author's name, but the contest between paper and flesh was a lopsided one. His eyes fluttered across the page, understanding nothing, then they returned to the source of the siren call.

The Gospel According to Jesus Christ, by José Saramago.

That's what he couldn't bring himself to read. A man displaying his contradictions for all to see. His psychoanalyst, if he has one, must take pure delight in him.

Just a regular guy, maybe better. A good soul, overflowing with noble sentiments that had always guided his course through life. But now there's no understanding what was happening, how could this wild beast have sprung inside him, come to claim its due? More often than not, he would loll in the sun like an old hippie, drooling over the girls. Horrified, he realized that the famous male mid-life crisis was not designed only for the proles, for hopeless jerks, for everyone else, but even for superior beings like himself. The Beast reared up against the Angel, and the two did battle. His stomach had probably started manufacturing an ulcer or two, subtly so far, and maybe that red patch on his nose was a symptom of psoriasis, and not sunburn. For him, the worst thing was not to be dragged down to the bottom, but to enjoy the trip.

He looked like a Philippe, or a Jean-Marc.

"Why are you staring at me like that?"

That's a surprise. His blue eyes left their moving target and homed in on me. There's been a mistake. I'm not there. I don't exist. I've traded my reality for his.

"Uh . . . I'm not . . . I noticed your book."

His gaze wasn't hostile—quite the contrary. He displayed that saccharine quality of melted candy that guarantees sticky openings.

"You know him? A great talent, like a cathedral, something modern but timeless. He's a bridge between eras, Saramago is. You don't know what to read after you've read him . . .

Want to sit down for a minute? Or maybe you like the benches better? *The Stone Raft* is a great work too. Have you read it? Are you a literature student?"

While he peppered me with questions in an attempt to make me stay, his eyes poked and prodded at my loose-fitting clothes for the promised protruberances, the distinctive signs of the human female. Though he found little, he persisted; maybe he was excited by the contrast between our two frames. Lisa nearly nude, and I like a veiled Muslim next to her.

He had sunk far lower than I imagined, much closer to feeding on the bottom. He had no ulcers, since he cruised girls with a clean conscience, each day with weapons as imaginative as they were varied. Today a literary masterwork, tomorrow a comic book by Hugo Pratt. You have to use every kind of bait possible to attract all manner of small fry. He attempted a quick move to get to his feet and stand next to me, but the lotus position reminded him that at his age, muscle elasticity was more dependent on willpower than on speed. My curiosity and good manners exhausted, I left him to untangle his legs, and disappeared.

That's when I caught a glimpse of Lisa. She had relocated onto the ground, and into the arms of a skinny young man who was kissing her the way Philippe or Jean-Marc dreamed of doing, stingers and mandibles fully deployed. She offered no resistance, consenting but distracted, indifferent, still chatting away on the telephone.

She wasn't much like the thumbnail sketch I'd made of her, but there was only so much you could do without pausing and retouching. Too bad if people won't sit still for their portrait. Photography without a camera lends images a certain instability.

I HEADED FOR the sidewalk café across from the park, where he promised to wait for me once I'd finished my curiosity detail. I went straight to Pierre Laliberté's side, filled with pride in my accomplishment. I had done it. I had plunged into the soft bodies of other people, risking death by suffocation.

I spotted him right off. Seated at the back, looking at the table, deep in concentration. He was writing. A girl with platinum-blond hair sat down at the next table, surrounded by her entourage, who were causing an uproar as they swirled around him. Ramrod straight, he was writing undisturbed in his notebook. For the first time I saw him actually being Pierre Laliberté, clandestinely practicing his magical trade in the midst of the blind. I alone saw him as he truly was, I alone had the power of life and death over his secret, and this knowledge made him seem so touching and dear to me, poor tiny sparrow shivering in the palm of my hand, poor vulnerable fifty-five-year-old creature. I approached silently and stood before him.

"What are you writing?"

The question, as falsely innocent as a question can be, touched off an extreme reaction. He leapt to his feet, pressing his notebook to his chest, pushing the table against his platinumheaded neighbor, who protested loudly. He stared at me, terrorstricken. I was at a loss. Didn't he know who I was?

"You scared me," he said drily.

"Why?" I asked, laughing without pleasure. "You think I've gotten too curious all of a sudden?"

He let out the beginning of a laugh that was barely under control. Then sat down. He tapped his closed notebook with his fingertips, then opened it again.

"No, not at all. It's just that . . . Uhh. It's . . . It's a shopping list. Whenever I come to Montreal, I try to get in some shopping."

He handed it to me.

There it was, in black on white, set down in a firm, polished hand. Two leeks, three yellow bell peppers, two pounds of ground lamb, turmeric, a bunch of coriander, olives stuffed with cheese and prosciutto, veal shanks, Italian tomatoes, gorgonzola. And, underlined, that weightiest of questions: Yellowfin tuna or Atlantic salmon?

I handed the notebook back to him. Personally, I'd take the tuna.

I WAS DRINKING lemonade. He was drinking beer. I was talking. I assumed he was listening. Every once in a while, with a flick of his wrist, he shook salt into his beer. The salt touched off a revolution of hissing bubbles; he contemplated it with delight.

I had almost finished with Lisa. Every last detail of her. Under the spell of my late-blooming lucidity, I added a few elements that made her little hungry auburn head glow like a stained-glass window. For example: she was anorexic. For example: she attempted suicide at age fourteen (on her wrist I SAW the scar that my mind had passively registered earlier). He listened, but did not react. When I finished—still no reaction—I quickly turned my attention to Jean-Marc and his fake-Buddha blubber crushing the grass. I had just started in with the color of his shirt when he interrupted me.

"No. No, stop. That's not it at all."

I suppressed the words that were so prettily waiting to take flight.

"Why? What did I say?"

"That's not it," he repeated obstinately. "It's not your fault. I told you, I'm useless as a teacher."

He gulped down the rest of his beer and got up without a glance at me. He's walking away from me forever, leaving me dangling, one half of an aborted liaison. I got to my feet too, panicking, following him, fastened to his back like a tick that will hear nothing of separation.

"Why? What did I do? Did I see too much? Mention too many details?"

"You saw nothing," he said grudgingly, stepping up the pace.

I refused to let him dump me.

"Wait! You're saying I invented what I saw? Is that what you're telling me?"

I was so panicked at the thought of losing him forever that I cast about in desperation for anything that might pass for mental quickness. I dug deep down, I begged my condor, who is never far away, to drop me some enlightening food, and that is what he deigned to do. He dropped upon my head fragments of outlandish hypotheses, in tune to the ironic beating of his great wings.

"I look at myself too much, all I see is me. Isn't that it? Isn't it? I'm obsessed with myself, I make things up because, because, because... That's it! I look for shortcuts. I make things up instead of really looking. I don't see anyone or anything because my vision is blurred by judgment, by comment... Emotions! That's it, isn't it? Emotion. I show too much emotion, and it blurs the people I look at. Yes, no, all of the above?"

He stopped suddenly on the sidewalk in front of a café teeming with alcoholics. Turned to me, grinning.

"Bingo!" he said. "Too much emotion. Come on, let's sit down here. You want it so bad."

It's true, he was right. I wanted it very powerfully. I want *him* very badly, not the tasteless marrow of those unknown humans he's making me scrutinize.

We sat down all over again, endangered by rising liquid levels. Nothing happened. Silence from his end. Conversation wasn't his strong point, that much was clear from the start. I snuck a glance at him. Why did I want him so powerfully? What did I want to be powerful about him? The beginnings of a pot belly? A roundish face that would soon collapse under the weight of senile gravitation? The skin of his hands was beginning to wrinkle, liver spots starting to appear. His clothing was shapeless, his appearance nil. He guzzled down his beer just like all the other lushes.

I wanted the thing hidden inside this nondescript envelope. I wanted the diamond at the heart of the stone. I wanted the celebrated author. I wanted to hold the mystery in my hand.

"Don't stare at me like that!" he snapped.

I quickly turned my wayward eyes to the bowl of peanuts. Damn, this was no easy matter.

"So," I began in a carefully modulated voice, "we have to put our emotions aside. If the idea is to be insensitive, let me inform you that I already am, abundantly. Becoming even more insensitive is not exactly what I need."

I ventured a glance in his direction. He was watching me, shamelessly. Actually smiling.

"No need to add any more," he grinned. "On the contrary. You have to subtract, you even take away the insensitivity, you take away everything. All you keep is curiosity."

I had no clue what he meant, but I pretended to understand. In an attempt to achieve partial osmosis, I grabbed his beer glass and took two swallows. The foam's nauseating bitterness brought tears to my eyes.

"And so, bare naked, with no other instrument but curiosity, you begin to see everything. What exactly am I supposed to see?"

"You'll see," he smiled.

"You're not interested in giving me a hint?"

"No."

Well, then. That's that. But his eyes, like two tropical lagunas, urged me to travel in the most preposterous directions.

"Is it anything like the other night?"

"You're getting warm."

"It's like the first time, but minus the frogs and the stars. I'm supposed to find the same . . . the same . . . uh . . . the same . . ."

"Space," he whispered. "The same space."

Oh, no. Not space. That space of his irritated me to a hyperbolic degree. Still, I tried to remain involved, my face as open as a slice of ripe fruit. I must have failed, because he started laughing. I had no idea why, but I laughed too. We laughed for the sake of laughter, like drinkers when the party's over. At least we were back on dry land. Right now, I'd give anything for him to talk to me like an earthling would to another earthling, a guy full of ordinary testosterone chatting with a nubile female of the species: Do you have any brothers and sisters? What's your sign? Comforting banalities coated with a superfine layer of seduction that might lead to something vulgar. Because right now I was dying for a good dose of vulgarity. The heat, I guess. Or the homeopathic quality of beer.

"You know," said Pierre Laliberté, "I never did this with anyone. What I'm doing with you."

"Why not?"

"I'm actually an ordinary guy. I shoot pool with my buddies, I go to the movies. With the women I meet, if it's going well, I, uh, I never do this. I never talk about this kind of thing."

"What do you do?"

"Well, I kiss them. I hold them. Stuff like that, ordinary things. Excuse me."

I grabbed his beer and knocked back what I needed for its bitterness to match mine and let my eyes dry out. All kinds of people drink beer. Pierre Laliberté likes beer. Why not me? Pierre Laliberté and me. What would a flesh and blood entity called *Pierre Laliberté and me* look like?

"How come it's different with me?"

"Uh, well," he said, "you were the one who asked. And besides, after all. After all, I like it. What about you?"

What about me? I'll tell you. I never asked not to be kissed, not to be treated with a touch of everyday vulgarity, not to be caressed where my nerve endings are farthest from my brain. I never demanded that people not fall in love with me.

"With you," he went on, "it's really refreshing. Plus a good-looking girl like you must be tired of men trying to pick you up."

"Yeah," I said darkly. "It's too much, really."

Yeah, really. As a mind reader, Pierre Laliberté was worth zero.

He was sitting there, gazing at something outside my field of vision, and suddenly his face froze. I followed his glance, and saw a pleasant-looking, anonymous guy across from us, probably a tourist, ready to strike up a conversation with anyone, meaning us. He was holding a camera in his hand, and suddenly he pointed it at us, as a joke. Pierre Laliberté leapt to his feet. He waved an awkward goodbye, and before I could answer, he was gone.

Well, well.

As a gentleman, Pierre Laliberté was an even bigger zero.

Then I remembered.

That was no man sitting next to me. That was a hunted animal, big game for some, doomed to flee as soon as the prying lights are switched on him. An escapee on the loose, pursued by anxiety. A poor deer, a poor, scared, little cub.

I DON'T KNOW exactly what happened then, in the transitional time after his departure. I started walking, with no particular direction. Transitions are dangerous, they leave us hanging in the middle of nowhere, we've lost the temporary strength we'd gotten used to, we have to face the nonexistence that follows (do we eat? work? weep?). During transitions, depressive personalities sink into depression, criminals into crime, artists worthy of the name into illuminations that will shake their lives and those of others.

I experienced none of that. During my transition, someone in my mind took control of my nonfunctional steering system and guided me where he thought I should go. I never go near places of worship, but I found myself in a huge baroque temple swarming with the faithful and those who had come to make offerings.

A shopping center.

Old condor of mine.

NOT A HALF-BAD CHOICE. Ideal, actually, with air-conditioning even, a place where I could continue Pierre Laliberté's lesson and fine-tune my curiosity, while getting a closer look at what the zeros that pile up on my bank statements feed on. It was time for me to return to the ranks of functional humanity. Time to learn how to spend, the better to give.

How strange. How perfect. I should have come here long ago.

Immediately, I was captivated. Light fell from the sky and splashed across glass walls, opening up the space before me (space, space . . .) like a luxurious carpet. I did not see a shopping center. I saw a city, a transparent city laid out horizontally, the better to exhibit its glistening entrails. Such beauty, such fervor displayed for me and me alone. Here—I felt it immediately—I would be loved, people will bend over backwards to please me. Not a single crumb of space (space,

space . . .) has been left, tightfisted, to its own devices. Delighted, I strolled along, taking all the time I needed, trying
to miss nothing. Everywhere, the cutest, most colorful things,
and all of them brand new, fresh from the hands of the Creator, as inviting as a salacious wink, expressly conceived to fit
every part of my body, or dwelling place, every hour of my
every day and night. Most marvelous of all, none of these
treasures has been designed simply to be looked upon, like the
exhibits in a museum that leave us empty at the exit. No.
Everything here was mine. Everything, as long as I wanted it.

And I did want it. I wanted everything because I had
nothing. How could I have survived so long with absolutely
nothing?

I had no crystal, no porcelain from the Linen Chest, no silk
sheets, none of crimson flannelette either, no plush ocher and
pale lilac towels. No Epilady that makes the skin of your legs
as smooth as your bottom, no Retinol Triple Action cream or
ginseng poultice without which the tiniest wrinkles soon become crevasses and beauty a distant memory. I have none of the
fishnet garments that Claudia Schiffer claims you must in order to uncover your true self, no brassieres to uplift that which
barely exists, no transparent placemats with dragonfly and la-
dybug motifs, no tea service, no coffee service, no cocktail,
fruit, sushi or pot service, no fluorescent sandals with gilded
soles, no fake leopard-skin handbag, no Kenneth Cole sun-
glasses, no binoculars for magnifying the bricks of the house
across the street two hundred times, no Posturepedic mattress
to provide my potential lovers with a firm welcome, no lambskin loveseat, not even a one-square-meter Hitachi D3 Digital

Display Drive television with Ultrascan HD. From what planet of deprivation have you fallen, Florence, you miserable bag lady, from what Cro-Magnonic cavern have you escaped, that all life's essentials have been hidden from you?

I had no twenty-five-speed bike outfitted with a mini-motor for climbing the most aggressive escarpments, no travel plans for Bangkok or the Philippines, no membership in a fitness club, no space reserved in the Cote-des-Neiges cemetery.

I am completely disqualified from existence.

THE MAGNITUDE OF THE TASK was overwhelming. Where to begin acquiring the countless things I did not have? Where was the moving van I would need to transport all these new articles, so necessary to my domestic well-being? And where was I to find a place for them in my monastic apartment, my wretched non-possessor's apartment?

Priority One: move into a giant space (space, space . . .) to accommodate my new life and its multitudinous appendages. Look, a real estate agency on the second floor.

That called for some thought. I sat down on a bench on the mezzanine, in the tinkling shade by a natural fountain. As in every self-respecting city, there were banks and a fountain here. Everything was designed to encourage leisure and numb the spirit. Angelic music welled from the walls and filled the mind with contented frivolity. I struggled hard to think, and I succeeded. Here, thinking constitutes a threat to the smooth functioning of the city. The thinking mind does not look at display windows. Outside their displays, the fine objects with their urgent colors quickly give way to pallor, their siren's song turns to a fast-receding and ghostly whisper. Before I know it, I've forgotten everything that was so essential to my survival. Change places, good God! But why? What exactly do I need at this very moment?

A vanilla ice cream.

HERE IS THE CULMINATION of civilization. Here, Florence, you bear witness to the accomplishment of the labors and dreams of millions of lives. At the far ends of the earth, in distant villages the names and insalubrious geography of which you cannot even begin to imagine, men, women and children are, even as we speak, shackled to machines that weave these exotic fabrics, polish the bolts that hold this furniture together, grind the roots and flowers from which these ruinous perfumes are distilled, turn the soil to extract the gold from which this jewelry is fashioned, harvest the latex that will take solid form as the tires of these automobiles. On the other side, in the West and the North, in Montreal and elsewhere, men, women and soon children are, even as we speak, squandering their vital energies in jobs that denigrate them, chasing after overtime hours and lucrative contracts, dying of powerlessness in aseptic offices and exhausting factories, getting their boobs pinched by dimwit bosses, moving around too much and growing old too fast, selling out their ideals and integrity to be able to buy the exotic fabrics, the furniture, the ruinous perfumes, the gold jewelry, the polluting cars, the travels and getaways that are never enough, even at the start, and always have to be replaced.

Where are the losers? In the North or the South?

Here, Florence, you are seated at the very spot where the four points of the compass come together, and all human activity converges. Aren't you impressed?

Yes, Condor, immensely impressed. But to tell the truth, the whole business makes me feel queasy.

In fact, everything makes me nauseous, even vanilla ice cream. I don't know why I'm here, or why my purse is stuffed with bank statements on which the zeros and the hours worked add up.

Then I remembered. I was here in this shopping center, which is a city in itself, for the people thronging around the objects on display, not for the objects themselves. I was here to develop my deficient curiosity, to watch people and penetrate their peripheral space without getting lost myself.

That's the order.

I was off to a bad start.

Where was everybody?

There, there, and over there. Everywhere, a cloud of gypsy moths fluttering around bright baubles. Their mobility works against them, for it fragments them. Immobile things vegetate in all their glory as they pass by like so many shooting stars. There is no other difference between objects and people. All are dressed in bright colors. Clean. New (or if not, their shopworn appearance is impeccably concealed). Smooth. Pale. Light. Pretty. They all belong to the same realm, the consumer objects and the consumers themselves. The universe has been conceived so that the former will merge with the latter in perfect union.

Get a grip on yourself, Florence, you nearsighted buzzard—or are you a farsighted schizophrenic? Look around you, there are plenty of women, young and not so young, and a few men too, both young and older. Fragments of heaving, sweating humanity, as far removed from manufactured objects as they can be. How can you work on the way you see if you can't even see this basic truth?

But I can't. I can't see anything human in the humanity parading past me. It's because of their polished surface, their pasteurized-milk color, that well-fed appearance that smacks of polystyrene. What can you learn by penetrating a liter of two-percent milk? Here and there, some skins are a bit darker, some features more slant-eyed, but that doesn't change the self-satisfied whole, as little touched by anxiety as sixty-five percent nylon viscose. That's the problem. The absence of anxiety makes the difference. This pale-skinned humanity lacks the anxiety that separates man from plastic.

In shopping centers—breathtaking revelation!—humans are light and airy; imminent consumption has wiped away their existential wrinkles. Satisfaction, or the promise of satisfaction, has momentarily reduced their anxiety to zero.

Nothing is less remarkable than satisfied humans.

My eyes flit from one to another, unable to alight anywhere, on any sharp edge. There is no danger of getting snared in the details, for they escape me completely. Not just the details, the whole thing. Zero. Right now, a blind man would see better than I do.

Too bad. Seeking space among the followers of the cult of commerce wasn't such a good idea. They've all melted into a pastel goo. But it wasn't my idea to begin with. I give up on the job, and on curiosity too. When you get right down to it, maybe vanilla ice cream is the true goal of my existence on earth.

Below me were food shops and counters. From where I stood, I knew it would be difficult to restrict myself to ice cream, so abundant was the variety. Wouldn't it be better, Florence, to treat yourself to Thai, Turkish, sushi, smoked meat, whole wheat muffins, quattro stagione pizza, barbecued chicken whole or cut up, chocolate from Belgium, Holland or from the Trappist brothers of Mistassini? To make it easier to decide, tables were set up by the food counters. The people seated there were eating or contemplating what they were going to eat, unless they were already painfully digesting what they'd mistakenly decided to eat. I contemplated them from above. At rest, given over to themselves, humans were recovering a little of their humanity. Immigrants and old folks emerged from the formless crowd, adding coarse texture to the prevailing prettiness. Two men were playing chess, two others looking on, kibbitzing. Three heavyset, good-natured ladies, Italians probably, drinking cappuccino. A well-dressed older man reading *Le Devoir.* Another, far less elegant, eating an ice cream cone, sitting off to the side in his threadbare topcoat.

No.

It can't be him.

I should never have come to a shopping center, especially not this one. When he was still alive, he loved shopping centers, this one in particular. Why should he love them less now that he's a ghost?

Pepa was nibbling away at his ice cream cone, holding it in both hands, like a squirrel.

That's how he always ate apples, cakes, whatever was small enough to hold in one hand, and which seemed to double in volume when held in two.

Pepa was alone. Other men around him are alone too. But Pepa is most alone among the alone, the only one of his kind, the one and only to be alone that way.

Pepa looked poor. A spotless new topcoat was hanging forlornly in the back of his closet, but he always chose the old, threadbare one when he went out.

Pepa rubbed his hands together to scatter the cone crumbs.

Discreetly, Pepa watched people passing by, turning away when someone's eyes threatened to collide with his.

Pepa stood up. Made his way among the tables with infinite precaution so as not to interfere with their wave patterns.

Such humility.

Such humility is monstrous.

What would happen if I suddenly shouted his name from the edge of the railing?

What would happen if I rushed down the escalator and ran to him—dared do something both inconceivable and indecent, the act of a desperate woman, what would happen if I embraced him?

Pepa walked slowly, arms held tightly against his sides, slowly enough to give me all the time I needed to risk everything, and do nothing.

I was afraid.

Down below, his chest protected against assault, his pace designed to save his strength, he was afraid too. Our fear was the same. There was only one fear. Our fear was what bound us, Pepa and me.

Pepa stopped in front of a shop window. Stared intently at the goods on display. Seen from behind, he was a frail, nameless old man, enfeebled by solitude. Mister Pepa.

Poised in front of the shop window, he looked and he thought.

He must have been thinking.

What was he thinking?

Why was it less painful to imagine he was thinking of nothing, unformulatable trifles, the murmur of ideas, rather than hidden flashes of brilliant intuition?

I was afraid of what he was thinking.

The heart is an involuntary muscle.

Emptiness opened up at my feet, and in it were contained all the words Pepa never spoke in his life.

HOW LONG CAN the illusion of his body remain, pressed against the shop window? Already, his topcoat was growing paler, and the passersby were making less effort to step around him. Quick, Florence. If you want to catch up with Pepa before he dematerializes, it's now or never. Heavily, I began to move, keeping my eyes on Pepa's frail gray back, sketched against the window like a mirage of solitude. He's waiting for you, Florence. You're the one he's waiting for. I began to run. I'm the one he's waiting for, me, Florence, it's not too late to make up for lost time, *it's me, I'm coming, wait for me, it's Florence, Pepa!*

Out of breath, I reached the bottom of the down escalator and rushed headlong towards the fading shape standing against the shop window in front of me. The faster I moved, the fainter and more insubstantial the shape became. When I got to the spot where I should have been able to reach out and touch him, there was nothing to touch, there never had been anything to catch up to, or embrace.

I leaned against the window, at the very spot where Pepa's ghost had fraudulently agreed to meet me. The window belonged to a bookstore. There were stacks of books for sale. *Gardening with the Birds, Put Green on Your Table, The Lakes of Quebec,* summer books napping among artificial daisies and cardboard blue herons.

In the middle of the display, a small white stack of books bearing a glorious red sash: The Grand Prize of the Americas. A small white stack of books entitled *Falterlust.*

Well, well. The news entered my mind, but it left no trace, as if it were sand, and I, air. So, *Falterlust* just won the Grand Prize of the Americas. Well, well, well. Just what is this Grand Prize of the Americas? I would have to congratulate Pierre Laliberté. Well, not really. You can't congratulate Pierre Laliberté because no one can congratulate a ghost, no matter what form it might appear in.

I sat down on the chair Pepa had occupied. It would be easy to say that the spot was still warm. But the feeling of warmth is deceptive, as are all the feelings that brought me here in the first place.

A moment of transition. All around, people were eating, getting up, sitting down, empathetic music stirred the air, keeping everything light. I'd forgotten the instructions for living. I didn't know how to think anymore, or how to go from one point to another.

Then it all came back. Be patient during transitions, wait for it to came back. It always does. The habit of being.

I bought myself a vanilla ice cream cone, which I devoured, holding it in one hand.

Pepa and I always had a weakness for vanilla.

11

SUZIE MAHONE

---

*A*PPARENTLY WE HAVE a new office. A hundred square meters of high-tech floor space lorded over by the high burnished ceilings of a neo-Gothic building in the heart of the Montreal financial district, ten minutes by foot from everything.

So how is it that, having a pricy, fashionable office only ten minutes from everything, as I just mentioned, Zeno and I were holed up in a tiny suburban bungalow, at the far end of two bus lines and one subway line? How is it that, having at our disposal a high-tech environment that cost us an arm and a leg, we were forced to work on an Arborite kitchen table piled high with pots and pans, amid the smell of fried eggs and the obtuse buzzing of a refrigerator?

"I asked you to come here because I can't go out," said Zeno succinctly.

Another irritating mystery. And just why couldn't he go out?

"My mother," he replied. "I'm taking care of my mother."

I saw no trace of his mother. Though we were at her place, there was no doubt about that. I recognized the surroundings, having explored them in a previous life, when I yearned to be adopted by them.

"Where is your mother?"

"In her room."

"Couldn't we have met in a more comfortable room. The living room, the office... Or outside even, on the picnic table?"

"No, we couldn't have."

That was that. Zeno did not invent democracy. And to illustrate to what extent that was that, Zeno leapt immediately into the agenda. One: the neo-Gothic office on Sherbrooke Street at the corner of McGill College. Two: the three interns hired to inject some new blood into Mahone Inc.'s tired staff. Three: me.

"As you can see," stated Zeno, "I won't be able to work at our Sherbrooke and McGill office for the near future. Nor meet the three interns I hired to inject some new blood into our tired staff. Which brings us to you."

"Me."

"Until further notice, you will have full responsibility for our geographical and human infrastructure. I'd like you to catch on fast, because time is flying."

I could have gotten irritated with his cavalier tone, but there was something tense and swollen to the bursting point in

Zeno's voice. He wouldn't say anything about what's poisoning him unless I went looking for it. That was a big job, so I might as well get to it right away.

"What's going on? Is something wrong with your mother?"

"Out of order," said Zeno crisply.

"What do you mean, out of order? It so happens that life is of a piece, and that we're at your mother's place, so there's no use pretending we're not."

"What's the difference," Zeno asked. "Here or there, it's mind space we're talking about. We have work to do, Flora. We don't give a shit about the physical space that happens to contain our bodies at the time. I beg you, make an effort. A little discipline, please. So, next Wednesday, in other words, tomorrow, a whole batch of computers will be delivered to the Sherbrooke office. You'll be there to supervise the installation. According to plan, if you remember . . ."

Then the knocking began, close by. The knocking of someone who wanted to come in, but who was already inside. For a moment, Zeno's eyes cut away, but his voice went on delivering directives and calmly unrolling our plans while the knocking, insistent and restrained, accompanied him with percussive regularity. It was all I could hear. When would Zeno decide to stop pretending he didn't hear it? I stared straight at him. He finally let out a sigh of exasperation, as if I were to blame for the diversion.

"You just can't concentrate, can you?"

"Someone's knocking."

"I know," he hissed angrily. "You think maybe I don't hear it?"

"When there's knocking, it means someone wants something. So someone wants something."

"I know!"

He pushed away his laptop and his pretentions to work. Finally surrendered.

"Go on, open the door," he said darkly, "since you're dying to see who it is."

"Open for who? Your mother?"

"Of course, my mother. Who else do you think it is?"

"Where does she want to go?"

Zeno took off his round glasses and rubbed his eyes, hiding nothing of his exhaustion.

"She wants to leave her room. I locked her in."

"You locked your mother in her room?"

"Yes," he said with a thin-lipped smile. "I'm a no-good bastard who locks his mother in her room."

I made no move. I didn't understand what was going on. He nudged my arm gently.

"Go on. She'll be happy to see you."

As if to prove his point, the knocking stepped up in intensity, in a polite and muffled way. How could the sight of me make her happy, she who never once said hello to me? Why was she locked up if she wasn't dangerous? Maybe she'd jump at me, claws extended like a rabid raccoon.

Out of bravado more than anything else, I took a few steps towards the racket. I looked back towards Zeno. He was observing me with an ironic glare that augured no good.

"What's her first name again?" I asked, feigning a sense of assurance.

"Suzie."

The way he said it: *Suzie*. As if she were a young girl, full of provocative laughter and hair streaming over her shoulders, a graceful girl he'd once been in love with.

I moved towards her room. For the first time in my life, I would free someone from captivity. Suzie, Suzie Mahone. In my memory, Suzie Mahone's house smelled of order and liquid disinfectant. But nothing was the way I remembered it. I saw things scattered every which way, clothing thrown over arm-chairs, papers on the floor. The knocking was steady and weary. I cleared my throat and tried to put on my everyday voice, the one I used to say "Hello!" to the mailman and "Isn't it a lovely day?" to the Vietnamese who runs the corner store, so that no rough edges, no mistrust or suspicion, are perceptible. "I'm coming, Mrs. Mahone, I'm coming," I called. I couldn't call her "Suzie." That was no way to address a mother, a woman I hardly knew, a Mohawk to boot.

The door was held shut with a latch so flimsy that the nudge of a shoulder would have been enough to force it. But women have never learned how to break down doors. I kept talking as I unhooked the latch, letting her get used to my voice, so she wouldn't put out my eyes at the first opportunity. The knocking stopped. All I could hear was myself, my blood pumping in terror through the plumbing of my veins, my words that filled the silence. "Here I am, here I am."

The door opened. Nothing happened. A woman was standing there, small and ordinary-looking. Zeno's mother, in a pretty turquoise housecoat, her features sharper, with more white in her black hair, but soft-spoken and smiling, more pleasant than I'd remembered her. She was in no hurry to emerge. She stood a few steps from the door, her hands folded. Her room was in darkness, like the cage of a nocturnal animal.

"I know you," she said. "You're a friend of my son's."

Then she stepped out of the room, carefully closing the door and drawing the latch behind her. She looked at me briefly with a peaceful smile I'd never known she had.

"Don't tell him I'm out. My son is a little strict with me."

She smiled again, then her smile faded abruptly, and she trotted off towards the living room and disappeared. When I went past the living room, I stole a glance inside. She was sitting on the sofa, leafing through papers with the classic expression of a worried mother, intent on understanding, and finding what she was looking for. This was the savage beast that had to be caged?

Zeno had switched off his laptop and filed away his papers. He was waiting for me in the kitchen, as if ready to face the accusations that would be sure to follow. Instead, I sat down in front of my computer.

"What's going on?" I asked. "Aren't we working anymore?"

"That won't be possible now," he said, resigned.

"On the contrary. So, tomorrow morning, the computer delivery. And the interns, when am I supposed to meet them? I suppose you hired three of the biggest bimbos you could get your hands on."

His eyes full of blame, he sat down.

"Flora," he grumbled, "I hired three guys. We're in business, let me remind you. Serious business."

"Thanks for the consideration. So girls are incompatible with serious business?"

Go ahead, kill me. He gave it serious thought, judging by the acid that welled up in his black eyes, but there wasn't enough time to put the plan into effect. The sound of breaking glass brought us to our feet. It came from the living room.

"Don't worry," he said in a calm voice. "I'll look after it."

As he left the kitchen, he told me, "You can go now, if you like. I'll see you this evening."

If I like. How could I like anything else? Of course I'm leaving. What business do I have in his family life? Everyone has his own family to face, including the melodramas, everyone's alone like a prizefighter in the ring. I heard Zeno's voice, muffled and taught as a drumhead, and his mother's voice answering it in short, staccato bursts. I could feel the anguish saturating both their voices.

Of course I didn't leave. When you go and do something as definitive as releasing a latch and opening a door, you enter someone else's life. You're not allowed to not share the experience.

The living room was no longer the same one I saw fifteen minutes ago. A stealthy tornado had touched down there, flinging all the objects into the middle of the room, disemboweling the cushions, slicing the bases of the lamps in two. Hard to imagine that the person responsible for the upheaval was the tiny, quiet woman seated on the sofa, head tilted slightly to one side, submissive, accepting her son's reproach with a kind of deference.

"It seems a little unreasonable to me, Mama," Zeno was

saying in a soft voice. "Look, look around. Doesn't it seem a little unreasonable to you?"

Suzie Mahone retreated further into herself, if such a thing could be possible. The sweet tone of criticism made it all the more humiliating.

"I have my reasons," she declared. "And you know it."

"Tell me again. Here, tell Florence. Tell Florence what you're doing."

She cast her humiliated eyes in my direction, and I hated Zeno for inflicting my presence on her. And I hated myself infinitely more for being witness to her humiliation.

"I don't know her," she snapped.

"Sure you do," Zeno said. "It's Florence. You know Florence."

"She's not family."

The wind of humiliation started blowing in my direction. Why didn't I listen to the voice of cowardice when it ordered me to get out?

"Florence is a part of me," Zeno told her.

"She's your wife?"

"She's much more than that."

I sat down on a chair heaped with newspapers and tried to blend in with the surroundings. Maybe in the meantime, Zeno's words would reveal their true nature: deceitful and excessive. Suzie Mahone looked at me; there was nothing humiliated about her anymore.

"I'll tell her because you asked me to, son. That's the only reason. I'm looking for an important paper. This is my house, and I'm looking for it, wherever it might be."

"Including inside the sofa pillows," Zeno added without irony. "And in the drapery linings, and the circuits of the television set."

"Everywhere it might be," said Zeno's mother, staring straight at me.

"She slices open the mattresses," Zeno told me; now I was his witness. "She disembowels our mattresses with a knife. Go look in the bedrooms, it's quite the sight. She rips the upholstery off the furniture one piece at a time. She pries up the floorboards. She's hurting herself and destroying everything."

"It's my house," Suzie Mahone repeated fiercely, "and I'm looking for an important paper."

"Florence, we file away papers in drawers in our desks, or in bookcases. You do agree, don't you? Not inside boxsprings, not behind the wallboards."

"It all depends," Suzie said to me with a wavering gleam in her eye. "It all depends on who's doing the hiding."

What did they want from me? What weird and impossible role did they expect me to play, what kind of judging was I supposed to do? Separate absurdity from coherence, sincerity from dementia, condemn without knowing the facts. What would Solomon have done, except threaten to slice the baby in half—in other words, that damned important scrap of paper no one was talking about?

"What kind of paper is it?"

My question threw both of them into awkward silence. Beneath it loomed the bitter discussions of the past that neither was in any hurry to reveal. Zeno's mother straightened in her seat, regaining all her dignity.

"That paper was given to me at birth by my mother. She rolled it into a talisman, and I wore it on my chest when I was a girl. It says I was born in Kanesatake of an Indian father and an Indian adoptive mother. I have to find it so my real citizenship in the world will be recognized."

As she spoke, a cloud of suffering rose in Zeno's eyes and spread across his face.

"Her citizenship," he said in a muffled voice.

"Yes, my citizenship," she repeated. "You're still too young and too ignorant to understand how important the pedestal is that life places us on."

"Mama," Zeno burst out, "aren't all the terrible things that have happened in the world in the name of citizenship enough for you? Why do you insist on entering that prison?"

She shook her head stubbornly, and wouldn't answer. He let fly his most poisonous arrow.

"I knew you when you used to be free, Suzie."

"Don't you talk to me that way," she said firmly.

For a time, the only sound was Zeno's footsteps as he paced the living room. His pacing took the place of further recriminations, but he poured all his unreleased tension into it, deliberately colliding with obstacles, thrashing underfoot the old newspapers, crushing the glass and plastic fragments of the broken lamps. He stopped cold in front of his mother.

"For twenty years, Mama, for twenty years you didn't give a damn about that paper, about that damned Indian status of yours, twenty years you lived a free life. Now why is it so important?"

She took her time answering. A slow, calm smile spread across her face.

"Do they accuse a chrysalis of being a chrysalis before it becomes a butterfly?" she asked.

I could hear Zeno cursing inwardly, but not a word escaped as he collided with a legless footstool. I'd kept silent as a stone, as if both distant and hypnotized, fascinated by the exchange but unable to participate; each argument seemed as convincing as the other. How alive both of them were, though life's intensity colored each one differently, and drove them apart.

"Who could have hidden the paper?" I asked.

"Tommy," Suzie replied immediately. "Tommy hid it."

"Come on," sighed Zeno. "When? Twenty years ago?"

"Yes," Suzie told him. "Twenty years ago."

"Who's Tommy?"

They looked briefly at one another, taken aback, as if no question could be more incongruous than mine, and no one more recognizable in the world than Tommy.

"My dad," said Zeno. And he smiled broadly, as did Suzie, as if struck by a current of strange complicity.

"Your Italian father?" I ventured.

"Yes," Zeno answered, "my only father, who's Italian. I never told you much about him, actually, because he left when I was four years old."

"Five," his mother corrected him in a soft voice. "You were five. We lived together six years."

"Suzie could sure tell you plenty about Tommy," Zeno went on, not letting the smile fade from his face, "but don't count on it. She has never said a word to me about him."

"I never said anything bad about him," Suzie protested.

"True," Zeno conceded. "Nothing good either. He's an empty space. You can imagine anything you want. Too bad I don't have any imagination."

"Your father was a man of quality. I already told you that."

"Of quality. I see. Maybe he was. When words are as vague as that, I don't have much memory."

"A strong man, a good man. Strong enough to turn a woman away from herself," she added with a touch of blame.

"Oh," said Zeno appreciatively. "You hear that, Flora? There it is, the perfect definition of love. That which turns people away from themselves."

Obviously I had plenty of catching up to do before I could walk beside them, at the same level as the Zeno I'd always known. Didn't he tell me, one day long ago when I was listening with only one ear, that his father was dead? How was I supposed to find my way along a pathway full of lies?

"Did I say that? Are you sure?" he said with exaggerated concern. "Really? Maybe it's true. After all this time, he must have died."

"Zeno," Suzie reprimanded him. "Your father is alive. Don't speak so lightly of death."

"You're right. Forgive me."

He took her by the shoulders and pulled her to him. The movement was so natural, so warm that she melted, and blushed with pleasure.

"Still, the bastard stole your citizenship paper and hid it in the joists of the house," he pointed out, half serious, half joking.

She stiffened in his embrace, then freed herself.

"He did it out of love for me," she insisted. "Out of jealousy."

"Then why wouldn't he have torn it up in a thousand pieces, burned it, thrown it in the garbage like we do with any normal scrap of paper we want to get rid of? How come, Mama?"

And they were off to the races again. Zeno's growling irritation, his mother's mulish silence, each in his corner, and me in the no-man's-land between them. Zeno ground the debris of the living room beneath his feet to stoke his anger.

"Look what you did to the house, Suzie. What a mess! That damned paper doesn't exist, aren't you ever going to get that through your head? Dad threw out your goddamned paper. It was probably the only sane thing he ever did!"

"No," said Suzie. "You don't throw away a talisman. It's bad luck. Your father would never do such a thing. The paper exists."

"Where?"

"In this house."

"How do you know?"

"I just know."

Her voice was so assured that Zeno waited for more; he was almost moved.

"I saw it in a dream," she said.

"Oh," Zeno chuckled. "That's a good one."

He sat down next to me, his shoulders shaken by a poor excuse for laughter.

"What can I do?" he asked me. "How are you supposed to argue with someone who gives you her dreams instead of an argument?"

"Why argue?" I whispered, but he wouldn't listen to me. He was totally absorbed by the unfinished struggle with Suzie and her unconventional weapons that were twice as deadly.

"In this dream of yours," he turned to her with a cruel smile, "did you see exactly what part of the house we should tear down to find the paper? That would save us a lot of wreckage."

"No," Suzie said softly, "I haven't seen it yet."

She was undeterred by his sarcasm, and kept a contemplative silence as darkening swells rose within her.

"My head is all mixed up," she admitted, her eyes glistening. "My head is like a blocked tunnel. The light can't get through."

She grabbed a cushion and pretended to search it, to unstitch it, then suddenly the pattern on it made her stop. It showed a symmetrical flight of ducks that her work of destruction had caused to disintegrate. She stroked the cushion, patted it back into shape and set it down on her lap. Her eyes scanned the room, picking out each of the objects dismembered by her search, then they glazed over, lost focus, swept over me blindly and came to rest with the full weight of their anxiety on Zeno.

"So many things, so many places," she sighed. "I'll never manage it. What's happening to me? I've gone crazy, isn't that true, son? What's happening to me?"

He stood up and ran to her side. They were so close they made a single entity of pale flesh, black hair and silky fabric.

"No," Zeno protested ferociously, "you're not crazy. Never say that. You're sick, but I'll cure you, I'll cure you, Suzie."

I could not understand the other words he spoke to her. They were whispered in music unfamiliar to me, a language of vowels and fluid syllables to which she responded with pacified noddings of her head. He was speaking to her in Mohawk, and the sounds that clothed her emotions were his sounds too, as if he had only now remembered them.

They rose to their feet together, then moved apart.

"It's time for my medication," she said. "Come. Come lock me in my room."

They left me in the dismantled living room with nothing but rubbish and desolation to keep me company. Poor, poor Zeno's mother. If I let myself get carried away, where would it all end? It begins with curiosity. You don't run when you could have made a getaway, you remain to broaden your gaze and your space, you dive into a universe of tumult and bitterness. Zeno's mother splatters me with her turmoil. Goodbye, blissful indifference. Now that I've seen Suzie Mahone, how am I supposed to stay on an even keel?

Poor, poor Zeno's mother, once so insignificant in her rapture as adoring mother, who baked Zeno enough pies to feed a tribe with. (A tribe, aha! Even then tribal longings had begun to open a dark breach in her simple soul.) Suzie Mahone who gave her front lawn and cedar hedges the disciplined forms of sentinels, under whose care each piece of furniture, every ornament in the house, had been apportioned an underlying order that inspired respect. Poor Suzie Mahone who seemed not to have suffered from her Italian husband's desertion, nor from being deprived of her origins, nor from having only one son who would stiffen beneath her caresses and impetuous kisses. But now, at an age when other women doll up their grandchildren with hand-knit baby clothes, she disembowels her delicate velvet cushions and buries her hatchet in her fine maple tables. She might be dressing up suicide the same way. For all that mind-dulling medication, she may still be contemplating the thought.

Zeno made his way silently back to me, in that supple, Indian stride of his. Why hadn't I ever noticed the exoticism of his prominent cheekbones, the coppery tint of his skin, his black eyes? Zeno Mahone, half Mohawk, half Italian. A hidden continent unto himself, teeming with wild lakes and smoking volcanos that I'd never cared to explore.

"She's asleep," he said with a tender smile.

Asleep. Fine. Good for her. But how long would that last? And what happens when she wakes up?

"What are you going to do?" I asked.

He righted an endtable and picked up a pair of shredded magazines, grains of sand in this desert.

"I guess I'll clean up," he said with a pained look, "until she starts all over again."

"What about tomorrow, Zeno? What about next week?"

He examined the shade he recovered from the shards of the lamp, as if looking for a way to reassemble reality—or an answer to my question.

"I don't know," he admitted. "Honestly, Florence, I don't know."

I had never seen Zeno so disarmed, so humble in the recognition of his impotence. To hide my own emotions, I started clearing up the refuse on all fours.

"You don't have to do that," he said. "You should go home."

"Yes," I agreed, but I didn't stop.

"I can't just dump her in the hospital, you understand, I'm not going to get rid of her like a . . . like a broken ashtray," he said, tossing the remains of a crystal ashtray onto the scrap heap in the middle of the carpet.

"I understand."

"I keep telling myself that with patience and conviction, and with the antidepressants she's taking, the storm will blow itself out. There's an end to everything, right? This isn't the first time, anyway."

"No?"

"I've seen her crack up a dozen times before. More than a dozen times since I've been old enough to understand. Fifteen times, I'd say, in the past twenty years."

I looked at him; I was stunned into silence.

"If worst comes to worst," he added with a threatening laugh, "I'll help her. I'll tear the house to pieces so we can get it over with once and for all."

Our hands met on an overturned chair. Together we set it upright. I kept his hands in mine.

"Zeno, Zeno."

"Don't worry about it, all right?"

"Why didn't you ever tell me anything?"

"Look at you. You're too impressionable."

What was that like? A childhood spent taking care of a disturbed mother, and no other parent than a father who's run off God knows where and with whom. A ghost of a man who never gave off the faintest light, or even a word, ever.

"That's how it is," said Zeno. "When I was young and helpless, I used to hope for something from him. Finally I stopped waiting. He must have made a new life somewhere else."

My eyes must have been full of horrified anathemas and curses. He pulled away from my arms and started to laugh.

"See how you dramatize things? A man is human, Florence. A man has the right to leave and not turn back if that's all he knows how to do."

I don't understand anything about humanity. If humanity has permission to jettison its human responsibility and scurry away like a louse, then I execrate humanity. I didn't understand Zeno's attitude either, his total lack of resentment towards the man who behaved like a louse to him. Zeno's attitude, bracing and marvelously non-resentful, left me more stunned than the most stunning of catastrophes.

"Why are you looking at me that way?" he wanted to know.

Just then I would have given him anything. The hidden face of his planet glowed so bright it completely transfigured him, the man I was convinced had sunken forever into pettiness. I would have given him the most precious thing I had— I loved him that much.

I pulled him to the sofa and sat him down beside me. He was serious, alert, a monolith of attention directed at me. As if he knew I was about to hand over what was most precious to me.

"Pierre Laliberté won the Grand Prize of the Americas."

He nodded slowly.

"I know. Finally he got the recognition he deserves."

"What is the Grand Prize of the Americas?"

"It's the equivalent of the Pulitzer, but for all languages. Plus two hundred thousand dollars American."

"I met Pierre Laliberté."

The words moved across his face leaving not a trace. Then he sank back onto the sofa, convulsed by silent laughter.

"I knew it. I could have sworn. So, finally, now you tell me."

He waited for the rest, still smiling. Convinced that the rest would follow in rapid fire, drowning him in ornamental details, where how with what exact words and gestures and most of all what does he look like what does it feel like to be around him where are the photos you took of him when he wasn't looking with the pricy Canon Mahone Inc. gave you for that express purpose and, above above all, when will the next meeting take place, the one he can attend too? I didn't know why, but once the cat was out of the bag, the rest decided not to follow. How to describe Pierre Laliberté without making him pale and dull? How to talk about the circumspect chaos of our meetings without deadening them? What true thing could I say about him without succumbing to the wild inventions of my twisted imagination? I sat there for endless seconds, my mouth shut, looking for something to say, and the longer I was silent, the harder it was to speak and the stronger the tension I felt in Zeno, stiffening his body as he sat on the sofa. Strangely, the more tense he became, and the more forced his smile, the greater the temptation to remain silent.

My silence was gifted with frightening power.

"You slept together," Zeno said suddenly, his voice blank.

Now that was as tempting as it was unhoped-for. I prolonged the tension, savoring Zeno's avid eyes upon me as if upon some wonderful dessert, or upon his beloved. Then he caught himself in time, voice rich with respect.

"It's true," he murmured. "That kind of thing is nobody's business. But yours. But the two of you."

What do I do now?

I could deliver the reality, which wasn't all that shoddy. Pierre Laliberté has a house in the country, exactly halfway between sky and frogs. Pierre Laliberté has six dogs, each as foul-smelling as poor Pokey, Pierre Laliberté's eyes and laughter are much younger than the rest of him. Pierre Laliberté didn't hump me. He did much worse: he inflicted me with the snakebite of curiosity, against which there is no known antidote.

Think carefully, Florence. Explore the space rich in possibilities that is opening before you. Reality has its limitations, while whatever you invent has none, and never will.

I looked at Zeno dressing me in the velvet of his eyes, in the power of his gaze. Finally he saw me the way I'd always wanted him to see me till the end of my days.

Or at least for a couple of hours.

"We didn't sleep together. That's not where it's happening. Not now, anyway."

Silence. Each sentence I spoke would be lodged in silence like a planet taking shape, organizing its gravitational field and gases around it.

"First there's a ritual. Then he speaks."

Each sentence was an unstable world that could explode at any second.

"What ritual?" Zeno asked impulsively. "I'm sorry. Go on, go on."

He bit his tongue at having broken the precious thread I was unwinding. And I bit my tongue with the effort of finding something startling to say.

"I'm not so sure I feel like telling you everything. Right away."

"I understand, I understand," said Zeno. "But give me a little, a little bit more. Just one thing, please. Just tell me what he talks about."

"He talks . . . he talks about himself."

It came into being like a whisper out of nowhere. And now it grew and spread like a giant construction, like the central sun of the cosmos.

"You mean, about himself? About himself as Pierre Laliberté?"

"He admitted who he was right away. I don't think he had any choice in the matter."

"Wait, wait," Zeno blanched. "You mean he told you he was Pierre Laliberté the Writer, and afterwards he kept on seeing you, is that what you mean?"

"Yes."

Zeno leapt to his feet and took a few wobbly steps across the room, quickly impeded by the obstacles. He began to quiver in place, the way you'd imagine an epileptic about to go into a seizure, or a junky craving a fix. In other words, I was such a total success I was beginning to worry I'd gone too far.

"Florence, do you realize?" he marveled. "Do you understand the degree of trust he showed you? No one before you, we don't know ANYONE who ever managed to approach him like that."

He jumped up and pulled me from the sofa with nothing but the strength of his overexcitement.

"No, really, do you realize? Look at yourself! Don't you understand? You achieved something no one could imagine, my magnificent little magical Flora, you enchanted him, there's no doubt about it, you're extraordinary, my adorable little sorceress, my Flora, my one and only, my shining one . . ."

He kissed me and squeezed me, he rocked me back and forth and kissed me again. I let myself be worshiped, as blissful as a starving woman being plied with sweetmeats. I let him look longingly at whatever part of me suited him until it was too late.

"What are you doing? Are you crazy?"

"I'm undressing you, and I'm not crazy. All the other times I didn't undress you, then I was crazy."

"Mahone, stop it!"

"I love it when you call me Mahone, say it again, Mahone, Mahone, I feel like a macho man when you call me Mahone, I feel like a superstud, hung like a bull moose!"

He began butting everything he could get to at hip level, the cushions, the sofa itself, me as well, to make me laugh and get me in the game, and when I started laughing and lowering my guard, he got all serious and hot-blooded, full of caresses as if I were his favorite stuffed animal. In the middle of the living room laid waste by a mother on the verge of dementia, we wallowed lasciviously on our poor excuse for a nuptial bed.

I almost felt like letting go. What irreparable risk would I run? Florence, you irascible old broom handle, you cerebral virgin, let yourself go for once. When was the last time someone actually touched you, actually gave you the slightest wave of pleasure? And who ever gave better proof than Zeno that he knew how to give you pleasure?

I have nothing against pleasure. Pleasure is pleasurable. If pleasure could free us, if pleasure could infuse in us more than fleeting strength, the kind of joy into which we could dip to our heart's content when no more remained, how I would love pleasure!

That's not how it works. Pleasure is pleasurable, but the after-pleasure lasts longer than pleasure itself. The after-pleasure lasts a lifetime, a life spent in desperation, recreating something that can be experienced with such intensity only once or twice, or maybe a hundred times, to put a nice round figure on it, and being generous.

Step out of your head, Florence.

I did. I stepped out where dangers take on all kinds of re-pellent faces, where an expert caress, a tongue, a cock can drive you into slavery. Zeno is so tiny and irritating when he's standing up, but when he's got you underneath him he's a gi-ant. His art is wrenching from you the vibrations caught in the wooden frame of your Stradivarius, for beneath him you become a precious Stradivarius, a black tulip, a diamond's heart, a goddess for the worshiping at whose altar love's votive lights burn bright.

Zeno wasn't making love to me. He was uplifting the woman who'd won the trust of Pierre Laliberté. Impossible to believe I was the one, especially when he put his words to movement.

I love you Florence.

Whatever else you do, don't cling to those words born from the short-term slipping and sliding of our skins one against another, from the fever of our senses, words stammered so often by so many couples playing on the Monopoly board of lasting passion, even as time has begun to dismantle the molecular structure of their orgasms.

Don't cling to those words, but listen to them again, hear them anew at least once more. If need be, become the girl they're meant for, the other Florence who can do anything, who conquered the inaccessible trust of Pierre Laliberté, and the occasional love of that half-Mohawk, half-Italian bastard, that totally Zeno Mahone.

12

RASPBERRIES.COM

---

*I*N *Recreated Creatures,* Annie and Anna, sisters by blood and mind so close-knit that nothing can happen to one without the other experiencing it, Annie and Anna, as I was saying, can cause the most extraordinary phenomena to occur each time they separate. Showers of shooting stars, gaping crevasses in downtown streets, mass die-offs of goldfish . . .

And we believe it. Even goldfish suddenly going belly-up in their bowls, even shooting stars in broad daylight. We believe it all.

In *Raspberries,* a conscientious child psychologist, who is also the mother of a five-year-old girl, gets felt up every rush hour on crowded buses by hands she cannot see. She spreads her thighs to make the anonymous feeler's job easier, she spreads her thighs and comes, fraught with an overwhelming sense of delinquency, shame, perversity and delight.

We love her unconditionally.

In *Go Run Fly,* a man raises homing pigeons that end up teaching him to fly, while making him forget how to walk.

We never doubt his capacity for air travel, but we do wonder how he'll ever go shopping again.

In *Morbid Martha,* not a single character, living or dead, is named Martha.

And we don't care.

WHO HAS GREATER powers than Pierre Laliberté? Who among the politicians and certified gurus of this planet can boast of bringing his supporters to accept, in such short order, so many fantasies and convoluted inventions?

I look around me. Here I am, at the new Mahone Inc. headquarters. More than nine hundred thousand dollars in sales, two hundred clients to date and three devoted programmers hunched devoutly over the computers, sophisticated scanners and laser printers that have laid waste to our credit line, the gleam of oak and copper, ceilings with vaults and arcades so high that the human neck lacks the elasticity to admire them, rare and gigantic plants that are bound to die within the week without a competent gardener to tend them. And on the outside wall, a solid brass condor—that's my obsession—a condor that tells Sherbrooke Street that it couldn't care less about the old and the servile.

All the same, Pierre Laliberté, sitting stiffly on his rickety wooden chair in his seedy rustic work space, has more power than Mahone Inc.

I considered our aggressive young interns, bundles of

nerve endings searching the immense sky of the Web in an effort to pinpoint new and unknown constellations. Sensing my
eyes upon them, the eyes of authority, each of them smiles a
brief, deferential smile without missing a beat. How serious
they are, how intelligent, what nice ties they wear. Humor-
lessly they amuse themselves by creating useless bytes and
sites in universal space. Is that reality? How much can humanity be worth when our clients like Pierre, Martine, Jackie and
Bashi-Bouzouk, respectively thanatologist, chocolate-maker,
lawnmower mechanic and ventriloquist, will make their appearance tomorrow on the computers of the planet to flog
their insignificant merits?

What if none of that were real? What if, flying in the face
of coherence, the realities imposed by Pierre Laliberté—twins
who create cataclysms, a flying man, a woman who has orgasms on crowded buses, the moribund elderly getting off by
themselves—were more real than our reality?

That's the way I'd been thinking, ever since I started carrying Pierre Laliberté's books around in my handbag like some
stupid groupie, like Zeno. Ever since I'd started rereading
them instead of working, slouched in an armchair that's too
comfortable for me right in the midst of our magnificent digs
on Sherbrooke Street at the corner of McGill College.

I read the third title, *Recreated Creatures,* and it literally
came crashing into me. Maybe because I wasn't as alert as I'd
been with the first two books, maybe because I thought it
would have the same effect on me, the same bewildering,
perverse effect as before.

Well, it didn't.

As for the destructive, torrential impact it had on me, I'd rather not talk about it.

If we know someone powerful, do we obtain power ourselves?

I CAN'T EXPLAIN WHY, but I knew we would meet again. The summer had waned since our last encounter, and his panicked flight. I hadn't received a single sign from him, but I never doubted that one morning, or late one afternoon, he would surprise me, standing on the sidewalk next to his hybrid vehicle. This must be what they call hope, the kind that takes the place of a pact even when there are no signatories.

It happened this morning as I was leaving the house. He stepped out of his car that was parked right in front of my door. He startled me. He was wearing a blue sweater, as baggy as the forest-green one, and his brown eyes glowed restlessly.

"Are you going to work? Do you want me to drop you off?"

I said Yes, without thinking.

He drove slowly. My place was only five blocks from Mahone Inc.

"Listen," he blurted out, "I came to tell you that we can't go on like this. I can't give you what you want. When it comes to conveying information, I'm one big zero. You're going to end up disappointed. And despite all appearances, I've got a lot of things to do."

I counted to five. I bit my tongue. But inside I was grinning from ear to ear. I didn't believe a word he said. When you don't want to see someone, do you take the trouble to seek that person out and tell him you don't want to see him?

Then right away, while we were stopped at a red light, he took my forearm. He'll kiss it, I thought with the first whisper of a beating heart. But he only sniffed at it, then deposited it carefully on my lap.

"How old are you?" he asked.

"Twenty-five."

"You smell so young," he sighed. "You smell like fresh-baked bread, you smell like a fragile new building. I love that smell."

I didn't react. Any reaction was beyond me.

Besides, Mahone Inc. was close by. I asked him to drop me off before we got there. I was afraid that Zeno, who was about to move back into our magnificent office, would see me with the only man in whose company he longed for me to be.

"Listen," said Pierre Laliberté. "If you promise not to expect anything from me, and not expect me to show you things, or try to cruise you, if you want us just to be together and not necessarily say anything, well, uh, maybe tonight."

"Tonight?"

"Tonight," Pierre Laliberté agreed.

TONIGHT FINALLY CAME. When it did, I was in the subway, on my way back from the far reaches of the city, still reeling from my encounter with a jeweler customer who created toothbrushes, combs and toilet seats—so far, so good—but in his case he decorated them with lapis lazuli, diamonds and fine skeins of fourteen-carat gold, for the sake of lending refinement to the utilitarian. What bitterness he displayed. In this society of handout seekers, he has no buyers. In this country of duct tape and bailing wire where no true wealth is disinterested, in this country of skinflints, he goes unrecognized. Where are the Arab oil nabobs, where the African dictators with the class to appreciate pearls and sapphires that would line the toilet bowls into which they piss? Now it's up to Mahone Inc. to put him in touch with authentic fortunes.

That was his message, well and duly registered on my cellphone. It turned my knees to rubber.

He was the reason Mahone Inc. existed.

I took the subway against Zeno's will. He wanted me to travel by taxi or hired limousine, he wanted me to throw a little money around. He understood nothing of my fear of private chauffeurs, who were ready to drive me around like an heiress or a lady nabob, far above the termite mound teeming with lower forms of life.

I am one of the poor in spirit, I fear.

Poor in every respect, spirit included, especially when I considered with a quivering heart that Pierre Laliberté was waiting for me in the same bar where he'd attempted to inculcate in me the art of peering into the souls of others. What did I have to offer? How could I bring anything to someone of his type, and still claim a place at his side? The only thing I gleaned at the shopping center was the threadbare ghost of Pepa. As for everyone else, all the living beings who inhabit this planet, I still had nothing to declare.

In the subway, I raised my eyes and grasped at all that fell within the purview of my gaze, in a last effort to see something. I wanted to give Pierre Laliberté something, even if he'd asked for nothing. I wanted to be his brilliant, inspired disciple even if he didn't give a shit. I wanted him to take me into his trust and reveal to me, alone among all others, his true identity.

Nothing less.

I am Pierre Laliberté, the writer. I admit it. Yes, it is I, Pierre Laliberté, who wrote Falterlust. *I'm telling you, Florence, but don't tell a soul. Yes, Florence—Flora—you deserve it, you alone deserve to hear my secret.*

How about a soul kiss to go with that?

In the subway, as grim-faced, crowded passengers vanished from my field of vision, I wandered through this wonderous fantasy, I heard the soft voice of Pierre Laliberté telling me what I wanted to hear. What more powerful sensation could there be, what in all existence could be more gratifying than the trust of an exceptional, powerful and mad human being who shared it with no one else? What love, after that magisterial gift, could I possibly lack, what other part of my life could possibly seek nourishment? None, I swore it. Not one.

Pierre Laliberté had the power to free me from hunger.

Two stops before my journey's end, I awoke. Panic kept me on the edge of my seat. Adrenaline surging, I threw myself in with the other passengers as if they were life-buoys of last resort before the ship slipped beneath the waves.

Quick, Florence, you're running out of time. Your ability to see clearly is fading before your eyes.

The dense crowd that thronged the subway was made up mostly of workers from the garment shops of the north end. Hindus, Sikhs and Pakistanis. Brown-skinned men and women, eyes more opaque than black olives. Exhausted, the lot of them. Their eyes, lost in inward contemplation, gave off immense exhaustion, as did their hands that drooped disjointedly wherever the laws of gravity made them fall.

I stared at them greedily, hoping to capture whatever fiber of the spectacular might lie dormant, sparkling beneath their dull surface. I looked at them so intently, unblinking, that soon I lost any sense of their individual shape. I saw only an animal mass of heaviness and fatigue at the center of which beat a single giant heart. *Pumppump. Pumppump.* Beneath the clatter of the subway, its external fibrilations, beat the slow heart of the beast, indefatigable for all its fatigue.

The heart of the beast transmitted its lethargic beating to me, and soon a leaden veil fell around me and I closed my eyes. I opened them just seconds before the subway doors slid closed on my station.

Too bad. My last chance to be brilliant just got snuffed out.

I dragged myself along the street, despondent and heavy, overcome by everything that whirled past. What happened to my legendary quickness, my vivacity that used to send me rushing to the front? I felt so much like an overcooked vegetable that I wondered if it was even worth trying to wrestle with Pierre Laliberté's crackling intelligence.

I paused at the door to the bar. Going inside demanded a superhuman effort. Then a hand fell upon my shoulder, and a whole body attached itself to mine, and I found myself turned all the way around.

"Flora! What the . . . What are you doing here?"

Zeno. Of all possible catastrophes, this was the least predictable.

"What about you?" I stammered. "And your mother . . ."

"I found her a sitter," Zeno rejoiced. "Freedom is a wonderful thing. So, you hang out at Raspberries.Com, do you, my dear? Are you going or coming?"

"Raspberries.Com?" I repeated stupidly.

"Uh-oh. What kind of illicit substances have you been consuming on our respectable premises to space you out so totally?"

With a laugh, Zeno snapped his fingers a few times in my face, while my glutinous mind flailed in its sticky bog in search of an escape route, a brightly lit EXIT through which I could flee as fast as my legs could carry me. Before me, the bar's smoky, shadowy maw gaped open. The place called itself Raspberries.Com, a wildly improbable name that reminded me of the title of one of Pierre Laliberté's novels. The very place in which Pierre Laliberté was expecting me. The coincidences were too frequent to stand.

"I was . . . I was just going in. No. The truth is, I'm meeting a client. You know, the jeweler who makes razors out of precious stones."

I smiled, though it would have been such a relief to burst into sobs. Zeno, that horrible man, idled at my side.

"Oh, yes," he said, pretending to peek inside. "I'd be curious to see what he looks like."

I commanded my smile to stay just where it was, as immutable as a death mask. You never know. Sometimes catastrophes vanish by themselves if we simply refuse to accept them.

"But I've got to run," Zeno said miraculously. "Tell me all about it later."

Saved but shaken, I stepped into the bar called Raspber-ries.Com alone. I'd burned off all my adrenaline, and now I was as floppy as a mop, dog-tired and inwardly somnolent. Pierre Laliberté's blue sweater appeared in front of me and pulled me along in its wooly wake to a booth at the farthest reaches of the bar.

"Is this okay?" he asked.

How could I say no? His things were strewn around this shadowy grotto, including his notebook. My eyes went imme-diately to it; maybe there were some hieroglyphs to decipher that were better than a shopping list. He slid over to make room for me. Wrapped me in his benevolent gaze. I could set-tle in right here and sleep against him like on a soft comforter.

"You're tired," he told me.

It's not me. I tried to explain that the condition isn't the real me, I caught it in the subway the way you catch the flu in winter, it infected me as I was working on my vision. Nothing turned out, that's what I'm trying to tell him. I couldn't sur-render to the curiosity experiment as instructed, I couldn't keep his instructions in my mind. I felt so much like some slithering thing that I wanted to crush myself.

His deer-eyes came to rest on me for a moment, laying their perplexity before me. Then he pushes a little glass of am-ber liquid in my direction.

"One swallow," he ordered. "It won't kill you."

Alcohol, alcohol, always alcohol. Why do I always meet the poison of alcohol on my path, along with its brigade of fa-natics who are never satisfied with tasting it in private? It's not enough to be drunk, they've got to get others drunk too. I took a swallow. The stuff was as unpleasant as ever, with a peculiar bitterness I hadn't tasted before.

"Fruit schnapps," said Pierre Laliberté. "Good, eh?"

"Too good for me."

"I'll order you a glass."

"No, thanks. I prefer my fruit unadulterated. In the form of lemonade, for instance."

I don't drink, I'm not the kind of woman you want to feel up or seduce—what does he possibly hope to gain? I assumed he thought that way, in any case. Meanwhile, I had everything to gain, since I had nothing to offer.

"Very good," he said. "Your perceptions in the subway were very good. But you can't leave it at that, in suspended animation. Drink, breathe—but do something."

I didn't know if I understood him. What did I do so well in the subway besides catch the chronic fatigue of worn-out passengers?

"You're gifted," he said, smiling. "Stop looking at me like I am lying."

"Gifted at what?"

"You saw, right? You saw exactly what there was to see, without adding anything, right?"

I stared at him, eyes wide, shot through by this stunning insanity: You can see without seeing, and without remembering not having seen a thing?

"What did I do?"

"You removed your little blinders. You took everything in, right in the face. Everything that everybody could throw at you, right in the face."

"That's seeing?"

"What more do you want?"

He wasn't making fun of me; he wasn't even smiling.

"Let's stop here," he told me. "We agreed we weren't going to talk about it anymore."

Very well. We won't talk about that, or anything else for that matter. We'll just sit here elbow to elbow like an old couple dessicated by promiscuity, without ever having enjoyed the pleasures of youth together. A kind of accelerated aging. I buried my chin in my palm and prepared to die of boredom. I should have brought a book. One of his books, so I wouldn't be bored with him. The irony made me crack a smile.

"You're tired," he said into his glass. "It's because you're new at it. You don't know yet how to transform it into something else."

"*It.* What's this *it?*"

"Sometimes it's fatigue, other times it's fear, other times— but not often—it's delight. It all depends on who gives you the energy."

That was it. He looked away, signaling that the tap had been turned off once more. I said nothing. I sat stunned on the padded bench. Let me recapitulate. If I understand correctly, we receive, assuming that we so desire, providing we adopt a propitious attitude, energies from people around us. Just go and sit down beside someone when you know that. Just try and keep away from the ugly, the old, the bikers, the crazies, the maniacs, the depressives and the nasties, three quarters of the population you don't want to receive the slightest energy from. So far so good. But let's say you receive a jolt of energy, bang! and after that you transform it into all sorts of derivatives if you're an old hand like him, and not a harebrained novice like me, you transform it into sweet cream, natural yogurt or a fifteen-speed bicycle. How far will the alchemical process go once you set it into esoteric motion? Go figure.

I was so amused at being the sole recipient of his fabulatory follies that I cackled at the private nonsense of it all.

He finished his fruit-flavored poison and ordered another with a minimalist gesture that immediately captured the waiter's attention. Once that was done, he turned and gave me a long, hard look, taking all the time in the world to focus his liquid eyes on mine.

"You know what I'm talking about. You understand intuitively everything I'm saying, but your reasonable, certified accountant's little mind isn't interested in going deeper. True or false?"

"I'm not an accountant," I responded, hurt. "I'm a Web surfer."

"Of course," he said with a thin smile. "I wasn't talking about your job, but your state of mind. I like it that you're a Web surfer. They work sitting down too, right?"

Like writers, I wanted to say. But I bit my tongue, and that kept the words in.

"The Web has made travel obsolete," I said, as sententious as a used car salesman.

"Obsolete," he chuckled. "But what about the smells? The smell of rain on the spruce trees? The smell of Venice in July? The smell of traffic on Sixth Avenue in New York? If you don't go anywhere, you'll never have any new smells."

The thought of Sixth Avenue in New York set me back a little, as if he'd thrown me a line I didn't know how to grasp.

"It's a matter of time," I said cautiously. "It won't be long before we'll have access to everything with one click. The smells, the landscapes, the New York smog, just like you were there."

It was preposterous, and fast too: he grabbed me by the shoulders and kissed me on the mouth.

"What about that?" he asked, releasing me. "The Web can never give you that."

"That," I said, shaken, "that, well, of course, it's a matter of time too."

He began to laugh, and I laughed too. We laughed like a couple of nutcases, even after the waiter put four glasses of schnapps in front of us, mumbling something about two-for-one, or all for one. Pierre Laliberté slid two of the glasses over to me. I stopped laughing.

"Not for me."

"On the contrary," he said with the remains of a laugh. "It's part of what comes next."

"What's next?"

"The next phase of our work. This is a working session, let me remind you."

How about that? I didn't think we were playing that game anymore. His tone was easy, his eyes were warm and friendly, but I felt a wave of cold breaking against my insides. Fear. I feared what would come next, what could happen. Pierre Laliberté's black magic frightened me very much.

"I can't drink alcohol," I said feebly.

"I know. You're allergic."

"Yes," I said, as vehemently as I could. "Mortally allergic."

"Like you are to rubber."

He went on smiling with all his sweetness, but the threat was everywhere, it came especially from what was sweet and benign in appearance, like his smile, like the schnapps that so treacherously teamed up with fruit.

"Here," he said, taking one of my glasses. "We'll make a deal: I'll drink three, you drink one. That way I'll get drunk before you do."

I fingered my glass, nauseous before the fact, my stomach gripping with anxiety. There's no reason to put myself in this position, no one has the right to impose it on me. I moved the glass over to where its brothers stood, in front of Pierre Laliberté.

"What happens if I refuse to drink? Because I do refuse to drink."

"Nothing," he said, smiling. "Nothing happens. We stop working, that's all."

"Why? Why is it so important for you that I drink?"

He took a swallow and savored it, just to irritate me. Then he took two more before deciding to answer.

"Because it's so important for you *not* to drink."

The way he said it, in that tone of clinical conviction, I had no way out, not even with myself. I grabbed the glass I'd pushed over to him and, holding my breath, downed it in one gulp. There, that's done. Now can we change the subject?

I surprised him. He began to laugh again. He lifted his glass to me.

"Bravo!"

Then he did something fast and terrible. He gulped down the three glasses of fruit-flavored whatsit and motioned to the waiter.

"You'll have another," he said to me. "We'll make it tequila this time."

He turned to the waiter to place his order: four tequilas.

It wouldn't kill me. Just make me sick. Everything quietly hiding inside me will try to escape my body, I'll lose awareness of everything except utter and total nausea, I won't know where I am nor why, nor even if it's worth existing, and no one will come to my aid in that vale of misery where I'll huddle for hours, certainly not him, because he'll be in worse condition than me. But it won't kill me.

I'll just lose control. Knowing I'm about to lose control of the situation is terrifying.

I watched his smile as fear churned my belly, swimming just below the surface of the bitter syrup I choked down. I'd love to receive instruction, and be introduced into the mysterious heart of life, but please spare me this, spare me the fear. I can't stand fear, and it's all too familiar. Familiar in the root sense of the word: part of the family. I knew that fear when I made love to Zeno for the first time, for the first fifty times. And I saw that fear every day of Pepa's life, disguised behind his little multicolored pills, his hands protecting his chest, his crab-like evasions.

Fear of dissolving into nothingness. Fear of falling so far out of sight that I'd never be able to find myself again.

"Don't be afraid," Pierre Laliberté told me.

He took my hand, squeezed it, held it in his. A wave of warmth flowed into my stomach, smoothing out the tensions.

"You'll just loosen up a bit," he said, as if he could read my body. "You won't drown. I promise I'll keep your head above water."

He's a magician. Should I tell him I fear magicians almost as much as alcohol? I do tell him.

"A magician!" he guffawed. "I invent nothing, especially not magic! It all exists, the magic is already there!"

He kept my hand, and my eyes. I couldn't tear myself away from what he was saying.

"Let's stay in the realm of the concrete. The rational. What's underneath your leather bench?"

"Concrete?" I ventured.

"Concrete! Concrete, the foundations, and then what?"

"Then... then..."

"What's the concrete resting on?"

All of a sudden he seemed to take great pleasure in his role of dispenser of information—the very role he claimed he wanted nothing to do with. Might as well make the most of it.

"Sand? Earth?"

"The earth!" he said with delight. "Let's work our way down through all of it, the concrete, the foundations, the earth. And beneath the earth is still more earth, and then fire. All the scientists tell you so: There's fire at the center of the earth, otherwise everything would have grown cold and dead. Right?"

"Right."

He was off to the races. God only knows when he'll stop.

"Let's go deeper still: There's fire, and earth, and lots of water, and maybe after that more concrete, and other foundations on which rest a padded bench on which is seated a posterior certainly less shapely than yours, but let's keep going, let's make our way through the padded bench and the Patagonian or Australian posterior, through the air, on and on, until we come to the void, the void where the packet of earth on which all our posteriors rest is floating, the void where nothing exists, but where absolutely everything can come into being."

He swallowed down his first glass of tequila, releasing me and smacking his lips.

"That's the magic," he said triumphantly. "It doesn't belong to me or to you. It simply is."

Space. The void. Twice now he's mentioned those two creepy crawlies. The first time around, I gave him one of my sardonic laughs, the kind I reserve for out-and-out fraud. Now I'm not laughing, I've never felt less like laughing. I see that space as if I were there. And that's exactly where I was. In a terrifying no-man's-land where people and tables and glasses of beer float in the solitude of nonexistence.

How can you float in the middle of empty space, in a capsule of stone and earth you know nothing about, that's heading towards an unknown objective, accompanied by a body and mind whose origins and destination are as singular as all the rest, and not be galvanized and overwhelmed, the constant prey of dizzying mysteries? How can you be endlessly surrounded by incredible immensity, yet live in a tiny, miserable box as if locked in by a torturer, to contemplate the walls and repair the cracks and do your best to decorate that box so you feel less like breaking free—unthinkable, but true.

I considered Pierre Laliberté with new respect.

"Do you think about that a lot?"

"Yes," he said. "Every time I'm tempted to be petty."

He caught me gazing at him with adoring eyes, and he shrank back into the far corner of the booth, as distant as if he were in a bar in Patagonia.

"Don't look at me like that," he said, darkening. "I'm an ordinary guy, as ordinary as the next guy."

How fragile things were between us, how close to extinction. I quickly turned my admiration in another direction. Among the shot glasses on the table glistened the black moleskin cover of his closed notebook. Pierre Laliberté, the shy and secretive writer, was sitting right next to me, and from each word—spoken as well as written—that fell from his lips, gold flowed, and I received the precious droplets without having done a thing to deserve them. A wild joy surged through me, which I concealed in my glass. I, Florence, slowly swallowed two mouthfuls. They were hot, strong and intolerable, then tolerable. Like fear. Fear is hard and impenetrable, but if we charge straight at it, we pass through it as if it were a sheet of paper on which some practical joker had drawn bricks.

"A kind of warmth," I said without looking at him. "A kind of warmth that could change into strength. Is that what you mean? We could feel the waves of emotion that come from other people, towards us, their fatigue or their fear. We could feel their warm matter as if we were immersed in it ourselves."

What was I talking about? I surprised myself. I had no idea where all this twiddle-twaddle was coming from, I didn't have a clue what I was saying.

Yet it all rang true, more real than reality. And so simple. All we need do is step outside our little box. When we do, we find ourselves in space, our space, their space, the only space that exists, and everything is given to us, other people, frogs, stars, because everything is connected. So simple. How could I have avoided that truth for so long? I stared at my glass. In addition to stepping outside the box, maybe it's also essential to soak yourself in alcohol to reach a few crumbs of truth.

With the greatest precaution, so as not to spook him, I raised my eyes to Pierre Laliberté. He was smiling, smiling at me as if he wanted to kiss me. Kiss me for real, not like a few minutes ago when all I got was the prickliness of his lesson and his beard, and not the smoothness of his skin.

"Yes," he said. "Yes, exactly."

"What does it mean? What's the use?"

"All kinds of things," he said seriously. "You could cure people. You know, lay your hands on them. Stuff like that."

I didn't miss the mocking effervescence in his eyes.

"Or you could make money off them. Use them, exploit them. People do it all the time. Or you can walk for miles without getting tired. Or you can sit down and write. Some people do that."

Nothing could have been more offhand than those last words. He dropped them into his glass instead of speaking them in my direction. Should I pursue them, or let them steep in silence for a moment?

"What about you? What do you do?"

How will he wriggle out of that one? I wondered.

"A little bit of everything," he joked. "I take long walks, I cure Oldsmobile motors and sick plants, I write little things."

He writes little things. My dear underground genius, Grand Prize of the Americas. *Falterlust, Raspberries, You Love You,* little things jotted down at a table in some café, in between a long walk and curing an Oldsmobile motor. My heart surged wilder still in my chest. Now we were drawing closer to the beating heart, the center of all that will be ours to experience together. I swallowed two more gulps of pale arsenic to give me the courage to push him into the confessional.

"And at the hospital?"

He looked at me quizzically.

I wanted to ask, What were you doing at the hospital, what did you hope to find among the elderly, rotten with age, among the moribund who'd exhausted their resources, what did you extract from Nina and all those other dissolving individuals who earned a mention in your notebook, how many notebooks did you fill in their quavering presence, how many wounded creatures have you vampirized over the years to nourish your seven books of 300 pages each with their captive strength?

But just then, the alcohol I'd rashly trusted reared up and betrayed me. A fog descended upon the sunlit clearing where my spirit played, and I couldn't see any of the things I wanted to say, I saw only the main character from that hospital that I resuscitated from the shadows. Pepa emerges from the haze of alcohol, lying on the bed of our final encounter, and he opens his eyes to me, I who bombard him with my supplications, *say my name, say something.* He opens his eyes and never speaks again.

Pepa, his eyes wide open, like a vial of evaporating perfume. Pepa is dead, and now he stands between Pierre Laliberté
and me. He blocks every way out in every possible direction, he
stands alone and sovereign in the center of my mind. Why did
he wait to die before coming this close? Why, in life, did he
never sit down with me in a dim bar to teach me and give me
instruction, to give me a father's nourishment? Should I have
pursued him, harassed him, beat him until he passed on a few
drops of knowledge and warmth? To see him again, so open
and spread out in nothingness, his essence forever wasted, and I
forever unable to taste or touch it, and draw any strength from
it, leaves me with a sense of unending sadness.

"Please don't cry," Pierre Laliberté told me, touching my
hand.

"I'm not crying."

It's only my eyes. They're crying, not me. My eyes, and the
storm inside me that must pass, and will pass. Pierre Laliberté
caressed me with his hand and his smile of regret, and his
deep and compassionate eyes. Pierre Laliberté was a pure caress, my one-night mentor, my master of a few truths. Why
was my father never my master?

"How old are you?" I asked him between two sobs.

"Fifty-eight."

Fifty-eight, of course. Fifty-eight, because there is no such
thing as coincidence. At fifty-eight, a Daughter was born to
Pepa, throwing the Hell of a Lover into disarray, giving birth
in turn to a faded man who every night for the rest of his life
would repair to the basement to steep in misanthropy. Pierre
Laliberté is the same age as my father was when he began

teaching me nothing. A strange, strange correlation that must bear out something decisive, some revelation, if you know how to read those kinds of things, if you have the correct optical instruments.

Pepa stands between Pierre Laliberté and me. Or is it Pierre Laliberté standing between Pepa and me, like a bridge between our two silences, bearing from Pepa's shore those impossible, detestable, excessive words that perhaps were meant for me?

I laughed. I laughed as hard as I'd cried, my brain saturated with alcohol and nonsensical speculation. What remained of my consciousness was relieved to discover that we were still sitting in the booth, the living with the living, and the dead with the devil, and that everything was as normal as it had ever been, totally normal, as in totally drunk.

"I was thinking of my father," I said in a thick voice.

"I thought as much."

"One of these days, Pierre—can I call you Pierre?"

"Yes, Florence."

"One of these days you'll have to tell me what you did with those words, that frigging sentence that you know exactly what I'm talking about."

"Yes," said Pierre Laliberté. "One of these days I'll have to, for sure."

He didn't run away this time, he looked upon me with an outrageous smile, or was it benevolent, it all boils down to the same thing. I had this overwhelming desire to confront him, brutally, right then and there. I sat up straight in the booth.

"Hold on," Pierre Laliberté said. "I'll be back in a couple of minutes."

I watched him make his way towards the bathroom. I saw the moleskin notebook lying closed on the table, forlorn among the empty glasses, offered up as a diabolical temptation to a lucky sinner. What do I do? Open it, read the last few pages, memorize it, or just steal it?

I held it between my fingers. It was softer than a baby's skin. Then I don't know what happened, I absolutely don't know. The table plowed into me like an iceberg, and I was crushed, collapsed, liquified. To make a long story short, I passed out.

13

JEEP

As EXPECTED, I did not die.
I returned to the world the next day just before
noon, half-dressed beneath the bedclothes, a damp washcloth
still on my forehead, a liter of water still cold on my bedside
table. My head was splitting, but otherwise I was intact. At
first, and it felt endless, I knew nothing of myself, but otherwise I was intact. Elsewhere in the bedroom, I came across a
bottle of tomato juice and a message scribbled on a paper nap-
kin with a ballpoint pen: *I have something for you. I'll give it to
you tomorrow night when you come home from your Web-surfer's job.
Drink the whole bottle of tomato juice as soon as you wake up.*

A note from him, unsigned. I drank the tomato juice and
filed the precious note in the drawer reserved for the handful
of desirable objects I own. Gold and silver in the form of jewelry I never wear.

It was time to think things over.

He was here. He was here with me, slobbering and unconscious me. Maybe he even carried me on his back like a sack of flour to be dumped in a warehouse. The question is: did he see anything incriminating? The question is: where were the seven books I'd been carrying around with me, the tangible proof of my duplicity?

No books on my bedside table or on my desk. No books in my purse that he must have searched to find the number of my apartment. Through my fissured skull a pale light gleamed. The books were at Mahone Inc., on the luxurious marble table of my luxurious office.

All was safe, even my honor. My chaste and unsullied undergarments attested that he did not undress me with anything more than cold efficiency, his eyes prudishly shut like a woman-fearing Hassid.

Under a cold shower, I energetically rubbed my fog-shrouded head, and a moment later the information lodged there shone like a fragment of new sky: *I have something for you.*

Pierre Laliberté had something for me. Something he'd give me tonight. This something had to be the recompense for my efforts at clairvoyance, the diploma that will certify that the bearer is both assiduous and curious. Pierre Laliberté is going to give me his last book. What other gift could better celebrate everything we share? His last book contains it all: my father's words, and a declaration of total trust.

I stood there in front of Zeno, luminous with serenity and fatigue. Afternoon in our air-conditioned office, and we inside it as if it were the final scene. Mahone Inc. now featured a solid brass condor beneath which two hundred square meters of professional success stretched in all directions, and I had Pierre Laliberté in my grasp. Almost. Lounging in Zeno's presidential suite, we discussed the only subject that meant anything, while outside, three conscientious employees toiled their souls out for us.

"Tell me about his secret life. Did he tell you why he lives in secret? After all these years in the shadows when he could have been shining in the light, hasn't he had enough?"

There indeed turns the tale. Why is Pierre Laliberté *Pierre Laliberté,* a being repelled by what others covet? I nibbled on tamari-flavored almonds with an air of deepest concentration. Zeno slurped cherry Coke from a can. We still looked like the commoners we are. The only thing different was the decor: the soft leather, the copper and marble, the glass that divided the space with its distinguished transparency.

"You see, he has this . . . this enormous feeling of unworthiness."

I started by weighing my words. Straightaway, Zeno wanted more, and faster.

"Unworthiness? Him? The greatest living writer? Unworthy of what? How come?"

"When he writes, he feels like he's the repository of an energy much greater than he is. That's what he told me. An energy much greater than he is."

"Tell me more."

"That's all there is. The rest of the time he sees himself as quite ordinary, a nobody, just like everybody else."

I stopped there, proud of my performance. Zeno twisted and turned on the lambskin of his executive sofa.

"Everyone knows all that," he erupted. "All writers write

with an energy bigger than they are. Big deal! That's who we want to know about. The guy who has heavenly manna falling on his head, not the ordinary guy, not the nobody!"

Ouch. I'd better do better. My turn to wax lyrical.

"But that's not at all that happens, and you know it! The first thing that happens is we start worshiping the least significant parts of artists, their haircut, their clever banter, their brilliant smile, the way they light their cigarette . . ."

"Does he smoke?" Zeno interrupted.

"No," I answered, taken aback.

"Go on."

"You see? Even you're interested in insignificant details."

"Go on!" Zeno warned.

"You made me lose my train of thought."

I maintained a sullen silence and waited for Zeno to calm down, but mostly I waited for inspiration to pour down its buckets of holy water upon me, instead of this pathetic trickling of clichés. From deep within me, from my innermost, openmost being, I summoned forth the ordinary face of Pierre Laliberté, his handsome deer-eyes, the flame that despite the ordinariness set everything alight in its unassuming way. What would he say if he allowed himself to speak? What would he say without speaking, what would he reveal in his concealment?

"Praise horrifies me, almost as much as the absence of praise. The fact that praise exists, that you can be showered with it, or deprived of it, makes creative life impossible."

My voice was so soft that Zeno had to bend forward. A sugary brown trickle of Coke dribbled onto the expensive carpet.

"The spectacle of writers lording it over their writing, over the evanescent vapors left behind, is pitiful to behold. The public life of a writer is time lost to vanity, time during which he is nothing but a turgescence waiting to be stroked by the tongue."

"Did you record all that?" Zeno murmured.

"Shh!"

"Excuse me."

"The public life of a writer removes him from the only space that counts, and delivers him over to his most abject, seductive weaknesses, ah, how handsome I am, how you must contemplate me endlessly, how ugly I am, how spineless, how you must pity me cajole me envelope me with love, how badly I need love . . ."

"He said that? He really said that?"

"Of course he said it," I shot back, irritated at being interrupted just when I'd struck it rich.

"Did you record it?"

"Of course not. I'm quoting from memory."

"Wait. We've got to get it all. Absolutely all of it."

Zeno rifled fast and furiously through the drawers of his marble-topped mahogany desk. He was so flustered that he actually looked for pen and paper in a place where these ancient instruments had been abolished. He finally ended up in front of his computer, where his fingers moved quicker than his thoughts.

"The public life of a writer . . . No, it began with something about praise . . . Can you repeat what you said?"

I repeated it all. Every one of the sentences I made up, coated with the same epithets and identical punctuation, down to the smallest comma, because all my invented sentences had been given the seal of approval by Pierre Laliberté, who was seated comfortably in the back of my mind. Who knows? They might all exist in his mouth—he just hasn't spoken them yet. But tonight, when he surrenders himself to me, he will confirm my premonition. Actually, I have invented nothing. I've only beaten him to the punch.

"But what about the prize, the Grand Prize of the Americas? He won it, he accepted it, didn't he? Was he happy to win it?"

Zeno had saved everything onto his hard disk, down to the tiniest reconstituted syllable. His fingers fluttered above the keyboard, impatient to be off and running again.

"Of that," I said succinctly, "I have no idea. He didn't mention it."

"Next time, ask him."

I eyed Zeno haughtily. Who did he think he was? Was he going to start dictating my own tall tales to me?"

"He does all the talking. I never ask anything."

"I see," Zeno said humbly.

"But I can tell you that he lives quite simply, without luxury. I would be surprised if two hundred thousand dollars changed any of that."

"Two hundred thousand American," Zeno pointed out.

"Two hundred thousand of whatever. Conquer that which is not your destiny, by sheer willpower, for what purpose?"

"Is that him? Is that him talking?"

I nodded my assent. Zeno's fingers, like docile gazelles, gamboled over the keyboard.

"What to make of all the beautiful women so far removed from your obsessions? How to administer the sumptuous mansions that creak at the seams with rooms and furniture you never use, surrounded by gardens you didn't design, that you don't even know how to fertilize? How can you endure this bourgeois life, oozing guilt from every pore?"

I stopped. Zeno stopped. That was no good. Those grandiloquent, flashy words lacked authenticity.

"Something like that," I said, disgusted with myself. "Accumulating things means nothing to him."

"From now on you've got to record it all, Flora," Zeno bellowed. "You've got to record EVERYTHING!"

How far we were from the cuddlesome excesses that had been his recompense when I first shared Pierre Laliberté with him. Since then, there had been three or four episodes of epidermal friction of variable intensities, a couple confessions of love muttered without much conviction, and plenty of physical distance due to mother-sitting. We seemed to have returned to our comfortable old norm. He thundered. I flashed back. Together we produced a dry storm that fertilized nothing.

Around us telephones were ringing crazily. We never answered, we acknowledged nothing that came from telephones. We had telephones because our clients were stuck on these PRE-CAMBRIAN INSTRUMENTS and their hoary rites, all to our good fortune. One of our three slaves would eventually put aside his work to empty the voice mailboxes and deliver us the contents. Zeno plunked away distractedly at his keyboard as he slugged back the cherry Coke. I nibbled on tamari almonds, lost in melancholy.

"Did you know," Zeno suddenly announced, "that there's a price on his head?"

I waited. He shouldn't count on me to play his little mind games.

"After he won the prize, a New York newspaper put up a fifty-thousand-dollar reward for anyone who discovers his real identity."

"Good God!"

"Fifty thousand American," Zeno emphasized.

I turned pale with forboding. What chance did Pierre Laliberté have, innocently, foolishly grazing among the crowds, while fifty thousand U.S. dollars awaited some clever big-game hunter.

"Don't worry," said Zeno. "I'm sure it's only a promotional stunt by his American publisher. The offer ends next month. No one has a chance."

He gave me a jovial wink.

"Except you," he pointed out.

"You're not funny."

"I know it."

He propped his legs on his mahogany desk, and leaned back against the lambskin of his chair. Contemplated the softly lit ceilings. Waved his hands as if to catch the delicately perfumed air coming from the air-conditioning ducts. Then he sighed and stood up.

"Let's get the hell outta here," he said.

FEET BRACED AGAINST the windshield of his van, rear ends compressed by the narrow seats, windows rolled down to capture the cordial pollution of Sherbrooke Street, finally we were back in our natural element. Zeno parked in a no-parking zone, faithful to his nonsensical principles that forbid him from parking lots. He pasted a huge CAR TROUBLE sign in the rear window to avoid parking tickets, that useless little runt, and for the past week he'd gotten away with his delinquent behavior. We could see our office windows. The solid brass condor looked to be snared by the windows, a prisoner of its own success. We turned our eyes away. Zeno set out two cups on the dashboard, into which he poured equal parts of cherry Coke and rum.

"Oh, no," I sighed, "not you too."

"Why?" aked Zeno. "Does Pierre Laliberté drink?"

"He does."

I immediately regretted my outburst of openness. Be careful with the splinters of unadorned truth. Don't give Zeno any fragment of a real image that might help him reconstitute a likeness.

Zeno drank with one hand, while he fingered the book in the glove compartment with the other. *Falterlust,* badly worn from rereading and red highlighter pen.

"Do you think you could get me his autograph?"

"Come on, Zeno. You know he would never do that."

He didn't challenge my peremptory answer. He stroked the book with his thumb, his expression more reflective than demanding.

"Does he like to write? Why does he do it? After all, he doesn't have anything spectacular to show for it. Why? Did he tell you?"

I could answer that one. It might be difficult at first, but all I'd have to do was look at Pierre Laliberté, watch him closely while his eyes were trained on mine, brimming over with everything he is, and ask him the question: Why *do* you write, Pierre Laliberté, why do you throw yourself alive into that fiery furnace, for it is a furnace, isn't it, and isn't it even sometimes hell?

"He doesn't want to write," I began slowly. "It's not an act of the will. He goes through terrible days, days of terrible resistance to writing. Flat days, empty of all will, except the will not to write."

"Is that true?"

"He feels such revulsion, such nausea at the very idea of approaching writing, the barbarity of writing . . ."

"The barbarity of writing," Zeno echoed. "In his case, I'd say yes. It's a wild kind of writing, with nothing comforting about it."

" . . . and it grows larger and larger, it becomes unbearable, resistance becomes more painful than the work to be done, and at that moment he no longer has the option of not going forward, not moving towards revulsion and beyond, and that's exactly what he does, he sits down and accepts that he must write and resistance melts immediately, like a pat of butter, for it was never anything more than warm butter in the sun, or a breath of wind. All he has to do is put one foot in front of another, move forward and enter the jungle."

"The jungle? Is that what he really said: the jungle?"

Zeno had twisted his body towards me; his attention was so extreme he'd even forgotten his computer. I imagined Pierre Laliberté leaning towards me at the very same moment, but with an attention full of ironic surprise, as if he couldn't get over the suffering I'd worked so hard to invent, as if he were just about to burst out laughing. ("Smile," he joked. "You're presently floating on a ball of earth.")

"He writes because he loves life," I quickly corrected myself. "He's madly in love with life. With real life, not the imaginary kind."

"Real life? Like what?"

"Cows. Sheep manure. Automobiles. Everything. For him, life is a symphony orchestra. Writing fiction is a way for him to step far enough back from reality to grasp its totality, the music of all the elements combined. The farther away you are, the clearer everything becomes."

The more I improvised, dipping at random into an invisible reservoir that filled as rapidly as I emptied it, the closer I felt I was getting to the core of Pierre Laliberté. He writes the way I described it. Just as he juxtaposed stars and frogs, he gave those impossible stories of his a panoramic vision in which everything was related to everything else, and all that produced disconnected fictions that had the authentic taste of reality. I was so amazed by what I'd discovered that I tossed down my rum and cherry Coke in one gulp.

"So he lives in the country," said Zeno.

"What makes you think that?"

"The cows, the manure, the sheep . . ."

"That was a figure of speech. Details, details, that's all you care about, poor Zeno."

"But that's what I want—details," he barked. "People reveal themselves in the details. He doesn't smoke, he drinks, he lives in the country, and you meet at your place, or in a café, or a bar?"

I responded with silence, to make it clear I intended to remain Mistress of All Revelations to Come. His appetite for the insignificant would find no nourishment here.

"What's his voice like? At least you can tell me that."

"It's a voice. What can you say about a voice? Not too high, not too low. A normal voice."

"There are mini-recorders you can wear around your wrist like a watch."

"I wouldn't do that."

"I don't imagine you took any photos of him either?"

"No."

"And you don't intend to take any?"

"No."

"You really want to keep him for yourself."

"I didn't say that," I protested feebly.

Zeno stroked his chin thoughtfully, dangerously calm. A century later he broke his silence.

"So, you sleep together," he decreed.

I shrugged. What am I supposed to tell him? What would win me the greatest long-term advantage, without necessarily turning against me like a decapitating boomerang? Yes? No? Maybe so? None of your goddamn business?

"That seems to be the only kind of relationship you know," I said through clenched teeth.

He threw me a sidelong look, which I fielded in exactly the same way. For a few silent seconds we hated each other intensely.

"Did you tell him about me?" he asked.

"No."

"He thinks you're free?"

"But I *am* free."

"What about us?"

"What about us, Zeno?"

"You're right. We're zip."

His voice fell, as neutral as a piece of metal, a total absence. He started up the van and we drove off.

I slumped against the door. We rolled on in apocalyptic silence. This time we've had it, the blow is fatal, we won't be able to recover from this *coup de grâce* as if it were more play-acting, we're not going to get up and dust each other off. I was stunned. So that's how it works. Everything is smooth and peaceful, then it all collapses. With no warning, like a piece of crystal that falls from our hands and shatters on the ground. The acid taste of rum and fresh blood meld in my mouth.

"Can I drop you off somewhere?" asked Zeno, as polite as a hired killer.

"If you like."

It had to end somewhere, the two of us, it had to end at a specific point that our comings and goings both foreshadowed and contradicted. Now we're there. Shelve your astonishment and your horror, *Flora-at-your-service,* and prepare to get out of the van.

"I want to change my life," Zeno blurted out.

"Oh?"

He spoke to the street in front of us, but I acted as if his words were meant for me.

"Change your life how?" I fired back.

Every word has its uses, every word communicates a stimulus that attracts other words to it in equal reaction. And as they travel back and forth, a fragile bridge takes shape, spanning the abyss over which we might cross with the most infinite of precautions.

"I feel like selling Mahone Inc."

A groan of protest escaped me. Sell Mahone Inc. just when it was taking off? Work ourselves to the bone down in the dungeons, then leave the ecstasy of the dizzying summits shimmering on the horizon to someone else?

"In a couple of years, it'll be an excellent deal," I ventured.

"I want to sell right now."

No doubt about it. This time, he was talking directly to me in that Siberian tone. Inwardly, I shrugged my shoulders and bit my tongue hard to keep from arguing. The breakup is consummated; all that remains is to sever all connections, and knock over what's still standing. How can I fight this crisis of his, this outbreak of suicidal masochism? How do you treat the Bishop Syndrome when it appears in its most splendid paroxysm?

"What would you do?" I said in a toneless voice, hoping to put off the eternal silence between us.

"Anything but what I'm doing now. Everything's possible. I could take to the road in my van with a load of . . ."

"A load of dogs."

"No," he said emphatically. "No more dogs. Nothing to tie me down, no demands. Free."

I played dead. His words must not touch me. I must not give him any purchase. I managed to listen with an appearance of genuine interest.

"I could travel around in my van with a load of books. I could be an itinerant bookseller, like in the book by Jacques Poulin you never read."

"No."

"I could head out for the other side of the continent, or cross an ocean or two. Like in Nicolas Bouvier's books. Which you haven't read either."

"No."

"I'm just saying that, but you're going to read plenty, now that you're getting it on with a writer."

I didn't answer. Listened indifferently. Keep on knocking, friend, it doesn't hurt a bit, there's no one there where you're pounding. My house came into view at the next corner. Soon I'll be walled up in my own apartment, tearing out my hair in proper fashion, with all due excess. Meanwhile, dry eyes and stiff upper lip.

He slowed well before reaching my door, the fateful threshold where we would part ways forever. Unexpectedly, he started whistling. Eyes straight ahead, he spoke.

"If I leave, will you come with me?"

"Me?"

"Yes, you, YOU," he said, exasperated. "You know very well we can't get rid of each other."

"Yes."

"Yes what?"

"Yes, I'll come. I'LL COME. Are you deaf or what?"

On we rolled, preposterous and buoyant, beyond my apartment, as far as the highway that follows the river and flirts with space. Zeno pulled the van over into the first available parking area so we could watch the sun sink into the red waters of dusk. Then he returned to Montreal. We won't go any further, that's understood. We won't be going anywhere else. How much farther could we go than this state of grace, each of us slumped against the door as if they were two islands, each connected to the other by an invisible, tenacious umbilical cord that pumped the blood of the universe into both of us?

One day, Zeno and me. One of these days.

IT WAS ELEVEN O'CLOCK when Pierre Laliberté came calling.

I was sure I'd missed him, since it was much later than usual when I came home. I paced from one window to the other, examining the cars below from all possible angles as they parked and pulled out. Then peace came over me. He said he would come. Had he ever stood me up since our first meeting, unlike some other people, unlike the guy I'd just broken up with and gone back to for the two-hundred-thousandth time in my life? I sat in my favorite chair and waited.

IT WAS SO RARE to be at home, sitting in my favorite armchair, indolent, remote from the complex world of the Web. I felt like a stranger in a strange town, relaxing in a hotel room. Hey, let's turn on the television like a stranger in a strange town. I switched on the TV, but turned off the sound so I wouldn't miss the squeal of tires down below, and the eventual drumming at my door. On the screen, men paraded by, one after the other, clean and smiling. Judging from the frenetic movement of their mouths, that contortion of faces turgid with the need to communicate, it must have been a talk show. I scrutinized the faces, each one in turn, with the insight of a stranger in a strange town. What do you say when you don't talk?

You lie, you lie, you lie.

Then Pierre Laliberté was knocking at my door. The television with its solicitous faces and illusions of being a stranger went blank. Now I am the resident of this apartment into which the greatest invisible writer of our era was about to set foot.

He was wearing his green sweater, the one he wore the first time. Let it never be said that the two hundred thousand U.S. from the Grand Prize of the Americas launched him into a spree of wasteful spending, at least as far as clothing was concerned. His gaze was as open and chocolaty as ever.

"Is it too late?" he asked.

"Too late for what?"

That was answer enough for him. He stepped inside with a smile, without closing the door.

"I can't stay long."

As long as the intensity was there, I couldn't care less about quantity. I noted with some anxiety that he had come empty-handed.

"What I have for you is in the hallway," he said, reading my eyes like a novel.

"Oh."

No bowing and scraping. No offers of hospitality, "Can I offer you something?" We stood facing each other with no discomfort. Whoever wanted to sit down first could without disturbing the other.

"You're looking a bit fresher this evening," he said, the corners of his mouth turned roguishly upward.

"That would be a change from last night."

"It's true, you were a bit the worse for wear."

He stood and looked around with friendly interest.

"So, this is where you live?" he asked.

I followed his eyes, and saw what he did. What I now only rarely saw. A handsome, pale hardwood floor, white walls, nothing pretending to be pretty. No photographs, no plants, no living things. The cell of a working humanoid, too cold to be inhabited on weekends.

"You were here last night."

"I didn't look at anything, I promise."

I believed him. Poking around in the absence—the mental absence—of the owner would not be in character for him.

"Do you like to walk?" he asked me abruptly.

"Um . . . sure. I always walk."

What kind of a question was that? Was he insinuating that my apartment was so unhealthy that I should get out as often as possible? Did he want to invite me to an upcoming speed-hike up Mount Royal? I would never find out. With the same impetuous manner, he hit upon the idea of going back into the hallway and picking up what he intended to give me.

"It's true," he said, his eyes serious now. "I know you weren't really yourself last night, but I wonder if you might know what happened to my notebook."

"Your notebook," I repeated.

"Yes, an ordinary little black thing made out of fake leather. I always carry it with me. I jot down stuff in it. Important stuff to me. I guess it doesn't ring a bell."

Gleaming in the darkness, the notebook floated to the surface of my memory. Ring my bell if it doesn't ring a bell. I could still feel its texture smooth between my fingers, like skin endlessly stroked, worn soft by constant caresses. Pierre Laliberté's notebook must be the thing he'd touched the most over the last few weeks. What happened when the soft skin of the notebook found itself between my fingers, what happened then? Did I pick it up, throw it to the floor, eat it? If I took it, where would I have hidden it in my woozily spectral state?

"You're talking about the notebook where you write down your shopping list?"

"Yes, exactly," he said drily.

"I recall it spending the evening on the table, among the many glasses."

"True, it was on the table. But later, when I left with you under my arm, it wasn't there. And I didn't drink that many glasses."

"Seven, at least."

He started laughing.

"You have one stiff upper lip. You can't understand excessive people like me."

I listened to him, nodding, mesmerized by the fact that he was really talking about himself, and about us, and not the stars of the firmament. He was saying how contradictory we were, him outgoing, me nunnish, yet we were still something together, some kind of temporary formation made up of mutual sympathy. He disappeared into the hallway. I sat down, just to be careful. When it comes to emotion, you never know what inelegant way it might find to cut your legs out from under you. He came back with a box.

A box. Will it be full of his books, from the first to the last, with a word to me in each, to guide me even more deeply into his dangerous magic, and transmit a little more of his power?

A box full of books doesn't make noise. It doesn't shake. A box of books doesn't smell like that.

"I think she went and pissed out of excitement," Pierre Laliberté laughed. "Come on, Jeep, out you come!"

And out of the box, terror-stricken, fur unkempt, slobbering already, popped one of those larval blond heads spotted in the shed at the beginning of the summer. Uno or Duo or Trio—there were no individuals in that undifferentiated mass—the real bobbing head of a real dog.

"She's yours," Pierre Laliberté told me.

14

RENAMING JEEP

OW EXACTLY DID I contrive not to react? Actually, I did react. I said: *Oh.* How could he have interpreted my *Oh* of motionless trauma, my *Oh* of a woman who found herself knocked to the ground and trampled on? As an *Oh* of delighted surprise, as an *Oh* as in "what a nice thought"? In any event, he left and the dog is here.

The she-dog.

She's weaned, her name is Jeep, one day I'll tell you why. She's housebroken, she needs the kind of dry dog food you'll find in this sack, she's easy to handle, all she wants is to run for an hour every day, at three different times if possible. Here's a leash for taking her out, the rest of the time she'll be a nice addition to your apartment.

Where was I when he dumped the dry dog food, the advice, the leash and the dog, then cleared the hell out?

I sat down on the floor, too stunned to make it to the nearest chair, and tried to put my thoughts in order. In a flash, the dog was all over me as if I were a toy thrown on the floor for her enjoyment, something to be gnawed and soaked with slobber. The more the toy resisted, the more it pushed her away, the happier she was. I got to my feet, offering her only my calves to saturate.

First rule of survival: Keep yourself standing straight and tall like a skyscraper to ward off the assaults of creatures that crawl.

Second rule: Get it out of my apartment right now. Get HER out. It's a her, after all—could anything be more insane? *Her*, just like me, as if we were the same species, as if I hadn't reached this acceptable shape after millions of years of evolution, polishing and finishing, while *that, that thing* was still obviously mired in the first rough draft of creation.

Stuff her back in the box and get her out of here. There! So simple that it almost didn't occur to me. Later, we'll see about the next step—how to get rid of the box and its contents. We'll see, and tough luck if we don't, but nothing beats this total relief, because at least I hit upon some course of action. Happily, I called her name, *Jeep!,* and she came dashing out of the bedroom she'd already chosen as her home, she came running straight for me with a trophy swinging from her yap. What's that you've got there, canine? My only presentable silk scarf was what she had, now hopelessly saturated with her digestive juices. You're welcome to it, kid. Keep it to remember me by. As a way of getting rid of you, it's pretty cheap.

Hard as it was to get rid of her when I didn't want her, it was even harder to get hold of her now that I do. Let's play. For her, life is a game. Let's play you run away and I chase you and I chase you and you run away and you run away and I lie down on the floor and you jump on top of me and I grab you and stuff you in the box.

She didn't like the way the game ended. She was a bad loser, whining and scuffling when I closed the cardboard flaps of the box over her.

I shook the box a little to change her mood, and spoke firmly. "Listen to me, Jeep, we're just not made for each other." She had no choice but to yield to the inevitable, and while she kept quiet for a few minutes, we left the house.

I didn't know where I was going until I hit the sidewalk. We were headed for Zeno's place. Every dog worshiper must always have a dog in his life; otherwise he'll lose the minimal amount of harmony that keeps him from destroying the lives of his friends. Zeno had gone without one for too long, and so had his friends.

The box and I walked along the sidewalk, carrying on a dialogue. She whining, I attempting to reason with her. "Now, now, you'll be happier where you're going, and we'll see each other again, I'm afraid we'll be seeing plenty of each other." I crossed paths with three teenagers stuck full of nails and rings who laughed at me after they went by. I crossed paths with a big black dog with his master in tow; the former immediately realized that inside the box was a fellow-creature to be sniffed. Then I crossed paths with a taxi that picked us up, the box and me, without any unsolicited questions. Real gentlemen, these taxi drivers, at least for the first few seconds. But pretty soon I noticed a brambly look in the rearview mirror, sizing me up with a mixture of hostile concentration and question marks. I stared out the window while the box, miraculously, balanced on my lap, the way a real box should.

"There wouldn't be something in your box..."

"Pardon?"

"... something that would be pissing?"

"What could you possibly mean?"

Pretending to be offended, I ordered him to pull over. Thank God we'd arrived.

The box was soaked with urine, but I carried it as if it were a cloud. Let her piss to her heart's content. Where she's going, she'll be welcomed with open arms.

I rang once at Zeno's door, then rang again. That animal's a heavy sleeper, unless he was in there dallying with some young thing, some novelty picked up during the evening who hasn't yet realized what she has or hasn't gotten herself into when she landed in his bed. Not a ray of light was visible, which didn't jibe with his exhibitionist voyeur side, that preferred to disport itself under the floodlights. Then I noticed his van was not in the parking lot. Where could he be, past midnight on a weeknight, if not about to return home? All I needed to do was wait. I looked at the box, shifting quietly on itself at my feet, lulled by its own whimpering. "You're wasting your time," I admonished her bluntly. "You'll have to learn patience. Life is a bother for me, why shouldn't it be the same for you?" Every time I raised my voice, hers weakened, as if by coincidence, or by cause and effect, as if a true grasp of things could possibly emerge from this rough assembly of wiry hair and viscera. I decided to walk away, just like that. The whining rose to the high end of the scale as I went down the stairs alone, then returned to rebuke her, "Shut up and wait. Your future master is on his way."

She shut up. I left.

I headed home, humming loud and clear. There's no dog here, I told myself, and there never was one. Do I look like the kind of person who would abandon a dog, do I look like the kind of person you'd leave a dog with? What's all this inner turmoil about a dog, when we live in an implacable universe where the children of Iraq have nothing but the dried-up breasts of their mothers to gnaw on, and the children of Palestine play games with rockets instead of soccer balls, and the ones in South Central Montreal guzzle beer next to their heroin-addicted fathers?

There is no such thing as minor pain. The harping voice of my condor. He materialized out of nowhere, after having disappeared God knows where, to wag his finger at me. Him again.

You should have left Zeno a note. I'll send him an E-mail from home. *You should have left some dog food in the box.* It would be soaked with piss by now.

The least you could have done is wait with her.

It was past midnight. Hadn't I done enough already, hadn't I had to digest the disappointment inflicted by the great writer whom I'd begun to believe was my friend, before that beast turned up in the form of compensation? What was I doing on the street instead of sleeping quietly like I deserved to? Slogging from one end of Montreal to the other to find a home for this object that had nothing to do with me, a home where it would be so happy that its brief stay at my place would have left her with nothing but golden reminiscences, assuming that beings of its species are capable of reminiscing?

Don't make me laugh. A home. What if Zeno doesn't come back, what if he doesn't come back for two days, or until next week? What if he's at his mother's dealing with a new outbreak of acute Amerindianitis? What if he's with that young thing he met earlier this evening, who has an apartment so far out he'll never want to leave? That's why you didn't wait with her, you ninety-pound weakling, you heartless lump. For fear Zeno wouldn't show up.

Worst comes to worst, someone else'll take care of her, goddamn it! Someone else will spot the box, hear her squeaking and release her. Neighbors, dog lovers, the planet is teeming with them.

Someone more humane than you.

Shut your big mouths, all of you, I shouted at the pale moon that arched an anemic crescent high above me, and at Pierre Laliberté, and at Jeep, and at Zeno who's never there when I need him, and at that part of me that was betraying me now.

They won't get me this time.

By the time I reached my front door, they'd gotten me.

I turned around and ran off.

Fifteen minutes later, Zeno's front porch came into view, but no box. No box, of course, and no need for all those useless scruples that are dangerous to the stomach. The little beast was probably cuddled warm and dry in the bed she'd soon begin to soak with her overflowing fluid. Zeno's bed.

Zeno's van wasn't in the parking lot. The dog must have been at some neighbor's place, someone who just adores dogs, someone who's already serving her hot milk and filet mignon cut into small cubes to soothe her ruffled emotions.

Then I spotted the box. Halfway down the stairs, wedged between two steps, upside down but visibly still full.

What kind of a neighborhood was this, where people pay no heed to anyone or anything, where they leave things that have just happened to fall onto the stairs in the night? I hurried towards the box. I touched it. Sounds of distress escaped, tiny piping sounds so faint they were twice as heartbreaking, like darts that could find their way to the heart of a stone. I turned the box over and opened it. Matted and pathetic, stinking stronger of piss than ever, the little creature broke into sobs when it saw me, the heaving mute sobs of a baby who has no more voice with which to cry. I wrapped her in my sweater. Too bad, I really liked that sweater. Now I'll have to throw it in the garbage. I picked her up, sodden and quivering, and carried her back to my place. We were so exhausted that neither let out a peep during the long walk home, and when we got there, we dropped to the floor and lay there, so destroyed that we didn't have the strength to throw ourselves into each other's arms.

I washed her in the bathtub. Rubbed her dry with my best towel. Upgraded her dry food with something more comforting. Rummaged through the fridge in search of animal protein—look, a leftover chunk of filet mignon. Why not mix in some warm milk? You don't tumble down the stairs at the controls of a cardboard box soaked with dog piss every day.

I watched her eat. She recovered all the energy she had be-fore the fall from earthly paradise. Tail wagging like a mad feather-duster, she guzzled, lapped, shimmied, ran to me to share her enriched slobber, bellied back to the dish then tipped it over, nibbled, sniffled, licked, chewed, gurgled— she'd lay eggs if she had the equipment. I watched and yawned. This wild-eyed joy was beyond my comprehension; it exhausted me. I liked her better depressed. "Jeep," I informed her solemnly, "Jeep, bright and early tomorrow morning we're going looking for your brothers and sisters and your mummy, not to mention Grandpa who really put his foot in it when he brought you here." She listened to me as her tail dis-located with pleasure, bestowing approval as approval has never been bestowed before.

For the rest of the night I slept fitfully, pursued by night-mares in which I was a torturer, tormenting a moaning vic-tim. Each time I awoke I realized my dream was reality. I am Bluebeard, my victim is groaning in the bathroom where I imprisoned her. With nothing to rip apart or chew on, noth-ing to flood but the tile floor protected by old newspapers, she sobbed in despair. I resisted, and returned to my guilty som-nolence. Finally she gave up and I fell asleep, deep in the black hole of innocence.

In the wee hours, my dreams turned around, awarding me the victim's role: I am tied to the floor, while they apply water torture. Unbearable. I much preferred being the tormentor. I awoke with a start. Jeep is standing foursquare atop me, copi-ously licking my face. How did the demon manage to escape her dungeon? She must have figured out how to turn the doorknob, unless the door grew tired of her constant whining. I pushed her away, wiped my face, she leapt back and started all over again. I pinned her to the floor with a war cry— *Jeeeep!*—and there we were, the two of us, starting our first morning together. And our last.

The bathroom was intact, the newsprint dry and odorless, the towels and shower curtain undamaged. I was about to be pleasantly surprised when surprise took on another complexion. She had held her bladder in check for the long hours of her incarceration, all the better to baste every corner of my apartment at dawn, distributing its contents equitably in four parts. Luckily I lived in a rectangle instead of a dodecagon.

I lowered myself to her level, hand brandished in dire threat. *I'll kill you!* She flooded my hand with joyous saliva. I wiped my palm on her head; she took it for a caress. I insulted her. She wagged her tail gleefully. Just my luck—stuck with one of those congenitally jovial types.

But that didn't matter, since our paths would soon part. I'd clean up later, when I was free and alone again. Time for a walk, I promised her, waving the leash under her nose. She could hardly contain her enthusiasm. Me neither. Whistling, I packed her bags. This time she'd travel in a knapsack lined with absorbent towels, all the way to the house of frogs and dogs. Where exactly was it, and how was I supposed to find a microdot on the map, lost in the wet origins of summer and darkness? I'd find it, I'd find it for sure, my memory would awaken to guide us. My optimism flowed forth, now that the final outcome was within sight. I wanted to send Zeno an E-mail, just to check the pulse of his existence. My computer refused to boot up. My computer, my telephone, my printer, my fax: with her fangs, she had severed the wires that connect me to the world. Not only is she a jovialist, she's a Luddite. Two irreconcilable destinies. The hot wind of anger swept over me, this beast must be chastised, such acts must not go unpunished, otherwise the world will fall into chaos and inefficiency. I said *Jeep!* once, without shouting, in my exacto-knife voice, deliberate and sharp enough to slice its way through anything. She came running. One glance, then she threw herself on the floor at my feet, ears flattened, muzzle quivering in a silent *mea culpa,* spine curved in a general decline, crawling and wriggling with contrition. She ventured a whine that begged forgiveness for existing. But a tiny tip of tail fluttered beneath this humiliated heap of existence, a tiny tip of tail that couldn't keep itself from wagging at the future pleasure that would follow this fleeting instant of disfavor.

Okay, then. What part of this pile of excess mortification should I strike first? How can I exert authority over this caricature of repentence? I let fly with a few timeworn insults—filthy cur, damned mongrel, ringworm-infested mutt—then walked away, my motivation exhausted. She crawled after me with the same attitude of penitence, tail nearly motionless so as not to disturb the overall emotional effect. She wriggled after me until a burst of laughter escaped my lips, which brought her immediately to her feet, biting my calves as if life had become beautiful all over again.

Too bad. I won't be the one to train her, I said to myself as I left the house with her stuffed into my knapsack without a whimper of protest. Her head knocked against mine in cadence. I wasn't thinking about her. In my widening irritation, all thoughts were for Pierre Laliberté. Him and no one else. Venerate him for his clairvoyance, and this is your reward? Of all the flawed and negligent things he could have done, this was certainly the most unpardonable. Bit by bit, my pace slackened. I pictured him as he departed, leaving me the dog, and for the first time I saw what I'd missed, caught up in my distraction: that malicious laughter hidden in his cow-brown eyes. It was all so obvious. He'd planned the whole catastrophe, he knew how much I hated things canine, and he'd made up his mind to push it to the limit. But he didn't know how I do things. He didn't know what *docile-Flora-at-your-service* could do, he'll get his dog back all right, along with some dry bones that will stick in his craw. Now that I'd recovered my combative drive and warrior-woman's walk, I winged straight towards Pierre Laliberté like a deadly arrow, the animal's docile head flopping from side to side behind my neck, mouth shut, as the survival instinct commands. The passersby smiled warmly at me, unaware that I was heading for an assassination. When I passed by a store window, I saw what they were smiling at. What a pretty picture we made, her and me, our blond heads bobbing, one in front, the other behind, a pretty picture if you're the sort who pins SPCA calendars on your walls.

The first three taxis at the stand turned me down categorically when I approached them with my animal cargo. I couldn't hold it against them. From the fourth car leapt a smiling driver who opened the door for me. As I settled into the seat, doggy bag on my lap, he wanted to know everything there was to know about her even before I told him our destination: What's her name, is she really a golden retriever, how do I manage to keep her coat so glossy? (We'll see if this caninophile's politeness will survive the murky directions I'm about to give him.) "Head out of town," I instructed him brusquely. "Keep the river on your left, and then we'll see as we go. We're looking at two hours, round trip."

"Two hours!" he exclaimed. Would he kick us out of his cab? No, he took off like a shot, delighted. "A fine day for a drive," he remarked.

He talked as he drove. About dogs. Once he had three, now he has two, he sleeps with the two dogs and his wife in the same bed. Montreal isn't a town for dog lovers, you can't let them defecate as they please on the sidewalk, even if it is the most natural of functions, and landlords—can you imagine?—won't allow dogs in their miserable apartments, but they will accept criminals. It's because of the smell, I ventured. What smell? he asked, so indignant I let the matter drop. I told him three different times that the dog in the knapsack on my lap wasn't mine, but he wouldn't let up, he addressed me as a member of the confraternity for whom no detail of pedigree, coat or urinary disease is too repulsive, he'd have shown me his photos of Castor, Pollux and the late Fedor if his hands weren't taken up by the steering wheel, and if only he'd thought to bring them along.

Meanwhile, I leaned against the door frame and closed my eyes halfway, to remove myself from a detestable conversation, true, but mostly to immerse myself in the atmosphere of that faraway night when Pierre Laliberté drove me to his house. My memory lit up, flickered out, then sank into an Impressionist gloom. A minute later it alerted me to the familiarity of a curve in the road and the shape of numbers on an exit sign—they might be missing pieces of the puzzle. Mostly, though, the world looked foreign. The trees had asserted their presence since my first visit, and I would have recognized nothing if I'd trusted my senses alone.

The whole time she sat on my lap, floppier than a stuffed animal. Not a whine nor a shiver, only her eyes gazing at me. Her head was tilted at a forty-five-degree angle in the effort to concentrate on me, and she was staring. With her way of seeking out my eyes, I'd almost believe that somehow intelligence hummed in her heavy little head, that it wasn't just a holding tank for peepee in a subliminal form. I stared right back at her, to let her know who was boss, and make it clear we weren't of the same realm, nor even the same universe. Then, with a shock, I received the *dogness* that shone in her eyes, an undeniable state of being through which energy and aspirations percolated, and the perplexity of the moment, a kind of quivering reality of the senses, as real as me. She *is*. I may well be, but she is too, and not one whit less.

I shifted the knapsack so she could look out the window. Let her implant her triumphant existence somewhere else, not on me.

I recognized nothing. Not the green clumps of bushes, nor the road vampirized by trees, nor the house near to it, but I asked the driver to stop for a first attempt. I got out, took a few steps, looked at the field behind the house but located no shed that might possibly house a dog colony. I climbed back into the car. The she-dog in my knapsack had picked up a scent, or an atmosphere, or the moist texture of the rain-soaked countryside of her earliest days, and she began to wriggle and whimper in disappointment at the prospect of returning to the car seat. "Keep on," I told the driver.

"Yes, ma'am," he said, enjoying himself, and not at all irritated by having to wander the countryside with a lunatic who hadn't the faintest idea where she was going. But the meter knew what was expected of it: we were nearly up to fifty dollars. A bit farther, and we were there.

"This is the place," I told the driver. "Wait for me."

This was where, most times, Pierre Laliberté wrote and breathed. I recognized nothing, but this was it. A wood two-story house with a sun-yellow facade and a slate-gray roof, simple, hardly memorable, except for the splashes of flowers sprouting everywhere, even from beneath the windows, filling every bit of space. I'd never seen so many flowers at the same time. I spent a moment or two observing them in amazement. Did he raise them commercially? Eat them? Did he care for them, fertilize them and water them for no reason at all, asking only that they be beautiful? That could be. That could be the reason his books were so few and far between. Isn't it a pity, isn't it downright criminal for a being filled with such power to squander his time on decorative pursuits, instead of pumping earth-shaking works from the depths of his brain?

Jeep wriggled on my back and allowed herself a bark, the first of our brief cohabitation that had been distinguished principally by whining, licking and whimpering. Maybe the contact with her birthplace suddenly brought her maturity. So much the better—or so worse—for her, because here was where I was taking my leave. Setting her free. Here you are, canine, home again. She galloped in circles, discovered her tail for as long as it took her to not catch it, and finally she flopped down in the grass and rolled around like a mad cow, filling her snout full of smells. I began to walk. Not towards the house. I was too afraid I'd meet him. Instead, I made for the shed in the middle of the field, a hundred meters away. This was it, I recognized it. Then I spotted Pierre Laliberté's car half-hidden behind the house. The entire puzzle, impeccably solved. Now, another can begin.

Maybe he was out with the dogs. Maybe I'd run into him by trying to avoid him. Probably he was in the house writing—he has to write now and then, in between repottings. He wasn't with the dogs: they were alone, the whole family. Blondie, the mother, snoozing. Her yellow-furred offspring tussling. I pushed on the half-open door and set off the alarm. I'd forgotten that dogs are barking creatures, which was not the least of their flaws. They started barking, the lot of them, exposing me to deadly fire from the watchtowers. But the barking came to an abrupt halt when Jeep barged in between my legs. All their attention was for her. Where-were-ya-whadya-eat-whadya-smell-like? The four others shoved my little pup around, and she went all coy, flattened by their nuzzling snouts. Blondie pushed everyone out of the way and took the prodigal pup aside, sniffing, licking and rolling her over with her muzzle as if to make sure she was all in one piece. The little one submitted to the examination with tiny, happy sobs that would have brought tears to the eyes of the SPCA calendar crew. I had to get out of there before it caught up with me. I looked around just long enough to see how the shed was converted into a kennel, complete with exits in the form of trapdoors, mounds of food and doggy litter. One last look at the dog named Jeep, who had become just like the others—well, almost, because she had acquired something more evolved and less formless from her brush with adventure, and with me. Then I stepped outside.

"Can I help you?"

That voice, all honey and metal, with distrust so courteous it was more like an invitation to tea than an order to clear out. That amiable voice sent me higher into the air than a blast of buckshot in the ankles. Melody. Of course, Melody. Part of me had forgotten, for lack of concrete proof, that their existences— Pierre Laliberté's and her own—were very much entangled. Now, the concrete proof that had been missing stood staring me in the face. Why did she confront me like an intruder? She was the intruder, not me. I was gambling with Pierre, Pierre who was on his own and free, and no more players can join the game once the bets have been placed, and the cards turned face up.

"Can I help you?" she repeated, a notch more impatient.

She had emerged from behind the shed astride a bicycle, hair unkempt like a young girl, in sky-blue coveralls. The dogs rushed out to greet her with an enthusiastic din, all except for one, who'd missed the mark and was thumping my legs with her tail. That would be Jeep for sure, a meager, flawed consolation in this off-kilter moment.

"It's this dog," I stammered, "it's on account of this dog."

"What dog?"

The more time elapsed, the more suspicious and ill-tempered she became. A watch dog. As if there weren't enough of them already.

"Pierre gave me this dog, but I can't keep it. I'm here to return it."

Her face lightened.

"You're Florence," she said.

So. He told her about me. He told her what I haven't told a soul, not even to Zeno, my ramshackle other half, but my other half all the same. Talk about a sucker punch, talk about new and unsuspected depths of treachery and deception.

"We know each other," she stated. "We've met, haven't we?"

"Have we?"

She squinted with the effort of fitting the images together. I didn't help her, but she didn't need my help.

"New York," she said. "The Washington Irving Hotel."

"Yes, yes . . . That must be it."

She laughed, and I burst out laughing as well. The dogs joined us in their primal voices, but I kept up my guard. Everything about Melody drew into perfect focus, her explosive, irradiating warmth, and her genius for sucking energy from other people, carried out with both finesse and curiosity. Curiosity. Curiosity made it easy for her to digest. She could lick her plate clean and come back for seconds. Did Pierre Laliberté teach her, or did she rub off on him? How did she use the raw material she appropriated from other people? What did she change it into?

"What were you doing in New York again? You did tell me, didn't you?"

That genius of hers. No one else, with such an artlessly inquisitive question, would have gotten an answer.

"I was working. I'm in Web sites."

"Oh, yes," she said, pupils dilating with delight. "Web sites."

She waited for me to repeat or contradict my previous confessions, smothering me preemptively with affectionate interest. I chose to counterattack, since we were grappling out in the open, matching indiscretions.

"Curious, isn't it?" I remarked. "What a contrast. New York and . . . here. In St. Firmin-des-Anges."

"Des-Maures," she corrected, and smiled.

I dove in, minus the life jacket.

"Are you Pierre's wife?"

She gazed upon me for a moment, then laughed lightly, indulgently, as if entertaining the blunder of a small child, or a member of the simple-minded set.

"I'll tell him you were here," she promised.

Then she showed me her back, and trotted off towards the house alongside her bike. I stood there, arms at my sides, paralyzed by her bad manners. Is that how she dismisses me, tolerating no indiscretion from others, while she displayed it in abundance? I can slug it out as well as the next guy.

"Are you sure he isn't here?" I called after her.

She turned around slowly.

"His car's here," I insisted clumsily.

"But he isn't."

She went on smiling with that exaggerated cheeriness of hers.

"Please excuse me, but I must go inside. I'm looking after someone who's ill."

I didn't move. Let her know that I was ready to step through any opening she might provide. Even transform myself into a compassionate nurse to help her care for someone ill. Even if that person didn't exist.

"It's not Pierre," she added, politely mocking.

She walked away. She had no concern for me, she didn't want to know whether I was lost in this nowhere hamlet of St. Firmin-des-Maures, or if I could find my way home again, if I wanted a glass of water or a crust of bread. Not a shred of hospitality, zero. But wait, she was coming back.

"It's too bad," she began.

"Yes," I said weakly, full of hope.

"I'm talking about Jeep."

She pointed to the roiling pile of pups flopping over one another, gnawing at each other in mindless exhilaration. You would have to be pretty canny to recognize the dog called Jeep in the middle of that rudimentary mass.

"Too bad you can't keep her. We named her Jeep because she's rugged, built for off-road. And she always gets what she wants."

Really? Well, I'm touched. Where can I shed my tears without fear of flooding the flowerbeds?

She grasped the handlebars of her bike and threw me one last smile.

"A little like you, if I'm not mistaken."

She whistled and the dogs charged after her, Blondie hugging her side while her quarrelsome progeny brought up the rear.

I retraced my steps, heart sinking, appalled as much by myself as by her, as by him. Nothing was possible, everything was compromised, everything ruined. She saw in me everything she needed to see, then discarded me like a spit-soaked handkerchief. He rejected me too, and now he was hiding in there, somewhere behind the curtains, laughing to himself at how he made a fool out of me with his ridiculous gift, and just waiting to laugh along with her. I could picture them, arm in arm, snickering at my transparent lies, the poverty of my strategies, my youth—the two of them had more than 110 years between them, 110 years of stratagems and wily schemes that easily trumped my know-nothing quarter-century. All was lost, starting with my honor.

As I stood there, sniveling, a smell ambushed me and left me nonplused. I stopped for a moment and tried to understand where this perfumery fragrance came from, sugary and warm like a fresh-baked cake, the kind you want to slather over everything, and I can't even stand perfume. My nose on high alert, I sought out the source, sniffing high and low. Then I got it. It was the grass. Ordinary green grass that had grown so high you'd have to call it hay, for all I knew. The ordinary grass was exuding luxuriant emanations. Even the mind-dulling countryside has its share of surprises. I continued walking, and with my steps, my thread of bitterness, but my despair lacked conviction. Blame it all on that triumphant fragrance. Then I grasped what Pierre Laliberté, that master of deceit, meant after all. Space. Perspective. I saw the infinite field and in it a single clod of earth living its life among so many others, and on it a plethora of smells, plants, moisture, living creatures with legs and mandibles among which I clung to a handhold, tinier than the tickle of a tick, an enzyme churning out its proteins. Could there be anything more insignificant? No, there could not. I might as well start walking again, whistling, forgetting everything, looking for new fragrances, new spectacles, looking for my taxi. Me, an anxious enzyme. Here in this oversized universe, a taxi was waiting to return me to a civilization that knew nothing of St. Firmin-des-Maures. Wasn't that an excellent reason to whistle a happy tune, even to smile?

I walked past the house as if it wasn't there, though I had the feeling someone's eyes were following me. It would have to be him, of course, watching undercover, true to form, the cowardly schizophrenic I'd always suspected him of being. He disappointed me so deeply that I'd almost given up blaming him. But I decided to take him on. I looked up and caught sight of a head quickly withdrawing from the second window on the first floor, but not quickly enough: on my retina remained the ghostly afterimage of a black-haired head, a woman's head. A head so ferociously black that I recognized it immediately.

So began the second puzzle, in family fashion: Gina Da Sylva was staying at her sister's place, either ill or convalescing. But her sister's place was also her brother-in-law's, for among his diverse and illustrious titles, Pierre Laliberté was also a family man. And tonight the three of them would raise a glass together and trade information. Melody, Gina and Pierre.

The three of them, members of the same clan, under the same roof, were too powerful to get anywhere near. So powerful, when you get right down to it, that all I could do was run, find some neutral ground and collect what was left of my strength. If Gina was there with them, my anonymity, or what was left of it, would sustain fatal damage.

Too bad, but what does it really matter? Keep your chin up and scurry back to the safety of your burrow, climb into that taxi from hell and clear the hell out of here.

But the taxi was not where I left it. Anxiety or not, I kept on whistling. If you owe somebody a hundred dollars, he's not going to run out on you. It turned out I was right. The taxi came into view from around a curve and described an elegant loop before curtseying to me. The driver got out of the car, in high good humor.

"Nice part of the country," he said, opening the door for me. "I wouldn't half mind having a place out this way. Not you?"

"No, not me."

I sat down. Not he. He closed the door, took a deep breath and stretched.

"I was looking around, maybe there's a house for sale. The meter's off, don't worry."

"Did you find anything?"

"No," he said, disappointed.

"Good! So it's Montreal, on the double."

Reluctantly, he understood the order: Get into the car and get going. He sat down with a sigh, turned the key and let the motor idle. I caught his sidelong glance in the rearview mirror.

"Didn't you forget something?"

"No."

"Sure?"

Why was he staring at me in the mirror? Couldn't he see that every second meant that much less of a tip? No, he couldn't. Anyway, he wasn't looking at me. He was looking beyond me, at that portion of the universe that stretched out behind me. I turned around. Still far across the field, but rushing onward with rabid determination, a tiny dog was speeding towards us at full tilt.

"Get going!" I shouted at the driver.

"What?" he growled.

I repeated the order in my most colorless, threatening voice, and he pulled out, his disapproving glance oscillating between me and the space behind me. We moved off, God be praised. Thirty seconds and thirty meters farther, I turned around. It had reached the road, smaller than before because of the distance, but still running, running after us with all the unchained power of its tiny legs.

"Faster!" I ordered the driver.

He threw me an indignant look in the rearview mirror, and put his foot on the accelerator. Then suddenly we came to a stop.

"No, no, I won't do it."

The mutiny was on. Not only did he stop, he got out of the car. He knelt beside the open door, bleating and laughing tenderly.

"Poor little doggie-dog, my poor little puppy-poo . . ."

A panting, wheezing shape raced up and flung itself onto driver, door and front seat all at once, whatever was separating it from the object of its search, its ultimate target. The shape threw itself crying upon me as if I were the promised land. I sat there stiffly, my foundations shaking, as the tiny ball of sobbing fur covered me with kisses, trampled me, enveloped me in its prehistoric breath. There's something wrong, something terribly wrong, I have nothing to offer that might soothe or comfort, I am not a valid destination, and still, it turns you inside out to be so wanted in defiance of common sense.

"What do we do now?" asked the driver, sitting down again, eyes moist in canine solidarity.

We're going to take her back where she came from. There's no other solution, we're going to take her back because that's what we came here to do. We've already squandered a hundred dollars and any chance of friendship with the Laliberté clan. So let's be consistent and take her back.

Jeep took possession of my bony knees and snuggled up in a ball to sleep until the end of time. The driver switched on the meter and accelerated. I let them get away with it. I protested and raised my voice—all in silence. I let them get away with it.

The driver didn't miss his chance. He launched into a long story, voice quivering, hanky dabbing at his eyes, an epic tale of heroic dogs, golden retrievers just like this one who crossed entire mountain ranges, continents and raging rivers to find their masters. Meanwhile, I gnashed my teeth for want of a bone. As he rattled on, I growled at the she-dog on my lap, "Don't think I'm going to keep you. You're not mine and you never will be." She wagged her tail weakly at the sound of my voice and sighed beatifically. "Your name is ridiculous," I told her. "You won't be called Jeep for the two or three days you'll be staying under my roof. There's a limit. Nobody's going to stick me with the name of a car and a dog at the same time." Her tail hit cruising speed. "Look at me, puppy-dog, dog-house, outside dog, get out of my house, outhouse." She opened a golden eye and looked at me. *Outhouse.*

I smiled an acid smile at my own inspiration. The triumph of revenge over adversity. *"Outhouse.* How do you like that? That'll teach you to glom on to just anybody." She closed her eyes, her tail fell silent and she slipped into slumber, as satisfied as anyone could be.

15

THE FALL OF THE SKYSCRAPERS

I DIDN'T SEE IT COMING.

Earthshaking events should emit a particular aura just before they occur. A tiny tremor that would register on the bones of those paying attention.

I picked up the anxiety in Zeno's hyper-intense manner when he appeared at my door that afternoon, but anxiety is part of our daily diet. And he did hug me with unusual intensity, but every time he hugs me I find it unusual. So what was the difference?

"Any news from him?" he asked, once he finished hugging me.

Then he saw the thing coming straight at him, something that had no place in my house. The former Jeep with her little body wagging every which way, and his attention shifted away from Pierre Laliberté.

It was two days after our taxi ride, hers and mine.

"A dog!" he said in wonderment. "Well, aren't you a pretty one, aren't you a fine one, nice doggy, nice puppy wuppy . . . whoa, you're a she-dog, aren't you? What's your name?"

"Outhouse."

"Outhouse," he went on, starstruck. "What're you doing here? Who do you belong to?"

"You."

For one enormous second, he abandoned his amorous tickling of Outhouse. All that passed for love, all the chinks in the carapace of his indifference, were focused on me.

"Florence," he murmured.

Then he regained his self-control.

"Where did you find her? Did you get her pedigree? Golden retrievers can have all kinds of hidden defects."

"Come on, Zeno! What was Pokey's pedigree?"

He laughed, then kissed me. Outhouse, sensing the moment was about to go down in history, slithered between us and began to gnaw at my calves.

"My fabulous Florence."

Then he tore himself away from the slippery slope down which he had begun to slide, and began bestowing less compromising caresses on the head of his new animal.

"So, no news from him," he said, in the form of an afterthought.

But the tiny gleam of anxiety—I should have been more concerned—reappeared in the dark pupils of his eyes.

"I told you I'd let you know when I had any."

Then he explained why he'd been away for three days. It was all because of Suzie.

No matter what they say, Hollywood-style happy endings, dripping with special effects and saccharine tears, do exist in real life. The proof? Suzie discovered her birth certificate. It had been well and truly hidden, deep in the viscera of the house, between the wallboard and the bathroom mirror, the spot where a dream more premonitory than the others had led her, to the very spot where Tommy, the vanished Italian father, the grudging groom, had hidden it twenty years before. Suzie, armed with her founding document, her seal of authenticity, returned to claim her place in Kanesatake, which they agreed to give her. At last report, she was living in a dim two-room apartment that belonged to an old medicine woman, and a healing circle was looking after her neuroses after convincing her to throw away her antidepressants and similar ineffective white expedients. At last report, she was in seventh heaven in her tiny semi-basement, and her past in bleakest suburbia was up for sale.

"Wow," I said, completely shaken. "How are you taking it?"

"It's just fine for her," concluded Zeno tersely.

He looked at his watch and let out a brief, theatrical exclamation, as if to inform me that a life of excitement awaited him elsewhere, far from the boredom of my place.

"Why did you ask me to come?" he inquired in his bossman's voice.

"To take delivery of your new dog."

"Oh."

Meanwhile, Outhouse was noisily and showily displaying her existence, attacking both our heels equally in the interests of fairness, spewing her saliva over whatever seemed to lack moisture, ripping with theatrical fury into the scarf that had been her constant companion ever since I abandoned it to her and upsetting every apple cart she could lay eyes on. Zeno patted and contemplated her a little longer than necessary.

"Could you keep her for me for a while?" he finally asked.

"A while?"

"A day or two. Two weeks at the most."

"No."

"Look, right now I'm putting up somebody who's allergic to dogs."

"Somebody? A he or a she?"

I listened to my own irascible voice, and it left the taste of rusty sheet metal in my mouth. It wasn't exactly thrilling to hear.

"Listen to you," Zeno laughed. "You're like a shrew waving her rolling pin, a sex-starved biddy pushing sixty . . ."

"But I *am* sex-starved," I said with a clench-toothed smile.

We kicked each other a couple times for show, then laughed for real, then he dropped a kiss on my forehead.

"Pighead," he sighed. "You want me to tell you everything? I'll tell you everything. Maud's at my place. She helped me a lot with mother. She was the one who looked after her while I was at work."

Was he talking about the same Maud, our good friend Maud, the same Maud who drowned in her tears and was flushed down the drain a few months ago? Alas. A woman raised from the dead into a world already saturated with the living is never good news.

"You have to understand, Florence," said Zeno, repellent

in his shiny-faced good-fellowship, "that we have a few loose ends to tie up, her and me, we were interrupted halfway through, before we could reach closure . . ."

I looked at him with great attention, hoping he would at least realize what he was and wasn't saying. What about the two of us, when do we tie up our loose ends, haven't we been stuck in one big coitus interruptus for the last few centuries? He didn't even notice my look. He'd started teasing Outhouse, trying to pry my tattered scarf from her mouth, and Outhouse and he were enjoying every minute of it. My scarf and I were getting the short end of the stick.

"Do you want the dog or don't you?" I barked at him.

"Of course I want it."

"Then take it right now."

"Florence, two weeks at the most."

"Since when is your lady Lazarus allergic to dogs?"

"Since the beginning."

"What about Pokey?"

"She put up with him."

"And she can't put up with this one?"

"No."

"Why not? Will it kill her? Will she break out in hives? Will her teeth fall out?"

"She's allergic, Florence."

"Why two weeks? What are you going to do after two weeks? Flush her down the toilet?"

"She's moving into her own apartment."

"You mean you're breaking up? How sad!"

"Flora."

"Are you separating after two weeks or not?"

"She rented an apartment."

"But you're going to go on seeing each other."

"It all depends."

"On the weather conditions? On the value of the Canadian dollar?"

"On where we're at. I'm really being patient with you, you know."

"How can I thank you?"

Par for the course. One of our best-loved numbers, with me in the role of the crawling slug, and he as the lipstick-smeared supermale. Then suddenly the wind shifted, and I didn't even know why. Zeno got all nervous and self-righteous.

"What right do you have to put on a scene? Did I ask you any questions about the last night you spent with Pierre Laliberté?"

It was nothing short of a gift, a chance to win back a little vertical dignity. I drew myself up to full height.

"For me, it's been ages. But with you, it's nonstop."

"It's been ages," he repeated, suddenly very quiet. "So you're admitting it actually happened?"

"What?" I said cautiously.

"You and him, screwing away in the same bed instead of talking philosophically and platonically about writing and fate, like you pretended, and like I was naive enough to believe."

"One doesn't rule out the other," I replied.

To this day I'm still convinced that the collapse had already begun, that I had added nothing to it. Even today, I try to see myself as innocent of all that followed, as if I did not belong to this ball of earth wobbling through the void among all the other bodies, as if we weren't all hopelessly tangled in a cosmic organism so monstrous that the faintest breath, the most innocent lie, would touch off a blaze, even from an incalculable distance.

"Do you love me, Florence?" Zeno suddenly asked.

"What does that have to do with it?" I stammered, taken aback.

"Because if you loved me, if I knew for certain you loved me, things would have been different from the start."

He couldn't have meant that honestly, spoken in the middle of the afternoon in the middle of my living room. I blushed, then turned pale. I couldn't put on a convincing face.

"You know I do, Zeno Mahone," I blurted out angrily.

"So say it. Say, Zeno, I love you."

"I've said it a million times."

"Never! Not once!" he retorted, serious.

I burst out laughing to show him how grotesque the situation was. He didn't move a muscle. He expected something from me, but I knew he would stop at nothing to humiliate me.

"I know you think you love me, Florence," he said softly, "and that's why you get so upset when other women turn up."

"I don't give a shit about your other bimbos!"

"You'd like to love me," Zeno continued, his voice soft and despairing, "but it never gets any farther than that. It never got beyond intentions, never."

"You don't know what you're talking about!"

"Say, I love you, Zeno."

"What do you want? Do you always have to win every single argument?"

He'd driven me back into the corner where it hurt the most. My eyes were wet and my voice quavered, but he showed me no mercy.

"Do you love me, yes or no?" he asked.

"There are lots of other ways of saying it besides saying it," I argued plaintively.

"No. Sometimes words are everything. Only words count."

He waited, standing before me, a weak, defeated smile on his lips, as if he were the one who lost something, and not me.

But he could wait all he wanted. I didn't say, *I love you, Zeno.* Even under torture, I didn't say it.

Afterwards, we each went our own way, in the pay of Mahone Inc. A little stunned, for sure, and relieved, him no less than me, to be temporarily apart. But I saw nothing virulent or irremediable in the mutual abrasion we seemed to thrive on.

Immediately afterwards—and we know there's no such thing as chance—I met Pierre Laliberté.

I was on my way to meet someone else, a client, a woman my age who went by the same name as me, which she revised and updated to Flore Crystal, because couldn't accept the dishonor of platitudes, or so she'd informed me over the telephone. That made me feel just fine, thank you. She agreed to meet me in the far eastern reaches of the city, on a street corner where I couldn't miss her, for she'd be performing her act there.

That was where I found Flore Crystal, an emaciated, angular young woman who dreamed of being big big big by "unveiling the ambience" to the astonishment of a handful of passersby. Every street corner in the universe has a secret soul, upon which the strata of past and future accumulate, and which lie waiting to be laid bare by a visionary. That was Flore Crystal's concept. She aspired to invitations from around the world, to scan the depths of street corners in foreign cities. She had the highest expectations of Mahone Inc. I spotted her from a distance, on top of a rough stage, swaying to some faintly Arab-sounding music. She'd set up pots of plastic flowers and palm trees on the sidewalk, baskets of fruit and used books among which anybody and his brother could rummage. Behind her hung a backdrop of sand dunes.

She'd gone to a lot of trouble. That was the most I could say.

First her, then him. He was winding his way through the crowd of the curious, shrouded in his blue sweater, eyes concealed by dark glasses, about to continue on his way. I headed straight for him without any strategy.

He recoiled when he saw me.

I'll always remember that reaction with a lump in my throat.

He had recoiled. But immediately, or almost, he righted himself and met me head-on. He even removed his dark glasses.

We looked each other over, as cautious as cats. I waved vaguely in the direction of the performance artist, and mumbled that I was here to see her. What a coincidence, running into him in this part of town.

"True coincidences are rare," he said in his serious voice.

Filthy liar, was what he really thought. I could tell.

As stoically as possible, I held my own against his gaze. I was completely convinced that he could find no fault with me.

Well, almost nothing, maybe a few little secrets, but certainly nothing greater than his.

"Let's go for a drink," I implored.

He put his dark glasses back on, and turned away a moment to consider the offer.

"Now?" he said, hesitating.

Of course now. Now, because anyone could see that later might never exist. When it came to us, "later" was a risky proposition. I stared at him without looking away, wanting to preserve the imprint of his ordinary face, fearing that this time really would be the last.

"Okay," he relented.

"Where? The usual place? Raspberries.Com?"

If I'd hoped to touch him by summoning up fragments of our mutual past, I was sadly mistaken. With a categoric wave of his hand, he brushed aside my nostalgia-soaked proposal.

"No, no. I don't go there anymore. Let's make it somewhere close by."

We started walking, side by side, stiff and silent. Gradually we relaxed, our arms touched accidentally, we lost our self-consciousness. The sun poured down on our heads, surprisingly triumphant for this late stage of summer. It was so warm and quiet that everything seemed to have turned its back on chaos.

In the distance, not far as the crow flies, New York was still intact.

We stopped at the corner, in front of a tavern converted to a topless bar. From inside came the pungent odor of smoke, beer and urine. He started to go in, but I grabbed him by the sleeve to hold him back. I thought of Flore

Crystal disporting herself on her pitiful stage in a demonstration of her art. Once you give your word, even to a stranger, you have to keep it.

"I need to tell the performance artist," I said.

He considered me briefly through his dark glasses.

"Go ahead."

"You're not going to run out on me?"

He took off his glasses and gave me an unfiltered smile. There was still a chance I might get back into his warmth.

"I'll be at the back, as far from the door as possible," he said.

Outside again, revived by the raw light of the sun, I thought not of Flore Crystal, but Zeno. His look of defeat returned to overwhelm me as his voice sprung up inside me, a tragic echo spreading sadness: *Do you love me, Florence? Do you love me?*

There was only one way to answer him, right now, to break my own mean-spirited, cowardly silence, my refusal to commit. With tears in my eyes, I squatted down right there on the sidewalk and connected my laptop with the hateful cellphone I used only for such purposes. I reached him immediately, on line as usual.

;-)? I entered. (How are you?)

;-)! he answered. (Not bad)

PL! (Pierre Laliberté is here.)

??? (Where? When? Are you serious?)

1394 FRO! I ended.

That's all I needed to say for us to share the world again. I got to my feet and headed for the topless bar at 1394 Frontenac where Pierre Laliberté was waiting, without a thought for Flore

Crystal, who was still disporting herself atop her sidewalk stage, for I'd exhausted my last reserves of honesty.

Entering the darkness of the bar after blinding sunlight was like penetrating the perfect opposite of our galaxy, a place where all things had been turned inside out like a glove, the better to reveal their true nature. Guided by the television screen on which stark-naked girls were dancing, and by a swarm of tiny lights blinking in the gloom, I found my way between the tables to the farthest extremities of space, where Pierre Laliberté was sitting. Two of those mysterious little lights gleamed close by him. It took me a while to realize they belonged to the fluorescent pasties stuck to the nipples of the girl who was taking his order.

"Lemonade for you?" Pierre Laliberté asked, more jovial than a few minutes ago.

"No, whatever you're having."

He ordered two whiskies and the lights flitted away.

"Do you bring your wife here?"

My question took him by surprise. I hadn't expected it myself. It popped up and I'd latched onto it as the first step towards a possible ending between us, happy or otherwise.

"You mean Melody?"

"Isn't she your wife?"

He thought it over for a moment.

"Yes, yes," he concluded, with a smile.

And in the same breath, still smiling, he added, "Women in general don't like it here."

Women in general, meaning not me, meaning instead the wives and mistresses and all the others he might have given vulgar kisses to, but never brought into this fetid place. I was none of the above, I was undefined, a living aside, maybe not even a woman in his eyes. Instead of being insulted, I appreciated the privilege of having indeterminate status. I wasn't threatened or miserable or even in love. Suddenly I realized that all that had gone on between us from the very beginning was nothing less than freedom. He put his hand on mine. The sheer spontaneity of it was a confirmation of the rightness of our curious association.

"I'm glad you decided to keep Jeep," he said.

Over my dead body, I said silently. Better not contradict him. The expression of frustration on my lips was enough.

"Quite a gift," I muttered.

His smile broadened into happiness, and the undressed waitress returned just as we were about to break into laughter. Four glasses full of ice cubes tinkled at the same level as her luminescent breasts. She put our order on the table, but kept her breasts for herself, after dangling them negligently over the table.

"It isn't happy hour yet," she said cheerily, "but I'm giving you the special, seeing as there aren't too many customers."

"You're very kind," replied Pierre Laliberté, handing her a twenty-dollar bill, completely at home amid all the exposed skin.

He eyed her most strategic places as if she'd been dressed, and the next minute looked away. My horizons were more restricted. The girl's right buttock rubbed amicably against my shoulder while she made change, as though we were recently separated Siamese twins longing to share the same circulatory system again. I dared a sidelong glance. Her body wasn't that young, though with the plump ones you never can tell. Having a lot of flesh attracts so much attention that it ends up adding weight, whatever the age. She wasn't completely naked: a tiny flesh-colored triangle lurked between her thighs, in addition to the two fluorescent pasties that so successfully focused attention on what they concealed. Those three minuscule zones, the only ones hidden from view, seemed to concentrate all her sensuality, as if sensuality needed a whiff of the forbidden to survive.

That's what I thought, but what did I really know?

I had one last intuition as I watched her leaning against the bar, scratching a breast absentmindedly. She was no longer in that naked body offered for display. No one had access to the place where she was at that moment, least of all the men who were looking at her. When it comes to hiding, nudity was just as effective as an Afghan burka. Then she moved away, breaking off the communication.

After that, all my attention went to divining the early warning signs of revelation or catastrophe, and I lost sight of the afternoon's other living beings.

"Melody treated you a bit coolly the other day," Pierre Laliberté began, halfway through his first whisky.

Melody. Yes. We had to speak of Melody at this point in our confused relationship, if we wanted to disperse the fog. Yes, Melody had treated me coolly, quite cavalierly in fact. Melody had judged and condemned me based on an accumulation of coincidences too rare to be true. Directly thereafter, Gina, sister-in-law and queen of the tarantulas, would have driven the final nail into my coffin. My credibility in the eyes of Pierre Laliberté?

Zero. Yet he'd just clinked his whisky glass against mine, and his soft buffalo eyes gazed benevolently upon me.

By then it was obvious that neither he nor I had any interest in displaying the naked truth, the topless truth. What use truth if not to tear away the thick cushions that protect us against unbearably sharp objects? Let the hard truth dissolve at the bottom of our shot glasses, I begged him in silence.

"Melody is very protective, very maternal," he went on.

Where was he heading, if not towards confession? I felt my heart struggling to break away from me, to break free from this place.

"What does she protect you against?"

"A couple is more than just two people who snore in the same bed because they've known each other for twenty years."

I pictured Melody in Herald Square, melting euphorically into the arms of another man. What did he know about the other half of the couple when she was beyond his grasp?

"A couple isn't a prison cell either," he concluded, emptying his first glass and starting in on the second.

He knew.

"What is a couple, then?" I ventured, relieved that the careening conversation was heading away from us.

"You and I, for instance, we're a kind of couple," he said with soft, mocking laughter.

I blushed, as if he'd declared his love for me.

"You and your computer are a couple. We're constantly forming couples with whatever we do. Then the couple breaks up, or doesn't break up, depending on the time allowed it."

Very well. Me and my laptop make a couple. Him and his whisky. Outhouse and my shredded scarf. Taken that broadly, a declaration of love was completely devalued.

"Florence, I really like what's gone on between us, what's going on between us."

Back on familiar ground. His way of putting my name at a distance, conjugating it in the past tense—it was all heading for a dismissal. I awaited the next step with something bordering on curiosity.

"But it's all based on a misunderstanding," he said, finishing off his glass in one gulp.

I stared at him intently. Now what? His brown eyes were distant, floating, troubled.

"What misunderstanding?"

A pause. He scratched his nose, picked up one of my glasses of whisky, then applied his liquid gaze on me.

"I'm not who you think I am."

Behind him, a backwash had deposited new customers at several tables. The girls with the starry breasts began to waft through space, quenching thirsts as rapidly as they could. I could see the tiny lights blinking like distant beacons, calling me back to the surface, warning me not to slip beneath the dark waters of Pierre Laliberté's words, and his eyes that opened onto the abyss.

"It's not me, Florence."

He jarred my hand, forcing me to react.

It took a hell of a lot of energy just to dare to understand the meaning of his words. The moment of truth was nothing like I imagined it would be. If he wasn't Pierre Laliberté, the invisible writer who had despoiled my paternal inheritance, who was he, and what was I?

I withdrew my hand from his grasp.

"What did you do with my father's last words?"

That was the point to which we had to return, the source of all possible misunderstandings.

"I passed them on to someone else," he sighed. "Someone else used them."

And then Zeno showed up.

I needed only a fraction of a second to see how shocked he was. As he headed for our table, he was looking at me alone. "Flora," he stammered, "Flore Crystal told me to tell you . . ." Then he halted, long enough to improvise the aria of the tenor who has just realized that his duet is a trio. He turned to Pierre Laliberté.

"Excuse me, I won't be disturbing you for long."

Pierre Laliberté raised a friendly hand to indicate that the disturbance was bearable.

"Flore Crystal will meet you tomorrow at the office," Zeno concluded in a tremulous voice.

As a performance, it was zero to the nth degree.

Calmly, I did the introductions.

"Zeno, Pierre."

Then I added, "Zeno is half my work couple," which was intended as an in-joke between Pierre Laliberté and me, but Zeno nodded vigorously, words failing him.

"I remember you," Pierre Laliberté smiled. "From Therios's place."

Zeno collapsed onto a chair between us, then stabilized himself long enough to stare shamelessly.

"I'm afraid I don't recognize you."

"Would you like a whisky?" Pierre Laliberté asked.

I proceeded to withdraw. I didn't go too far away, I could return any time, and I certainly gave every appearance of being there. But in reality, I was perched high atop an observation tower, trying to understand, intent on remaining motionless and attentive until the slippery truth could be pinned down by fact. Something palpable had to exist in the situation we found ourselves in: Zeno making contact at last with Pierre Laliberté who had just told me he wasn't Pierre Laliberté. But that something escaped me.

Zeno had managed to restore a semblance of self-control, but he was still as tense as an overstrung violin. Pierre Laliberté displayed the lightness of a prisoner emerging into fresh air. From high above, I observed them both.

They were talking about Therios.

"He's back," said Pierre Laliberté. "I saw him on the street, but he didn't see me."

"Impossible," said Zeno.

"It was him, for sure," said Pierre Laliberté.

"He must have had some things to settle before going back to open his inn."

"I've got the feeling he's back for good," Pierre Laliberté insisted.

They were nattering away like a couple of old biddies, but their shared delight was suspicious. Only a dispassionate observer could appreciate the efforts both were exerting to paper over their dishonesty. Of the two, Zeno's struggle was the more heroic. A part of him had managed to stay afloat and speak, and be reasonable, bring his glass to his lips and return it to the proximity of the other glasses on the table after having swallowed a mouthful corresponding exactly to his ingestive capacity. The other part—the part caught up in wild emotion, that threatened to faint or to explode—had sought refuge in his eyes, and it avidly devoured everything in sight. Pierre Laliberté's hand lying on the table, the sleeve of his blue sweater, a fragment of his face. Then, slowly, the second part, the starving part, began to overtake the first, successfully prodding him, inch by inch, to draw his chair nearer, so that he was constantly rubbing against Pierre Laliberté's arm. What did he look like? Some shameless gay pick-up artist, the kind who always gets the quick brush-off.

What about Pierre Laliberté? Nothing was clear, except this: No matter which way I reshuffled the available hypotheses, I reached the same conclusion. From the start, he played the wide-eyed innocent grafted onto the head of a colossal liar. One: he wasn't the great invisible author, though he'd known all along that I thought he was, and done nothing to dispel my illusions. Two: he *was* the great invisible author, he could feel things heating up, so he clumsily invented a way out that I swallowed hook, line and sinker, like a hungry carp. The more I watched him trying to be a regular guy, all palsy-walsy with Zeno, who kept stroking his arm, the more I was sure that his final turnabout was so much hogwash, the more certain I was, deep down in the gut that never lies, that no else one but him, the illuminated grand master of stars and frogs, could have written the books I'd read.

Zeno had skated over to familiar ice that demanded little. He was talking about Mahone Inc. with a few non-compromising generalities: what a curious job it was, what strange people you meet, each a self-contained universe, a universe we had to size up in a few hours and sum up in a few bytes, the kind of work only a fool or a maniac would get mixed up in. Flora excelled at this kind of work, by the way. Pierre Laliberté seemed extraordinarily interested.

"What kind of people come to you?" he asked with a glance in my direction.

"Everybody," said Zeno. "Artists, mechanics, restaurant owners."

He could have said, People like your sister-in-law, Gina Da Sylva. Instead, he added, quite deliberately, "People who are dying for visibility. We sell visibility."

Pierre Laliberté nodded, then looked at me, encouraging me to join the fun. I motioned that I would pass, pointing to my glass of whisky.

"Florence, are you sick?" asked Zeno, falsely solicitous.

"Not yet."

Pierre Laliberté bathed me in his chocolate gaze once more, that deceitful gaze. This time I endured it with the greatest transparency I could summon so he could read, if indeed he could read the tormented auras of human beings, in my sardonic smile and hard stare, that I had seen through him at last.

He could read. He was troubled. He looked at his glass of whisky, then abruptly stood up.

"I've got to be going," he said.

"No, please," Zeno insisted. "I was just leaving. Stay."

He put his hand on his arm with enough pressure to force Pierre Laliberté to stop, neither standing nor seated.

"Stay," Zeno reiterated.

His voice dropped a notch, and with it his self-control. He turned to me, begging for help.

"Tell him to stay, Florence," he implored. "You haven't finished . . ."

"Nothing is ever finished," I volunteered, more bitch than philosopher.

Pierre Laliberté picked up his bag like a fugitive determined to flee. Zeno grabbed him violently by the arm.

"Wait! Do you have a pen?"

Pierre Laliberté hesitated between perplexity and concern, then opened his briefcase and pulled out a black ballpoint pen. He handed it to Zeno. Ever so slowly, Zeno took it. He squeezed it in his hand. Instead of using it to write, he slipped it into his pocket.

"I'm keeping it," he said, his voice bordering on exultation.

Pierre Laliberté suddenly realized who he was dealing with. Zeno was a rabid admirer, a dedicated Lalibertophile. A flash of sheer terror swept across his face, then he departed like a shot, without so much as goodbye for me.

He did not get far.

Violent light flooded the place. Every fluorescent tube in the bar was switched on at once, and in a hubbub of chairs being pushed back from tables, people who'd been sitting got to their feet, they were pointing lights at him, and cameras, and microphones, several men and a woman, all equally determined.

"Are you Pierre Laliberté the writer? Can you look this way, please? Are you really Pierre Laliberté? Could you say something so we can hear your voice?"

I'd never seen a cornered animal before. The terrifying spectacle must be the same for deer, or foxes or hare. The same agony, the same terror when the trap snaps closed, or the shot is fired.

Pierre Laliberté tried to retreat. He collided with a table that had been pushed against the wall. He wheeled around in search of an escape route, but no escape was possible, except at the far end of the bar, which was as tightly sealed as a safe. One of the journalists, more clever than the rest, blocked the door to the toilet, his camera still running, and Pierre Laliberté took refuge against the far wall, trying with all his strength to claw his way out. The pack followed him, blinding him with their lights.

I watched him shrivel up like a caterpillar touched by a burning match. I watched him gasp in the rarified air, suffering the kind of panic attack that could cause death. I stood up and shouted, "Leave him alone! Leave him alone!" Then I lost sight of him beyond the circle of hunters.

I grabbed Zeno's arm. He had to do something! I saw he was crying. He turned to me, streams of tears flowing down his cheeks but cleansing nothing. Dirty water cleans nothing. I collapsed onto my chair. The floor seemed to fall away.

"Zeno, you didn't do it, did you? Tell me you didn't do it."

He continued to cry silently, without answering me. That was his answer.

Then the circle of hunters began to move and cracks appeared in their wall. Pierre Laliberté burst out, butting and punching with the strength of desperation. He broke into a run, pushing past the people blocking the door, overturning anything that stood between him and freedom.

The hunters dashed off after him.

The bar lights switched off. Everything went back to normal, quiet and sordid. The real customers returned to their seats. The girls began to flit through the darkness, decked out in their little falling stars.

Zeno and I finally got to our feet. We went out, mute and delirious as zombies. On the sidewalk, I didn't even look at him. "Don't you walk beside me," I told him, and he immediately obeyed, letting me take the lead towards nowhere. One of the photographers from the pack came towards him, and I stopped to listen. He was wearing a *New York Times* jacket.

"That's not him! The guy claims he didn't write that stuff!"

"Sure," mumbled Zeno. "What did you expect?"

"He claims his wife did. Apparently his wife wrote all his books, using his name. Do you know his wife?"

For a brief instant no one else existed on a street normally so crowded at rush hour. Even the sun had sunk from the shock of the impact, leaving no one but Zeno, the photographer and me standing in opaque silence. I looked to Zeno; sharing was an old habit. He was looking at me, his eyes wide with amazement, seeking my reaction too, out of the same instinct.

"Melody," we both whispered.

I didn't protest, not even deep inside. All at once everything about this bomb blast was probable and enlightening.

"No," Zeno told the photographer. "I don't know her."

ON THE NEXT DAY, only a few hours later, in New York, the monstrous event took place that sent the known universe veering off in a completely unknown direction. Like so many people, I withdrew from life to track the ebb and flow of the catastrophe on the television screen. Without wanting to be cynical, I was not surprised at not being totally surprised. All worlds are destined to collapse. It is only a matter of time.

But I never imagined I would feel so much pain. In that gaping hole where once there had been splendor, there lay so many corpses, so much agony, an opaque energy so dense it could never dissipate. I wept for the magic. The pure magic of catching sight of the lacy Manhattan skyline from the air, the sacred magic of a mountain 110 stories tall witnessing the prodigious fact of human birth, the magic that now lay buried deep beneath the ruins.

The terrible parallel was obvious. True coincidences are rare indeed.

I could not help but see beneath the rubble, among the wreckage of the magic, the smoking remains of the man who, for me, had been Pierre Laliberté.

16

WE'RE ALL POOR SLOBS

———————

*T*HERIOS IS BACK for good.

He acquired another taverna a few doors north of the old one, on Saint Denis, and opened it after a few slapdash renovations. That was where we all regrouped, former regulars, a couple dozen dedicated skordalia and garidosalata eaters. Zeno and I were part of the group, together at the same table for the first time since the Catastrophe.

But not Pierre Laliberté.

Therios wandered among the tables, regaling us with the final morsels of his personal epic, setting off laughter and lifted glasses of retsina. Soon it would be our turn. As we waited, we'd just have to put up with being together, Zeno and I, in the new booth Therios set aside for us, as if our tandem hadn't been flattened by a steamroller, as if we could still possibly be what we no longer were.

We ate without looking at one another. Zeno, a shadow of himself, wan, pitiable, the battered-child eyes beneath his glasses constantly begging for something, a glance, a caress. I no longer had anything to give him. Not even pity, that ugly remnant that sometimes flickers on when love has been extinguished.

In the middle of the meal, with an unsteady hand, he took out some pages printed off the Web and laid them close to my plate.

"Did you read it?" he asked, exhausted by the hunger to communicate.

I threw it a glance.

"Yes."

A piece of the *New York Times,* a short article buried among the reports on the aftermath of the Catastrophe. It would take an eagle eye to find. I had the eye; Zeno too. A fragment of the telephone interview Melody had given the newspaper to relieve her partner once and for all of the immense false responsability that had been his. She had confessed to being the reclusive author Pierre Laliberté, but refused to give any other details, be they salacious or bizarre. Cold fury dripped from each of her words. She concluded by saying, "This is the last time you'll hear my voice, and I swear you'll never see my face."

"Really, it's incredible. Don't you think it's incredible?"

"No."

I pictured her again, tripping the light fantastic along the sidewalks of New York, gleaning the humanity of human beings with total impunity, taking notes in the unutterable comfort of secrecy. Such power flowed from her that if I'd looked on her with truly open eyes, if I'd already known how to practice the peripheral gaze that the other Pierre Laliberté, the counterfeiter, had taught me later, I would have seen beyond all doubt that hers was the power of a creator, of a writer.

"It's true," said Zeno. "I reread all her books from the new point of view. It's clear as day, the writing is that of a woman. It has all the baroque savagery of a woman. What I don't understand is how I could have missed it all this time."

I turned my head in his direction to stab him in the eyes.

"Did you get your reward?"

His gaze fluttered uncomprehendingly.

"My reward?"

"Your Judas money. Your fifty thousand U.S."

He slumped back against the upholstered booth and pushed his plate away.

"No," he said. "Thank God, I got nothing. After all, I didn't deliver the right . . . the right . . ."

"The right victim," I concluded.

"Yes."

Impulsively, he grabbed my hand. I pulled it away in disgust.

"Flora, Florence," he said in a broken voice. "I'd give anything to take it all back, to never have done it. I don't know what got into me, Florence. It was like a blackout, like I'd lost consciousness. An attack of madness. Help me, Florence, help me, please."

"The Bishop Syndrome," I muttered coldly.

He stared at me, shattered. Suddenly Therios appeared before us, bantering and overflowing with warmth, an extraterrestrial from a happy planet from which we'd been expelled long ago.

"Well, if it isn't my little flower, along with her pine-eater," he cooed. "How are my little lovebirds? Not married yet?"

A sob rose in my throat. I masked it as a hiccough of laughter. Zeno began talking fast.

"We've got an office now, you know, a superb joint, bigger than your restaurant."

"Bigger!" roared Therios. "So, playing the snob, are we now? You're not trying to tell me you won't be coming to my place anymore, when the only reason I came back was to put the two of you up for free!"

He sat down at our table to deliver the rest of his spiel.

When Therios returned to his island a few months earlier, everything was as blue and beautiful as he'd remembered it. He spent his first weeks swimming in the sea, getting sunburned, whiling away the hours in tavernas around countless shots of ouzo and plates of meze, splicing together the thread of his previous existence with his old pals, none of whom had left their homeland, not even to be buried. That was when the first error insinuated itself into his ideal postcard.

"Once you start wanting to move, you can't put up with people who sit around all day."

Specialists at sitting around all day they were, every last one of them, people sustained by a rhythm so deliberate, so different from his, that he'd begun to feel more a stranger in the land of his birth than in the other, the gray snowy one he'd never stopped complaining about.

"They don't know anything if they haven't seen it on television. Can you imagine, they didn't even know people speak French in Montreal? Plus those Mediterranean types are nothing but trouble. I couldn't stand myself if I had to put up with so many lousy copies of me all at once."

Beneath the jokes and laughter, you could sense the heartbreak at having to abandon the dream he'd maintained with such longing during the long Quebec winters, pulling himself away again from his universe of origin, knowing this time would be the last. He'd held on as long as he could, refurbishing his house, drawing up plans to enlarge it, hiring carpenters and masons. Then he got out of bed one morning, looked in the mirror and could not recognize himself. He decided to pay a visit to the graveyard.

"I had a talk with my father," he said, getting to his feet. "I asked him, 'Babba, does a son have the right to change this much? Can a son feel so uprooted from the soil of his ancestors?' Well, you won't believe me, but a fabulous cloud floated over the sun, and in July in Argostoli there are never any clouds. Dimitrios was telling me to leave. Dimitrios would have done exactly the same thing. The truth is," he added, topping up our glasses of retsina, "I was starting to get homesick for our referendums, for our slush. Anyway, I didn't make the trip for nothing, I brought back some new recipes. You know what's the lastest word in the fish restaurants, in Plaka?"

He pretended to wait for our answer, then dropped it on us with a gale of laughter, before accosting the next table.

"Sushi!"

Then we were alone again, feeling a little lighter in spite of ourselves, thanks to the Therios Express, a hint of a smile on our lips. Zeno looked at me and mistook my expression for openness.

"I've got my tank. I'll give you a lift to Mahone Inc."

"I'm working at home from now on."

My answer removed any hint of a good mood from him. He watched as I conscientiously deposited my share of the bill on the table, as I stuffed my stuff back into my bag, as I threw my coat over my shoulders. You could have heard a ghost flit by.

"I don't want to see you anymore. We can keep in touch on the Web. If it doesn't work out, I'll let you know, I'll look into finding another job."

My voice was steady, free of belligerence. From where I stood, on the dry ground of lucidity, there was no more room for sloppy or aggressive sentimentality. Zeno got to his feet, even paler than a few moments before. He left a huge bill on the table. He picked up his personal effects, his laptop and the keys to his van. He followed me out, a couple steps behind. We waved goodbye to Therios in perfect synchronization.

He couldn't help himself. He trotted after me when we got outside. I stopped to dot the *i*'s and cross the *t*'s one last time.

"I want to walk. Alone."

"I understand," he stammered. "I understand. I . . . I'm going to work."

That was how we separated, without a drumroll or weepy violins. You couldn't have imagined a scene more ordinary.

SINCE OUTHOUSE TOOK me by storm, I've been doing a lot of walking. Every afternoon I take her out for a walk, sometimes until nightfall. It's the only time of the day I know she won't be inventing some new and original way of tearing the house apart. Besides, walking calms the sense of fear and keeps it from turning into pure angst.

Here I am again, stagnating in an intolerable transition. Where can I possibly go? Should I do something, or abstain from doing anything? Transitions are booby-trapped tunnels. If you're in a hurry to reach the other end, you might fall into the abyss. You don't know what's ahead, you don't know what's chasing you. No matter which way you turn, you smell the scent of sulfur.

Before, I had Zeno. There could have been stronger guardrails, but at least he fit my shape, and my modest requirements.

Then I had Pierre Laliberté. Briefly, without ever really having him, the residual gleam of a diamond in a strongbox snapped shut too fast.

Now what?

I stroll along, the dog nipping at my heels, each of us caught up in her own concerns. She sniffs, chews, urinates, dashes back and forth, but never lets me out of sight. I let her run free, so as not to impede the flow of her karma. Who knows, maybe today's the day that a fabulous fate will be hers, far from my side. But she's no mad dog: she hovers close to my wake, indifferent to the praise dispensed by dog lovers as she bounds by. You could swear she's gotten wise to the fact that her loss would not be the cruelest blow to my existence.

When I'm out walking, I can accept the idea of having nothing, no guardrail, no certainty, no treasure I can call my own. I'm willing to feel light, since the tireless earth continues to support me.

Not this time. This time, out walking, I take a sledge-hammer to the statue of Pierre Laliberté. To do that, I need to make myself heavy. All that had been ours together, from the first liquid glance at the hospital to the dog trotting along behind me rubbing my leg, all the words, spoken and written, the broad space between us, the ease, the temperature of his hand when it touched mine, the magical underside of life I saw thanks to him, the glowing current of his eyes mixed with the sweetish burn of tequila. All that added up to a reinforced concrete idol that wouldn't be easy to topple. But I was working at it, and I'd succeed.

He wrote nothing. Neither *Raspberries,* nor *Falterlust,* not *You Love You,* nor the seditious *Recreated Creatures.* He'd usurped floodlights that were not meant for him. What did he look like without the artificial light that gave him his brilliance? A dead star, a black dwarf. A poor slob.

Of course, something remained. The warmth of his gaze, his intuition for the invisible that had led him into such over-heated soliloquies, his pure curiosity, powerful enough to keep him standing watch over the decomposing bodies of perfect strangers for a month at the hospital.

Admit it. A nice enough guy. A nice guy a little more awake than the rest, a bit freer, but that's it. The kind of nice guy that the baby boom generation produced by the shovelful, former hippies who have recycled themselves as businessmen or consultants. Unless, like him, they're too socially maladjusted to make their peace with money and power.

Maladjusted—that's clear enough. More than maladjusted: a failure, a guy on the dole, a would-be street person, a drunk pretending to be something else, a guy without a job and without a cent, a liar inventing conspiracy theories in bars instead of putting his shoulder to the wheel of the grand global machine. A loafer, a parasite.

A parasite, yes, that's it, a parasite. A marital parasite.

What has he been living off of all these years? Off Melody. Melody's royalties, that's for sure, but less prosaically and more fundamentally, he was living off Melody's radiance, relying on the oxygen she generated, depending totally on her quest. She combusts and burns and invents everything. He's just the spear carrier, the talentless assistant. He was happy just to lug his meager combustibles to the central burners, stuff he'd gathered nosing through rubbish heaps and dumpsters, a sentence gleaned at the bedside of a dying man, a flash of genius floating on the surface of his tenth whisky. He fetched it and brought it home, his mistress's good doggy and faithful helper, and mistress gave him a pat or a biscuit or a kick in the ribs, and doggy crawls back to his corner, tongue dragging to the ground in search of new scraps of refuse.

Not surprising he loved dogs, the kind with real fur that go *woof woof* and produce slobber by the gallon.

A poor slob.

Walking and walking, and not looking where I was going, I found myself on Sherbrooke Street, not far from my high-tech stable. How long did it take me to topple that other magnificent statue, the high hope of guaranteed happiness that was Mahone Inc., finally ensconced among the old stones and mahogany, here in a district that struts and boasts, We've made it at last?

Two days, I think. The third time I stepped into the incarnation of my sumptuous dreams, the third time I sat down at the desk that had been outfitted in thousand-dollar increments, I realized that this was not it.

Two days. Not much pleasure after all.

Has anything remained standing among the fallen statues? Did anything endure? Beneath the incessant coming and going of forms that rise, the better to fall to pieces, can we count on an unalterable core, a truth to which we can direct all our powers and hopes?

The corner of Sherbrooke and McGill is usually quiet this time of day, its office workers and its transactions safely stowed away until tomorrow, but I saw a crowd. Police lights flashing in the middle of the street. I drew closer. It must be a film shoot. The Americans are always coming here to buy their fake European cityscapes for half price.

It wasn't a film. It was real life. Close to Mahone Inc. Right in front of Mahone Inc.

The people on the sidewalk and in the middle of the street were looking up towards the windows of the building, towards our windows. I raised my eyes too. I saw a man crouched on the cornice, what a crazy idea, what a dumb way to get a breath of fresh air. Then the amused revelation sunk in. Zeno, priceless buffoon that he is, what's he doing up there, clinging to the window ledge above our brass condor? I was the only one smiling. No one else seemed to find the joke even remotely funny, especially not the firemen and the police who were pushing back the curious to set up a security cordon, spreading tarpaulins on the ground, leaning ladders, creating an incredible circus. My smile faded. Zeno. Zeno, that numb-skulled gnome. What the hell is this ridiculous ploy! He's not actually pretending to kill himself, is he? Boiling over with fury, I pushed aside the spectators and headed for the main entrance, which was blocked by the animalian mass of a policeman. I shouted at him to let me by, I know the guy up there, fucking shit, stand back! He held me back, his tiny canine eyes full of mistrust, then finally called over a fellow cop who looked me over from head to foot.

"You know him? How? What's your relation with him?"

In my state, bursting with exasperation, what was I supposed to say? Our relations are infinite and unending, he's my colleague, my associate, my former and occasional lover, my accomplice, my companion in breakup, he'd be my husband if marriage weren't such an over-starched institution, and if it had ever occurred to him to propose to me!

"He's . . . he's my man!" I blurted out, overcome with emotion like a girl, my voice shaking with sobs.

They let me pass.

Behind me, howling broke out. Outhouse, left at the threshold, wailed at the injustice.

"That's my dog," I shouted. And immediately, I corrected myself. "That's *his* dog!"

Outhouse, wearing her seal of approval, barged into the theater of panic and raced ahead of me into the elevator, as if she knew every square inch of our office.

UPSTAIRS, BARBARIAN STRANGERS, some in uniform, were brazenly sprawled across our lambskin armchairs and on top of our marble-topped desks. They had infiltrated our tony office space. A cop armed with a walkie-talkie met me at the entrance and guided me to my own desk, where all the activity seemed to converge.

Nausea flooded over me when I caught sight of Zeno's small form about to topple into the void. What had gotten into him? What syrupy novel, what tearjerker of a movie did he think he was starring in? Then I saw his things, his brief-case, his coat, his laptop, all lined up in perfect order on my desk, a large solemn sheet of paper lying on top of them with my name in flamboyant letters, FLORENCE, my name written on a sheet of paper he took the trouble to fold after having taken the trouble to scribble down some kind of surreal non-sense, some insane last will and testament. A plainclothes cop stepped up to me and disturbed my meditations.

"Is that you? Are you Florence? Good, that's great."

He was practically rubbing his hands in delight, then he shoved me towards the window.

"Talk to him. Gently, gently. He won't jump, I'm sure, but we have to take precautions."

As I was trying to string together a few words in my fear-parched mouth, the plainclothes launched in first, in a stento-rian voice entirely devoid of precaution.

"Sir! Sir! Someone is here for you, sir. Florence is here."

No reaction from the other side of the window. Zeno's hair, his fine black half-Mohawk, half-Italian hair, was danc-ing in the stiff wind. His leaf-green silk shirt billowed out like a hot-air balloon ready for lift-off.

"Zeno! Get back here! Zeno! ZENO!"

My turn to shout, casting all caution aside. But my cries sounded like pathetic mouse-squeaks in the thin-air universe where he hovered. We needed a loudspeaker, an ultrasound machine, the thunder of God to rip him away from what was pulling at him. I grabbed the man and begged him to find something better, because it's obvious that whatever was pulling on Zeno was speaking more convincingly than we were.

Overexcited by my hysteria, and all the commotion about the shape silhouetted against the void, Outhouse began yelping in her strident dog's voice, the only one she had. Zeno turned around.

I could hardly recognize that distant look. Only one antenna still connected him to the world I lived in, and that antenna was turned towards a barking dog, receiving a few fragments of happy memories. His face lightened a little, then he saw me. I had no idea what energy I was giving off, and what managed to flow from me to him, whether he could read the words I stammered, *I love you, Zeno, Zeno, I love you, you fool,* but his face brightened. Whatever had been pulling him into darkness loosened its grip. He made a move to return to us, and moved too quickly.

And slipped.

Slipped and caught himself, slipped again, and fell, fell and landed astride the brass condor where he lay, dumbfounded and stunned, while I died several times over, and a few of the police and firemen leaned out the window as if they were lifelines and hauled him back inside.

End of the incredible drama.

The last scene of this bad movie, against which the end titles would normally scroll by, showed us in one another's arms, as the police and firemen applauded.

"Took you long enough," whispered Zeno, clinging tight-ly to me. "Took you long enough to get here."

"You fool," was all I could sputter. "You useless idiot."

We didn't let go of each other until we reached the side-walk.

They were waiting for Zeno. You don't idly importune the suicide professionals without a proper explanation. A police car was there to take him to the hospital for tests and interro-gation, to make sure he would continue to function over the next few hours. I'd made up my mind to accompany him when Maud arrived.

I hadn't remembered just how average-looking a little brunette she was, her skirt short like that of a schoolteacher intent on seducing her pupils. But who cares? Someone from the emergency squad had called Zeno's house, and that's where she was, and now here she stood, all shaken and over-come by events. Zeno held her tightly to console her, winking at me over her shoulder, that randy old goat. And since she was the missus, the one to whom the thankless tasks fell, she'd get to spend the whole night with him in the emergency ward.

While I went home alone, just as I would after a normal evening of exhausting work.

ACTUALLY, I'D NEVER been less alone than since Outhouse moved in.

Dogs expand to fill all available indoor space. Indoors, they are at their most overwhelmingly present, in sharpest contradiction with quiet solitude. As soon as she enters the house, theoretically exhausted by three hours of walking, Outhouse begins her barbarian dance. She runs. Lap after lap in my rectangular apartment, twice, ten times, twenty times at a flat-out gallop, squeezing what remains of the juice from her energy core and sending it to all her cells—or maybe she's just happy to be back. Who knows. She runs forever, like a nutcase pursued by the monsters of madness, then collapses from exhaustion.

That's when you have to watch out.

The first few times, as she lay sprawled on the floor, I turned to my cyberjob and forgot all about her, figuring it would take her hours to digest her fatigue. Fat chance. Five minutes later, with the purposeful silence of a practiced miscreant, she would be gnawing my shoes to a pulp, or ripping the slipcover from my sofa while, in front of my computer, I told myself, affected by a shadow of tenderness, that there were far worse calamities than owning a dog.

This time, I forgot about her when we got back home. She roared off like a race car, but my inner panic kept me from seeing her. My thoughts were focused on the terrible sequence of events that had led me to Mahone Inc. on an evening when normally I wouldn't have gone that way. Is there anyone at the controls of this explosive game of chance, or is he blundering in the darkness, handing out catastrophes and miracles like a blind madman? If I hadn't shown up when I did, where would Zeno be now?

Took you long enough to get here.

I went and sat down in front of the dark screen of my computer, my therapist and primal point, my own personal altar.

For the first time in my life, I felt a sense of regret at being an impious woman without a sense of ritual. An irrational longing made me want to venerate with candles and incense, with whatever humble offering I had on hand, something greater that lies beyond us and that we call chance. There is a plan, Florence. In everything that lives, and that does not yet live, there is a terrible and subtle plan, starting with the giant construction of which you are a part, Florence, all those bodies spinning endlessly in space. Everything takes shape and communicates from that sole point, the burning conjunction of cause and effect that rises to the surface now and again with a clarity brutal enough for even you to notice. It is always there, lurking, where you cannot see it, Florence, working out of sight, beyond all control.

Took you long enough to get here. Against all logic, deep in our unconscious conjuncture, Zeno knew I would get there. It was impossible for me not to get there.

At the foot of my personal altar, briefly delivered from cynicism and rationality, I wept as I did not know I could weep, without selfishness, without despair. I wept at the grandeur of all that lay so far beyond me, and the tears, coming from a statue that had never lost its self-control, were the best offering I could have made.

Meanwhile, Outhouse had stopped running.

Outhouse had stopped running a long time ago. Finally, I took notice. I stood up, both feet firmly planted in reality. I called her, looked for her, cocked an ear as I'd learned to do from her. I heard a faint rustling. It came from my closet, a large space where I kept my clothes along with what I didn't need for working or cooking. A space I kept protected from that dog's snout of hers, constantly sniffing out for things to shred. That's where she was. I hadn't completely closed the door, and through that small opening I commanded her to come out. Pronouncing her name in a certain way is enough: out she popped, quite satisfied with herself, a scrap of torn coat-lining dangling from her jaws.

Dirty dog, Outhouse, you piece of shit. I bawled her out without much conviction. It has become our daily exchange, and she played the repentance game, haunches quivering in submission, belly scraping the floor, depositing her slobber-soaked trophy at my feet.

I knew where this shred of lining came from. A summer jacket with a few small holes in the pockets, now torn into strips, beyond repair. I bent down. There was something hidden in the piece of ripped silk lining, something black.

A notebook.

Pierre Laliberté's black notebook.

On that comatose night, I really had picked up Pierre Laliberté's black notebook and slipped it into my well-worn pocket, from which it had surreptitiously migrated down into the lining.

I was so beside myself that I kissed Outhouse on the side of her scatterbrained head. Then I remembered that the notebook wasn't really worth much. It was not the precious notebook of the great demiurge Pierre Laliberté, but that of the imposter, Melody's talebearer. I pushed Outhouse aside just as she was about to take advantage of my weakness, and opened the notebook all the same. Let's see just what this talebearer was reporting to his mistress, what shopping lists he was jotting down for her in the shadowy precinct of bars.

It began with this sentence. *We are all poor slobs, sheltering giants.*

That was how it started, and it never stopped. There were sentences like that, unraveling, raw and devastating, through to the very end, without weakening or straying from the path, until every last hole of nothingness was stoppered up. Then it rose and rose higher until it was brutally cut short because there were no more pages left.

It took me fifteen minutes to read the whole thing. I read it, reread it, read it again. It was a novel. A fragment of a novel. Every sentence, as hard as the core of a diamond, was written by the Pierre Laliberté I knew, whom I'd thought I'd lost. They had his firm handwriting, and the inimitable style of the seven novels I'd read. I sat on the floor, which is the safest place when you're about to collapse. Outhouse snuggled up against me and I let her. I even petted her to celebrate the occasion. It's not every day that you rediscover what you've lost. Your treasure.

17

NO FLOWERS, PLEASE

---

*T*HE FLOWERS HAD FADED in front of the yellow clap-
board house, and the house itself looked faded too. I
knew that when I rang the doorbell, there would be silence.
No barking of dogs from around the back, no clatter of human
heels across the wooden floor. I knew that, but I rang anyway,
my left hand clutching the black notebook in my pocket. I
rang a second time. The sound of the bell echoed within me
and hung there, heavier than an indigestible meal.

I paced back and forth on the front porch, not yet resigned
to leaving. Outhouse turned circles around my legs, her euphoria enough for two. Then I spotted Pierre Laliberté's car
abandoned in its usual place, almost out of sight. I walked
slowly towards it, as I would a relic that still might have
something sacred. I touched the hood. It was warm, as if the

motor had just been turned off, though the heat of the sun's rays was most likely the reason. Outhouse chose this moment of meditation to start yelping like a banshee.

"Why don't you shut up!" I ordered her.

She began barking with renewed ferocity in the direction of the house. And she was right to. In the doorway, around the back, stood an imposing figure, a woman with flame-red hair.

"How about a whisky?" she asked.

Gina Da Sylva. Gina Da Sylva may have traded the dark, mysterious version of herself for an incendiary one, but she couldn't change her voice. It was just as abrasive as I remembered it.

"Take your choice," she offered as I stood there, mouth agape. "Either it's whisky or a bullet from a .22 in the butt. You're trespassing on private property."

She gave me the finest smile in her repertoire, a grimacing slash through which the smallest suggestion of human warmth appeared. I responded with the same enthusiasm and moved towards the house.

"Would you mind leaving *that* outside?"

She pointed a hostile finger at Outhouse. Some obscure part of me rebelled at the idea of abandoning the animal outside, so close to the road. A rarely traveled road, fair enough, but one reckless driver speeding by would be more than enough to extinguish as small a life as hers. Then my senses returned and I remembered she was just a dog after all, a perfectly interchangeable sack of bones and guts. The proof: there had been five more exactly like her, right here, a few weeks ago.

"No problem," I said with a smile.

Outhouse howled with indignation as I left her outside, but she calmed down after a few muttered apologies. Then I stepped into the house.

His house. The citadel of his power. Where do the smells, the remains of combustion, the glow of the furnace of the creator in his state of trance—where does all that go when he leaves? I sought the answer in the pale wood walls, the pale wood furniture, the colorful rag rugs on the floor, the rumbling of the woodstove, in the absence of personal effects. Everything must have risen, just as warmth rises, all the scrolls of smoke that made up Pierre Laliberté must have risen to the second floor, where they still hung quivering in the air. But Gina Da Sylva discouraged my timid move towards the staircase.

"Sit down," she told me. "How does it feel to return to the scene of the crime?"

"I've never been in this house before," I answered laconically.

"Really?" she said, surprised. "I thought... Let me rephrase my question: How does it feel to visit the scene of the crime for the first time?"

She handed me a glass of whisky with overstated politeness, then sat down across from me. Beneath her makeup and red hair, she was emaciated.

"You've been ill," I stated.

"I almost left this life. That's why I dyed my hair the color of resurrection. Bright orange, like the sun. How do you like it?"

"It's striking," I said, not committing myself.

"Revolting, is what you mean. The truth is, I chose this grotesque orange because I can't get away with black anymore. I have to hide, I have to flee my former image, which I liked very much. And it's all your fault."

"Mine?"

"Because of you, I lost everything. They did too," she added with a wave of her hand towards the staircase. "You're a kind of criminal, in your sickly sweet way."

The game was going to get nasty. I'd come prepared to suffer Pierre Laliberté's lightning bolts, and I had the black notebook to offer by way of reparations. But I didn't know what to do about her. What did I have to do with the illness that almost killed her? She removed her scarf and let it drop to the floor. There, in all its theatrical glory, an enormous scar encircled her neck, a livid strip of flesh that clasped her throat like a flaming necklace.

"Good God," I said, stunned.

"They almost cut my throat. They laid me across an altar like a vestal virgin and sliced open my neck."

"Who did that?"

"Your Web pals, who else? The ones who visit your sites. Didn't I tell you that your marvelous site was attracting plenty of new readers? Goths, medievalists, satanists, voodoo cults . . . Now that's fame for you!"

"Good God," I repeated, short of exclamations.

"Except that the price of fame," she said in a broken voice, "was a lot steeper than I imagined."

We drained our glasses in silence. For once I wasn't the last of the pack to cross the finish line. I pictured Anthony's big athletic body pouring whisky into my glass with the ceremoniousness of a bad actor, the tiny tattoo stretched across his shaved head. Afterwards, when Zeno had enlarged the photos he'd taken, we discovered that it was a little devil tattooed on his head, a well-proportioned, rather cute little devil.

"Yes, of course, Anthony," said Gina, naturally reading the stream of my thoughts. "His veneration should have been suspect, if you're the kind of person who's suspicious of everything. But I was anxious to play another game for once in my life. I wanted to trust the adulation of admirers who were crazy about me. I'm no ingrate, by the way. I enjoyed every minute of it while it lasted."

It had lasted until the final tournament, among players enamored of Gina, who had been elevated to the rank of High Priestess in spite of herself. They were very young, very wild players who, ferreting out scenes of virtual death in her books, had decided to flirt with the real thing. What better than a good old sacrificial killing to provide some weekend excitement? They drugged her silly, she said. The whisky tasted like sheet metal, not a good sign, and after that she couldn't remember anything but the beginning, a big crowded hall full of happy people where Anthony had led her, eyes blindfolded. A huge ovation greeted her. One hell of an ovation, she said without irony. Unfortunately, she missed most of it, since she'd passed out. When she came to, she was drenched in blood in an ambulance rushing her to the hospital which was, as experiences go, far less triumphant. She never knew what saved her from being butchered: probably the clumsiness of the would-be killers.

"So here I am," she concluded in her harsh metallic laugh, "forced to adopt the Pierre Laliberté Syndrome, and hide from my readers as if I'd done something wrong. And it's all on account of you."

That was enough! She wanted to wash her hands clean, and leave me the dirty water.

"Just a minute," I protested. "There's an unspoken rule among Web surfers, and you didn't respect it. We never transform virtual encounters into real ones. Anthony is your mistake, not ours."

"I see! And where are these rules published?"

"They're unwritten because they're so obvious."

Unwritten because obvious. She spoke the words several times over, pronouncing them with such buffoonery that they turned into an unintelligible mishmash: *unrittinbekawzobvius.* Just when I'd started wondering whether the attempted throat-slashing had created collateral damage higher up in her skull, she broke off her nonsense and turned her brilliant black eyes on me.

"What do you think? I accept my share of the responsibility. They do too," she added, motioning towards the staircase. "They accept their share of the blame. You're nothing but an insignificant, interchangeable cog in the machine. No one can blame you for what happened. Otherwise, I would have filled your head with lead a long time ago."

She pointed to a shiny new hunting rifle leaning against the woodstove like a common poker. I ruminated on her words, very tempted to consider them as insults.

"But I'm not complaining. I'm beginning a new life, underground and redheaded. I've started a new novel. I'm going to use the whole incident, and for the first time I feel I've really got a story to tell. Trouble is, there's no way I can use my real name again. I'm looking for a pseudonym. Wait a minute! It could be *Florence*. Not bad, eh? *Florence*. What does your family name sound like?"

We traded caustic smiles, then the next minute, out of the blue, we both laughed. I disliked her a lot less, this Gina Da Sylva, now that I had nothing to do with her.

"I'm sorry," I spoke. "Terribly sorry."

And I was. Sincerely. Not only for her, forced to hide out in the back country and wear flaming orange hair to escape her rabid fans. For Mahone Inc. too. It had failed in its fundamental mission by casting down into a darker realm that which it should have raised up into light.

"It doesn't matter," she said.

"You never know," I offered. "Maybe your invisibility will end up turning you into a celebrity. There are precedents, after all."

We traded knowing glances. The presence of Pierre Laliberté fell between us like a wall.

"That's right," she agreed. "After all . . . look at my sister."

She sized me up with an acid look.

"You came to see her."

"I came to see *him*."

I'd shaken her, I could feel that much. I felt her wondering how much further she could push the stratagem, then I felt her giving in. She knew I knew that Pierre Laliberté really was Pierre Laliberté, despite Melody's allegations to the contrary. Now what? What happened next was an infernal racket at the other end of the house, and the tinkling of broken glass. Gina jumped to her feet and grabbed the rifle. She pointed it towards the hallway with a virile self-assurance I'd never thought her capable of. Outhouse came barreling full tilt into the room and leapt onto my lap, her muzzle dripping blood, like a pincushion full of glass fragments.

"Well, well," said Gina, lowering the rifle.

And she burst out laughing, relieved at having her window smashed by something other than a bloodthirsty satanist. I hesitated between consternation and open admiration for Outhouse's idiotic fearlessness.

"Add the window to the damage you've already caused," said Gina, almost cheerfully.

"Naughty girl," I scolded Outhouse. "Naughty, naughty girl. Now we'll have to take you to the vet."

"No need," countered Gina. "A pair of tweezers and a little Mercurochrome will do the trick."

She disappeared, then returned with a first-aid kit.

"Hold your mutt's head tight."

The mutt trembled a little as our four hands joined around her execrable head, then she calmed down. Gina maneuvered with the gentleness of someone who had bandaged and repaired two children. Our forced togetherness pushed us onto ground I'd been hoping to reach since the beginning.

"So, they're gone," I began.

Immersed in her nurse's duties, she didn't answer for a while.

"Of course they're gone," she said. "What did you expect?"

They probably had no other choice. They had to flee the scroungers who gave away their well-protected secret, scroungers like Zeno and me. I thought of Melody's immense sacrifice, how her life had been turned upside down, her joyous freedom eradicated. And I thought it was pure folly to take on someone else's identity, even to save him, a folly so magnanimous and grand that I would never be able to experience it.

"She must really love him," I said, melancholy.

Gina gave me a sidelong look, and went on mending Outhouse's snout with a disabused expression.

"Matrimonial servility," she muttered.

Roughly, she wiped away the coagulated blood from Outhouse's head, drawing a whine of protest from her. Then she got to her feet, exasperated.

"Why did you come here, anyway? Are you going to tell me or not?"

"But . . . I did."

"What do you love so much about Pierre Laliberté? His books, or the fact that he hides?"

I observed her carefully, in search of the jealousy behind her irritation. But I found nothing.

"I like his way of seeing. For me, his books are secondary. I guess the books look after themselves when you've got that way of seeing things."

She accepted my words begrudgingly. When I finished, she shrugged.

"The books are secondary," she repeated. "Good thing you're not around too much. But you're not wrong as far as Pierre Laliberté is concerned, when you get right down to it. Then again, I know him a lot less than you do."

I released Outhouse, who was beginning to find my bony

knees unbearable. She padded over to the foot of the stairs, sat down and started in whining.

"That's one of his mutts, right? You must've hit him right between the eyes for him to give you one of his mutts."

It was my turn to stand up, but with infinite slowness in light of what she said. I felt an acute sense of absence, a hole in the center of my belly. Perhaps it was the whisky. I'd never see Pierre Laliberté again, I'd never know for sure if I grasped the substance of what he gave me.

"We're even," I said, hesitant. "He owed me something."

I looked her in the eye.

"Where is he? Very far? Did they leave together? Are they in New York? No, they couldn't be, New York would be impossible."

Gina listened with a broad smile.

"Keep on looking," she said sarcastically. "You never know, and with your sense of smell, and a little help from your pooch, you might just sniff out a hint or two."

"Still, New York," I went on, my voice more bitter, yielding progressively to despair, "New York might be just the thing. Yes, I have no problem imagining them in New York after all, together or each alone, notebook in hand, sitting close to something that's suffering, notebook in hand, jotting down the color and the dimension of the suffering in the air. They'll be able to enjoy themselves for years to come."

Gina Da Sylva gazed at me. At last, I'd hit her where it hurt most with my words. My portrait reduced the masterful writer to a pile of rubble; my mortal blow to the nobility of writing. My assault was so effective she couldn't defend herself.

She moved to the door and opened it wide, showing me out. Outhouse ran ahead of me.

"And you," said Gina calmly, "what are you going to do? Are you going to do something? At least make an effort to participate in the world the way we do, even though we go about it clumsily?"

She had a point. Such a good point that it knocked me down and kept me from replying, even when I had time to think about it, in cramped proximity with Outhouse in the back seat of the taxi taking us back to Montreal.

NOT BAD. When it comes to recovering from the damage caused by the country, Montreal is not bad at all. The proof? A giant bouquet of white flowers was waiting at my door, with Zeno at their far extremity. He handed me the flowers and knelt before me.

"Oh, Queen," he declaimed, "your enamored vassal has missed you, three times he has come to pay his respects, and twice he has gone away empty-handed, so perhaps you would like to tell me exactly where you were?"

"None of your business, Vassal. What's the deal with the flowers?"

He gave me a quick kiss, thrust the flowers at me, then turned his amorous exuberance towards Outhouse, flopping her over and tussling with her to her delight.

"Because I love you, that's why."

Though spoken with maximum offhandedness, and without a glance at me, his words poured a warm, languorous syrup into my inner cavities. He didn't allow me to savor the feeling for long.

"And also to thank you for looking after her. I've come to pick her up, as agreed. I'm taking her off your hands."

I realized with a slight lag that he was talking about Outhouse. He'd totally seduced her already, tickling her in the funniest places, rubbing her the way she hadn't been rubbed since birth. Delicately, he lingered over her muzzle.

"What happened to her?" he asked with the caring tone of a true dog owner.

"She smashed through a window. A kind of Suzie, canine-style. I'm warning you: she busts through windows, eats clothes, tears furniture apart, she pisses on everything that moves. She's no soft touch, I'm warning you, nothing like Pokey."

He guffawed. Mussed her fur, rolled her over, scratched her tummy, pulled her legs, tickled her under her chin. She came back for more.

"Is that so, you little strumpet?" he said to her. "Is it so that you're a mean little strumpet-muppet-puppy-doo?"

I watched them pawing each other on the sidewalk in full view of every Tom, Dick and Harry. No dignity or modesty or anything like that, and I really didn't like what I saw. I sniffed at the flowers, then nibbled at one. It tasted like turpentine. It wouldn't take much for me to throw them on the ground and stomp all over them.

"So, Maud's gone," I deduced, for the sake of saying something unpleasant.

Zeno deigned to turn his attention to me. He was wearing a broad smile.

"Sure has," he said. "I told you she would. Admit it, you never believed me."

I shrugged. "I couldn't care less."

He took me by the neck and rumpled my hair, much less adroitly than with the dog's fur.

"Do I take her as is," he asked, "or do you have anything else for me?"

"Anything else?"

"Dog food, little things she likes, doggy toys."

"I don't have any doggy toys," I said haughtily. "Only my scarf. She's taken a particular liking to my scarf."

"Great. The scarf it is."

He waited. As did I. He was waiting for me to fetch the scarf, while what I was waiting for was harder to put into words. I was waiting for the right impulse to emerge from my confusion, the one that would tell me what to do to avoid all regret. As soon as it made itself felt, everything became clear, and I handed the flowers back to Zeno.

"Here," I told him. "I can't keep them."

"No?"

"No. Now that I'm not giving her to you anymore, she would just eat them, and get sick."

And Outhouse, whom he finally left to her own devices, ambled over and beat her tail against my calves. I was the one and only mistress life had assigned her.

18

START ALL OVER

---

*H*E FEELS PAIN DEEP in his chest, and that must be the dangerous kind. He's often in pain, but who cares? His joints ache, his hips, his knees, his neck, his hands. His throat hurts when he swallows, his skin hurts when his clothes touch it, his eyes hurt when he opens them in the morning. Before, living held more pleasure than pain. Living was sweet. Now he's consumed all the sugar in life, and nothing but gall remains. That's old age. It sucks life down to its bitterest core, and you taste every last drop. Anyone who doesn't like it is welcome to spit out the bonbon at its sweetest, in the bloom of youth.

Even so. He'd take some more if he could, the honey, the sweet. He'd devour every sweet thing he could. Just to be free of pain for five minutes, what sweetness that would be. And vanilla ice cream. And the few dreams that come to him like gifts during his brief rest, dreams of childhood or of love. Moments of grace, too, when his spirit is so young it swallows the grievances of his ancient body and changes them into experience.

As the Jacques Brel song goes, growing old means nothing, but to die, ah, to die. Or the other way around. But the other way makes no sense, harshness and pain are still part of life, infinitely more tolerable than the abyss that lies ahead, utter darkness.

Most of the time he is in pain, and afraid, but who cares?

Certainly not them. When they sit around the table like that, transformed into cannibals, they form a barrier, a living monolith that will not crack. They are on the life side, he on the broken side. He can't really hear what they're saying, they never make the effort to speak louder or repeat what they've said, they never have the patience to wait for him to speak. But to be fair, the only way he can utter a complete sentence is inside himself. Worst of all, they won't even look at him. Except her, except the Daughter.

The Daughter's glacial stare. A courtroom in itself where he is sentenced for sins he cannot remember committing.

He would like to say, *I am your father, I am your husband, pity, pity for what has befallen me,* and maybe their compassion would flow like a spring in the month of March. But he no longer knows how to communicate anything except bitterness. Bitterness flows from him without so much as being asked, and it endangers all attempts to draw closer to those nearest him. Where they stand now, dedicated to the violence of pleasure, the sweetness of life, they flee bitterness, they turn away from it as he had once done with all his strength, before.

They flee from him. They harry him out.

And he withdraws.

Withdraws into general indifference. Only the Daughter follows him down to the depths with her vengeful eyes. One day, he will have to ask her what reprehensible act he committed, or what it was that he failed to do. One day, he ought to try to pierce the wall of ice that separates them, like when she was a little girl and they chased one another through fortresses made from packed snow in the yard. But his mind is growing dim: it wasn't with her, the snow forts, it was with the boys. With her, he remembers nothing, nothing tangible, nothing warm to hang on to.

Fortunately, he has his space below. In every war, there must come a truce. Down below, his island awaits him.

"WHAT ARE YOU DOING?" my mother said. "What are you looking at?"

She was waiting for me halfway down the stairs that lead to the basement, but I was in the kitchen, conversing with the ghosts. The four of them, in their Sunday best, laughing and joking, taking up all the table, and me at the far end, like an added, ill-attached appendix threatening to fall away at any moment. They were laughing; I was not. For an endless minute of suffering, I was Pepa, Pepa withdrawing into his subterranean shelter before he suffocated from solitude.

"What are you doing?" said my mother.

"I'm coming down."

Here I am. In his lair, his den. The first time I've been here since I don't know how long. I maintained the silence. Curiously, I felt nothing. My mother had changed the basement into a gym, except for one corner, preposterous in the extreme with its rocking chair and ancient roll-top desk. It's difficult to feel anything besides fatigue in a fitness club.

"You have so little furniture," my mother said. "I thought maybe the desk would look nice with your modern things. It would be a memento of your father too. Sorry about the chair, though, I promised it to your brother."

I did not want anything. I told her so over the phone, but she insisted I come over. It would be the last time. She was moving in with her secondhand Romeo, breaking up the house like the old-timers used to say.

"Take it, take it," she insisted. "You're the only one who has the space. It would hurt me if his desk ended up in some stranger's place."

His writing desk. A dark, repellent piece of furniture with bulging sides, and tiny drawers that held nothing, and the strong smell of dampness when I rolled open the top.

"You could always sell it," said my mother, biting her lips. "One day, without telling me. It's an antique, you know."

Nothing seemed to have changed behind the roll top. A venerable glue pot with its thick, almost black contents, rusted paper clips, a pound of rubber bands, eraser wheels, lead pencils as sharp as styluses, a pencil sharpener overflowing with cuttings, sheets of blank paper—yellow, but like everything else, blank. A meager haul.

"There are some things in the bottom drawer. Things he wrote."

"What do you mean?" I asked, suspicious.

"Your father wrote. Poems, letters, notes about this and that, nothing special to judge by what he sent me when we first started to see each other. But I never threw away a thing."

"I never saw him write!" I protested.

"He wrote when he was alone."

Then she added, not realizing the hurt she was inflicting, "I think he stopped when you were born."

Another wound caused by my supernatural birth, the catastrophic event of my birth? One day she'd have to tell me what plague I carried even before I knew who I was.

"Why? Why me? Why when I was born?"

"Oh, it wasn't you," she frowned. "It was a coincidence. When you were born your father had a . . . a disappointment. A big disappointment. It broke his spirit just as he was getting going. It's crazy, crazy how easy it is to hurt a man."

She shifted from one foot to the other, fingering the pretty necklace of transparent stones that kindled fresh flame on her black mohair sweater. She was as embarrassed as a young girl. And her beautiful eyes looked twenty-five years younger when she turned them on me.

"I met Alonzo just before you were born. Nothing happened between us, nothing at all, just one of those uncontrollable desires I couldn't hide from your father. We never saw each other again for all those years, never, until just a while ago, I swear. I swore it to your father, but he never believed me."

Alonzo. Well-preserved Alonzo who'd been waiting on the side for twenty-five years. No wonder he had that faded, pretty-boy look about him. Alonzo did all right by waiting. She was selling everything and moving in with him, as though life could begin again after menopause.

It would have been a nice story if it had happened to someone else, not my mother. If she hadn't thrown my neat, proper, arid universe into disarray.

"And you've loved him all this time?" I asked, stunned.

"I was never unfaithful to your father," she swore, hand over her heart.

But there was such love burning in her eyes, brighter than the transparent stones, such an avowal of love in that confession that refused to confess, that I fell silent. Nothing more can be said about that kind of capacity for love, powerful enough to endure years without ever seeking the light. Nothing more to be said. Just be silent and regret not being made of the same flammable stuff. Or to put it another way, that really took the wind out of your sails, didn't it, Pepa?

I rolled down the top of the old desk.

"Very well," I told my mother. "I'll take it."

NOW WHAT?

As predicted, the writing desk, an incongruous presence in my Zen-like space, offended the eye. At first I tried to make it fit in, dissimulate it, blend it into the wall. But hypocrisy can't defeat excess; it only amplifies and renders it ridiculous. We have to accept the existence of that which won't fit in.

The writing desk stood serene in the midst of everything.

Outhouse was as shocked as I was. She attempted to urinate on one of its legs to change the smell, but I caught her in time.

There's a problem with such a massive body. It has that relentless power to draw everything lighter than itself into its gravitational field.

I sat down in front of it without any idea what I would do next. The bottom drawer was gaping open from my first summary inspection. I slid it closed with my foot. I knew more or less what it contained. A sheaf of papers covered with drawings and writings scribbled in lead pencil, most of them erased by time, some older, some more recent. What did this tall, backwards-leaning handwriting tell? Sooner or later I would find out, at the appropriate time, another day.

One day at a time.

I picked up a pencil. The characteristic yellow of old pencils, dark yellow with a red belt, and a small round rubber eraser at the tip like a clergyman's hat. It weighed almost nothing. How could an object so insignificant produce anything?

I pictured Pepa clearly. He was slipping the pencil into the sharpener, giving it three twists, blowing on the tip with obvious pleasure and then, braced upright against the back of his chair, he was turning the pencil between his fingers for a time, as if to allow the softness of the wood to permeate his fingertips.

After that, I could see nothing at all.

I put the pencil down. It truly was the weapon of another era, made for patient combatants, people who had time to take the measure of their adversary. Today's battles require something stronger, something with a quicker reaction time.

I fetched my laptop and set it up among the rubber bands, the glue pot and the lead ammunition dump.

To my astonishment, it fit easily into the ancient pedestal. Its flamboyant modernity gleamed like a fruit of the third millenium, a fruit born of the old writing desk, the glue pot and the pencils.

Of course, Florence, you grasshopper brain, my condor chortled in my ear. It's as plain as day, you're rediscovering the wheel all over again. The computer is the child of the pencil and the writing desk, its organic continuation, just as you are Pepa's child.

Banal as it sounded, my discovery threw me into an intolerable funk. I stood up, unable to sit at the bedside of past and present as they overlapped. I paced. I recognized the anxiety, the acidity in the pit of my stomach, the panic and dizziness of transition. I got out Pierre Laliberté's notebook and propped it on the desk. It was not much of an audience, so I called the dog over. Now was the time for her to perform her dog's work, and keep me in touch with the earth. She hurried over, shreds of toilet paper hanging from her mouth.

I sat down at the writing desk in the black light of Pierre Laliberté's notebook, my legs kept comfortable by Outhouse's hot little body.

I switched on the laptop. Entered the utter discomfort of transition.

Admit it. Admit that the family bond exists, admit that outside it nothing exists, admit that I am the continuation of Pepa and almost nothing else, not an autonomous thing that can gambol about irresponsibly, disconnected from its origins. What is to be done? Can anything be done?

Where to begin, begin again? I will have to pick up the thread of the story well before the petty little portion I know, that much is clear. I'll have to go to the source.

On the screen, instead of heading for the familar Mahone Inc. Web site, I hung suspended above empty space. The blue-gray space of the screen that is the child of the blank page. The blue-gray screen that creates a terrifying rush of vertigo.

In the utter discomfort of transition, the time has come to cast myself into vertigo, the only space infinite enough to hold all that I do not know.

The time has come to write.

To write something that would begin or end with these words: *Start all over, Florence. Start all over.*